Rampage

THE RISE OF AN EMPIRE

by

Cade Skoblar

DORRANCE PUBLISHING CO
EST. 1920
PITTSBURGH, PENNSYLVANIA 15238

The contents of this work, including, but not limited to, the accuracy of events, people, and places depicted; opinions expressed; permission to use previously published materials included; and any advice given or actions advocated are solely the responsibility of the author, who assumes all liability for said work and indemnifies the publisher against any claims stemming from publication of the work.

All Rights Reserved
Copyright © 2022 by Cade Skoblar

No part of this book may be reproduced or transmitted, downloaded, distributed, reverse engineered, or stored in or introduced into any information storage and retrieval system, in any form or by any means, including photocopying and recording, whether electronic or mechanical, now known or hereinafter invented without permission in writing from the publisher.

Dorrance Publishing Co
585 Alpha Drive
Pittsburgh, PA 15238
Visit our website at *www.dorrancebookstore.com*

ISBN: 979-8-8868-3190-0
eISBN: 979-8-8868-3763-6

Rampage

THE RISE OF AN EMPIRE

DEAR GRANDPA, *you have been the biggest inspiration in my entire life. You have nurtured me and helped me grow not only on the outside but on the inside as well. You helped me refine my creativity by playing with me every single day as a child, and continue to do so to this very day with the conversations we have every day. Words cannot describe how important you are to me and how you have effected my life in the most positive way imaginable. I dedicate this entire book to you and hope to imortalize you in my writing. Thank you for everything. Albert Fritsch, you are the greatest grandpa I could have every hoped for*

Love your Grandson, Cade

Council of Dragons
Matus
Jal
Holy State of Nidiel
Ul
Efdona
Olwen
Kingdom of Cade
Qeknur
Kingdom of Kret
Laug
Vojhan Empire
The Harmonian Empire
Kingdom of Gara
Kingdom of Gort
Republic of Khaic
Gluth
Kingdom of Shimia
Nigt

CHAPTER 1

Harmonia: a beautiful land of wonders, magic, and a boundless landscape, the full extent of which most would find impossible to explore in a lifetime. This vast world is one that is held together by magic. Magic is the lifeblood of the land of Harmonia. Almost all intelligent creatures have magical capabilities, whether they are the lowliest of goblins or the most ancient of dragons. Harmonia is home to many kingdoms and empires but the largest and the most powerful of them is the Harmonian Empire. The Harmonian Empire is a kingdom of elves, creatures who live for thousands of years, who proclaim it to be a shining beacon of the power of goodness and harmony.

Shatterstar, the capital of the Harmonian Empire, glistens like an ocean of stars whenever night falls. It is the shining beacon of all of Harmonia. A city of such beauty and elegance that it is rumored that travelers are brought to tears just by approaching its gates. Shatterstar, located at the center of both Harmonia and the Harmonian Empire, is an island city, completely surrounded by water. The only thing that rivals its breathtaking beauty is its unparalleled defenses. Even if enemy forces conquer the rest of the Harmonian Empire, which in itself would be a herculean feat with an infinitesimal chance of ever happening, the capital would prove to be near impenetrable. Towering golden walls surround the entire island to protect all that lies behind the massive silver gates of Shatterstar. The wall is fortified with defensive weapons along its entire length. Catapults and stationary ballistae are mounted on Shatterstar's boundary walls to rain down death upon all invaders. But of course, in the several thousands of years of the empire's existence, none have ever reached the capital.

Behind the walls is a glistening paradise of natural beauty with grass greener than the skin of a goblin and streams of the purest, most invigorating water flowing freely through the island. The builders of this ancient city have accomplished something extraordinary. The paradise-like Shatterstar exists in perfect harmony with nature, the skill of its ancient builders ensured that no harm came to the wildlife during the construction of the metropolis. The precious metals and stones used to build the houses and the gargantuan boundary walls are completely in tandem with all of plant life. As one steps through the silver gates of Shatterstar, they chance upon quaint houses and shops made out of stone and wood. The farther one moves into the city, the bigger the houses and buildings get, continually increasing in size and grandeur until one reaches the center of the capital, where stands the royal castle. A massive fortress as stunningly gorgeous as it is deadly, the castle is so tall that its towers can be seen from miles away, towering above even the colossal golden walls of the island. The castle is home to the ruler of the Harmonian Empire, Queen Ashehera Kelmoria. The Kelmoria royal family has governed the empire since its inception and Queen Ashehera has been at the helm for the past 100 years.

The inside of the castle is decorated with riches, collected over thousands of years, all throughout the course of the empire's existence. The court alone is so enormous that it would take hours to explore the entire place. The long hallways are adorned with riches beyond the imagination of commoners. The plush carpet, running along the floors of the hallways and extending along all the castle halls, is richly adorned in hues of crimson and gold. The castle is constantly rife with activity, servants and guards moving and patrolling amongst its halls. The guards, dressed in full gold-plated armor, wield keen-edged weapons, their red capes billowing behind them as they patrol the halls.

The tallest tower at the back of the castle houses the royal quarters, luxurious chambers befitting their royal inhabitants. Two beds fit for kings stand in a room of marble and gold, its walls sprinkled with massive, curtained windows and paintings of elven heroes and royalty. One painting stood out amongst all – a knight clad in silver armor, wielding a sturdy steel blade in his right hand and a shield in his left. A falcon is emblazoned on his breastplate and shield, the crest of the Harmonian Empire. A mantle below the paintings is home to numerous candles, their flames adding a warm glow to the complexions of the painted heroes. The room belongs to two young elven princes, sons of Queen Ashehera, their ramblings filling the marble room with happiness and warmth.

The elder prince is Arun. He is about 200 years old, which is considered the age of a young adult for an elf. He has long, golden blonde hair and is wearing leather armor unfit for one of his royal blood. Arun's eyes are green as emeralds, his demeanor stiff and severe. In addition, he has more muscle tone than would be expected of one of his title. His pale skin glistened slightly as he leaned against the window and continued to talk to his brother.

The second prince is named Adamar. He is 100 years old and is a child in elf years. He has a much livelier personality compared to his brother Arun. Despite how contrasting their personalities are, they look practically the same except that Adamar likes to keep his hair short and that he is wearing a suit made of the finest silks, attire much more for a young prince. Adamar was hanging upside down from the furniture, gigging uncontrollably.

"Ugh, get down, you moron. Mom's going to be mad at us if you break anything. Especially today."

"Huh? Why today? And when does Mom ever get mad anyway?"

"It's Reynard's passing day. Mom is always in a bad mood on this day," replied Arun, pointing towards the painting of the silver knight on the wall.

Adamar instantly dropped down from the furniture, frowning slightly. His long elvish ears slowly droop down, thinking about Reynard. He was just an infant when Reynard died, but from what he had heard, he was the greatest warrior the empire has ever had, with whom Arun was really close. Their mother doesn't like to talk about that day much. Suddenly, the princes heard a knock on the door.

As it slowly opened, it revealed the angelic figure of Queen Ashehera. Her black and white royal dress adorned with blue gemstones was simply designed yet breathtaking, sparkling and glittering as she walked. The queen had a depressed air about her as she gently touched her children's faces and forced a smile.

"Hello, young ones."

"Momma!" yelled Adamar as he jumped towards his mother and hugged her tight. "You seem sad… what's wrong, Mommy?"

Ashehera fought to keep her weak smile on her face as she was asked this.

"Come here," she gestured, calling her sons near.

Ashehera brought them over to one of the large windows in their room. From the window, so much of the city could be seen. A large stone crypt decorated with jewels lay in the exact center of the entire city and island. Ashehera tightened up the moment that she looked at the tomb. Even though she has seen it every day for over 100 years now, it never got any easier. Ashehera's hand rested on Adamar's shoulder as she stared at the crypt.

"Why did Reynard die so soon? And… why was he so different looking? You never tell us."

"Adamar!" scolded Arun.

RAMPAGE: THE RISE OF AN EMPIRE

"It's… okay… he died for this empire… that is all you need to know," she said through gritted teeth, her jaw clenched.

Ashehera's hand gripped Adamar's shoulder so hard he started to whimper in pain.

"O…o…ow…M…m…mommy?"

Ashehera instantly let go of Adamar. Her hand was shaking. "I… I… I'm sorry, I must leave now."

"Mother, wait! Dammit!" called Arun after Ashehera, but she had already left the room in a hurry.

"Now why would you ask Mother a question like that, especially on a day like today?"

Adamar held his head low as Arun knelt and checked Adamar's shoulder and found a red bruise left behind from Ashehera's powerful grip. Arun let out a shaky sigh as he held out his hand and gently led his brother to a cabinet on the other side of the room. It was full of herbs and medicines that were neatly categorized. Arun reached out to grab a small bottle filled with a paste of strange, crushed leaves and gently spread some of it on his brother's shoulder. The pain slowly started to dissipate in but a few moments.

Adamar smiled as he looked up at his older brother. "Thanks, Arun."

"Don't mention it."

The two brothers turn back to look at the tomb of Reynard Kelmoria. Every single year the entire empire is made to mourn his loss on the anniversary of his death. Adamar and Arun don't know much about Reynard. When he was alive, he was always away from home, fighting battles and bringing glory to the empire. He was the strangest elf the world had ever seen. He was massive – the most enormous elf to ever live, his musculature and physical prowess previously unparalleled in elven bodies. But that was only scratching the surface of the strange elf hero before he died.

CADE SKOBLAR

As Ashehera swiftly moved down the golden halls of her palace, she could not help but think of her deceased son. Her favorite son. Reynard. He had everything it took to be a fantastic leader and what he had accomplished for the empire was nothing but astonishing. A pang of latent guilt from his death still hangs over her head like a cloud of despair. She adored Reynard with all of her heart.

Ashehera slowly slumped into her massive golden, jewel-encrusted throne with a look of sadness stretched across her face. As she solemnly sat on her throne, an elf approached her, his body skinny, his bony face twisted into an expression of snobbish boredom. His nose was even longer than his elven ears, its tip red. He wore fine, delicately-woven attire.

"Your majesty?"

"Yes, Royal Advisor? What is it this time?" Ashehera sighed.

"Thank you for indulging me, your majesty, but I must bring up a primary concern once again."

Ashehera groaned, rolling her eyes, fully aware of what the royal advisor's nasally and pompous voice was going to put in front of her. She wasn't in the mood to hear the same song and dance she constantly heard. Not today.

"The empire is too big, your majesty! Our borders are so extensive and widespread that our outer territories are being constantly ransacked and pillaged by nations such as the werewolf kingdom of Shimia, the legion of giants in Olwen, and the centaurs of Buyantia. Furthermore, our borders are so far-flung now that we can't effectively send reinforcements to protect our border villages because it takes too long to travel! Even more, it takes longer for us to receive the messages that something has happened to begin with. By the time we even get to send help, if we do in the first place, it's far too late!

Instead of fixing the problem, you're making it worse. Your continued aggression against the Republic of Khiac, which was a neutral country, is now making the rest of Harmonia increasingly aggressive towards us."

As the royal advisor continued to rant, the queen started getting increasingly, visibly angry with his complaints about her methods. Her fingers tightly gripped the sides of her throne and her purple eyes glared at the advisor, who was completely oblivious of Ashehera's climbing rage, engrossed, and blinded by his passionate tirade.

"Don't get me started on your near-suicidal expansion into the mountains near the Dragon Council's territory! Not only will mountains not aid the empire in any way, but it just spreads our resources thinner than they already are. Oh, what else could possibly go wrong? Ah yes, of course! Stability is decreasing, we have uprisings and rebellions in dozens of locations all over the empire and there are increasing rumours of a coalition forming against the empire. I think the best way to alleviate this would be to start releasing territory a…"

Suddenly, a trident made of shining blue crystals materialized with a flick of Ashehera's hand and flew past the advisor. His pointed ear was sliced off the side of his head with the throw, pinning it against the wall. The elf screamed in agony and writhed on the floor. The queen slowly stood up with an enraged glare.

"How dare you?! How *dare* you insinuate that we GIVE AWAY the land that my dear Reynard worked so hard to give us *on his death anniversary?!*"

The royal advisor cowered in fear and pain as the queen loomed over him. His hand gripped the side of his head, trying to staunch the stream of warm blood. His breathing was shaky as he stared at the queen with fear in his eyes. Ashehera glared back. She tapped her trident on the ground and in an instant, two guards in golden armor stepped into the throne room.

"Take him to his quarters. Let him tend to his wounds," said the queen with venom in her voice.

The guards dragged the advisor away to his quarters. Ashehera slumped back into her throne with a pained sigh, sadly looking over to the empty throne next to her own.

"Oh, my king… I hope I am meeting your expectations… I wish you were here to guide me."

Her hand gently caressed the golden armrest of the second throne. She sat by herself with nothing but the silence and her thoughts to keep her company.

The royal advisor paced back and forth in his quarters, his features livid with anger. White bandages were wrapped tightly around his head, stained red at the place where his ear was once visible.

"How dare she? That maniac is going to drive the entire empire to the ground! She is just as unhinged as she is reckless."

"I agree."

The royal advisor stopped in his tracks, startled by the unexpected, feminine-sounding voice issuing from nearby. After all, he had thought that he was alone in his rooms. The advisor whipped around to see a mysterious figure wrapped entirely in a purple cloak standing in his large window. A hood covered all their features, making it impossible to know their identity.

"Are you Belas Petcaryn, royal advisor to the Harmonian Empire?"

"Y… yes? How do you know me? Who are you?"

"Who I am is not necessary. What is important is that we have similar goals. Saving the empire."

"What makes you take me for a fool? You have no leverage over me. Moreover, you are trespassing in her royal majesty's palace, and I just need to call for the guards to have you rot in the dungeons!"

"That would be ill-advised."

"And why would that be?"

The cloaked woman reached inside her cloak and threw a well-worn doll at Belas's feet, one of its button eyes missing. Belas reacted instantly, grabbing his knife.

"What have you done to her, you WASTE OF EXSISTENCE?!" Belas screamed, his insides writhing with rage and worry.

"Nothing as of now. An excellent start to make sure nothing happens would be to stop yelling like a moron. Now listen and listen closely. Depending on how this conversation goes and your actions in the hours that proceed, this discussion will determine if your daughter gets to eat dinner with you tonight or is left at your doorstep with a slit throat."

Belas was shaking with fear and anger. How dare this woman take his daughter? He can tell it's not a bluff though – that is her doll, down to every detail. She took it everywhere with her.

"What the hell do you want?"

"Simple. All you need to do during the festival tonight is make sure an entrance to the city is unlocked for the prince's passing ceremony. Think you can manage that? I know you can, so there is no point in lying. The amount of bribes and favors you have built up over the past thousand years is impressive indeed."

"...You said this would benefit me as well. How is that even possible with what you are asking me to do?"

"You think the empire is too large and hostile."

"What? How did you..."

"The people I work with have eyes and ears everywhere. If you try to betray us or tell anyone of our little transaction, your daughter will be dead before you can even utter a word. Now, back to the subject at hand. The empire is too big to protect its people and move soldiers and resources. Hostile nations surround you from all sides. We will start a chain of events tonight that will change history and make your dream come true. So… are you in or out? Not that you have much of a choice anyways."

"Yeah, yeah, I will have an entrance open tonight before the festival," Belas said, accepting his fate.

"Good. Be a good dog and your little daughter will be okay."

The woman walked towards the window, and she turned to look at Belas one more time. "Don't disappoint us. Tonight is going to be a show for the ages."

The woman turned and dived off the ledge. Belas ran to the window to see what happened. The strange woman was gone, leaving no trace behind her.

Ashehera stared at her reflection in the mirror as her servants fixed her up to look as stunning as possible for the festival. Her bedroom was massive, beyond the definition of luxury. The ceiling was made up of glass and had painted images of seven extraordinary, luminous beings. The great gods. Fierna of Fire, Aquanas of Water, Ental of Earth, Ventis of Wind, Lazgin of Beasts, Pertinus of Ice, and Azgus of Magic. The seven beings that crafted the world in their image. She was always nervous about this holiday that she had announced in Reynard's honor, one they had celebrated for 100 years now. Would he approve?

One of the maids handed her an armored vest. She was much younger compared to the other maids in the room with her. She was slightly paler than would be expected of an elf and had a nervous countenance about her. Ashehera looked to the maid with a raised eyebrow.

"What is this for?"

"Um… a… a… apologies, your majesty… I… I just wanted to make sure y… y… y… you were prepared for anything…"

Ashehera gave her a weak smile and put a hand on the young maid's shoulder. She let out a small yelp of panic as if she thought she was in trouble. She slowly opened her eye to see Ashehera's smiling face.

"Thank you, young one. Why don't you go back to your quarters? The festival is to start soon."

"Uh… uhm… yes, your h… h… highness," stammered the maid in a timid voice as she bowed and left the room.

Ashehera unfastened the top of her dress to put on the armored vest. She held her arms out for her maid to once again tie her dress up.

"I want to look my best. No exceptions."

"Yes, mistress."

Suddenly, Ashehera heard a timid knock against the door.

"You may enter," she said in a strong and bitter voice.

The door slowly opened to reveal Adamar. He was dressed in an outfit fit for a young prince. Ashehera instantly relaxed and let go of her tension as she saw her youngest son.

"Why, hello, little one," said Ashehera with a relaxed smile.

She brashly pushed one of the maids adjusting her dress out of the way. The young maid fell to the floor, letting out a whimper. She lay there trembling, her eyes closed tightly, until her fellow maids helped her back to her feet.

"Leave us. I wish to converse with my dear boy."

All the maids bowed quickly and exited the room, giving the queen the privacy that she so desired.

"So, young one, what is it you wanted to speak to me about so urgently? It would be good to tell me now, since the festival is going to be starting soon."

Adamar squirmed a little in his chair. He loved his mother, of course, but she always made him feel slightly on edge.

"Mama, can… can you tell me about Reynard? I don't… remember much about him."

Ashehera was a little taken aback at first at this request, but she soon broke into a smile.

"Of course, little one," she said as she placed him on her lap and brushed his hair. "Reynard was a fantastic elf. One of a kind. There was no other elf that looked or acted like him. Your brother was sent to us by the gods. He looked so… unique that many ostracized him and distrusted him. He was as big as a mountain and his skin was dark like tree bark. He rarely ever lost a fight against his enemies once he became the Royal Knight of the Harmonian Empire."

"W… woah!"

"Mmhmm! He was the beloved knight of our empire. He used to be dressed in all silver and wielded a large sword even though he needed two hands to pick it up! He won battle after battle to protect us and make the empire the way it is today."

Sadness crept into her eyes and she forced a smile as she looked out the window towards Reynard's tomb. The festival preparations were almost done. Soldiers and peasants had put heaps of flowers and jewels beside his tomb, but several citizens looked very unhappy doing so.

"Then Reynard was murdered by the humans," she said as Adamar tilted his head in confusion.

"What's a human?"

"Humans are a species that went extinct over 100 years ago. They were one of the most dangerous creatures ever to live. They couldn't use magic and yet…."

RAMPAGE: THE RISE OF AN EMPIRE

Ashehera's hand flew to her chest as dark memories from the past filled her mind.

"Humans were beings outside the understanding of this world. Everyone in our world has the capabilities of magic, except for the humans. The way their minds worked is something none of us can fully comprehend. Humans are weak… they have no claws… no fangs or spikes. Their bodies are fragile and break like twigs. They fought amongst themselves constantly for petty reasons and looked harmless. But there was something about them… some… dark and twisted thing that none of us could grasp. This indomitable desire of theirs was more potent than everything we know, than all magic. An unending desire to survive and control… no matter the cost."

Ashehera's hand was shaking, her heart thumping quickly against Adamar's back. Adamar looked scared.

"They were walking terrors. How the human mind worked was… beyond any of our understanding. If a human set his mind to something, they could do the impossible. Even break the fabric of reality and warp it to their selfish desires. Creating weapons of mass death only they could use."

"O… only they could use?"

"They crafted glyphs into their weapons—corrupted and unnatural magic mass-produced by humans so long ago. We could never understand the inner workings or even use the humans' strange weapons and technology because if any magical being touched it, they would start to rot away. They always thought ahead."

Ashehera's eyes looked wide and her pupils shrunk as her mind continued to fill with dark memories.

"To meet their desires and create new forms of technology that were beyond our comprehension, they tore our world apart—minerals, magic, land. But… but what I remember the most… are their eyes. Eyes filled with hatred and malice… and determination unlike any I have seen before. As small and weak humans are, they never stopped. No matter what we did, they never submitted…"

"Mama?"

"…They continued to clash against us like maddened animals. If we advanced, we fell into a trap. If we retreated, we were taken advantage of. If we stabbed them, they thrashed. If we broke their legs, they crawled. If they were about to die, they took their own life just to take as many enemies with them…"

"Mama, you… you're scaring me."

"They were an uncontrollable fire. They were chaos incarnate. Tools of death creating explosions, manipulating magic, bending the planet to their whim…" Ashehera was sweating and shaking. "A fire. A roaring fire of hate and carnage with the minds of scholars and the undying determination of gods… they deserved to die… they deserved to be annihilated! THEY DESERVED…"

"MOMMY!"

Ashehera, knocked out of her trance by her son's pleading cry, looked towards Adamar, who was shaking and bawling.

"I… I'm so sorry, baby. Come here." Ashehera picked up her son and held him close to her chest. "I'm… I'm sorry."

"The humans… won't come… back… right?" hiccupped Adamar between sobs.

"No, my sweet child, they are long gone. I made sure of it. Dry your tears, my son. We must prepare for the festival. They can't see this cute little face wet with tears now, right?"

"Y… y… yes, Mama."

Ashehera waved to her son as he sat up from her lap and quickly left the room. She let out a shaky sigh as she walked towards the window to look at Reynard's tomb.

"I hope I make you proud, my son."

RAMPAGE: THE RISE OF AN EMPIRE

Belas cried tears of joy near the secret passage that he had installed in the castle walls as he hugged his daughter close to his body. The young child had no injuries on her whatsoever and seemed quite calm for one who had just been kidnapped. She turned to wave at the strange woman from Belas's window, who in turn waved back to the small child she had recently held hostage.

"Oh, thank goodness, thank the gods," Belas cried, sagging with relief.

"You did well. You went above and beyond. You must have pulled many strings to ensure there were no guards on this side of the wall," said the cloaked woman.

As she spoke, several small boats could be seen rowing over to the secret passage and one by one, the people inside stepped out. They were all dressed in black cloaks. The secret passage made part of the golden wall transparent when Belas pressed one of the rings that adorned his fingers, specially crafted for this very purpose, against one of the golden bricks. By the time they all disembarked from the boats, there must have been almost a hundred of these black-cloaked strangers. Despite their large numbers, they could easily hide in the night due to their black cloaks.

"Leave now, Belas. You wouldn't want your daughter to miss the festival now, would you?"

Belas nervously shook his head as he picked up his daughter and hastily ran away. The purple-cloaked woman then turned around and stood in front of the others to address them.

"All right. Everything is going forward according to plan. I will go over it one more time before we begin. This is a suicide mission in service of our glorious master. All of your lives are forfeit except for my own, as was our master's request. It's going to be pitch dark soon, allowing us to blend in with the night. It's your job to silently take out as many enemies as possible until your presence is discerned. After we stay hidden for as long as possible and deal as much damage in the process, we need to have a final stand at the tomb of Prince Reynard. That is where I shall use the two glyphs that our master has provided for us. Our master used the last of his powers to store his magic inside of these glyphs for later use," she said, holding up two small pieces of paper with runes marked on them. "Remember, leave civilians out of the fighting unless they hinder you or fight against us."

One of the black-cloaked assassins raised their hand. "Mistress Nyana?"

"Yes?"

"Why do we not do this when there isn't a festival full of people? Won't the crowd make this more complicated for us?"

"The tomb is protected by the magic of Queen Ashehera herself. Every year the magic barrier around the tomb is taken down to redecorate the inside of the grave and clean it. It's part of the festival. If we had come on any other day, we would never have been able to access the tomb. Not only that, but with our master's current weakened state, he would not be able to destroy that barrier. This glyph has the last of our master's power. So even if we wait until next year, if we fail this, it all would have been for nothing. There is no second chance. The queen is a powerful magic caster," Nyana said, partly annoyed by the question, and turned back to the rest of the assassins.

"Anyone else?"

Another raised their hand.

"Yes?"

"Would it not be easier to go into the city using invisibility magic? It could save us a lot of trouble and risk."

RAMPAGE: THE RISE OF AN EMPIRE

"We need to save as much magika as possible for the final fight. We can't risk wasting so much of it on upholding an invisibility spell. This is also why we couldn't bring armor with us; it is too loud. The first part of the operation needs to be as quiet as possible. Then, when the time comes, we use all of our mana on offensive and defensive spells. We also could not risk making invisibility glyphs for everyone here. Glyphs are too expensive to waste, especially when it's the primary way to transport spells from our master." She seemed less annoyed by this question compared to the first one and once again turned to the crowd of cultists to address them. "This is our final chance. If this mission fails, all is lost. Your top priority is to keep me and the glyphs safe. Stealth is key. Stay in the shadows for as long as possible and take out as many as you can until we are caught. Now go."

The dozens of black-cloaked figures moved silently with lightning speed and melted into the shadows to do as their general had told them. All of them were fully prepared to die and would have no regrets. All of them were in full service of their master.

The commander held the two glyphs she was entrusted with close to her chest before hiding them away in her cloak and joining her comrades in the shadows.

Glyphs, small pieces of paper covered in runic symbols, stored powerful magic spells within them for later use that would usually take a ludicrous amount of magika and time to cast. The power from a glyph was released by deeply concentrating on the magic stored inside and beckoning it to come forth. This could be done by reciting the spell mentally while having physical contact with the glyph. Some glyphs were so powerful that one would need a mighty magic caster, or even several, just to release the spell.

Almost all creatures in the land of Harmonia possessed something in their blood called *magika*. Magika was the building block of life and magic in Harmonia. Certain creatures had more magika in their blood than others. The magika in one's blood enabled any creature to use magic. However, just because one has magic does not mean they learn how to use it. For example, an ogre has magika in its blood, but the chance of an ogre learning magic is next to none. Elves have one of the most potent concentrations of magika in their blood, second only to another creature. Over time elves learned how to increase the magika in their blood by performing lengthy and tedious rituals or taking perilous potions that could potentially end their own lives. Ashehera had taken many of these potions and performed these rituals throughout the span of her life.

The black-cloaked assassins were silently picking off guards one by one with their jagged crimson-handled daggers, going about their deadly work efficiently. Never stepping outside of their bounds and never taking risks. If they did, they would fail their master. That could never be an option for them.

Finally, one of the assassins appeared next to the commander and bowed. "Mistress Nyana, the perimeter of the wall has been cleared of guards. How shall we proceed?"

"Excellent, relay to everyone that they are to try and stay as hidden for as long as possible to pick off as many as they can. The less there is to fight in the end, the more of us can survive later on. Got it?"

"Yes, mistress."

Nyana untied her purple cloak to wear it like a cape. Underneath her disguise she was wearing light leather armor with several pockets and compartments on the sides. Around her body is a bandolier of throwing knives. Golden gauntlets cover her hands and her face is completely enveloped in a golden mask. The mask is simply designed with wavy lines running along its outer edge. It roughly resembles the face of an owl. Even Nyana's hair is hidden inside the golden mask, the only feature visible being two void-seeming green eyes peeping from the eyeholes of the mask.

"Now... I shall not fail you, master," she whispered under her breath as she walked closer and closer to the sound of instruments and the hubbub of voices.

Ashehera was looking over her dress one more time with a nervous, pained look in her eye. This day always brought out the worst in her. She looked over as she heard a knock coming from the door.

"Come in."

Arun gently pushed the doors open and stepped inside his mother's large personal chambers. The walls were covered with overgrown vines and stunning flowers that glistened like crystals. In the center of the room was a pool of water that looked purer and fresher than any natural spring in Harmonia. On the ceiling were murals depicting the history of the empire and all the massive battles and tribulations the country had to go through to get where it is today. The center of the ceiling featured the murals of the seven gods.

"Arun? What is it, darling?"

"You seem to be on edge. Adamar came to me in tears, Mother. What is happening? Every year since we lost Reynard, on this day, you have been... eccentric. Mother, whatever you are doing cannot be a normal grieving process."

Ashehera tightened her fist into a ball and inhaled with frustration. It took a moment for her to compose herself, to try and hide her anger.

"And what would you know of loss, son?"

"What? What are you even saying, Mother? I lost my father! And Reynard was my brother! Mother, it has been a hundred years since

Reynard died. You have had a hundred years to grieve and instead, you force people to perform this ceremony, to give up their money and jewels just to decorate a tomb that is closed for 364 days a year and then opened for mere hours at best. You have done this every year. This is not healthy. Our home is falling apart! The people hate this! The empire cannot sustain itself with how far we expand our borders There are no profits. Our citizens are starving and being raided daily and there is nothing we can do about it. Almost every other country in our world loathes and despises our very existence and who can blame them?! You are worried about one festival when, right now, our empire is currently at war with four other nations and is on the verge of declaring war with the Dragon Council and the Kingdom of Cade? This constant warmongering has no benefit. The Harmonian Empire used to mean something besides despair and death once! Mother, you have to—"

SMACK!

Ashehera slapped Arun and he stumbled back. Arun squinted and stared at his mother with surprise, a surprise that quickly turned into contempt.

"Get out of my sight, you ungrateful swine!" hissed Ashehera.

Arun turned away and walked towards the door. He turned back to look at her one more time.

"Well… can't say I didn't try. See you at the festival, *your highness*," Arun said sardonically before leaving his mother's private quarters.

Ashehera fell to her knees and let out a sob. She sat alone with only her thoughts to keep her company.

One by one, more golden-armored bodies fell to the ground and were pulled away into the shadows. The black-cloaked assassins were silently killing off any that would impose on the will of their master.

RAMPAGE: THE RISE OF AN EMPIRE

The perimeter of the city walls has been cleared. No sign of any bodies is left. Now all they must do is wait for the signal to begin their plan.

Nyana walked amongst the citizens of Shatterstar, keeping to herself and inching ever closer to the tomb of Prince Reynard. She thought about the two glyphs of stored magic that was entrusted to her. *You have one chance. If this fails, it's all over. I must not fail. People are going to die today because of me. I have come to accept this. People who have done nothing wrong will be slaughtered like livestock without a second thought. You can't panic now. I won't allow myself. This is going to be the beginning of the end. You know you wouldn't hurt the undeserving… but this is different… the master… he can come back. I must do this,* Nyana thought to herself as she blended in with the crowd.

From the balcony of one of the smaller castle towers, Queen Ashehera and her two sons walk forward to start the ceremony. Ashehera stepped in front of her two sons to address the crowd of citizens gathering around the city's central courtyard. Reynard's tomb was in the center of the town, protected by the powerful magical barrier that is only taken down for a short time every year.

"Greetings to all the fine citizens of Shatterstar, the capital of our beloved empire."

Most of the citizens began to cheer, but a large portion of the crowd was silent. For several decades, Ashehera's rule had been put into question. Despite pleas and begging from her citizens and advisors, she refused to change how she ruled. Many saw her as a mad queen who lost all reason after the death of her husband and son.

"Thank you to all that have come to enjoy the festivities. We have gathered once again for the passing of our dearest prince. He who brought glory and riches for the empire and bravely gave away his life to fight off the human scourge a hundred years ago. Today we shall honor his sacrifice and let his bravery live on in our hearts."

The crowd did not seem too ecstatic about the celebrations, but forced smiles nevertheless. As the queen continued to talk, shadowy figures slowly started to sneak closer and closer to the festival, staying completely quiet in the process. They were vipers, waiting for the chance to strike.

"Today is the 100th anniversary of the death of our prince. Shall he be remembered for all time!"

Ashehera lifted her hand to the sky and a beam of bright light erupted from her hand and blasted into the clouds of the night sky. Her magical powers were astounding. Suddenly, the clouds parted as a beam of pure energy shot down from the sky and slammed into the ancient shield that encircled the tomb. The invisible shield burst into an eruption of pink flower petals that rained down on everyone standing in the vicinity of Reynard's tomb. Ashehera stumbled back into her eldest son's arms, practically out of breath. The shield was made of ancient and powerful royal elven magic. When the queen made this barrier, she used all of her magical power into one massive spell.

The moment the shield went down and Nyana watched the queen fall backward, she lifted her hand and bellowed to the sky. "NOW!"

Dozens of cultists revealed themselves from the shadows and took advantage of the queen's weakness from her spell. All of them gathered around the tomb and assumed defensive positions.

"Hold them off! We must complete the ritual!" barked Nyana as the cultists clutched their daggers and swords firmly.

Ashehera watched in horror as the tomb of her son was defiled, on this holiday no less. Her eyes filled with rage as she yelled, "Stop them! Kill them now! I want them rotting away in the dungeon and executed! NOW!"

Ashehera was screaming so loudly her voice started to crack and her two sons pulled her away in a panicked state.

"Mother, stop this! This is not good for your public image. The guards will stop them," Arun panted, buckling from the effort of restraining Ashehera.

"THIS IS UNACCEPTABLE! I'LL HAVE ALL OF THEIR HEADS!"

"M… mommy, you… you're scaring me… w… what's going on?" Adamar whimpered.

Ashehera pushed her two children away and started limping her way towards the entrance of the castle. Civilians started running away and screaming in a panic.

Nyana placed one of the glyphs on the door of the large stone tomb. Four cultists joined Nyana to unleash the powerful spell stored inside the glyph. They started chanting as the rest of the cultists stayed in formation around the tomb to ensure that the mission was successful. Arrows from soldiers in the towers rained down on the cultists wielding throwing knives, daggers, and their own deadly spells. They cultists surrounded by golden-armored warriors with the highest quality weaponry.

One cultist lunged at a soldier and shoved his knife deep into his throat, killing him instantly. Blood poured from his throat and the knight fell to the ground, only for arrows to come flying down and piercing the chest of the cultist who had had just killed him. After that, spells started flying back and forth between the cultists and the knights.

"FIREBALL!"
"ICY BREATH!"
"WATERY BARRIER!"
"WARRIOR'S FURY!"
"FURY LIGHTNING!"
"ROCK SHIELD!"

A cultist stumbled back and fell, the hilt of a knife protruding from his stomach. He could barely breathe as he lay on the ground, both friend and foe trampling him. Then, as blood spilled from his mouth, he was able to utter a spell.

"S... strength of the berserker!"

The cultist suddenly felt his pain melt away. He forced himself to stand back up once again and roared triumphantly as he charged into enemy lines with his sword and chopped down any living thing dressed in gold with his newfound strength.

Meanwhile, inside Reynard's tomb, Nyana was in a panic. The spell stored inside the glyph was so potent that it was taking her ages to cast it. She usually would not have enough magika to cast a spell of this magnitude, but the spell has already been completed and stored inside the glyph. Since the spell is so large, it was taking her and four other cultists a long time to cast it. As Nyana watches their numbers begin to dwindle more and more, blind panic and anxiety start seizing her. And finally came the moment she was dreading – arrows zoomed past her face, one of them lodging right into the neck of a cultist who was helping her release the spell from the glyph.

"No, no, no... I can't fail... not again... please... PLEASE!"

More arrows are fired. Two more cultists who were helping Nyana cast the spell get killed. The soldiers had a near-unencumbered shot at Nyana. Five arrows come flying towards her, but a cultist instantly blocked the path, sacrificing their life to protect hers. Nyana hated this, seeing her allies getting butchered like this. But they knew what they were getting into and she couldn't stop now. She couldn't even turn around to see how many of her friends were still alive. All she heard were screams as she turned around, the only one left to try and release this massive spell inside the glyph.

The main doors to the castle open and Ashehera marched outside, grasping her crystal trident, another platoon of knights marching behind her.

"STOP HER! I WANT HER ALIVE AND IN THE DUNGEON RIGHT NOW!"

There were only about thirty cultists left, all of them tired and injured, but determined to make sure this plan was seen through.

"You can do it, mistress! We will hold them off. Just do it!"

All the knights charged with a mighty war cry. Ten more cultists died instantly, their corpses held up in the air by triumphant golden lances.

Nyana could feel the spell being near completion. She was so close. She could feel herself getting more and more terrified. She had thought she was prepared for this and yet she was panicking. All she could do is trust that she would be able to finish this in time, even if she gets killed in the process.

A knight headbutted one of the cultists with his hard helmet, splattering his brains all over the ground. The cultist's hood fell off to reveal an elf. Ashehera was taken aback at the sight.

"My own citizens? What madness is this? STOP THEM NOW, MY KNIGHTS!"

A cultist sheathed her dagger to focus on a spell. "BLAZING INFERNO!"

An explosive blast of hellish fire erupted from the ground, blowing away several knights and killing many others. The pile of bodies around the tomb grew higher and higher, the cultists on their last legs with their backs pressed against the wall.

"GENERAL, PLEASE HURRY!"

Nyana was shaking with fear as a cultist's head was pinned to the wall next to her by an arrow. She concentrated with all her might on the spell, not scared of these enemies but of failing her master. Suddenly, the ground started to shake. The glyph went up in green flames, shriveled, and burnt to ash.

Nyana shook and collapsed to the ground, knowing that she had completed the spell. The other cultists were all dead. It was just her.

Ashehera walked over the dead bodies to confront Nyana. "Do you understand what you have just done?! What spell was in that glyph? What did you just do?"

"Heh… hehehehe… my purpose, nothing else," said Nyana through her golden mask, laughing maniacally.

"Guards, take that mask off of her face and…"

Suddenly, the ground started to shake again. A green fog began to roll in. Ashehera and her knights looked around in confusion as the mist got thicker and thicker. Nyana tried to crawl away, but a knight stomped on her chest to stop her from escaping. The soldiers start to panic from seeing strange magic the likes of which none of them had ever seen in their extraordinary life spans.

"What… what in the seven's name is this?"

"I've never seen anything like this!"

"Green? Why is it green?"

"Is this magic?"

"Something is wrong… something feels very wrong."

Suddenly, a blinding light erupted from the tomb of Prince Reynard, followed by the most monstrous and horrific scream imaginable. It sounded like the disturbed and tortured cries of a crowd of banshees. The night sky started getting cloudier by the second, the darkness deepening. The sky started flashing green and plants began to wither and die. The ground continued to shake violently and cracked apart.

Ashehera stood spellbound, shocked by such unknown and powerful magic. "What kind of power is this?!"

Arun and Adamar watched from the tower with confusion and horror as the sky changed color in a way it never has before. Nyana started laughing as she coughed up blood that dripped out from the bottom of her mask.

Ashehera kicked her in the stomach and growled, "WHAT IS

THIS? WHO ARE YOU? WHAT DID YOU WANT WITH MY SON'S BODY?"

"Heh… hehehehe… Your majesty… the spell has only just begun."

CHAPTER 2

"Where am I? Who am I? What am I? Blackness... all I see is pitch blackness. Is there screaming outside? I can't think... I can't think. Do I have a purpose? Do I have a name? Why can't I feel anything? Why can't I smell anything? Why can't I see anything? Why am I not scared? No... it's not that I'm not afraid... I simply don't care. All I know is that there is an impulse rising within me. A beckoning voice calls me to break free and tells me to indulge a fury that is not my own. The war horns are sounding. Calling me to my purpose. I'm being given commands by a general I don't even know... and yet I must obey. I don't care about where I am anymore... I only want BLOOD. I don't care about who I am... I just want to SLAUGHTER. I don't care about what I am anymore... all I know is that I'm ready to GO ON A RAMPAGE!"

From outside the tomb, the stone door started to crumble. A loud slamming noise could be heard from the inside. Suddenly, an explosion of dust and stone propelled from the tomb, revealing a large frame. Standing amidst the ruins of the stone tomb is a towering, humongous, skeletal being. Its breathing was heavy and it slowly looked down at the elves surrounding him. A steaming red fog poured from his eye sockets and agape jaw. The strange being's boney fingers ended in sharp talons and even the 'ends of its ribs were pointed enough to rend flesh. The skeleton's empty sockets glowed a vicious crimson as the fog dissipated from its face. The giant skeleton was only dressed in ragged trousers that had somehow survived one hundred years in a sealed crypt.

Ashehera was stricken to silence. It didn't make sense. The power to bring the dead back was one that not even she knew existed. Ashehera was almost 1,000 years old and even with that extraordinary lifespan, she has never heard of such a power. Ashehera was slowly starting to realize what was happening. Its frame. Its posture. It was her son.

"R… R… Reynard? M… my son, is that y—"

"Reynard? Who… is… Reynard? No… I don't care… I only crave… blood. I only desire… to rip apart elves and bathe in their intestines."

"R… Reynard?"

"DIE, ELVEN SCUM!" the skeletal being roared.

Knights started to back away in fear as the corpse of Reynard started moving towards them. Nyana held onto the second glyph in her pocket with dear life. She had succeeded, but this would have all been for nothing if she wouldn't be able to pull off this second spell. It was not as large as the first spell, but still just as important. She could use it much quicker than the first, but seeing how Reynard had already gone on a rampage, it could prove challenging to pull it off.

Reynard charged and grabbed an elven knight by the throat. He picked up the knight so high that his legs were no longer touching the ground and snapped his neck with the ease of a child breaking twigs. Reynard violently threw the dead body straight into a stone wall. The impact was so hard that the stone wall cracked and left a crater of impact where the body hit. The other knights were terrified, but some still had the will to fight. An archer shot arrows right at Reynard, but he used his claws to slice the arrows in half before they even hit him. Another knight charged at Reynard, but the behemoth undead punched him, his fist going through the knight's armor, straight into the elf's chest until his hand was on the other side of the elf's torso. Blood and intestines gushed everywhere, staining his white bones red. Reynard then grabbed another knight and shoved his claws into her eye sockets. Then, with a jolt of superhuman strength, he ripped her head off, cracking the skull in the process, and threw it to the ground.

The green fog started seeping into the pores of the many corpses on the ground. The dead bodies started to shake and twitch until they eventually stood, each a smaller likeness of the undead Reynard. Knight and cultist alike were being risen from the dead by the green mist. Slowly, each undead warrior started attacking anything with a heartbeat while letting out a bone-chilling breath.

Nyana jumped out of the way and did a backflip onto the top of the crypt. She turned her head to see several guards chasing after her and archers ready to fire. She had plenty of magika, but casting the first glyph had taken a lot out of her. Nyana eyed her opponents and slid off the tomb. She moved with incredible agility and speed as the knights started to chase after her. As she ran, arrows whizzed past her, one of them lodging into her shoulder. She gritted her teeth and continued to move with lightning speed.

Ashehera was shaking. The power to bring back the dead was something far beyond her imagination. She has always been a master of magic. She had spent hundreds of years experimenting on herself to increase her magika and had studied every spell possible and yet her son was standing before her, reborn into a bloodthirsty beast. Ashehera shakily stood back up and watched in horror the monster that was apparently her son continue to massacre her knights. However, the only thing she could think of was how she had so many things she wanted to say to him. Could she bring him back? Was this some kind of dream?

Reynard shoved his boney talons into a knight's neck and decapitated the knight with a single slash, splattering the knight's blood all over his skull.

"My son? R... Reynard? It's me... it's Mommy... do you remember me? Please stop this rampage... please... come ba—"

"RAAAAAAAAAAAAAAAAAAAAAAAAAAAAAAAA AAAAAGH!"

The moment Reynard saw Ashehera, some kind of uncontrollable rage filled him. He charged at her like a mad rhino, shoulder-butting her through two stone walls of the castle.

Ashehera, lying in a pile of rubble, coughed up blood, her body aching with agonizing pain. She was lucky to be alive. She opened some of her dress to see the armored vest completely cracked open like a shell. It was useless now, but it had taken the brunt of his attack, saving her life in the process. Reynard was being surrounded by more and more knights pouring in from every corner of the courtyard.

Ashehera got back to her feet with difficulty and with a flick of her finger summoned her crystal trident. Her body was filled with pain and her legs wobbled, but she stood her ground.

"My dear son... I promise you that I shall find the person responsible for all of this. I will make them suffer the pain of a thousand deaths and make sure they feel nothing but ceaseless agony for years to come. I will make this as painless as possible. I refuse to give up on you, my son. I finally have you back and I shall NEVER lose you again. Guards? Where is the woman I told you to apprehend?"

"We... lost her, your majesty."

"WHAT?"

"I'm going to rip out your spine and use it as a noose to hang you from!" snarled Reynard.

Reynard lunged forward, but this time Ashehera was ready. She flawlessly dodged his brutal attack and countered by slashing at his bones. The trident slashed against his back and sent sparks flying off of him. Usually, her trident would obliterate bones, slicing cleanly through them, but it didn't work this time. Why? What has happened to her son?

RAMPAGE: THE RISE OF AN EMPIRE

Reynard grunted in pain from the attack. It was more excruciating than his mind could keep up with. It was as if all the fight in his body was being taken away. But his rage willed him to fight on. He twisted around to try and backhand Ashehera. She once again flawlessly evaded his attack and slashed at his hand. Again, the trident sparked against his bones, but this time too, only a small crack appeared on his skeletal hand.

"RAAAAAAAAAAAAAAAAAAAAAAAAAAAAAAAAA AAAAAAGH!"

"GIVE UP! I only want to help you!"

"I'll feed your intestines to the crows!"

"…Very well, my child. Our duel shall continue. But know that every moment this duel continues, my heart aches unbearably."

"COME CLOSER SO I CAN RIP IT OUT FOR YOU!"

Nyana was able to escape to a good hiding spot. An arrow was lodged into her shoulder and she had lost track of Reynard. She will not allow herself to fail. Nyana twisted around to look at her shoulder and firmly gripped the arrow. She gritted her teeth as she prepared herself to pull on the arrow. She could hear footsteps near her. No matter how painful this was, she can't utter a sound or she would be as good as dead. She would normally have waited until they left so there would be no risk, but the arrow was already halfway out and she was losing blood. Without hesitation, she pulled on the arrow until it sliced its way out of her flesh. Every cell in her body told her to scream in pain, but she willed herself not to. She let out a shaky, pained breath as she ripped a piece of cloth from her pants and tightly wrapped it around her wound. Blood stained the ragged piece of cloth, but it would have to do for the time being.

Nyana heard footsteps getting closer and quickly began to sneak away. She needed to find Reynard fast. Nyana took out her dagger and held it close to her chest. Its hilt was golden and encrusted with rubies. The blade was curved and made of silver. Suddenly, she heard more footsteps approaching. She jumped behind a barrel, holding her breath.

"Have you seen the spell caster yet?"

"No, sir! We are continuing our search for her now."

"Very good. Remember, Her Majesty wants her alive."

"Uh… permission to speak freely, sir?"

"Granted."

"Why are we looking for this woman when the queen is in trouble? She just told us to find…"

"Because if this woman can create monsters from the dead one time, she can do it again. Plus, it was a direct order from your queen, anything else you want to say?"

"No, sir."

"Good. Dismissed!"

The knights scattered once again and Nyana took the opportunity to make her way back into the palace. The quick and agile Nyana started sprinting and jumping on small ledges and boxes to get to the top of houses and jump from roof to roof. As she ran, she reached into her pocket and gripped the final glyph tightly. She was lucky the spell inside the second glyph was not as powerful as the first.

Usually, one could automatically use a glyph. This was because the magic was already completed, cast, and stored inside the glyph to make sure that it would automatically get activated when the time was right. That being said, the spell inside of the first glyph was so large and powerful that it still took a long time just to get out of the glyph. Nyana looked at the castle and grit her teeth under her mask. She was going to succeed whether the gods wanted her to or not.

RAMPAGE: THE RISE OF AN EMPIRE

The golden knights of Shatterstar panic as the undead corpses of soldiers and cultists swarm them. No matter how much the undead were shot and stabbed, they kept standing back up and continuing their advance. Reynard groaned as he looked at Ashehera standing above him, a pained look in her eyes. Several of Reynard's bones are now cracked and his skeletal body was coursing with pain. Ashehera could not help but wonder what kind of undead he was. She didn't have much of a frame of reference, since she had never seen any undead in her entire existence of a thousand years. She could tell he was different though. The undead outside acted mindlessly and didn't seem to react to pain and yet her son was still talking and grunting against her blows.

Reynard was on the ground, defeated. He tried to lunge at her neck one last time, but she easily dodged his attack and slashed him with her trident.

"I'm sorry, my son. I cannot allow you to do that."

"I... HATE... YOU!"

"Why, my son?"

"I... don't know... I DON'T CARE! I MUST KILL YOU!"

He lunged at her once again, only for her to dodge and slash at him once again. Reynard fell backward with a snarl and looked up at Ashehera.

"I'll... RIP... YOU... APART!"

Ashehera stared down at him with tears in her eyes. Each slash of her trident was breaking her heart. This was not what she had in mind in her fantasies of him coming back to her. She looked to the knights surrounding him.

"Keep him there. Make sure he doesn't move while I handle the others."

Ashehera turned towards the horde of undead outside of the castle and charged. She masterfully dodged and countered most of the attacks dished out by the undead with quick, decisive movements. Nevertheless, undead knights viciously lunged out with their sharp blades and cultists with mangled and broken bodies lashed out at the elven queen. Despite her prowess, skill, and her mighty trident, she was hopelessly outnumbered.

Ashehera's formal dress was hindering her movement. Seeing how she had no real chance to go and change, she was forced into a defensive position. A knight slashed at Ashehera's arm, making her yelp in pain. She quickly decapitated the zombie-like knight, slicing through the golden armor like butter. If her crystal trident could slice through metal with ease, how come it could only just crack the bones of her son? Another knight came from the side and with a twirl of her wrist, she cut off both of the undead knight's hands and sliced him in half. The knights pressed in closer and closer around Reynard. He was covered in cracks and could barely stand. His glowing red eyes showed nothing but hate and contempt for all around him.

"Snap your bones like twigs… choke you till your eyes pop out…"

The knights seemed intimidated by him but were bolstered by the fact that he was on the ground, defeated, and their numbers were far superior.

While Ashehera was distracted, Nyana was getting closer and closer. She finally came upon the view of the defeated Reynard splayed on the ground. Then, of course, there was the problem that was a horde of undead, the queen, and a legion of imperial knights in her way. Nyana pondered, looking around for an opening as she scratched the golden chin on her mask. Nyana had saved up almost all of her magika. Usually, one would not need magika to open a glyph, but since the first glyph she used contained such a powerful spell and her four assistants died while releasing the spell, she had

had to use some magika to successfully cast the spell that had awakened Reynard. Nyana quickly started hatching a plan. She still had magika to spare and all she needed to do was touch Reynard with the glyph for the mission to be a success.

"Invisibility," Nyana whispered softly.

In an instant, she turned completely invisible and jumped down from her perch. She moved with lightning speed, making sure not to bump into any of the undead, but it was getting harder and harder the closer she got to Reynard. Finally, she stopped running and had to move against the wall as Ashehera and the walking corpses battled inches away from her face. Nyana quickly dodged as the end of Ashehera's trident almost slammed into her eye, accidentally knocking the back of her head against the broken stone wall. The noise of Nyana's golden mask clanging against the stone caught Ashehera's attention, making her turn around immediately. Nyana bolted, running and flipping over the knights as quickly as her injured body allowed her. Her invisibility spell ended and without hesitation, she grabbed the glyph from her pocket and slammed it onto Reynard. Sparks of lightning started flying around them and Nyana, along with the undead Reynard, vanished, leaving a soft curl of smoke behind them.

Ashehera turned around as the knights surrounding them leaped back in surprise. "NO! REYNARD!"

The knights left their post to run to the queen's aid. Ashehera retreated as she ran to where the spell had just taken place behind her. She looked at the ground where Reynard was lying just moments ago with pained eyes as she fell to her knees. Tears dripped from her eyes.

"You're gone…again? I failed you again? DAMMIT! DAMMIT DAMMIT DAMMIT!" Ashehera violently punched at the wall until her knuckles started to bleed. Blood seeped from her mouth from biting down so hard.

"Your highness! Please, we must get you to safety immediately! Let your loyal warriors finish this fight."

Ashehera looked down at her bloody knuckles and let out a shaky and pained sigh, "…Yes…. please…take me to my throne."

"At once, your highness."

As Ashehera was escorted away from the battle, more knights were being killed. It was a full-on clash between golden-clad warriors and bloodthirsty corpses. The rest of the night was filled with the sounds of screams and clashing iron. All civilians were forced into lockdown on the other end of the city, far from the fighting. The undead horde was heavily outnumbered, but they dragged the fighting out just by the simple fact that they wouldn't stay down. Delivering blow after killing blow did nothing but stop them for a moment.

By the time the sun was back in the sky, all the undead had finally been destroyed. The casualties from the night were catastrophic. Bodies of at least 173 dead knights and twelve dead civilians lay strewn around Reynard's tomb. The royal courtyard had been destroyed and the castle walls by the courtyard were damaged. Bodies littered the courtyard and castle. The delicate flowers of the courtyard gardens, the priceless carpets of the castle, the finely-woven garments – everything was spattered with blood and gore.

Ashehera sat on her throne, devastated. She didn't get any sleep last night. There was so much to think about and try to fix in such a short amount of time. The doors to the throne room slowly creaked open to reveal Belas, his head still bandaged from the events that happened in the throne room the previous day. Belas knows that last night was all his fault. He let the group into the city. He would take that secret with him to the grave.

"Ahem… good morning, your majesty. We have… things to discuss," he said in a slightly nervous voice. Something the queen quickly caught on to since the royal advisor rarely sounded nervous.

RAMPAGE: THE RISE OF AN EMPIRE

"Yes?"

"Well… I know you already got the casualty and damage reports, but there are other things to go over. It has been confirmed as of today that several of the cloaked assassins who attacked you last night were… your citizens. Out of the maybe 100 or so attackers, over seventy of them were registered Harmonian Empire citizens."

Queen Ashehera was reduced to a stunned silence. While she had uncovered the identity of one of the cultists and found him to be an elf, the fact that most of the assassins were her citizens was incomprehensible to her.

"Your majesty, I see you under a… ahem… a lot of pressure. I will conclude my report quickly. As for the undead, we are still searching through our records and getting in contact with as many historians as possible. We can still find no official documents confirming the existence of magic that can bring back the dead. There is something that I found fascinating, though. When you were fighting… Prince Reynard… and those other… corpses, your exceptional trident hurt and destroyed them quickly, yet the other knights struggled to fight the undead and their weapons seemed incredibly ineffective. What is your trident made out of, your majesty?"

Ashehera examined the crystal trident that she summoned to her hand from thin air and looked back to Belas. "I know not. This weapon has been passed down in the royal family by my father and his father before him. This weapon is more ancient than any elf. Not even I know how old this trident is. These crystals do look similar to the ones growing inside the mountains of the Dragon Council. If these crystals can hurt the undead, then we need as many of them as possible."

"You mean the same Dragon Council that you have been trying to annex and are on the verge of war with?"

"The very same."

"My queen… in times such as these, would it not be wise for a truce to be struck? Thankfully war has not started yet and seeing how the empire is already currently involved in four separate wars right at this very moment… maybe a different approach would be viable?"

"FINE! We shall talk with the dragons. They should not pose much of an issue. They have stayed hidden away in their mountains since before I was even born. All they do now is squabble amongst themselves and play nice with their pet snakes in the Kingdom of Cade."

"That may be our best course of action. We will establish diplomatic relations with the Kingdom of Cade then. The Nagas that live there are for the most part peaceful. Your majesty… under no circumstances can you attack the Kingdom of Cade. Overall, their power as a country is weak, but they are inseparable allies of the Dragon Council."

"Agreed. We shall depart soon. I have some things to attend to before then."

"Yes, your majesty," Belas said with a bow before leaving the throne room.

Ashehera slumped over and massaged her temples roughly with her fingers. She gave a shaky sigh as she sat up and left for her sons' private chambers.

Arun was lying on his bed, still at a loss for words from the events of last night. His mind could not wrap around it all. His brother rising from the dead with dozens of others? Their own civilians trying to overthrow the queen? It's as if everything wrong that could have possibly happened did so in one night.

Arun stared up at the ceiling with a longing look, then turned his head to look at his brother's bed. Adamar had cried himself to sleep and that too when Arun used sleeping herbs on him. Arun had tried to cover his brother's eyes last night to shield him from the horrors unfolding before them, but Adamar had already seen enough for it to be too late. Arun stood up and kneeled next to his brother's bed. He gently brushed his brother's hair with his fingers and held the fast-asleep Adamar close to his chest.

"Don't worry, my brother... I shall protect you in these dark times. I refuse to let any harm come to you."

The door slowly creaked open to reveal Ashehera. She knelt next to Arun and held him close to her.

"Arun, I have to leave to figure out how to get your brother back and save our kingdom. You must stay here and help search through the historical records to find any kind of magic that can bring back the dead."

"Mother? You're... leaving? I don't understand. There was just a tragedy in our capital that almost reached 200 casualties. You're needed here! You have thousands at your disposal and you choose now to leave? After we learn that most of the attackers were civilians? The public will think you're running away!"

Ashehera grumbled in frustration and leaned against the wall. "Arun... my son... why do you have to make everything so complicated? I'm only trying to do what is best for our kingdom. If there were that many undead... and my son is still out there, we need to find out why my trident can hurt them."

"You're worrying me, Mother. Our country is already embroiled in four wars right now and what if you start a fifth with the Dragon Council? Why don't you just leave this to the professional diplomats?"

"PROFESSIONAL DIPLOMATS? MY OWN SON SEES ME AS A FOOL!"

Adamar jolted awake in fright from the yelling. "M... M... Mommy?"

Before Arun even got a word out, she was gone from sight and out of the room. Arun clenched his fist, but softened his demeanor the moment he spoke to his brother.

"Hey... it's okay, brother, you can relax. Nothing is wrong."

"B... but I heard Mom yelling and... and what about Reynard?"

"Hey hey hey, none of that, okay? We don't need to worry about any of that right now. A lot has been happening and sometimes we just have to not think about it. You'll just end up making yourself upset and getting nothing done. Here... want me to read you another story?"

"Yes please."

"Okay... here we go. Once upon a time—"

Ashehera angrily walked down the marble and golden halls of her palace while yelling frustratedly to herself. "How dare he? Who does he think he is? Questioning me? The most powerful person in all of Harmonia! The mistress of an empire that is vast enough to control almost half of the continent! How dare he? What has he accomplished besides being a constant thorn in my side and questioning every damn decision I make?! It's so easy for him to judge me while all he does is lounge about and gorge himself on my riches! Mine!"

She looked up at the ceiling with tired eyes. Jewel-encrusted chandeliers hang from the top. The walls are adorned with golden statues of elven heroes. At the far end of the hall was a silver statue of Reynard the knight. His armor was all silver and on his chest plate was the crest of the Harmonian Empire, the falcon. His helmet entirely concealed his face and was adorned with a crimson feather. In his hands was a massive silver greatsword that he held to his side with both hands.

A small tear fell from her cheek as she pressed her head against the statue. "Oh, Reynard… what happened to you? Where are you? Please… let me find you… let me know you're okay."

Ashehera started to walk away. She turned around to get one last look at the statue before walking out of the palace to the royal carriage. It was going to be a long trip to get to Cade. But even if it took her ages, she was willing to go through with it if at the end of it she found her son and finally had him back after a hundred painful years.

CHAPTER 3

BAM! Suddenly, an electric spark flashed, teleporting both the massive undead Reynard and Nyana into a strange, dark room. Nyana let go of all the tension in her body once the realization hit her that she had succeeded. This aura of calm was quick to diminish, however, as she suddenly felt a cold and firm grasp around her neck. Nyana was slammed against the wall, her feet dangling off the floor from being held up so high. She felt the air in her lungs rush out, leaving her gasping for breath. She desperately tried to free her throat as he started to squeeze tighter.

"Who… are… you? Where am I? What… am I?" said Reynard in an angry and confused voice. Pure anger was pushing him forward. Many of his bones were snapped and cracked from the fight with the queen.

"You… are mine," said a voice far away in the darkness behind Reynard.

The voice sounded decrepit and ancient. Suddenly, Reynard's hand was forced open and Nyana fell to the ground, fighting to get air into her lungs. Reynard looked down at his hand, confused. How did his bony fingers obey a command that was not his own? Nyana slowly stood up. She gently massaged her bruised neck, staring coldly at the skeletal figure.

"If the master didn't want you, your skull would be in twelve places by now. Don't EVER try that again, or you will regret it."

"I would heed her advice, revenant. I have invested much magika and planning into this and I would be most displeased if your rude actions caused my second-in-command to die. I would hate to punish both of you."

"R… revenant? What's a revenant? Is that what I am? Is that my name?"

"Follow the path to me… and all answers shall be revealed to you," said the strange ancient voice.

Neither Nyana nor Reynard could see anything since the hallway they were in was so dimly lit. Slowly, the hall started to light up with torches erupting on their own in sickly green flames. The walls were adorned with strange, disturbing statues of demons and monsters of unknown origin. The ground was decorated with a long red carpet that was covered in dust. Everything Reynard could see was covered in thick dust and cobwebs. The hallway led to many rooms, some of them empty, some full of broken, rotting furniture. As Reynard and Nyana walked down the hallway, torches started to light up in front of them, lighting their path. Cages hung from the ceiling, swaying back and forth, with skeletons inside them.

"How long is this hall? I want answers now, woman."

"You will hold your tongue, undead brute! My master has gone through a lot of trouble to obtain you."

"Not much farther, my child," said the decrepit voice from the shadows.

As the two walked farther and farther ahead they could see an entrance to a large room. The two massive double doors, embedded with skulls and bones, were already open. As the two approached the doors, they could see the inside of the room. While Nyana kept up her brisk pace, having been here dozens of times before, Reynard grew more apprehensive with each step he took.

This room was the cleanest of them all. Imposing statutes, contorted in disturbing ways, protruded out of the walls as if trying to climb their way out and cling onto anything to escape. The floor was cold and a few inches of a green, murky fog covered it like an ever-moving carpet. The ceiling was decorated with murals of ancient battles between armies and massive dragons. In front of the two was now a large pit. The pit was wide, about ten by ten feet. The perimeter of the pit was decorated with skulls and black gothic spikes. Behind the strange pit were three staircases. One to the left of the pit, one to its right, and one directly in the center behind the pit.

Reynard walked towards the right staircase with his heavy footsteps and Nyana took the left. At the top of the stairs was a long row of giant statues of skeleton knights along a long red carpet leading to a throne. On both sides of the throne were gargoyles with green flames erupting from their mouths and eyes. The throne was made of stainless black steel, with large spikes erupting from its back. Behind the throne is a glass mural depicting a strange-looking woman with blue skin and four red eyes, wrapped in a cloak the color of midnight. Resting upon the throne was a withered and frail body. Its skin was greenish brown and so old that it was practically see-through. Its fingers ended in long, sharp talons. The figure was dressed in a blood-red robe. Bugs crawled on its face. A centipede slithered from one of the body's eye sockets and entered its agape mouth. The figure's face was a skull unlike any other. Its mouth was full of razor-sharp teeth and upon its head were two jagged demon-like horns. The ancient corpse's head was leaning on its right shoulder, slumped over and lifeless. There seemed to be a faint, dimly shining red light coming from the right eye of the corpse.

"Where is your master? There is nobody here."

"You're looking right at him."

"You serve a corpse?"

"Says the walking corpse."

"Hmmph."

The light coming from the eye socket of the corpse started to glow slightly brighter and the strange, decrepit voice filled the room. "Welcome, my revenant. I am your new master. Zithoss. Son of Goddess Nioxis and master of the dead."

Reynard stared at the corpse and got closer. "Master? Those are bold words indeed, coming from a withered husk of a man. Do tell how you are my master."

Suddenly, with the force of an entire mountain crashing down, Reynard slammed to the ground and bowed to Zithoss. He struggled to get up, but he could not move a single inch of his undead form. Reynard snarled and struggled more, but to no avail, as Zithoss talked over his struggling, unyielding form.

"There is no point, my revenant. If you stop struggling, I shall release you."

Reynard let out one last roar of frustration and let the tension release from his body and just as Zithoss said, the force that was holding him down vanished.

"I am sure you have plenty of questions right now. Ask, and you shall receive the knowledge you seek."

Reynard paced back and forth like a cornered animal ready to attack at any moment.

Finally, he clenched his bony fist and began his questioning. "Who am I? I remember nothing. I woke up and all I felt was… rage."

"Who you were before does not matter. Your old name does not matter. You are someone entirely new now. All I shall say is this: your rage is why I picked you. Your old life is no more, but fragments of your past life remain. Such as the pure rage and agony you felt towards elves when you died, my revenant."

Reynard clenched his fist and glared at Zithoss the moment he brought up elves. "You keep calling me your revenant. What does that mean?"

"It is what you are now. You are no mere undead. You are a unique undead endowed with my magika. I'm sure you have already met some of your undead counterparts. Thoughtless and expendable. I crafted you the way you are. Made it so that you have a consciousness and are imbued with the blessings of Nioxis herself. Your strength is superb, and your body of bone is sturdier than steel."

Reynard looked to his clawed hand and moved his fingers to examine them closely. When he was done, he looked back towards Zithoss.

"Where am I?"

"Halfway across the continent whence you awoke. This is one of the largest mountains that separates the lands of Whita and Nigt. This mountain has been my home for longer than you can possibly imagine."

"Huh... some home. You live in squalor."

Nyana punched the giant skeleton on the side of his head. Reynard snarled and whipped around to turn towards the woman with the golden mask. Nyana was secretly glad of her mask because it hid from Reynard the pain she had felt on punching him.

"Stupid girl. I will—"

"You'll do no such thing." said Zithoss in a calm, dismissive manner.

" Nyana...refrain from acting out in such a childish manner again. " Zithoss said while still looking to Reynard. Nyana gently nodded her head in response.

"Hmmmph... I'm not done with you yet," snarled Reynard at the silent figure of Nyana. Turning back towards Zithoss, Reynard demanded, "Why did you bring me back from the dead? Why are you being so vague, you bastard?"

"You are going to be my general. My overlord."

"...What?" Reynard was at a loss for words.

"Hundreds of thousands of years ago, this entire continent was mine and mine alone. For millennia I was the master of all. The years have been long. I am a concept long forgotten to time. Time has not been kind of me. I cannot die of age, yet it has been so long since I have been able to move my own body. Before you died, you were a famous general and an exceptional warrior. You may have lost your memories, but those instincts are still inside you. You are going to be the face of my new empire. You will take back the land that is rightfully mine and, in the process, collect the souls I need to get my power back."

"Souls?"

"I. Am. ZITHOSS! The elder lich. The son of Goddess Nioxis. Down those stairs is my well of souls. Souls that fuel my all-powerful magic. My source for magika. You will go out into the world, build my empire, and give me the souls I require in order to use my magic again."

"So, you're powerless, huh? What is stopping me from killing you now for dragging me all the way here, then?"

Zithoss let out a derisory laugh. "Stupid boy. I am the son of a goddess. I cannot die. I may have no power left... but as I said before, I have control over you. I gave you life and I can take it away."

Suddenly, a cold and crushing feeling overcame the revenant as he fell to his knees in blinding pain, fully convinced that his second life too had come to an end. Then, in an instant, the pain stopped, leaving Reynard panting on the floor.

"Grrrrrrrrr... Understood, master," breathed Reynard in a pained whisper.

"You are reluctant, I see. I apologize for the aggressive display of power, but I cannot allow you to doubt me. You should know that you will be the one who benefits more from this than I. I already said you shall be my overlord. My existence must be hidden for as long as possible. I admit it was a risky gamble I pulled in Shatterstar, but seeing the outcome I would say we have gained. They will find out eventually. My magic of the dead has not touched the soil of elves for thousands of years… until this night, that is. I have been working from the shadows in my mountain ever since. Failed plan after failed plan led to you—my perfect plan. As my overlord, you will be the leader of my empire… or should I say, your empire? All I need are the souls you collect in battle. The riches you collect, the territory you claim, and the glory will be yours and yours alone. They have no meaning to me. Just my power. Not to mention… there will be plenty of elves to slaughter. Their souls make for the best source of magika."

Reynard thought for a moment. What choice did he have? If he refused, then he would be destroyed or controlled like a puppet. On top of that, there was the ever-increasing urge for violence and killing growing inside of him. An emotion that he couldn't control or understand. He wanted to kill this golden masked woman badly, but he would be destroyed if he did so. He would just have to take this rage out on elves instead. He paced back and forth, considering Zithoss's proposal. He glanced at Nyana, who was staring at the gargoyle statues, before finally looking back at Zithoss.

"I accept."

"Of course you do. I have willed it to be so, my overlord."

Nyana's face was hidden, making it impossible to know how she felt, but her clenched fist betrayed her emotions.

"You are the perfect candidate for what is in store. I know it to be true. Nyana, bring the three here."

Nyana glared at the motionless body for a moment before obeying her master and walking out of the room into another side room. Nyana entered what used to be a treasure vault right next to Zithoss's throne room. There was a time when he had so much treasure that gold coins would be spilling out of chests and would need to be piled on the floor. All the precious jewels and metals one could imagine would be in decadent abundance in this giant vault. Over the years, little by little, the treasure had to be spent on one failed plan after another. Most of the money was spent on mercenaries and for covering up Zithoss's existence. Finally, after so many failed attempts and the drying up of the treasure, Zithoss used the bold tactic that had actually worked. All that was left of the treasure now was cobwebs and dust. Several old chests lay around the floor, broken and crawling with insects and spiders. In the middle of the room lay a single chest. Nyana could feel the immense and overwhelming magical power radiating from the chest without having even touched it.

She returned, carrying the strange chest telekinetically. It looked to be made out of stone. The trunk was wrapped in chains and it had a peculiar lock that was shaped like a skull.

"What… what is this feeling?" mumbled Reynard.

"My revenant, what you are feeling is sheer magical power radiating from the three artifacts stored in this chest. Tools I used during an age where I could move more freely than I can now. Nyana, open the chest. I am sure that he is worthy."

As soon as Nyana opened the chest, Reynard staggered back from the sheer amount of magical energy radiating from the trunk. Whatever was in this chest held immense amounts of power. Nyana put her hand in the chest and slowly and carefully picked up what looked like a sizable gauntlet made out of gray steel. The fingers' ends were curved into hooked claws and in the center of the gauntlet was an orange eyeball. A moving eyeball. The iris was red, constantly looking around the room in a frantic manner. Nyana stared down at the gauntlet. It was impossible to tell how she felt about it all.

"What is that? It feels… sinister."

"That, my revenant, is the Gauntlet of the Overlord. An ancient artifact I created thousands of years ago which was used by the mighty human King Daemos to fight the Harmonian Empire. It was stolen by enemies of mine… they were the source of… my current state. It was treasured and zealously guarded by the humans after my age of power was forgotten, erased from time. It was then passed down from generation to generation of humans until it came to Daemos… and then was returned to its rightful side by me. I went through an immense amount of trouble to retrieve it after Daemos used it himself. Generation after generation, the gauntlet was passed down after King Sargon stole it from me and improved upon by the humans. By the time I got the gauntlet back… I had been reduced to this… useless state. Now, not even I know everything the gauntlet is capable of. How many tricks and purposes those humans have used my gauntlet for. Now… put it on. We must see for ourselves if you are worthy, unlike my servant."

Nyana growled and turned away as Reynard reached over, took the gauntlet from her and slipped it on. His hand was too big, but the gauntlet immediately resized itself to fit his bony hand perfectly. Reynard stumbled back as pure magical energy started coursing through his body at an immense speed.

"HA! Yes, yes, YES! It's working!"

Reynard stopped shaking as the gauntlet started to stabilize and he looked at Zithoss. "What kind of power is this?"

"The power of the gods. The power of my mother. It was initially used to store the souls of the dead, but of course when King Sargon took the gauntlet for himself, he proved once again how humans could accomplish the impossible. He improved the gauntlet. Altered an artifact created by my mother and me. He modified my gauntlet to allow a human to use the souls stored inside the gauntlet. These souls allowed even a human to perform magic."

Reynard looked down at the gauntlet and the eyeball on the gauntlet stared right back at him. "How… is that possible? Humans could never use magic. Wait… how do I know this? Grrrrrrr… what is happening with my mind?"

"Fragments of emotions and memories are coming back to you in increments. Stop getting distracted by illusions of the past, my revenant. The humans altered the gauntlet to use the souls inside as a power source, destroying the souls inside and being able to convert them into pure magika at will. Nyana, get the next artifact."

The next artifact was an enormous sword, so gigantic that Nyana's skinny frame was unable to lift it. Its hilt was made of a black, shiny metal, but the blade was pure crimson. The edge had a sickly glow coming from it.

"My sword, named 'Oblivion'. Stolen from me by King Sargon after our fight and later used by King Daemos. Passed down in the same way as my gauntlet. My mother crafted it and once again, it was enhanced by the humans. Pick up the blade, my revenant."

Reynard did as he was told and picked up the sword. Despite the blade's massive size and weight, he was able to lift it with a single hand and move it around as if it were but a light dagger.

"It's an impressive blade, indeed."

"Nyana, shoot fire at his sword."

"WHAT?!"

"Fine. Fireball!"

A blazing fireball shot from Nyana's hand and flew towards the sword. Reynard jumped, holding the sword in front him to shield himself from the fireball, determined to attack Nyana. But the blazing impact he expected never happened. Instead, Reynard watched as the fireball bounced right off the sword and slammed into one of the decrepit stone walls. Reynard stared at the blade with astonishment.

"How?"

"Humans. Despite my everlasting life, not even I understand how the human mind works. Just like the gauntlet, they were able to smash the laws of reality as they saw fit. Now… for the last artifact."

Nyana bent down to grab a small ring that was at the bottom of the chest. She held the ring out and Reynard slipped it onto his bony finger. Suddenly, a watery black substance spilled from the ring and started to envelop Reynard at a rapid pace. At first, the shocked and uncomprehending Reynard was on the verge of panic but, thinking it over, he deduced that there was no reason for him to do so. The first two gifts he received had caused no harm to him. He let go of the tension in his body and allowed the black fluid to envelop him. Suddenly, Reynard could hear clanking. He looked down to see black steel armor slowly starting to form over of his skeletal form. He now had pointed metal boots which had small spikes on their soles. Slowly moving up his body, the liquid soon formed a chest plate. The shoulder pauldrons were spiked and sharply arced to the side. The magical liquid did not overflow to his right arm since it had the Gauntlet of the Overlord on it, but his left arm was completely covered in the spikey and pitch-black armor. Finally, the liquid engulfed his head. A stunning black helmet formed around his skull, hiding his appearance. On top of the helmet are two sharp bull-like horns that protrude upwards. All that could be seen of his body now were his glowing red eyes shining from his midnight-black helmet. As the final touch, the tar-like fluid wove itself into a black cloak which flowed from Reynard's shoulders like a blanket of twilight. Reynard was at a loss for words as he admired his new dark and imposing appearance.

"A ring created by the humans over a century ago. Nyana was able to loot it from the late King Daemos before his demise. It is now yours. Now, my revenant, lets—"

"Not yet."

"...What?"

"I don't remember my name, but whoever I was before is long gone, just as you said yourself. I want a new name."

"It matters not to me. Do as you please."

"...I shall inherit the name of the man who used these artifacts before me. Daemos."

"Very well, Lord Daemos. Now you are equipped to do my bidding. You will venture out into the world and start a new, dark domain. You will be the face of this new empire, but you are still my servant. You will build yourself an army of the living and collect a bounty of souls for me."

"How will I be able to get these souls back to you?"

"For every foe you slay, their soul will be locked away in my, or I should say your, gauntlet. They will be safely locked away until you return them to me. How you do so is not my responsibility. That is for you to decide. I don't care as long as I receive what I deserve. Oh... and just in case you need reminding."

Daemos again felt his body fill with sheer blinding pain. He fell to the ground, feeling the very life draining away from him. Then, in a quick moment, all the pain vanished and Daemos was able to stand again.

"I'm able to rip away this life just as easily as I gave it to you. I don't need magika or souls to do so. The spell will be active as long as you draw breath, meaning I can continue using and controlling the magic that has already been cast. It matters not where in Harmonia you hide or how far away you are. My eyes and ears spread far across this ancient land. If you betray me, I shall know. Of course, I don't think we will ever need to go to such lengths. We see eye to eye, do we not?"

"Yes... master," Daemos replied, growling softly.

"No need for such formalities or hostility. You are gaining more than I. This empire will be yours. Whatever you gain in your travels is yours. You are my overlord, after all. This is but a precaution to make sure this transaction is not spoiled by renegade behavior."

"I understand."

"Now... Nyana, I hope you will be able to guide our new friend across this vast land and give him the proper magic training he needs?"

"Yes, my lord."

"Good. Now. Draw your weapons, both of you. I wish to see your sword fighting skills, Overlord Daemos."

"Heh... as you wish."

Daemos slowly drew Oblivion from its sheath and Nyana gracefully arched and grabbed her two daggers.

"You're no match for me, you undead brute."

Daemos charged at her with a guttural roar, but she easily sidestepped his attack and slashed at his ankles. The blades sent sparks flying against the black metal as Daemos whirled around and slammed his sword down, only for Nyana to slide under his downstroke and land another slash at his torso. Daemos made a two-handed swing, but she flipped over the attack and lodged both of her daggers into his shoulders. She then pulled herself up onto his body using the hilts of her daggers and flipped Daemos to the ground.

Before Daemos could do anything, she pulled his helmet off and pressed both of the blades to his skeletal neck. "You lose, brute."

Zithoss let out a low, frustrated growl that shook the room.

"That was pathetic, Overlord. Leave this room. I wish to speak to Nyana alone."

Daemos picked his helmet back up and snarled as he walked out of the room. Nyana walked towards Zithoss.

"I can tell something is troubling you, my child. Speak"

"You never told me that this is why we needed to resurrect the prince! You said that I could have been your overlord. I have served you almost my entire life and—"

"ENOUGH!"

The room shook once again and Nyana bowed her head.

"You know as well as I do that the gauntlet did not choose you. We have spoken of this over and over again. You are not the overlord. I have given you so much, but you insist on being selfish. I gave you a home when you had none. I gave you a purpose when you had none. I gave you power when you had none. I even gave you what you desired the most when you came crawling to me all those years ago, did I not?"

Nyana was silent.

"You are to teach the overlord what he needs to know. How to navigate this land. How to fight with a sword and how to use magic. It seems the resurrection took more of his memory than anticipated. So be careful, my disciple."

"Yes, my lord."

Nyana bowed to Zithoss before leaving the throne room and walking back to Daemos, who was leaning against the wall and admiring his new sword. He groaned the moment he saw Nyana.

"You were lucky, magic caster. Lucky."

"I care not about your whining, *Overlord*. If you want to cope with your loss, do it in your head," Nyana sneered.

"WHY DO YOU—" Daemos growled.

"Follow me. Our master has instructed me to train you. I'll teach you the basics of sword fighting and once you have some souls to use, I'll teach you how to use magic. It looks like we will be working together, however horrendous it might seem."

"...Fine."

Daemos followed her to an old and dusty training room. Targets were painted on the wall, but they had faded and smudged with time. Around the room were training dummies and there was a small arena in its center. Nyana stepped into the ring and Daemos was soon to follow her.

"Draw your weapon, you skeletal buffoon."

"That's Overlord Daemos to you, cur."

"You have the gall to call yourself overlord after I dispatched you so quickly?"

"Grrrrrrr… draw your weapon, hag."

Nyana took her two daggers and slammed the hilts together. A blinding light filled the arena. Daemos shielded his eyes from the light, but when he looked again, the daggers were gone. In their place was a thin, curved blade. Her saber was pointed outwards towards Daemos.

"Come at me, Daemos," Nyana taunted him.

"With pleasure."

"Heh… you won't land a single blow on me, you oaf."

Daemos slowly reached to grab his massive blade. His sword's sickly glow illuminated the whole room. He firmly held the hilt with both hands and immediately charged at Nyana. Nyana didn't move an inch. She stood perfectly still until the final second and then lithely dived under his attack and stabbed him. Daemos snarled as he wildly swung his massive sword with his brute strength. Nyana was dodging his blows with ease. She was smart enough to know that trying to fight him in a contest of raw power and strength was impossible. His physical strength had been increased manifold thanks to him being given Nioxis's blessing by Zithoss. If she got hit even once by these swings, she would be a goner.

Nyana moved swiftly and lunged right at Daemos's head. Daemos shoulder-charged Nyana and made her fly backward.

"Graceful Gust!" she said as she cast her spell.

A powerful wind surrounded and protected Nyana, preventing her from slamming against the wall.

"YOU COULD HAVE KILLED ME, YOU CHEAT!"

"Cheating? I've done no such thing."

"YOU SHOULDER CHARGED ME! IT'S A SWORD FIGHT!"

"I see no issue."

"Of course you don't. You're a brute, after all."

"No… I am your overlord."

Nyana clenched her fist and angrily yelled, "LIGHTNING STRIKE!"

The lightning bolt was too fast for Daemos to deflect and he snarled in pain as he was sent flying backward and into the wall.

"YOU LITTLE INGRATE! I'LL RIP OUT YOUR SPINE!"

"COME AND TRY, YOU—"

"ENOUGH!" snarled the disembodied voice of Zithoss.

The entire room started to shake and the training dummies began to rattle and fall over.

"Come to my throne room at once."

Nyana brushed herself off and walked past Reynard, who snarled and punched at the stone wall behind him, making dozens of cracks in the wall. Both made their way to Zithoss, who was still slumped over in his chair with insects crawling in and out of his rotting skull.

"Your childish foolishness is not going to benefit me in any way. I care not if both of you despise each other's existence. You are both my servants and thus you shall both end this useless prattle. Understood?"

"Yes, my lord."

"Yeah… sure, boss." Said Daemos as Nyana turned and glared at him.

"Good. I cannot allow your emotions to get in the way of my plans. Now. I want him trained in sword fighting, do you understand? I just need him to understand the basics. I have waited too long for all of this to fall apart because of the immaturity of my servants."

"It will be done, my lord."

RAMPAGE: THE RISE OF AN EMPIRE

Nyana once again left with Daemos to train with blades, both of them aware that they couldn't start any problems this time around. While their disdain for each other was constant, but Nyana and Daemos were smart enough to know that they both had far more to lose rather than gain if they didn't play nice for now.

After two weeks of rigorous training, Daemos was a much more adept fighter. He was still not nearly as talented with a blade as Nyana, but with her training and his immense strength, he had devised a new strategy to fight with. While the two have not grown to enjoy each other's company, but they have learned to tolerate each other.

Both Nyana and Daemos once again make their way to Zithoss's throne room.

His corpse sat on the throne, staring at both of them. "Have you finished your training, Overlord?"

"Yes boss, I did."

"Then prove to me that you are ready to serve me in your task once you leave this mountain."

"As you wish," said Daemos, bowing in front of Zithoss's throne. Addressing Nyana, he said, "Well, teacher? Shall we give him a show?"

"I'm more looking forward to watching you fail once again."

Daemos unsheathed Oblivion, but this time he held it with one hand. Despite the sword's massive size and weight, he could lift it with a single hand because of his incredible physical strength. His stance was a lot calmer and collected, but the undercurrent of impatience and an urge to showcase his strength was still present.

Nyana lunged at Daemos and he flicked his wrist slightly to block the attack. The large size of the sword allowed it to act as a powerful shield and not just a weapon. Plus, since he was so strong, he could swing the blade with complete ease. Daemos was blocking most of the attacks that the fleet-footed Nyana was delivering, but every couple of strikes would land a hit on him. He snarled as he quickly went back to a two-handed stance and made a mighty swing using all of his strength. Nyana flipped over his attack, but the swing was so strong that it made a gust of wind that pushed Nyana back ever so slightly. He then quickly switched Oblivion back to his right hand and started delivering powerful and quick one-handed attacks. The sword strikes were too mighty for Nyana to block, so she had to dodge every single one. She ended the duel by sliding under his legs, jumping on his back, and pressing her daggers against his boney neck.

"Hmmmph!" groaned Daemos.

"Told you I would win."

"Enough of that. It was an excellent show indeed. You have done well, my overlord. You are ready. On your conquest, you are sure to gain more powers and skills along the way. Nyana, you are his guide in the upper world. I hope the two of you will not fail me. You are going to have to start from nothing. Goblin souls have little to no power to make you undead warriors and my followers are all dead, it would seem, except for Nyana. That being said, the sacrifice was indeed worth the reward. Now go. I forbid failure. You will not fail… will you?"

"Of course not, master."

"Yeah… we won't."

Nyana bowed and Daemos lowered his head only slightly. Both of them walked towards the exit of the massive dungeon inside the mountain. Daemos had not seen the sun. He came to life during the night and for the past two weeks, he had been stuck inside this dungeon-like castle. The dungeon was much bigger than he expected. It turned out this entire time they were at the top of the mountain where the throne room was. The entrance was the front of the dungeon. There were several other secret exits and entrances to the dungeon, but none were needed for now. It was a nerve-racking thought to have to build an entire empire from seemingly nothing at all. That being said, Daemos was oddly content. Staying inside of the dungeon had nearly driven him mad when the uncontrollable urge to kill had been taking hold of him. He was ready to become an overlord. He was prepared to become this world's new Dark Lord. He could imagine it all now. Piles and mountains of gold and treasure, heaps of weapons and servants, miles of land and victories abound.

Nyana was less than enthusiastic. She had come to dislike Daemos significantly and was annoyed that she now had to babysit the wannabe Dark Lord. Nyana looked forward to seeing the front gates of the dungeon. As Daemos stared at the two large metal doors embedded with demonic designs of bones and skulls, he wondered how Zithoss and this dungeon had stayed hidden for such a long time. Without wanting to wait any longer, he forcefully pushed open the massive, rusty iron doors. A blinding light shone into the dungeon, making all the insects and rats scurry and panic. Daemos uncovered his eyes and walked forwards into the light.

CHAPTER 4

Daemos looked at the bright green plants and vibrant trees surrounding the mountain. He was not expecting the outside to be so stunning. They were in a massive forest—the Forest of Duma. A forest so large that it held the territory of three entire kingdoms at the edge of the Harmonian Empire.

The empire had not been able to successfully push into the forest any more than they already had since their resources were so thin and their power weak on the outskirts of their land. In fact, the other countries and the monsters in the forest constantly attacked the peasants and soldiers in the outer territories of the empire. The Forest of Duma was home to the largest population of monsters in Harmonia. Not just this but the monsters residing inside the forest are some of the most dangerous and fierce.

"We are right now in the nation of Whitia. The land of the goblins. This mountain is so massive that it spans between Whitia and Nigt, the land of the orcs. Our mountain is in one of the deepest recesses of the Forest of Duma. Three kingdoms control the forest. Whitia, the kingdom of the goblins, Nigt, the kingdom of the orcs, and Shimia, the kingdom of the werewolves. Shimia is the dominant power of Duma at the moment and is more focused on raiding the unprotected, weakly defended villages of the Harmonian Empire along their borders. We won't have to worry about them for now."

"You are well versed in all this, then?"

"I have traveled to every nation in Harmonia. My knowledge of the land will be needed in order to start our conquest."

"Anything else that you can tell me?"

"Whitia is overall a poor, pitiable country. It has survived only because it is on the edge of the continent and is far away from the Harmonian Empire. Whitia has a weak government. It comprises several isolated goblin villages with one representative and chief each. The representatives have a council where they can speak with the goblin king. Whitia is currently at war with the orcs of Nigt because the orcs are running out of food. They need to survive off of raiding the goblins. The orcs of Nigt are fully capable of farming for themselves, but why were forced to live in the swamps after Shimia took a plentitude of their territory. Being completely surrounded by two hostile kingdoms now, the only way they can feed their population is from hunting and raiding. Now the two have been in a stalemate for a while now. The goblins are smaller and weaker, but they have survived using guerrilla war tactics, traps, and low-level magic."

"Goblins know magic?"

"How much could you have possibly forgotten already? Every creature can use magic because every creature in Harmonia has magika in their blood. Intelligent creatures can use the magika in their blood to perform magic if they are taught. Different species have different amounts of magika in their blood. More magika means more powerful spells and being able to use more spells until you run out and have to wait for your magika to replenish. Goblins have low magika, but they have a lot more than the average orc. Orcs have a culture around being warriors and hunters. Add that to their meager magika levels and there is little to no magic-using orc anywhere. That's not to say there has not been any orc magic casters of course. Meanwhile, goblins have low magika, but they have mandatory magika practice. Mind you, goblins for the most part use weak and pathetic spells, but it is all they are capable of since they have such low magika."

"Hmm... it seems you do have your uses."

"And it seems you are still as annoying and arrogant as ever."

"So, it would make sense to start our advance on one of these villages. It's generous to call this place a country anyways. Just several tribes loosely held together by a so-called king. Let's get started."

"You really are a moron."

"I beg your pardon?"

"There are only two of us and no matter how much stronger we are compared to goblins, there are a LOT of goblins. It would be pure idiocy to charge in without a plan."

"Your ceaseless chatter annoys me, girl. Instead of giving me new reasons to want to crush your skull, you could share your information on our objective."

"Girl? Who are you calling a girl? I am far older than you are—"

Suddenly, Nyana and Daemos could hear the sound of clanging metal from the bushes. Both Nyana and Daemos whipped their heads around and drew their weapons. Nyana knew that this forest was full of monsters, but she had not expected to be ambushed so quickly. Or was it even a monster?

The clanking noise got closer and closer until….

"HEEEEEEEEYAAAAAH!"

A goblin jumped at them from the bushes. He was about three feet tall and his skin was as green as the grass he was running on. He had a long white beard and wrinkles from old age. His ears were more extended than those of elves and his nose was about the same length. This goblin had several of his teeth missing and an assortment of pots and pans tied around his body like armor. As he ran towards the two of them like a barbarian, he swung around a tree branch with butter knives hammered into it. He also had a large metal sheet nailed around his head. The goblin skid to a halt and jumped onto a rock. He then struck his nearest approximation of a heroic pose before speaking in the loudest voice he could muster.

"Strange ones, heed me now! You speak to the almighty Cling Clang! I am the unstoppable Cling Clang who killed five dragons with a single swing of my mace. I am the invincible Cling Clang who can crumble mountains with a breath! I am—"The goblin lapsed into a fit of coughing before continuing, "Ouch… um… sorry! Hold on… I ran out of breath there…" Fighting to catch his breath, he panted, "Just… just give me a moment, okay guys?"

Nyana and Daemos looked at each other, utterly puzzled, as this goblin was now leaning against the rock, breathing heavily.

"Man, I kind of got dizzy for a moment there. I think I'm good now… where was I? Oh yes! Okay, here we go in three… two… one." Cling Clang resumed his ear-splitting holler, "I AM CLING CLANG! God of this forest! I have watched over the scary door on the mountain for thousands of years and now you come before me from the pits of the damned. Come forth and die by the blade of Cling Clang!"

Daemos looked back at Nyana one more time and shrugged as he grabbed his blade. Cling Clang gulped the moment he saw the size of the sword the strange black knight was carrying. Nyana groaned and pushed his arm down.

"Idiot," she muttered under her breath. She kneeled down to Cling Clang's height and looked at him. "Cling Clang, is it? What exactly are you doing here?"

"STAND BACK, FIEND! Ahem… I shall grant you lower life forms the privilege of hearing my reasoning."

Daemos angrily clawed at the side of the rocky mountain, sinking his claws deep into the rock and leaving a deep mark on the side.

"I am the guardian of this door! I found it while on my patrol and I knew it meant bad business. I have been a guardian of this evil door for fifteen years… no… that's not right… it was…yes! I… I… I mean 15,000 years! Waiting for it to open."

"Why didn't you just open the door for yourself?"

"Alas, my god-like body was too short for the handles and too large for me to push. Of course I could have used my almighty powers to blow down that pathetic door at any time!"

"Why didn't you, then?"

"YOU DARE QUESTION THE MIGHTY CLING CLANG?!"

"I'm um… sorry?"

"Never mind, you are forgiven!"

"Well, thank goodness for that."

"Indeed. It would be unwise to anger one as powerful and mighty as I! Would you like to hear the perilous and mysterious backstory of Cling Clang?"

"Oh um… no, thank you. its fi—"

"IT WAS A DARK AND STORMY NIGHT! AFTER I SINGLE-HANDEDLY SAVED AN ENTIRE VILLAGE FROM—"

Daemos snarled and lunged at Cling Clang. He lifted his tiny body off the ground with one hand and slammed him against the tree. "You are going to listen to me and you are going to listen very closely. Your incessant prattling is annoying me more and more by the second. The urge to crush your windpipe between my fingers is similarly growing with each moment you continue to speak. Do you want to live?"

Cling Clang nodded slowly but surprisingly, he didn't seem scared at all.

"Good. So this is what you are going to do. You are going to give me simple 'yes' or 'no' answers to my questions. Got it?"

"All you had to do was ask, angry one."

Nyana leaned against a tree, groaning inwardly. She hated unnecessary conflict and complications. That is not to say she was unwilling to get herself into difficult situations. She had spilled much blood and performed many dark deeds for her master. Although, if it could be avoided, she would rather do things quiet and peacefully.

"Now, do you know the location of the closest village?"

"Yes."

"Good. This is what you are going to do. You are going to take us to this village and bring us to their leader. Understood?"

Cling Clang made a show of pondering on Daemos's words and finally said, "NOPE!"

"WHY NOT?!"

"Well, you see, angry one, many goblins are terrified of my mighty figure. Out of fear they have banished me from their villages because my godly stomach required too much of th…"

Daemos growled, throwing Cling Clang to the ground in frustration.

Nyana stepped in, having had enough of Daemos and Cling Clang. "I'll handle this, you moron. Cling Clang, come here."

Cling Clang, who had been examining his tiny body for bruises, shakily gathered himself up and approached Nyana. "Yes?"

"We really need to get to the closest village. It's essential and it would be lovely if a powerful god like yourself could take us there."

"Hmm… why do you want to go there? I am their guardian, after all."

"Oh… I just wanted to find some civilization, is all. I was just hoping you could help me…"

"This is tempting… gods always want to try and help the powerless, delicate mortals to the best of their ability, but I am afraid I cannot do that."

Daemos punched the side of the mountain, creating a large crater and drew his blade. "WE ARE WASTING TIME! I was promised the opportunity to kill elves… why are we wasting time with this buffoon when I have an empire to build?!"

Nyana stared at Daemos and threw her hands up in a flabbergasted manner. "ARE YOU KIDDING ME?!"

Daemos tilted his head in a confused manner.

"DEMONS! EVIL DEMONS! I SHALL SMITE THEE WITH A SINGLE BLOW! FOR MY NAME IS CLING CLANG THE MIGHTY, THE UNSTOPPABLE!"

He charged at Daemos's leg with his butter knife branch. The crudely constructed 'weapon' bounced off Daemos's armor and hit Cling Clang in the head. Cling Clang stumbled back, shrieking in pain and held his head. Daemos pressed his spiked boot on Cling Clang's chest and made him squirm.

"You are going to take us now."

"…Yes… yes," panted Cling Clang.

Daemos lifted his boot and the moment Cling Clang was standing up, he reached into his pocket and threw sand at Daemos's face. It missed, uselessly sliding down the breastplate of Daemos's armor.

Cling Clang started running while laughing maniacally. "HAHAHAHAHAHA! THE ALMIGHTY CLING CLANG WINS AGAIN! I SHALL SMITE THEE LATER, EVILDOERS!"

Nyana stood there, still speechless from the bizarre events of the past few minutes.

She looked at Daemos and threw her hands up. "Are you the stupidest revenant that was ever created?"

Daemos turned his head and snarled at her. "And what exactly is the problem with one goblin running off?"

"HE WILL ALERT THE OTHERS, YOU BUFOON!"

"…You are lucky I need you alive, or else I would have crushed your skull a long time ago."

"I'd like to see you try, you bastard. Come on. Let's see if we can even salvage this opportunity. I can't believe you made everything go to shit and we have literally just left the mountain! If we had gotten him to trust us, he could have led us right to one of the main tribes and THEN we could have started the conquest. All you accomplished was making it harder for us to find this place AND possibly tipping the enemy off to our existence."

Daemos clenched his fist and moved closer to Nyana, towering over her. "You finished?"

"I'll see if I can think of anything else. For now, let's move."

Daemos pushed past Nyana, taking the lead and the duo started walking through the forest.

Nyana and Daemos travelled through the forest at a brisk pace until night fell. Since Daemos was undead, he did not need to sleep or eat, but they had to stop for Nyana's sake. She caught a deer in the forest and cooked it over a fire as Daemos stood guard. He sat in silence as Nyana roasted a piece of meat on a branch.

"I can tell you don't like me," said Daemos as he stared into the blackness of the Forest of Duma.

"Oh really? What could possibly have given that away?" taunted Nyana.

"Well... I don't like you either, but it may be more beneficial for us to work together instead of constantly being at each other's throats. I cannot fail. In case you forgot, an ancient Elder Lich has my life in the palm of his hand. He can kill me at any moment he pleases. Knowing how the boss works, he must have something over your head as well, right?"

"No. He wouldn't do anything like that to me. Unlike you, I'm dedicated to my lord and would do anything for him. He was there when nobody else was. Gave me the chance to have a life... worth living."

"Eh? Is this some kind of a love story?"

"God, no! It's nothing like that, you oaf." Nyana flung a rock at Daemos. It hit the side of his head and clinked off his helmet.

Daemos snarled, angrily throwing the log he was sitting on far away and pointed his blade at her. "If you would STOP HITTING ME, I wouldn't be so mad!"

"If you weren't such an embarrassing screw-up, I wouldn't have to."

"That's it! I don't care anymore. I'M GOING TO KILL YOU RIGHT NOW!"

Suddenly, a thunderous noise could be heard from the forest.

"RRRRROOOOOOAAAAR! WHERE LOUD NOISE? SMASH LOUD NOISE! BREAK AND SMASH LOUD NOISE!"

"What is that? Look at what your incessant yelling has brought upon us now," Nyana jumped to her feet, cursing Daemos.

"It's trolls… AND THIS IS YOUR FA—"

"LITTLE SNACKS! CRUSH SNACKS! CRUSH CRUSH!"

The trees started to shake and then fall with mighty crashes, accompanied by heavy footfalls. Soon enough, two trolls emerged out of the trees and stood in front of Nyana and Daemos. Giant beasts with little to no magika or intelligence. The trolls were around fifteen feet in height and used small trees for clubs. Their skin was tough and brown like tree bark. Their eyes were yellow and they had the most horrible smell emanating from them.

"Dammit. You take the one on the left and I'll deal with the other!" yelled Nyana.

"Fine," said Daemos in an annoyed tone.

He drew his massive sword and charged at the troll. It was time he put his revenant strength to use. The troll wound his arm up and with a mighty swing of the tree, slammed it into Daemos. Daemos put his sword forward as a shield and took the brunt of the attack head-on. The powerful swing pushed Daemos back and even sent him airborne, but he was able control his fall and landed on his feet like a cat. The troll gave Daemos no time to rest. It immediately went for another swing. Daemos charged and slammed his body into the tree shoulder-first. On impact, the tree shattered into pieces and the troll stammered in surprise.

"STRONG SNACK! VERY STRONG SNACK! STRONG SNACK STILL BE CRUSHED!"

"You should be honored to be the first soul to be added to my collection."

Daemos charged at the troll and jumped into the air. His black cloak fluttered behind him like the spreading wings of a raven. He lunged downward and with a single downward thrust sliced off the troll's massive, muscular arm, making the troll scream in agony and anger.

Meanwhile, Nyana gracefully avoided attacks from the massive troll she was fighting. The troll's swings were broad and covered a lot of space, but she was simply too nimble and agile for him to land a single hit. Nyana flipped over, slid under and swiftly dodged the troll's attacks.

"SNACK TOO FAST! SLOW SLOW SLOW!"

"Sorry, you revolting cretin, but I am not going to lie down and allow you to eat me. I have other plans in mind. DRAGON LIGHTNING!"

Her left hand erupted in sparks as a powerful blast of electric energy suddenly shot from it and made a hole right through the troll's torso. The troll squealed in agony as Nyana continued her assault.

"LANCE OF THE KING!"

A portal opened out of thin air from which Nyana pulled out a lethal-looking lance made out of bone and black iron. She ran the lance through the troll's neck. The troll's lifeless body flopped to the ground with a thunderous noise. Daemos was distracted for a moment, watching how quickly Nyana disposed of the troll, only to be punched on the side of the head while he wasn't looking.

"KILL METAL SNACK! KILL KILL!"

"The only one that will die today is you, monster."

Daemos charged and with a powerful sweep of his sword sliced off one of the massive trolls' legs. The troll collapsed to the ground and as it wailed in pain Daemos sliced its throat open with his sword. Nyana approached and motioned towards the Gauntlet of the Overlord.

"Hold the gauntlet up. Allow it to take their souls. Troll souls are weak and will not be very useful to our lord or the gauntlet's magika storage, but every soul counts."

Daemos nodded as he lifted his gauntlet above his head. Suddenly the eye on the gauntlet opened wide and stared at the dead bodies. A strange greyish green mist shaped like the distorted versions of the trolls' faces started to get pulled from the corpses. They writhed in fear and pain as they were absorbed into the eyeball. Daemos watched the process with astonishment, feeling the difference in his connection with the gauntlet. Despite how weak the souls were, he could feel them inside of the gauntlet.

"What was that magic you used to end the fight? I have never seen the likes of it before."

"There are four categories of magic: elemental, universal, dark, and light. Almost all magic is universal. Shields, teleportation, telekinesis, flight, and so on. Elemental magic is control of the elements and is used for combat. Dark and light magic are a long-forgotten art. I was somewhat trained in dark magic from our master. Spells and powers that are granted by worship and favor of the dark goddess Nioxis. You were resurrected using dark magic. Our lord is the son of Nioxis. It's how he has survived for so many years. I have been alive for seventy years and yet I'm only a novice at dark magic. It's incredibly hard to learn."

At first, Daemos felt on edge, thinking that she was an elf for having a lifespan that was so long. Then he calmed down knowing that if she were an elf and seventy years old, she would look a lot younger.

"Then, of course, there is light magic. Magic and powers that are granted by worship and favor of Aidiel, the goddess of light, sister of Nioxis. Both dark and light magic are forgotten arts, just like Aidiel and Nioxis have been forgotten. Instead, the seven lesser gods are worshipped in Harmonia. Nobody knows if the seven are even real. They simply became the dominant religion as all the others were forgotten. There is a growing empire in the east, though, that apparently wants to reinstate the worship of the goddess Aidiel. I investigated them decades ago. None of them have light magic."

"I see. And will I be able to use these powers for myself with this gauntlet?"

"Yes, you will, but to use those powers you must expend the souls that you have collected, the same souls our lord requires. When you have some more souls I will teach you basic spells, but use them sparingly. The souls are for the master, not you."

"Understood."

The two of them returned to their fire and Nyana groaned. She had left her deer leg on the fire for too long and now it was burnt. She angrily gripped the leg and started cutting it up with her dagger. She wasn't going to waste the food. Nyana gently moved her mask to the side so she could eat but her face remained fully covered.

"Why don't you take that mask off?"

"None of your business," she snapped as she bit into the burnt leg.

"Hmmph… not that I care, anyways. If you know so much about this forest and the continent as a whole, why couldn't you just take us to the first goblin tribe?"

"I have a general knowledge of the continent and its denizens, not a complete and accurate knowledge of the location of every settlement."

"Of course you don't," chuckled Daemos quietly.

"Have something you want to say?"

"Nothing you would like to hear, but I do have more questions."

"Fine. Not like we have anything better to do."

"What kind of monsters live in this forest besides the trolls? You said before that the

Forest of Duma has the most monsters on the continent. What other kinds are there?"

"Several. Hydras, basilisks, wyverns, cyclops, direwolves, and many others. This entire forest is full of them."

"Is there a way we can use them for our own purposes? If we can use the mass supply of monsters in this forest for our armies, it would be near impossible to stop us."

"There is a dark spell capable of dominating the minds of low-intelligence beings, but it is very difficult to cast and takes a lot of training. I know the spell, but I am still trying to master it myself."

"How does one… cast a spell?"

"It's not as easy as just saying the name of the spell and watching it happen. You have to consistently visualize in your head the spell you are going to use and remain completely concentrated on casting it. You must focus on your magika and release the spell you focused on without distraction or wandering thoughts. Well, that's at least how almost everyone else uses magic. I have heard it is easier to cast spells with the Gauntlet of the Overlord. It was modified by humans for themselves, after all. I wouldn't know though. Apparently, I'm unworthy of the gauntlet."

"Easier?"

"The knowledge of all spells is inside that gauntlet. Every spell except for light magic. In short, the gauntlet does most of the work for you. You give the command and the gauntlet does the spell. It just needs the right number of souls to cast the spell. The stronger the spell, the more souls needed."

"And what about the other ability the boss was talking about?"

"The one about your troops? That is built into the gauntlet since the beginning. No souls are required for its use. You can pour your emotions into your troops and influence how they fight on the field. Increase their morale, drain their hope, or make them bloodthirsty monsters."

"I see. So, tomorrow, we shall start our conquest. I am looking forward to it."

As the sun rose on a new day, Daemos and Nyana continued to walk through the thick and unforgiving environment of Duma. Daemos and Nyana had already killed several giant beasts along the way in order to find the first tribe. As they moved deeper and deeper into the forest, they heard screams coming from the left of them. The two started running as fast as they could, stopping abruptly as a giant direwolf jumped from the shadows of the forest and lunged at Daemos. Daemos wrapped his black metallic claws around the wolf's neck and ripped out a chunk of its throat.

Daemos stood and followed Nyana, who was now ahead of him and was observing the source of the noise from the shadows of the trees. Daemos stood next to her and both of them watched what appeared to be a raging battle. A small fort made out of logs was being desperately defended by goblins against an invading force of direwolves – giant wolves about seven feet long who craved the blood and flesh of any kind of creature. The goblins were fiercely outnumbered and had already faced serious casualties against the vicious beasts. From atop their wooden walls, they shoot wooden arrows and dropped rocks on the wolves that were trying to scale the walls with their fearsome claws.

"How shall we approach this?" Nyana asked Daemos.

"We give them a show these lower beings won't forget." Daemos slowly stood up and walked out of the forest. He slammed Oblivion on the ground, getting the attention of the massive direwolves. "I have been in the ground for a very long time. This bloodlust that has been rising inside of me has done nothing but built up more and more. You should be honored to satiate my hunger."

A few wolves charged at Daemos. One of them jumped mid-air right towards Daemos who swung Oblivion down the middle of the beast's body, slicing the wolf in two perfectly symmetrical pieces. From Daemos's left, two wolves ran as fast as they could towards him, leaving dust clouds behind them. From the right came two more wolves. Daemos held his blade with both hands and with a mighty slash decapitated both the wolves to the left of him with a single swing. The wolves on the right jumped onto his back and tried biting his armor and ended up breaking their teeth in the process. Daemos landed on his back, crushing the wolves that clung to his armor. All that was left of the wolves were smashed intestines that were spattered in a red slimy paste on his back and on the grass under him.

Both the goblins and the direwolves were now intimidated. This strange black-clad warrior who wielded staggering strength is obliterating the beasts as if they were nothing at all. The pack of direwolves all but forgot about the goblins and were now encircling Daemos. Daemos lifted his gauntlet in the air and absorbed the souls of the wolves he had killed. Once again, these souls were nearly worthless. Just like the trolls, these souls didn't have much magika in them. But then again, he could feel the small simmer of power that was in the gauntlet now. Could he use a spell? Nyana had said that the gauntlet would do most of the work for him – he just needs to cast the spell and the artifact will do the rest of the work. That being said, Daemos did not really know any spells. Only one way to find out.

Daemos yelled the first thing that came to his mind when he thought of a spell, "FIRE!"

The Gauntlet of the Overlord started to shake and the eyeball etched on it opened wide, a violent red glow emanating. Daemos's metal fingertips started to smolder and spark and as he watched in wonder, a stream of fire erupted from his palm with an explosive burst. Flames engulfed the wolves and Daemos looked on as they squirmed and howled in agony. Five direwolves died slow, horrific deaths in front of the crowd of wolves and goblins. The rest of the wolves started to retreat into the deep recesses of the forest, cowering in panic.

Nyana stepped out from her hiding spot and looked at the dead wolves. "Huh... I guess the gauntlet does do most of the work. That being said, you should work on your control more. I also didn't expect that simple fire spell to be so powerful."

Daemos gave a noncommittal grunt and held his gauntlet up to absorb the souls of all the dead. The terrified goblins watched in astonishment as the velvet-black stranger ended a conflict the goblins had been locked into for weeks.

Daemos held his sword forward and pointed it towards the wooden walls of the goblin stronghold. "Bring out your master. I wish to speak to whoever they may be."

The goblins nervously looked at each other as the massive black knight continued to stare them down. "W... we will call him for you at once, dark one."

"HOLD ON!" a loud, singsong voice came out of the woods.

Everyone turned to see who spoke. It was Cling Clang, now armed with a frying pan with nails sticking out of it. His eyes looked determined.

"I told you the almighty Cling Clang was not lying. The scary door on the mountain did open!"

All the goblins started to mutter amongst themselves.

Daemos was getting annoyed. "You again. You escaped the first time, but now you shall die by my blade."

"HA! CLING CLANG WOULD LIKE TO SEE YOU TRY! My godlike body is impenetrable and soon you shall lie dead on the forest floor! I am the guardian of the goblins and you shall perish!"

Daemos drew his blade and started walking faster and faster towards Cling Clang. Soon he was charging like a bull directly for him.

Cling Clang did not move though. He smiled as he held out his hand.

"Thorn vine!"

The ground rumbled as serrated vines ripped from the ground and slashed at Daemos. Daemos looked back to call for Nyana only to see her resting on a tree branch, watching the scene like a spectator. He growled in frustration.

"What's the matter, dark one? Trembling in fear of my power? The power of THE MIGHTY CLING CLANG?!"

Daemos snarled as he ripped the vines out by their roots with his sheer strength and slashed his sword at the goblin.

Cling Clang jumped back and started casting another spell. "I won't let you hurt my people! Acid bolt!"

An acid-tipped arrow materialized out of thin air and shot right at Daemos, but he twirled his sword and deflected the magic right back at Cling Clang. His eyes widened in surprise as he jumped out of the way.

"WHAT? H… how is that possible?!"

"You will die never knowing the answer."

Daemos was about to deliver the killing blow to the gob-smacked Cling Clang until suddenly, they hear a battle cry.

"FIRE THE ARROWS!"

Small wooden arrows fired from the walls of the wooden fort and uselessly bounced off Daemos's armor. He turned around to look at the attackers and by the time he turned back, Cling Clang was already gone.

He snarled and kicked at the ground in irritation. "Why don't you help me deal with this, woman?"

"Why don't you fix your own messes, you mistake of an overlord?"

"One of these days I'm going to rip your head off."

Daemos charged like a bull and smashed through the thick wooden walls of the fort. The fort seemed to act like a gate to the entire tribe of about two hundred goblins and its settlement. Nyana watched with disgust as Daemos started his rampage. The small three-foot goblins were no match for the magically enhanced revenant. His sword swings eviscerated their small bodies and cracked their rusty daggers and wooden spears. Daemos was outnumbered and yet it was a massacre for the goblins. Their attacks did nothing to the hulking undead and only brought them closer to their demise. Goblins yelled spells only for them to be reflected right back at them by Oblivion.

"Spark!"

"Vine slash!"

"Gust!"

Dozens of spells could be heard but they were drowned out by the sound of goblins being slaughtered.

The slaughter lasted about a half-hour before the goblins finally surrendered. Out of the couple hundred goblins of the tribe, several dozen had been killed by Daemos, his gauntlet now brimming with souls. The goblins shivered and cowered as their leader was called out to speak with Daemos.

Nyana finally jumped down from the tree and glared at him. "This is all your fault. We could have coerced them into serving us. You have spilled the blood of many today."

"Did you not do the same to bring me back?"

"I did what I had to do in order to serve the will of my lord. That doesn't mean I enjoy it or will turn to it for an immediate solution."

"Perhaps that is why the gauntlet did not find you worthy."

Before Nyana could retort, an old goblin was carried out towards Daemos by two other goblins. He was wrapped in brown robes and could barely stand on his own without his walking stick.

"I am Chief Gobna, dark one. Why have you come here? Why kill so many? Why cause such carnage in the Saka tribe?"

"Simple. You and your tribe are now under my rule. A new power is rising in Harmonia. It shall start with the full annexation of the Forest of Duma."

The chief was taken aback by Daemos's declaration. "The entire forest? How is that even possible? Even just in Whitia, there are hundreds of monsters, several other tribes and of course, our king."

"They will all be taken care of. You shall all help in my conquest. I don't see how any of you have a say in the matter. Unless you want me to continue my assault on your home?"

"No… you have spread enough pain as it is, dark one. We shall serve you. Just spare my people."

"Wise move. There is going to be war soon enough but fret not, casualties will be minimal. I understand the importance of caring for the people. You're my subjects and soldiers now. That means you are under my protection. I shall care for your needs. We shall repair your homes and improve on many of the lackluster qualities of this… fort."

Nyana was thoroughly confused by now. How can this blood-crazed maniac suddenly get such a clear head and understanding of maintaining an empire? He had just been threatening them a moment ago, but the second they submitted to his will he became protective of them? She didn't understand until finally, something Zithoss had told her came into her mind. "A revenant will lose most of their memories, but fragments of their past lives will still shine through to the surface. It is why I chose him. It is how I know he will be worthy of the gauntlet." Nyana was relieved that the goblins will be given respite and Daemos will help them rebuild, but she was worried about what might happen next. He had killed so many of them and was now expecting them to just fall in line. Grudges and hate were bound to grow within this tribe of goblins.

"Now will be a time of rebuilding. The future has much to bring. In return for obedience and loyalty, you will have prosperity. But right now, it is the time to rebuild."

Two long weeks have passed and the power structure of the southern Duma Forest has drastically shifted. The goblins of the Saka tribe have worked heavily to rebuild and start extracting resources from the land and Daemos has helped them the entire way. Hundreds of trees have been cut down, the sides of mountains and rocks have been mined out for stone and a wider and more effective border perimeter has been established around the fort. Construction has been hard, but production has been rising quickly. The fort was now bigger with sharp wooden stakes along the walls, making it hard to climb. Watchtowers have been built behind the walls and stone walls were being constructed. Daemos and Nyana have been on a killing spree, eliminating the monsters near the Saka tribe and allowing them to expand their borders. More land has been secured to allow for more farming and Nyana has used powerful magic to create moats and provide easier access to clean water. She has also been training Daemos to use the dominating spell. It would allow him to control the mind and will of monsters and creatures of lower intelligence and of weak will. The gauntlet had almost all the spells already stored inside of it and did do most of the work, but mild training was still needed in order to use the spell properly. On top of one of the watchtowers fluttered a new black flag with a terrifying symbol emblazoned on it – a red skull, its lower jaw missing, and the upper ending in razor sharp teeth. The new flag of Daemos's empire.

In the two weeks, Nyana had been training Daemos to use magic efficiently now that he was collecting many souls from the monsters and still had goblin souls left over.

There were still many problems that needed to be fixed. The Saka tribe only had a small supply of rusted iron weapons and most of their armory consisted of wooden spears and stone clubs. To top that, most of the goblins were poor fighters and had insufficient training. The opinion of Daemos among the members of the Saka tribe has been mixed. While he did cause a mass genocide of almost twenty percent of their entire tribe and yet there have been immaculate improvements in the past two weeks. Not only this, but the rapid increase in the power of the Saka tribe has been unprecedented. However, many goblins were unhappy and angry with their new ruler and their fear of him was the only thing stopping them from rebelling.

A meeting of the goblin council had been convened. A large, circular table housed the leaders of the rest of the goblin tribes and their king. The room was loud, resounding with constant bickering and yelling.

One goblin covered in jewelry was yelling at another swathed in animal furs. "You are a fool! The orcs are in a weakened state. We should take this opportunity to raid them. They have just returned from their ocean raid of the dwarf kingdom of Gluth!"

"Why can't you understand the simple fact that we are running low on viable wolf cavalry. It would be a suicide mission. We have just conquered the resistance group in the South as it is! It would be the height of folly to jump into another war while we just got done with this war on our own land."

"Maybe for your sickly parasite-ridden soldiers constantly rubbing against flea-ridden animals, but the Nagana tribe has standards!" retorted the jewel-laden goblin.

"You are nothing but thieving pirates with no honor, Nomai."

"And you are a backwards woman who thinks mutts can win a war!"

"ENOUGH!" yelled the goblin king. He was wearing polished steel armor and had a crown of roots and vines and jewels. "This is not why I have gathered you all here. As you can see, Gobna of the Saka tribe is missing from our discussion. For unknown reasons, the Saka tribe has gone completely dark."

"You think they got wiped out? Those pathetic farmers know not what a real goblin should be like! I say they were given the short end of the stick. They don't even have viable iron deposits on their land, unlike mine," said Gogba, a goblin of large stature and covered in unknown stains.

"Quite the opposite. My liege, I already sent my spies to investigate," said a goblin with a quiet voice, wrapped in black robes.

"Against my wishes, Vesta?" snapped the king.

"Only in your best interests, King Krawl. You know where my loyalties reside."

"What did your spies see?"

"A massive pile of burning goblin bodies. Must be several dozen. Not only that, but the Saka tribe has changed. Spikes, walls, expanded borders and a new flag flying over the fort."

"...How is this even possible?"

"I KNOW HOW!" hollered a familiar, boisterous goblin.

"Who said that? Who are you to intrude in the king's private meeting?"

"IT IS I! THE ALL-POWERFUL CLING CLANG!"

"Oh god, not him again!" groaned one of the chiefs. Cling Clang and his penchant for trouble were apparently infamous across Whitia.

"Cling Clang, the mad, wandering goblin. You're lucky that your past deeds have given you leeway. If not for them, I would have had my guards kill you at once," King Krawl said exasperatedly and then sighing, he asked, "Why do you come here?"

"I know who did it! The one who destroyed Saka."

"Pray tell then."

"A massive black knight with an eyeball on his hand. Cling Clang saw it! I saw it! My god-like eyes do not miss details. He is going to conquer all of Harmonia. He came from the scary door in the mountain."

"What? How do we know he is telling the truth? He is completely insane!" barked Gogba

"He is insane, undoubtedly… but he's loyal to Whitia. He was once a great protector of our kingdom before madness took over him. Deep down, he would never betray Whitia," said Vesta.

"This is most troubling. I want a platoon sent out to investigate. Who knows what this supposed black knight is planning? Send the troops immediately. We will destroy this black knight and free our people. We are already facing a war with the orcs of Nigt, we cannot battle at another front at the same time. We must deal with this problem quickly and efficiently if we intend to survive."

After one long month of traveling across the Harmonain Empire, Ashehera finally made it to where she needed to go, the Kingdom of Cade, the home of the Nagas. While terrifying in appearance, they were one of the most peaceful kingdoms in Harmonia. Nagas were snake-like beings. They had heads of a snake and their entire body below their torso was a large snake tail. Their torso was humanoid with two arms which were covered in scaly skin.

The Kingdom of Cade was a place of scorching lava and fire. Perfect for reptiles to live in. The Nagas had learned to coexist with the salamanders, large fiery reptiles that exuded a massive amount of heat and bathe in lava. Salamanders had a reddish-orange coloration to them and the power to breathe fire. Salamanders were to the Nagas what horses were to the other intelligent Harmonian creatures. While salamanders were more common in western Harmonia, they had migrated to change the snowy and ice-covered north into a hospitable home for the Nagas, who were forced from their homeland during the expansion of the Harmonian Empire. The Dragon Council gave up their territory willingly to give the Nagas a home in their snowy mountainsides and they have been inseparable allies ever since. The magic of the dragons living next door to the Nagas kept the lava from causing environmental damage. It was a strange sight to see a valley of molten rock, fire, and lava in the middle of a wasteland of snow and icy mountains, but the Kingdom of Cade had been around for thousands of years before Ashehera was even born.

The kingdom was a major trade superpower that excels in crafting magic weapons. Of course, there was no doubt that the three dwarven kingdoms of Gort, Gara, and Gluth were superior in weapon manufacturing. The only reason the Nagas were able to stay competitive in weapon manufacturing was because they were able to imbue fiery magic into their thin sabers and curved blades which made them more valuable and powerful than the average dwarf-made blade.

The Kingdom of Cade did not have an actual military. They were a peace-loving country which tried to avoid fighting in every way. Some considered them hypocrites in that even though they refuse to fight, their country's biggest export was magical weapons. They were safe from invasion for two reasons. The first was that they were permanent and inseparable allies of the Dragon Council, arguably one of the most powerful forces in Harmonia along with the Harmonian Empire. The second reason was that they were known to craft stone and steel golems – statues of human and elven knights that come to life and defend their Naga creators when danger approaches. The number of golems in the Kingdom of Cade was staggering. The country was one of the heads of social progress and magical advancements. They were the only country to have elected officials, a focus on the equality of species and freedom of speech.

Ashehera stepped out of her royal carriage and cast a fire protection spell around her body. The ground was covered in prickly red grass and black rock. One guard at the front of the carriage brought out a red carpet with fire protection magic on it and rolled it out for Queen Ashehera to walk upon. As she walked down her carpet, she could see the large serpents poke out their heads in curiosity. They were very large. Their tails could grow up to six feet long and then their torsos were around the size of a human's or an elf's. Many of the Nagas seemed to be curious about their new visitor, but they did not show any signs of being scared. A Naga approached the guards that were walking in front of Ashehera. He had green scales and yellow eyes and was wearing an expensive cloak and dress shirt. The serpentine creature bowed his head politely.

"Welcome to our home. My name is Zacta. It's a pleasure to meet you. May I ask why you have decided to visit our home?" the Naga asked politely, his speech drawing out the 's' sounds, emulating the hisses of a snake.

"You are forbidden to speak to her majesty without—" interjected a guard, but was quickly silenced by Ashehera's raised hand.

"It's fine… ahem. I am Queen Ashehera Kelmoria of the Harmonian Empire. I wish to speak with your leader, King Renas."

Zacta arched his neck backwards and then tilted it to the side, wary of the new arrivals. "And why would you need to see him?"

"I must speak to him about passage to the Dragon Council. Your country is the only one with close ties to them and I must have an audience with Voxis, the Queen of Dragons."

Zacta squinted his reptilian eyes at her and hissed. "Fine, but we are watching you, bloodthirsty one."

As Zacta slithered away to lead them to the king, one of the guards approached her. "Permission to speak freely, your majesty?"

"Granted."

"How dare that animal speak to you in such a disrespectful manner? He should be charged and executed!"

"We have no jurisdiction here. The Nagas have a belief that everyone is made equal despite their class of expertise or species. The king still has legal power over the citizens, but he has no control over their speech. Now come. Renas is waiting for us."

The carpet was rolled out until it finally reached its length and after it ended, Ashehera had to walk on the black charcoal ground. Standing before her was a large castle with a multitude of sleeping golems scattered everywhere. The castle was surrounded by a moat of lava, with eight-feet long salamanders happily swimming around in it. The drawbridge to the castle opened and Zacta slithered across, motioning for Ashehera and her escorts to follow him.

The inside of the castle had a calming and awe-inducing air to it. Suspended from the ceiling were luminous balls of fire acting as chandeliers. A strange aroma filled the castle that seemed to force the stresses and anxieties out of anyone who breathed in the air. Down the long hallway decorated with golems and strange magical weapons stood the throne room. It was littered with gold and jewels stacked so high that they were spilling onto the floor from the chests they were put in. King Renas sat upon his throne, his tail wrapped around the seat and hanging off the side of the armrest, swaying back and forth. He was of one of the rarer breeds of Nagas, the proof of which was his head, a large cobra hood. His scales were blue, with stunning green patterns running along his body. His torso and arms were covered in golden armor and a golden crown gently rested on the top of his head. Renas's tail slowly moved over to a table next to his throne and gently wrapped around a teacup that he then brought to his mouth and sipped from. He looked towards the door and his face registered immediate surprise.

"Queen Ashehera of the Harmonian Empire? Well... I must admit I was not expecting such a visit. To what do I owe the honor?"

"I need your assistance. There is an urgent matter I must attend to and to fix this problem, I need to speak with Queen Voxis of the dragons."

"Well, this day sure got interesting. You must understand that this is a delicate situation you are in as it is. You have been colonizing the rightful land of the Dragon Council. The only reason that they have not spread death and flame upon us all is because I have been able to convince them to stay on the side of peace. I'm afraid that this peace would be ruined if you were to disturb the dragons."

"Well, I'm afraid that can't be an option, your majesty. Something sinister is arising. There is only one being old and wise enough to give me the information I need and that is Voxis."

"Do you not understand what you are asking of me? To help give you passage to the Dragon Council would be detrimental for everyone."

"I thought you would say this. GUARDS!"

Her escorts drew their weapons and Renas sighed, "Savages, the whole lot of them. There is no need for violence. Do you not realize what will happen if you hurt me or my people?"

"Yes, I do. But I am desperate. I need to talk with Voxis now. Inside my carriage is a glyph with an ice storm spell I poured all of my magika into. It will be enough to engulf your entire capital and consign you reptiles to a slow and cold death."

"You are an animal. A brute!"

"I'm merely impatient, your majesty. You can hate me as much as you want but I need results. The world itself may be at stake. I need to talk to Voxis. I don't care what way it happens. Either she comes to me after I freeze you all to death or you take me up the mountain the nice and painless way. Either way, I get what I want. It's up to you whether you want everyone in this city to die."

"You are despicable indeed. FINE. You win, witch."

"The names you call me don't bother me, your highness. I'm aware that going up the mountain will take a lot longer than having Voxis come to me, but I would rather stay safe and get my answers. Now move." Renas slithered off his throne and towered over Ashehera, who was not intimidated in the slightest. Renas turned to his advisor. "Have my daughter take the throne in my stead while I am gone. The journey will take at least a month."

"Of course, my liege."

Renas exited his palace, his uninvited guests close on his heels. He then whistled and two large salamanders dripping with lava crawled out from the moat of lava surrounding the castle.

They climbed over to Renas who gently petted their heads. "These salamanders shall be our guide. They will keep us warm and melt the ice and snow in our path up the mountain. Are you ready, cruel one?"

"Yes, I think I am. Shall we proceed, then?"

The salamanders roared as they walked in front of the group, melting ice and snow as soon as they came in contact with it. One salamander was at the front and one was bringing up the rear.

Ashehera formed a barrier around her body to keep her regal form from getting wet in the snow. "This is going to be a long journey.

RAMPAGE: THE RISE OF AN EMPIRE

A month, perhaps even two if the snow is particularly thick. I hope it will be worth it, cruel one."

"More than you can imagine."

CHAPTER 5

Daemos has been working to improve his goblin stronghold. The Saka tribe has continued to grow its borders and is working overtime to create guard posts and barricades. What was also in high production were cages. Daemos has been capturing low-level monsters in order to eventually convert them to his cause using domination magic. If he planned on having a powerful empire, he was going to need a mighty army. Domination magic was a long-forgotten form of dark magic. Similar to light magic, almost all of Harmonia has forgotten its very existence and most creatures have no idea how to use it. Without domination magic, it would be nearly impossible to tame and control a monster. This would mean that if Daemos could exploit this, he would have one of the only armies in all of Harmonia capable of using monsters of all kinds of caliber.

A problem that was still plaguing them, however, was the shortage of useful weapons. The only weaponry the goblins were capable of creating were made out of wood and stone. The small number of iron weapons they did have were rusty and barely salvageable. The Saka tribe were not the greatest warriors and their settlement was not near any known iron deposits. The tribe had one advantage over all the other tribes, however. They were the owners of one of the only three boats in all of Whitia. These boats were used to fish and conduct trade with the other tribes. Daemos used the boat to conquer a small uninhabited island to the east of Whitia. There were not many monsters on the island and it would prove to be a great source of wood, stone, and food in the future.

Daemos has been collecting more and more souls and now was the time to use them. He has been practicing his dominating spell with Nyana since the Duma Forest had so many monsters. They would make for a perfect army fodder. Daemos was in the fields with Nyana, practicing domination magic on direwolves that have been captured.

"There, there… damn, you almost got it. You're horrible at magic, though. How can you struggle this much with the gauntlet doing most of the work?"

"You're so lucky I need you alive, worm."

"Funny. Now try again. If you master this spell, then soon we can have a legion of monsters to do our bidding."

Daemos pointed his gauntlet at one of the caged wolves. He squinted his eyes and tried to concentrate as best as he could. "Dominate."

A red glow erupted from his palm and started seeping into the skin of the wolf. At first, the wolf snarled and struggled, but in a few moments, its eyes started to glow a dim red and it bowed its head to Daemos.

"Well, would you look at that? Looks like you finally did it after… however many times we tried. Too much to count."

"Shut up," Daemos said, but only partly annoyed this time as he looked at his gauntlet in wonder and relief.

He turned to see all of the caged wolves. He chuckled as his gauntlet started to glow red. One by one, he used the spell on all of the giant beasts. Since direwolves were weaker than most monsters, it would not cost as many souls to dominate their minds. Daemos now had at least two dozen giant direwolves fully under his control. This gave the Saka tribe an advantage over the other tribes. The ability to control monsters. Eventually, Daemos would control the entire Duma Forest and with it the multitude of dangerous monsters that live inside it. All he needs to do is harness the entire deadly might of this forest and soon his empire will grow with a force so massive that no army or empire will be able to stop it.

As Daemos was lost in his daydreams, a goblin scout ran up to him and saluted. He seemed scared just to be standing near Daemos. While it was true that during his rule prosperity has been at an all-time high, with both production and protection being massively increased, but this came at the price of very hard labor and a loss of many lives.

"M… My lord, our outer farms are being attacked by a hydra!"

"A hydra, you say? Perfect."

"W… what? E… excuse me, dark one, but I don't… I don't understand," squeaked the scout.

"You will soon. Nyana, come with me. This attack is a golden opportunity. One we must exploit."

Nyana was leaning against a tree; her hands were behind her head. When she heard Daemos, she straightened up and stretched her back.

"Fine. Let's get moving, then."

Daemos turned to the goblin scout. "You are to tell Gobna that I will be away for a short time. I shall return shortly."

"Y… y… yes, my lord!" the goblin stammered before he rushed to do as he was instructed.

Daemos was walking at a brisk pace, tingling with excitement. His hand gripped the hilt of his massive greatsword tightly. Nyana was talking to herself as she walked behind Daemos, her brain working rapidly to make sense of the latest developments. *Why would a hydra be near goblins? They live too deep in the forest to ever be near a goblin vil – the moron expanded the borders, of course.*

Nyana growled to herself in frustration and looked to her partner, saying with mock sweetness, "Sooo… a hydra, huh?"

"Indeed. I shall dominate it with my own hands and in turn use its power to dominate this forest. Soon all of Whitia will bow before me. Once we have our hydra, I will see to it that I deliver some of my souls back to the boss. I think he would be quite pleased with our progress."

"Would he, though?"

"…Are you suggesting he would be displeased?"

"I'm not suggesting anything. I was just curious if you thought governing over a tribe of battle-scarred goblins and working them like pack mules is progress in your eyes."

"Hmmph. You sure do have a lot to say for someone who barely helps."

Nyana drew her dagger and threw it with lightning speed. It missed Daemos's helmet by an inch and stuck deep into a tree behind him. Nyana pulled her dagger free from the tree and glared at Daemos.

"I will HELP when you earn my respect. I'm not one of your little minions. Of all the rotting corpses he could have picked from, my lord trusted YOU. You are taking the title of Dark Lord! That is not a title to be taken lightly. You have to earn it. You don't deserve to be called a dark lord after you scared a tribe of starving goblins that can barely swing a sword into submission. I have no clue why he chose you. Sure, you can use the gauntlet, but you fail to use it at its full potential because you are also a horrid magic caster, DESPITE the gauntlet giving you a boost! So no, I'll give my 'help' to a REAL Dark Lord, not some undead brute dictator that bullies starving goblins."

Daemos was completely silent. He didn't utter a word as Nyana continued on her fueled tirade about his performance thus far. He slowly turned his head to look at her. "Fine. Then I shall work harder. I will work towards the day that I 'earn' that title and when I do, I will enjoy watching you grovel at my feet."

"I don't care what you are. As long as you are useful to my true master, that is all I will see you as. A tool. Now. Shall we get going?"

"Yes... let us indeed."

The two traveled along the newly formed borders of the Saka tribe. Every here and there a poorly constructed watchtower or barricade was found. Without much iron at their disposal, most of these were held together by either magic spells or vines.

Nyana looked less than impressed at this expansion of the borders. "This is what you have your peasants waste away on? These are near useless!"

"I still say we are doing better than when I initially arrived. The tribe has grown and these barracks will suffice for now."

"You care about quantity, not quality."

"It's not like I have much to work with!"

"It's your job to work with whatever is at your disposal."

"You ingrate, I—"

Daemos was interrupted by a loud screech. Both of them whipped their heads around towards the direction of the horrible caterwauling. They started to run as fast as they could until they found it the hydra. The monster was massive and stood at a hulking thirty feet high, its body reaching the length of over twenty feet, not including the tail. The hydra had the body of a lizard with four strong legs to support its massive body. The tail alone was ten feet long and its tip was covered with barbed spikes. The hydra's seven vicious, horned heads all snapped and bit in random directions, trying to eat as many goblins as possible. The necks had a row of boney spines running along the back. Each head was serpentine-looking with a faint resemblance to dragons.

Hydras have the power to shoot pure magika from their mouths in the form of powerful beams of crackling blue light. What might be the most terrifying feature about the Hydra was their healing capabilities. Everyone knew that if one cuts off the head of a hydra, two more grow back. But this was the tip of the iceberg. Even if one was to slice and smash their way through the thick armored hide of the monster, its wounds would start to heal, no matter how deep or fatal. The only way to truly kill a hydra is to cut off all of its heads before they have the chance to grow back and while the creature has no heads, one must crush its heart. It is a nearly impossible task to kill a hydra, which is exactly why Daemos wanted one for himself.

"So… all I have to do is beat this thing into submission and then dominate it using the spell?"

"Yeah."

"And I understand you will sit out this fight as well?"

"Damn right I will. I am not stupid enough to fight a hydra without backup, unlike you."

"You only talk big. And what if I do beat this hydra and claim it as my own?"

"If you do that, then I may not view you as the worthless cockroach that you are."

"Heh… I will make you eat those words, hag." Daemos charged, letting out a demonic war cry which caught the hydra's attention.

The giant serpentine menace used three of its seven heads to shoot condensed magika at Daemos, who drew Oblivion and held the thick blade in front of him like a shield. The beams slammed against the red steel of the sword, deflecting wildly in different directions wildly and instantly cutting trees in half. The hydra tilted one of its heads in confusion, then roared and slammed Daemos with its massive tail. The strength of the attack caught Daemos off guard and sent him flying backwards, breaking through three trees in the process. The chestplate of his armor now sported a huge dent.

He groaned in pain as he pushed himself off the ground. The hydra prepared itself for another tail whip, but Daemos was now ready for it. Before the tail could make contact a second time, he grabbed the hydra's tail tightly and dug his claws through its armored scales and into the flesh. The reptile let out a pained-filled screech and started swinging its tail around wildly. Daemos was being flung around, but he did not let go and started climbing up the hydra's tail by digging his claws into his flesh, using them as a stronghold. He had almost reached the monster's back when one of the heads used the length of its neck to reach behind and bite down hard on Daemos. He groaned in pain as the fangs of the hydra scraped against his bones, powerful enough to puncture the thick black armor with ease. His bones remained undamaged but he felt the pain. Daemos was even more determined to claim this monster as his own now.

The hydra threw Daemos out of its mouth and onto the ground.

He slowly pushed himself back up, panting. "Heh… now this is a fight. You shall be worthy of joining my army, beast."

The heads of the hydra let out a loud hiss, eyeing their prey. Daemos used his godlike strength to rip an entire tree out of the ground and use it as a club against the hydra. He slammed the large tree against one of the heads. The beast reared back. Daemos looked at its tail, only to see that it had already fully healed. He groaned in frustration and gripped the tree harder.

Nyana watched the fight with an expression of slight boredom on her face. She stared at the Gauntlet of the Overlord and clenched her fist. She started thinking to herself, *Why? Why you? If what the master said about you is true, then why are you like this? He could have chosen any other rotting corpse to be his overlord, but the one he chose was you. Arrogant and rash. Has he really forgotten that much? You are so different compared to what I heard about you during your time in the world of the living. I know revenants lose their memories. I know they take traits from when they were alive. How did you die? What made you the way you are? Why… why did he pick you over me?*

Daemos was on top of the hydra now, clobbering its heads with his metal fists. His armor was shredded and some of his bones were visible.

The giant monster kept biting Daemos but with sheer willpower, he continued to shrug off the attacks. Daemos took his sword and plunged it into the hydra's back. It let out a roar and started spraying beams of magika in every direction. Daemos let out a laugh as he started using his sword like a saw on the hydra, spraying its blood all over. The hydra let out a pained whimper and start swaying back and forth. With a thunderous boom, it collapsed on the ground. This would not last forever, though. The hydra's body had already started to heal.

Daemos shakily slid off the beast's back and held the gauntlet out. "Dominate."

A red light starts to glow from the eyeball of the gauntlet and soon the hydra's eyes glowed red as well. The monster stood up and as Daemos stared, it slowly bowed to him. Daemos let out a laugh and fell to the ground, exhausted.

Nyana jumped down from her perch and looked down at him. "My my, I guess you're not useless after all. Dominating a hydra. I'm impressed. Your armor is destroyed though. Take the ring off."

"Why?"

"Just do it."

Daemos slowly took the ring off his finger and watched as his black armor and cape vanished in thin air.

"Now put it back on."

Daemos put the ring back on and the armor and cape came back as good as new.

"Nice trick." Daemos looked over his hydra, its wounds practically gone. If a skeleton could smile, he would be grinning from ear to ear. "Perfect. With a hydra under my command, these goblins will kneel before me and Whitia shall be all mine."

Nyana held out her hand to gently pet one of the hydra's heads. "You know… I was wondering. How did you get to know the boss? Does he have something over your head as well? If I do anything out of place, I'm going to be dead a second time, apparently. He has to have something on you too, right?"

"I've told you once, I can say it again. That's none of your business."

"Not going to tell me, huh?"

"I should be asking what is happening with you? One moment you're a bloodthirsty savage and now you're a different person. Well, not person. Different skeleton," Nyana chuckled.

"...I ...I don't know."

"You don't know?"

"What am I supposed—"

Suddenly, the air around them erupted in screams. Smoke could be seen rising to the sky in the distance. A black haze started enveloping the clouds and the sounds of screams could be heard.

"What is the name of Nioxis is that?"

"A fire? Did one of my useless subjects start a fire? Idiots!"

"No... no, I think it might be an enemy raid."

"Is that so? Well, we have a new friend for them to play with then. Let's go!"

Daemos climbed up onto his hydra as Nyana cast a spell.

"Fly!" Nyana levitated into the air and flew forward.

"Forwards! Towards the smoke!"

The hydra reared back and charged forward towards the screams.

The goblins of the Saka tribe were in a panic as enemy goblins started throwing torches at the half-repaired wooden stronghold from the backs of wolves. Hard work and toil of weeks was being burned to the ground in a matter of seconds. Gobna paced agitatedly as the goblins started to panic and flee in terror, one of them running towards the chief.

"Chief! Please take shelter! It's too dangerous!"

"So… this is how fate calls us. Conquered and oppressed, only for our 'master' to not be here at the end."

"I… what the? Chief, look!"

From the back of the fort emerged the two dozen direwolves dominated by Daemos. The enemy had regular wolves but direwolves could be from eight to ten feet in length and were more powerful than the average wolf.

The pack of direwolves jumped over the burning walls with ease and started running at full speed towards the attacking force. The enemy was a raiding party about seventy strong. Half of them were on the backs of wolves and the other half were on foot. Some of the goblins were wearing jewelry while the others were dressed in black cloaks. Watching over the fight was a goblin dressed in rusty armor and animal furs, riding a wolf. She watched in surprise as a pack of massive direwolves lunged into the fray and started tearing apart wolf and goblin alike. The massive beasts pounced on top of the first goblins they came into contact with and ripped their small bodies apart in an instant. The attacking goblins fell back in fear and surprise. *How are there direwolves here right now? And why are they helping the Saka tribe?*

The smaller wolves whimpered in fear of their larger and more deadly relatives on the opposite side of the battlefield.

The goblin watching over the attack started barking orders. "Don't falter! Burn their fur with torches! Aim for the eyes and keep as far a distance as possible!"

The retreating goblins got their arrows and doused them with fire magic. Twenty goblins took cover behind the goblin riders and pulled back their strings.

"FIRE!"

All the goblins let go of their bowstrings and shot the arrows. Most of them missed their targets due to the sheer speed of the direwolves. One of the arrows did hit a direwolf, however, and set his thick fur on fire. The wolf whimpered and shrieked in agony as its body started to burn.

"Retreat! Repeat the attack!"

The other wolves started to circle the attacking force and were slowly closing in on them. The direwolves snarled at the goblins and were getting ready for another conjoined pounce attack.

"Make a circle and hold your spears out! Archers in the middle and keep shooting flame arrows and spells! We can do this!"

Suddenly, the ground started to shake and screaming from the Saka stronghold could be heard. Even the direwolves stopped their attack and started to whimper and fold their ears back once they got a smell of what was coming from the thicket of trees. The ground shook more and more. Trees started to break and fall to the ground and soon enough, an ear-splitting roar was heard that sent chills down the spine of every creature, be it goblin or wolf.

From the thicket of trees emerged the massive hydra. Instant panic flooded amongst the attacking force of goblins. Hydras were extremely rare creatures and one of the apex predators of the Duma Forest. They didn't normally bother goblins because they were too small to be a good meal and they live further out in the forest, but the recent rapid expansion of the Saka tribe had disturbed the hydra and drawn it out into the open.

The goblin general watched in awe and terror as the massive hydra let out another monstrous roar. She had never seen a hydra with glowing red eyes and, above all, being ridden by a black knight!

"Beast, the one in the back is the general. Spare her life… slaughter the rest and bring me their souls."

The hydra charged forward, making the ground shake with every stomp of its mighty feet. Its long necks grabbed goblins, crushing their small and frail bodies in between its massive razor-sharp teeth.

Goblins helplessly attempted to shoot the hydra with arrows but they snapped when they made contact with the scales of the reptile. The goblin general watched in terror as the entire battalion entrusted to her was being crushed and devoured by one monster. As the hydra continued its rampage, the general was ready to flee, but her wolf's legs were stuck to the ground by magic. The general looked around to find the caster and saw Nyana casually leaning back in midair, she was still flying from her spell. The distraction worked, though, as the hydra has already stopped right at the hill of the general. All that there was left of her battalion were half-dead goblins squirming in pain and mangled bodies.

Daemos jumped off the hydra and landed on the ground in front of the general. The ground cracked beneath his heavy black boots. Deamos stared down at the general. As a show of force, he held his gauntlet above his head. The souls of her dead soldiers started to get sucked out of their bodies and swirl around his body like a tornado. When he closed his fist the cyclone of souls has drained away into the staring eye of the Overlord's Gauntlet.

"I am Daemos, leader of the Saka tribe and soon to be master of the entire Duma Forest. Who might be the foolish mortal that dared to threaten my inevitable takeover?"

"I... I..."

"SPEAK!"

"Fena... I... I am Fena, of the Ferak tribe."

"Fena, is it? So, Fena... why attack my lands?"

"I... um... it was my orders! T... to lead my force against yours. F... from King Krawl of Whitia!"

"Hmm... so you would know where I can find this king?"

"Y... y... yes."

"And you are a general, correct?"

"Yes."

"Perfect. I have a proposition for you. Are you interested in hearing it?"

"Y... y... y... yes, sir."

"Good. Starting now, you work for me. You will train my tribe how to fight properly. They are quite pathetic. You will give all information useful to my conquest and you will serve me to the utmost capacity, otherwise, your soul will be mine. Do you understand?"

"Yes, master."

"Good. It seems we have an understanding, general. So, join the others. You have quite a lot of information to unfold for me."

Nyana watched Daemos and the goings-on with interest.

Moonlight bathed the fort and village of the Saka tribe. Fena stared at the ceiling of the hut she had been given to temporarily rest in. She couldn't sleep. Her mind still couldn't process what she had witnessed today. The massive black knight was more terrifying than anything she had ever witnessed. He controlled beasts that could level entire goblin civilizations if given the chance. How could this be? She had helped King Krawl unite all of the goblin tribes to form Whitia. She was one of the most powerful and respected warriors and military leaders in all of Whitia and just like that, she had been defeated.

The door to the hut slowly opened to reveal another goblin. She had brown hair and blue eyes. She was gathering ingredients to make a stew.

"You're thinking about the master, right?"

Before Fena could agree, the goblin continued speaking.

"He is powerful... none of us are sure about what exactly he is. All we know is that we cannot stop him."

"How long has he been here?"

"A couple of weeks. He is a strange one. He killed direwolves with a single blow and then took over our town. He has been working all of us very hard, progress is being made. We have been seeing growth and security for the Saka tribe unlike anything before. Before our lord took these lands, we would be ambushed by monsters every day. They would kill us and steal our food. Now our lord is making those same monsters protect us and help us with manual labor. You're lucky he decided to spare you," the goblin said as she finished cutting up all of the ingredients she had and was beginning to make the stew.

"Does anyone know what he wants?"

"Well… to conquer all of Harmonia."

Fena was stunned and felt a chill run up her spine. "But… but that's impossible."

"I'd say he has a head start. No big kingdoms or empires are near the Duma Forest. Too many big monsters. It wouldn't be really worth it to take this forest. Only the strongest adventurers and warriors occasionally come here to kill monsters and even then, more than half of them end up dead. Our lord can control these monsters though. Imagine the power he will have once this whole forest is his!"

Fena thought this over, mulling over the words of the goblin. Just what had she gotten herself into?

"Here, the stew is done." The goblin wrapped the bottom of the bowl in a cloth and placed it next to Fena. "Eat well and I'll see you in the morning."

Fena stared at the bowl and started eating. She was scared. Unsure of what was in store for her.

The next morning was hectic for the Saka tribe. All able-bodied goblins were immediately put under combat training under the tutelage of Fena. Daemos ordered her to not give them the time to slack off. He wanted them ready for combat. He had a plan. If he takes out the king, then all of Whitia will fall. For most of the day, Daemos was out with a hunting party to capture more direwolves and other smaller-scale monsters. They were even able to capture drakes. Drakes were related to dragons, but while dragons were massive, intelligent, and skilled magic casters, drakes were much smaller, around ten to fifteen feet tall, had the brains of animals and were unable to use magic except for their natural ability to breathe fire. Also, while dragons had four legs, drakes had two. By the end of the day, Daemos was being followed by a horde of monsters he had dominated. Two dozen direwolves, two drakes, and a troll. With a small force of monsters, he would be more than a match for the king.

By the time he returned, it was night and the moonlight was shining down on the camp. He was pleasantly surprised to see Fena still training and Nyana doing more repairs to the wooden fort. Daemos knew that this was going to be a slow process. It was impossible to rush from country to country and constantly win. He needed time to gather resources and build his lands in a strong and sustainable manner. That being said, it would be useless to do so unless all of Whitia was his. The Saka tribe had no access to iron ore. That would need to change. He would start a deadly assault on the king of Whitia and knock out the entire small country with a single move. Once Whitia was his he would lay low and give time for his people to recuperate and his country to fortify.

Daemos approached Fena, who was just finishing a training mission with the villagers. She looked up at the black-clad warrior and slightly gulped.

"May I help you, my lord?"

"Yes. We need to talk. You have some information that I need."

"Of course, my lord."

"Tell me how to get to the king."

"His castle is in the center of Whitia. The fortress is made out of stone and is defended with guard towers and spiked barricades. There are lots of bushes and trees surrounding the area and the tree cover is used to ambush enemies. Many goblins hide in the brush to assassinate attackers before they even know what happened. On the top of the fort is an old rusty ballista. It was salvaged off the coast from a destroyed dwarven ship. Very powerful. I've seen it kill a drake with a single blow. Its weakness is that it takes a very long time to reload, especially with how heavy the ballista ammunition is. They still have plenty left over from when they first claimed the weapon because the castle is rarely ever attacked."

"Anything else you can tell me? What about the other tribes?"

"Of course, my lord. I am the leader of the Ferak tribe. My tribe is a group of hunters who use our knowledge of the Duma Forest to our advantage. My tribe crafts many different kinds of poisons and traps. We also tame wolves for riding."

"Does that mean that direwolves are of some use to you?"

"No, my lord. We can only tame regular wolves."

"I see. Carry on."

"Since I am now… your loyal servant, the Ferak tribe is no longer under my guidance and has most likely been put under the command of King Krawl since my disappearance."

"Hmm…"

"The next is the Nagana tribe. They are the territory farthest to the north and border Nigt. Their culture is all around thievery and hoarding. They are responsible for many of the stereotypes for goblins outside of the Duma Forest. They constantly steal from the orcs of Nigt who in turn raid the dwarven kingdom of Gluth across the shore by boat. Although the Nagana tribe is heavily criticized and hated by the other goblin tribes, they are fiercely loyal to the king and have been defending Whitia from Nigt for decades."

"This information is not useful to me. I need to know what they excel at."

"O… of course, my lord. M… my bad. The Nagana tribe excels in front-quarters combat. They are the front-line soldiers and use the weapons they steal from the orcs and the dwarves. They are also incredibly rich from all the plundering. They use this money to buy things from Gluth or even return some of the things that Nigt took from Gluth in their raids. The Nagana tribe plays both sides."

"Go on."

"The Soba tribe is weak, but has grown very rich through trade with other kingdoms. Soba has the largest iron deposits and mines in all of the Duma Forest. Most of the goblins there are not fighters, just like your tribe my lord."

"Something that you will fix… correct?"

"Of course, my lord. I will make sure that your tribespeople get ample training as warriors. The chief of the Soba tribe is brother to the king, which means that King Krawl gives 'unrestricted access to his ship in order to do any trading. Finally, the last one is the Zacta tribe. A creed of goblin assassins and spies who dress in all black. They are masters of ambush and stealth killing. They use daggers and sneak up on enemies from the dark."

"You do seem to know a lot about these other tribes."

"It was my job. I wasn't just the chief of the Ferak tribe, I was also the general of King Krawl's army. Whitia has had several rebellions since the king came to power. Just before you showed up, another rebellion uprising emerged from the south. It was crushed before you arrived. It was my obligation to know as much about my allies as possible given the chance they could rebel as well."

"Hmmm... good. Do you think we have sufficient numbers to take the castle?"

"Well, my lord, although your control over these monsters is highly admirable, I don't think we will be able to take the castle. The royal castle has several hundreds of able-bodied warriors ready to fight. Having a small army of beasts is great for a surprise attack and catching the enemy off guard, but we would still be overwhelmed by numbers."

"Now, your current task, besides continuing the training courses, is also to find a way to bring the Ferak tribe under my rule. I want as few casualties as possible. I will need every able body."

"M... my lord, I... I would not know how to do that. I'm a general but I rarely ever go into battle or enemy territory."

"I need soldiers. You are the best avenue of getting me hundreds without disposing of our anonymity. Go... NOW!"

Fena shakily nodded her head and jumped atop her wolf. She gently rubbed its ear as it started running on towards the Whitia Castle.

Krawl, the king of the goblins, sat on his throne with three goblin chieftains. He was getting incredibly worried. First, Gobna had gone missing and now Fena. The three remaining chieftains sat at the large table with the king.

"This is outrightly preposterous! Half of our government has been taken out, including the general of our army. Not only that, but an entire raiding party just vanished into thin air? It's impossible. I bet Fena betrayed us," said the leader of the Nagana tribe.

"This is getting worrisome indeed. The Saka tribe was the largest exporter of food and the Feraks were our largest military detachment," said the Soba chieftain as he greedily grabbed a handful of food from the large table and gobbled it down.

"It would be foolhardy to send out another attack. We need to stay together and destroy them by our numbers. Vesta, send out another scouting party. I want to know how they are going to hit us."

"As you wish, my lord," said the black-cloaked leader of the Zacta tribe.

Fena was sneaking around the side of the stone stronghold with a small militia of Saka goblins. She knew that once she was out of the picture, one of the other tribes would try to absorb Feraks within their own. That would mean that they would be temporarily housed at the capital.

From the side of the castle, she could see hundreds of tents set up. Her tribe had been made to camp out beside the castle. Fena watched closely to make sure there were no other goblins around.

Fena looked to the sky, waiting for the sun to go down. "Should we go now, general?"

"No, we wait until nightfall. Easier to not get caught and it will also make our escape easier to pull off if my former tribe sees me as a traitor. The other tribes have probably convinced the king that I am a traitor at the first chance they could get, so that they can take as much of my land and resources as possible. They have always had silver tongues."

"But... but you are a traitor."

Fena sighed. "That is not the point. Now stay quiet and hunt some game. We're camping out as well."

As night fell, Fena and her militia slowly approached the campsite. Many of the soldiers she had once commanded were already asleep, except for the few who were on guard duty. One of the Saka soldiers walked beside her, taking cover in the shadows.

"So how are we going to do this, general?"

"We have to reason with them. I just have to hope that their loyalties still lie with me and this can go as smoothly as possible."

Fena approched the guards on duty openly. They looked dumbstruck, assuming that their leader had died or was in captivity.

"Chief? What are you doing here? We all thought that you were dead!"

"I don't have much time to explain. I need you all to come with me. There is a new power rising in the Duma Forest. One you can't even imagine. I was… lucky enough to be spared and given a chance to serve under a new king. You are all family to me. Whitia is going to fall soon. I need to make sure everyone I care about is on the right side before the battle starts."

The guard was taken aback by how sudden and straightforward this was. He looked back to the camp and then to her. He nodded his head and motioned for her to follow him. When they made it to the camp, she explained everything the best she could to the tribe elders. About how two strange and powerful beings arrived seemingly from nowhere and were already conquering Whitia.

Suddenly, a loud horn sounded on top of the fort. One of the older members of Fena's tribe had sounded the alarm.

"Never surrender! Long live Whitia!"

"NO, DAMMIT! It's now or never! If you trust me and want to live, then run with me now! If you want to die, then stay at the castle! Come on! We have to move NOW!"

Fena mounted a wolf and charged back into the thicket of trees as fast as possible. Arguing and yelling could be heard from

RAMPAGE: THE RISE OF AN EMPIRE

the Ferak tribe as they quickly started splitting and choosing sides. Alarms and torches were everywhere as goblin soldiers started to awaken inside their fort. In the confusion, the Ferak tribe nearly split down the middle, with half staying loyal to the king and the others believing in their chieftain and following her into the forest.

The group vanished into the forest as spears and arrows were being shot at them from the castle. They didn't stop their retreat until the sounds of goblin war cries and alarms had faded. Fena dismounted her wolf and looked over her former kinspeople.

"A lot of you followed me. Good. I know what I say is hard to believe, but Whitia will come under a new power in a matter of days. A massive black knight and a mysterious woman in a golden mask have the power to control monsters… they even have a hydra!"

Whispers of confusion and panic spread across the horde of goblins.

"I can't have my tribe be destroyed. At least we will be on the winning side. Now come… he is waiting for us."

All the goblin chieftains once again met at the large table with the king on his throne, tiredness and stress writ large on his face. King Krawl looked at his last three remaining chieftains- Nomai, Gogba, and Vesta. In the corner of the room, Cling Clang the wandering goblin watched with interest. Normally he would have been kicked out of the castle already, but seeing how he was one of the greatest goblin fighters in his time and had the most information on this new, strange enemy, he was allowed to stay.

Nomai slammed his fist on the table and took charge of the conversation.

CADE SKOBLAR

"See! I knew Fena was a traitor. She switched sides instead of staying loyal to you. She must be destroyed as soon as possible. A large portion of her former soldiers stayed loyal to you, your majesty. I suggest that you give her land and armies to me so that I would be able to—"

"Not so fast, you greedy rat!" yelled Gogba, whose fat exterior almost made him roll off his chair. He used his grubby hands to hold onto the table and balance himself.

"You really expect me to let you get away with taking all of her land and soldiers for yourself? This is unacceptable, Nomai!"

"My forces have held back the orcs of Nigt on the front lines AND kept this country rich and prosperous by raiding the orcs who steal from the dwarves! All your goblins do is mine iron and make subpar weapons."

"Is that so? The dwarves certainly don't think so, going by our trade."

"ENOUGH! I didn't call this meeting to listen to the both of you bicker like children! The only reliable ally I have is Ve—"

Suddenly, a poisoned dagger was shoved into King Krawl's throat. Blood started gurgling from his mouth and the poison quickly infected him, making him foam at the mouth, his blood now slightly purple. Krawl's body fell to the ground, lifeless. Standing over his corpse was Vesta with a psychotic smile on his face.

"I have stayed loyal to the king for too long… watched him make a fool of himself. Now, I am the king. If you two do everything I say, we will win. I promise you that. The old fool was willing to surrender soon. I would die before allowing the pride of our kingdom to be snuffed out. Now, be good dogs unless you want to die as well. Your king commands it."

CHAPTER 6

Daemos swung his sword with incredible strength and control as he chopped down four trees with a single swing. Nyana was leaning against a boulder, reading. She looked up at Daemos and threw a pebble at his head.

"Hey Daemos, check this out."

"What is it, woman? I'm trying to gather wood. I don't have time for your books right now."

"Why? You're the lord of the tribe. Just order the goblins to do it. Also, stop it with the 'what is it, woman' crap. It's annoying."

"They are too slow. I am preparing for a fight soon and I want to be ready. I have the beasts hunting for food and my people rebuilding and fortifying as much as possible."

"Right. Well, I have been studying some new spells in this ancient book. I want to see if you are able to cast them."

"And waste the souls that I have to bring back to Zithoss? No, I intend to surprise him with a bounty of souls. I prefer to use my sword anyways. I just use the souls I need to build my army of monsters and that's it."

"Suit yourself. Oh, by the way, I think the goblin general is back."

Daemos turned around to see Fena returning with a large number of healthy goblins and wolves. Daemos was impressed. With every step that he took towards her the ground shook a little bit. The massive black knight stared down at Fena with his glowing red eyes. The goblins who arrived with her nervously looked at the massive hulk of black steel with fear.

"You did well. Prepare the rest for battle. The attack will commence tomorrow morning."

"Yes, my lord."

"When all of Whitia is mine, we shall use some time to grow and rebuild. The next target is Nigt."

Goblins start to mutter in panic when he brought up the idea of invading the orcs of Nigt. One of the new arrivals stood up and looked at the black knight.

"How is that even possible! We have been in a stalemate with them for ages! Invasion is imp—"

He was silenced as Daemos let out a laugh. He lifted his gauntlet and the eyeball on it started to open wide and look around. The goblins were suddenly covered in a shadow as a large drake landed next to him. Then another. Then another. Soon, a small flock was circling in the sky. The trees fell down as the massive hydra let out a hissing roar and dozens of large direwolves let out howls. All the goblins were shaking by now.

"This forest is filled with some of the most dangerous monsters in all of Harmonia. Monsters talked of in legend and story. Some of the greatest heroes and adventurers died in these forests. Soon this entire forest will be the start of my new empire. When this forest is fully under my control, I will have an army unlike any this world has ever seen. Once this forest is mine, we will strike our main target."

"W... who would that be, my lord?"

"The Harmonain Empire."

Fena was in the cottage that was provided to her with a look of dumbfounded dread on her face. What had she just done? She thought she was saving her people, but she had just dragged them into a war that she didn't think was possible to win. How can this maniac take on the entire Harmonian Empire? The Harmonian Empire had made several attempts to annex the Duma Forest, but had failed every single time. The first country any invading force encounters in the forest is Shimia, the land of werewolves. They fight so well in their forest that not even the powerful magic and the overwhelming numbers of the Harmonian imperial army could make a foothold in the forest. Between the werewolves and the massive monsters, they have deemed the Duma Forest a lost cause for the time being. But leaving the safety of the forest and invading the empire on their territory? That is a suicide mission.

Fena groaned as she sat up and massaged her temples. She was filled with fear and grief. Has she doomed her people in an attempt at giving them a chance to live? She rolled over in her bed of furs and tried to close her eyes and sleep, but to no avail. The anxiety of being prepared for the coming battle had banished sleep.

Daemos sat on his throne of stone, fur, and wood. It was not much of a throne, but it was a start. His goblins and monsters have been working overtime to build and construct a fortress. It has steadily become more and more difficult to do so without access to the iron mines on the other side of the goblin country. The only way they have been able to bind materials together is with earth magic to create vines or to scavenge other rope-like plants from the forest. The building is unstable and crude at best. Nyana walked into the unfinished fort, a little annoyed, and strutted over to Daemos.

"Yes? What have you come to bother me about this time?"

"What the hell are you making your troops do before the battle tomorrow?"

"I am preparing in case the enemy strikes. We have no defenses."

"This pile of sticks is not going to provide any sort of *defense*," Nyana mocked.

Daemos grunted in annoyance and stood up.

"Why must it be that at every possible chance you have, you continue to question me and act as if you are superior?"

"Because you are just proving that I am! Why would you have your soldiers build this in the middle of the night when they are about to fight a war the next morning? Plus, if we win tomorrow, we will finally have access to iron so you can build all you damn want! Even better, why not just take the king's castle and use it as your own from tomorrow? WHY ARE YOU DOING ANY OF THIS? WHY ARE YOU A COMPLETE MORON?!"

Daemos clenched his clawed fist. He had only been trying to build a fort to intimidate the enemy if they were ambushed. Every time she made a valid point it annoyed him further.

"Why would he ever choose you? He said that you were once an accomplished general when you were alive! So how do you make these horrible decisions that even I can tear apart? What is wrong with you?"

General? What was she talking about? Daemos remembered nothing of his past. He was a general when he was alive? He wanted to know more but... his anger was consuming him. He hated her so much. Always whining and yapping. Always getting in his way. Daemos grabbed his sword and slowly approached her.

"I have heard enough of your incessant prattling. You have insulted me for the last time."

Daemos raised his blade and slammed it down in Nyana's direction.

She quickly dodged and the blade slammed into the stone, cracking it with ease. "WHAT ARE YOU DOING!?"

"Swatting an annoying gnat."

RAMPAGE: THE RISE OF AN EMPIRE

Daemos made a large overheard swing with his blade and nearly hit Nyana, but she dodged and slid under his legs. She then stabbed him with her dagger. He made a grunting noise as the weapon sparked off his armor. He whirled around and threw her off his body. Nyana was sent flying into a wall and she let out a pain-filled yelp. His strength was beyond reason. Daemos slowly approached her as he started dragging his blade behind him, making a trail of sparks as he did.

"I have listened to you time and time again talk down to me and treat me like dirt. But no more. Now I will cut your head off—"

Before he got the opportunity to finish his threat, Nyana stood back up and jumped from wall to wall with incredible speed. Daemos held his blade to his side. Nyana shot from the wall like a cannonball and Daemos was ready to intercept her with his blade. Just as the two were about to make contact, a powerful force overcame them both. They dropped their weapons and groaned in pain. Daemos felt like he was dying. It was the most excruciating pain he had felt so far. A voice echoed in their heads.

"Meet me in my throne room. We must talk."

The voice faded and Daemos felt his body released from the pain. He shook and tried to gather his bearings for a moment before reaching for his sword. Nyana was standing before Daemos.

"The master wants to speak to us. Let's not keep him waiting then."

Daemos and Nyana walked through the heavy stone doors to enter the dungeon of Zithoss. When he had summoned them, he didn't sound pleased at all. Daemos felt a wave of anxiety hit him. He knew that Zithoss had given him life and could just as easily take it away. Nyana, on the other hand, looked mortified and ashamed of herself. Daemos still couldn't understand her that well. He couldn't read her at all.

The two approached Zithoss, who had not moved a single inch from the last time they had met each other. The only sign of any life inside the horned skeleton was the faint and dim glowing red light coming from one of his eye sockets. His ghastly whispering voice filled the room as if he were a crowd of people surrounding them.

"Release the souls into the well," Zithoss commanded.

Daemos looked down at the large pit in the center of the throne room. Whenever one stared for too long into the pitch-black depths of the pit, an unexplainable ominous dread overtook them, forcing them to avert their eyes. Daemos approached the pit. Around the pit was a spiked iron railing and a stone pillar. The pillar had a handprint engraved into it which was too small for his hand. When Daemos had first got the gauntlet, it had resized itself to fit his hand. The stone pillar started to shake. The engraving on the pillar started to get larger, its outline withering away into dust. In a few moments, the handprint on the pillar was the perfect size for his hand.

Daemos looked to Nyana, who motioned him to do as Zithoss had said. Daemos lifted his arm up and placed the gauntlet into the stone groove. The eye on the gauntlet instantly opened wide and started glowing green. The ominous pit started to fill with a strange green liquid, as if from thin air. Green smoke arose from the liquid and ghosts and spirits started to circle the pit. The distant and quiet sounds of pained moans and screams could be heard from the pit. The liquid in the pit had a powerful glow that illuminated the room fully. The cold and chill of the throne room were now replaced with an unnatural warmth. The pit was not nearly close to being full. It looked incredibly deep as well, now that the bottom could be seen covered in the strange green liquid.

Nyana started to cry tears of joy that dripped out of the bottom of her mask. She ran to the edge of the railing to stare at the pit and then ran to Zithoss.

"My lord… you did it… you finally did it! In all my time serving you I have yet to see the beauty of the well of souls! It's… it's beautiful!"

Zithoss looked towards the pit. A dozen souls were ripped from the liquid and were sucked away into Zithoss's body. Nyana was speechless as she watched her master and mentor shakily start to move his bony hand. Nyana started to weep more. In the several decades of serving Zithoss, he has never been able to move a single inch. More joy than she could possibly contain was filling her.

Zithoss shakily moved his hand upwards with great struggle. Nyana had to restrain herself from helping him. She only stopped because she did not want to ruin this moment for him. Zithoss reached out and pointed at Daemos.

"You have given me something that has been locked away for… longer than I can remember. I have not been able to move for a long, long time."

Zithoss slowly moved his head to the left to look at Daemos better. When he moved his head, dust and insects spilled out of his skull like sand. The bugs crawled away in a panic once they were thrown out of his skull.

"The joy I feel is immense… but that is not why I called you here. Both of you are beginning to disappoint me."

Nyana felt her heart shatter. Her body shook and she instantly fell down to her knees to bow.

Daemos tilted his head to the side. "Disappointed? What madness is that? Almost half of Whitia has been conquered and you can move once again! What more can y—"

Daemos was interrupted by Nyana running up to him, attempting to stab him. Before she made contact, however, Daemos's body was slammed into the ground with a force unlike anything he had felt before. Nyana fell back in surprise and looked towards Zithoss, who was still pointing at Daemos. Zithoss simply flicked his finger and Daemos was sent flying into the wall with incredible force.

Nyana was stunned by his all-powerful magic, but she snapped out of her amazement to speak to him. "My apologies, mighty one! This insect still does not know its proper place! I've been trying to do as you tell me but he— he—" the flustered, angry Nyana could barely finish her sentence.

Zithoss simply lifted his hand for her to stop and she fell silent instantly. Daemos continued to struggle against his magic grasp, but he could not move his body an inch. Zithoss's one glowing red eye started to glow even brighter and erupted in a demonic red flame.

"My revenant… you will listen and listen properly. You will stay completely quiet. You will not disrespect me with your foul language and you will heed my words. Understand?"

Daemos was silent.

"Good."

Zithoss put his finger down and Daemos fell to the ground, released from his telekinetic grasp. Daemos hadn't even given him that many souls. Only a few weak ones and yet he could stop him with a flick of his finger. He still hadn't comprehended how powerful Zithoss was.

"Now. Although I am incredibly satisfied with being returned to… a fraction of what I once was, you are both underperforming. You fight amongst yourselves. Nyana, you act as a bystander. Quick to anger. Daemos… it appears the loss of your memory was greater than I had first anticipated. You were once a great leader. A general. You act like a brute with no strategy or brain. You're stubborn and foolish. You have been reborn for less than a year and yet you act as if you are superior to all. When you are out there you are the overlord. When you are in here you are MY revenant. I have watched you make foolish choice after foolish choice and turn down all sound advice. This will not stand. I refuse to lose my last chance because of your incompetence. Understand?"

"Yes, master."

"Good. Then we have an understanding. I don't want the two of you making fools of each other in my name. Now go. Conquer Whitia and bring me the souls that I desire."

The two bowed their heads and left the dungeon in the mountain. Nyana and Daemos were both quiet as they pushed open the large stone doors and entered the sunlight once again. Nyana let out a shaky breath and leaned against a tree, her head lowered to look at the ground. Daemos stood still as a statue with only his massive cloak flowing in the wind behind him.

"This can't happen anymore. I refuse to bring shame to his name."

"I think we have no choice in the matter either way."

"THERE SHOULDN'T…" she breathed deeply, trying to get rid of her frustration. Nyana lowered her voice and continued, "There shouldn't be a choice. He gave you a second chance, just like me. We are loyal to him. No matter what!"

"…What has he done to earn your—"

"I already told you, I am not telling you. Now, I will strive harder to work with you. You on the other hand must heed my advice!"

"Fine. We have a war to win."

Daemos turned around and walked away to return to the village. Nyana sighed and stood up so she could follow Daemos. Daemos clenched his clawed gauntlet into a fist as he thought of the coming battle. This was going to be his first large-scale war. It was a war he was positive he was going to win. He had every advantage imaginable.

Just then, a faint thought tugged at his mind. There was something he wanted to ask her. Daemos didn't turn to look at her and he spoke as they walked forwards.

"When we spoke... you said I was a great general... yet I remember nothing. Who was I?"

Nyana tilted her golden masked face to the side as he asked the question. She really didn't feel like talking to him right now, but she had a duty now.

"Who you used to be does not matter. That man died over a century ago. You are Overlord Daemos in service of the Elder Lich Zithoss. That is who you are and that is who you will remain. Now listen. There is a battle ahead of us. We have an overwhelming advantage, but we can't lose our heads. Do you understand?"

"Yes."

"Good. Then let us return."

When Daemos returned to the village, he immediately halted the construction of the poorly made fort and called for a band of goblin wolf riders from the Ferak tribe to do some reconnaissance and spying. When the spies eventually returned, he looked over the collected intel and prepared to address his army.

Daemos stood in front of the goblins that he would be commanding tomorrow morning. He could sense the fear they had for him. He paced back and forth and watched as they trembled in place staring at their new king. Daemos lifted the Gauntlet of the Overlord over his head. The eye opened and started to sporadically look everywhere.

"Tomorrow will be the first of many battles, yet this may be the most important. With this battle, we will control all of Whitia in a single offensive measure. This battle will be fast and is expected to turn heavily in our favor. Despite this, every single one of you will be expected to fight at your utmost potential. Only the best will suffice under my command."

RAMPAGE: THE RISE OF AN EMPIRE

Daemos sat down on the throne that was made for him and continued his speech.

"Our spies have informed me that the enemy is in a state of panic. They are aware of our power and their troops' morale is at an all-time low. We have found that traps have been placed around the battlefield, so the beasts will start the charge to reduce casualties. On top of the castle is an old ballista. An ancient human weapon, from what I have been told. We will use the drakes to burn it down. When the beasts have cleared a path and caused significant damage to the enemy, then the infantry will charge in and finish the fight. This will be an easy victory. Tomorrow is the start of a new dawn."

Very few of the goblins cheered. Daemos grunted and was about to stand up. Seized by panic, the goblins broke into a cheer which continued until Daemos left. Daemos entered one of the empty tents and sat down. He grumbled in frustration.

"You don't have the love of your subjects yet, huh?" said Nyana, who was hiding behind Daemos, an invisible spell cast over her. She ended her spell after she stopped talking. Daemos harrumphed as he looked at his gauntlet, staring at it in its single large eye. He turned back to look at Nyana. He was annoyed he had to ask for advice from her, but it was the best option he had.

"You're welcome for helping you make the plan and speech, by the way. Fena is a good general. Thank her as well for planning that with you. A bit more practice and I'm sure you ca…"

"I have brought great amounts of land and resources for this tribe. Created a powerful army. And yet they are not grateful."

"Grateful? You really are clueless. They are scared."

"Is that not the point?"

"Not if it is your own soldiers, I'm sure. I mean, right now, they are just terrified of you. I think it should be a terrified respect instead. They don't even know how to act around you. You just kind of barged in, conquered the entire village and made a bunch of drastic changes in a matter of moments. Now they are in a war. Sure, you have made them bountiful with wood and food, but you still work them to near death on forts and defenses that couldn't stop an angry bear. Maybe after this fight, when you become the king of Whitia, they will see the fruits of our efforts more and come to respect you? I get you're an overlord but there's… I don't know, a process to this? You can still be threatening and be a symbol of fear while also being a good leader that has the respect of your people."

"Perhaps there is some validity to your words, woman."

"Again with the woman talk? Just call me Nyana."

"…Fine…Nyana."

The two sat in silence for a good minute listening to nothing but the sound of crackling campfires outside and the noises of nature.

Daemos broke the peaceful silence. "Your loyalty to the boss… it's quite powerful. How did one such as yourself come to devote their very being to one so dark?"

Nyana responded with only a sigh. Her fingers started to tap against her knee with a fast and aggressive rhythm. "Are you going to constantly ask about and pry into my past till the battle starts?"

"Until I get an answer I am satisfied with."

"Well, you're not getting one," Nyana said as she stood up and stretched her back. She opened the flaps to the tent and looked out at the night sky. She turned back to look at Daemos and tilted her head to the side. She let out a groan and spoke. "If you answer one of my questions, I will answer one of yours."

"What kind of child's game is this?"

"Do you want to know or not?"

"…Fine. Ask your questions."

"I know you don't have any memories of your past. You lost them when you became our master's revenant. But when you were first revived, you acted differently… far different compared to any revenant I have seen before. Yet, as we speak, you are once again nothing like the revenant I first met at Shatterstar. What happened back there?" Nyana asked as she sat on the grass outside of the tent and crossed her legs. Her face was hidden because of her strange golden mask but from her posture, she seemed intrigued and curious to hear the answer.

Daemos stepped out of the tent and sat opposite to her. He had been taken aback by the question. He was not fully sure how to even answer it. He pondered over it, trying to formulate his thoughts. Daemos thought back to that moment. In the courtyard of the elven castle. Violence, anger, rage. Horrible cyclones of emotions had swirled in him that night. Merely thinking about it now was almost dragging him back into that moment.

"I… don't know. I felt… hate… rage… I wanted to kill…rip and tear. I wanted to kill every elf I laid my eyes on."

Simply saying the word 'elf' made his body tense up. He stared at Nyana as he continued to speak and relive his memory of the night of his creation.

"Every elf I looked at… deserved to be crushed like an ant under my boot. They deserve no happiness. I don't know why but… I know at least that to be true. Especially… that queen! Every elf… should be killed." Daemos suddenly had an epiphany. He stared at Nyana. "Are you… an elf?"

Nyana had been listening with great interest. Although, she also seemed apprehensive and cautious. She slowly stood up as Daemos reached for his blade. Nyana jolted and went on to take off one of her golden gloves in a very unwilling, skeptical manner. As she watched Daemos wrap his fingers around the hilt of his blade she pulled off her glove to show him her hand. Her skin was green and patterned in scales. She did not have scales, but the patterns on her arm looked like scales. She quickly put the glove back on.

"Th... there. I am not an elf, okay?"

"Very well. Now it is my turn to—"

"You already asked your question."

"...What?"

"You asked me if I was an elf. I showed you I was not. No more questions."

Daemos stamped his feet in frustration and groaned.

"Oh, don't whine now. Go on, leave me to sleep. I get an undead like you doesn't need to eat or sleep but that's not the case for the rest of us. Now leave me alone and get ready for the battle tomorrow. We have a lot of preparations to do."

CHAPTER 7

Terrified goblins stand at the Whitia Fort the next morning, anxious for the upcoming attack that would inevitably come for them. They have trained in combat and strengthened their defenses for days and nights in order to prepare for the attack. Ever since Vesta took the crown by killing Krawl, the kingdom of Whitia has become heavily militarized. Dozens of traps and defenses have been erected in a rushed fashion. Multiple rounds of ammunition have been created for the old and worn ballista on top of the fort. Civilians have been brought to the castle to prepare for the attack. Practically none of them knew how to fight but were forced to do so anyway. Inside the castle, the last remaining leaders of the goblin kingdom discussed and planned for the defense of their capital inside the castle.

Vesta was the leader of the king's personal clan of assassins. Being the leader of some of the most dangerous goblins in Whitia had its advantages. Years of combat experience and stealth training made planning for the coming attack much easier.

Vesta sat in his new throne as he watched the last two remaining chieftains bicker amongst themselves- Gogba the gluttonous merchant and Nomai the pirate raider.

"For once Vesta… I mean King Vesta has the right idea. They don't even know they are being led into a trap! You are paranoid, Gogba! Have some trust in our new king!"

"Don't speak of the death of my brother so lightly! It may have been a… necessary death since he became so soft… but he had a point! I have connections! I can ask for aid from the king of Gluth! Better yet, we can evacuate!"

"Silence!" yelled Vesta.

"We are going to be fine. Now listen. We know they have at least one hydra in their forces. That is one of our biggest priorities. Hydras are nearly unkillable because of how fast their bodies heal. It is also obvious that it is maybe one of the first times a hydra has ever been weaponized for war. Nearly no one knows how to properly kill a hydra. From what we know, they have a warrior amongst them who can control the beasts of the forest. Our scouts have two primary targets. The first is the strange black knight with an eye on his hand. The second is a mysterious woman with a golden mask. Those two are definitely the ones controlling these monsters. They must be our primary targets. The traps we set up can halt the beasts and slow the hydra and in that time, we must destroy those two. The enemy has the Saka tribe and half of the Ferak tribe as their infantry. We obviously have the advantage in the infantry, what we don't have is the amount of powerful cavalry that the enemy does. We know they have direwolves. As for us, we need to always stay on the defensive. I want our ballista in constant use and as many of our soldiers as possible shooting arrows and casting spells. Furthermore we—"

Vesta was cut off by screams and the sound of trees falling over with thunderous booms. Cling Clang ran into the meeting hall with an excited look.

"THE DARK ONES ARE HERE! YOU SHALL STAND BACK AS THE ALL-POWERFUL CLING CLANG WILL DESTROY THE ENEMY!"

"It seems our meeting has been cut short. To battle, then."

Arrows filled the sky as the large army of monsters and goblins started to approach the Whitia Castle. Right in the front lines was the mighty hydra. The seven serpentine heads of the monster were shooting its concentrated beams of magika towards the castle. After every blast from the hydra's breath, a small explosive impact followed. Following the hydra were large trolls using logs and trees like clubs. The sound of howls filled the air as dozens of massive direwolves ran with incredible speed towards the castle. From the sky, loud roars could be heard as two drakes swooped in. Vesta was taken by surprise as he was unaware of trolls or drakes being in the attacking force. He did not let this stir him, though.

Vesta watched from the peak of the stone fortress with the two chieftains. The attacking force was larger and more diverse than he had anticipated. He pointed towards the drakes, seeing them as the biggest, most immediate threat because of their flight.

"Let the ground troops fall into our traps. Focus our fire on the drakes. ATTACK!"

The ballista fired a massive bolt at one of the drakes. Caught off guard, it was impaled in the neck. The flying reptile was pinned to a tree, gurgling on its own blood as it wiggled and writhed. The other drake let out a roar and flew towards the fort.

The hydra continued to bombard the fort with his powerful magika. As the hydra advanced, it hit a trip wire and two large sharpened logs came swinging from the trees on both ends. Both the logs slammed into the hydra's necks and ripped off three of the heads. The hydra stumbled back in a panic as its blood started to spill all over the ground.

Vesta watched with great interest. The fight was starting out exactly as he had planned despite the unexpected forces of the enemy. His attention was brought to the forest as he saw their main targets begin to approach the battlefield. The castle of Whitia was perfectly constructed for defense. Its back faced the ocean, meaning the only way to attack the castle was a frontal assault unless the invaders possessed a navy.

Daemos walked out of the forest menacingly with his troops following him. His large black cape flowed behind him. His hateful red eyes could be seen glowing even from across the battlefield. Walking beside him was Fena of the Ferak tribe and Nyana.

Vesta smiled and pointed his finger towards them. "All archers, fire on them!"

A volley of arrows fired directly towards the group. Fena ducked for cover but Daemos simply looked at Nyana.

Nyana held up her gloved hand. "Wall of water!"

A stream of water from the ocean shot into the sky from behind the castle and flowed towards the three of them with great speed. The water formed a bubble around the three and the arrows slowed down the moment they entered the water.

Daemos lifted his gauntlet up, its eye glowing green. "Drake, destroy the ballista. Trolls, pelt them with boulders. Wolves, scale the walls. Hydra, attack."

All the beasts let out ear-splitting roars at once, making the enemy goblins tremble in fear. The drake swooped over to the castle roof with stunning ariel agility and showered the castle with hot flames. The ballista fired once again, this time only grazing the drake. The airborne reptile let out a screech when suddenly boulders started to be thrown at the castle. The large trolls shoved their meaty fingers into the earth and ripped out chunks of ground and rock, throwing them into the enemy lines. The direwolves started to run as fast as their bodies could towards the walls of the castle. Some of the wolves were picked off by fireballs being thrown over the side of the castle. Arrows and throwing spears were not strong enough to pierce the thick fur and hides of the direwolves.

RAMPAGE: THE RISE OF AN EMPIRE

Most of the direwolves latched onto the walls of the castle with their large claws digging into the stone like hooks. They slowly started to scale the wall to reach the other side. In a panic, the goblins started throwing fireballs at the wolves, some flinging anything they could lay their hands on over the side of the wall.

The hydra's heads had regrown and the massive monster started its advance once again. Vesta grits his teeth with frustration. There was something different about these monsters. He has fought the beasts of Duma before. They were powerful and dangerous, but at the end of the day, they were still animals. Yet these beasts act like the pain meant nothing to them and their fear has been stripped away, no matter how many of their friends are lost. It was as if animal instinct had been completely stripped from them, leaving them mere weapons. This went against Vesta's plans completely. He knew that the enemy could control monsters, but not to this extent. He had planned that if he injured the hydra enough, it would go into a frenzy and start attacking the enemy as well. All it was doing was attacking his castle and ignoring its allies. Vesta let out a shaky breath and clenched his fist. This was not going according to plan.

The hydra let out a roar of agony as its massive body was entrapped once again and it fell into a pit full of sharpened logs. The hydra's body was impaled on dozens of massive spikes, but as it tried to climb its way out of the pit, its body had already started to heal.

The drake swooped down to the castle, grabbing a goblin with its feet and flying away to eat it alive. Its jaws crushed the bones of the goblin instantly before turning back around to continue its attack. The ballista fired a mighty bolt at the drake, piercing its neck and killing it instantly. The victory shouts of the ballista operators quickly turned into screams of panic as the carcass fell from the sky and dive bombed right into the ballista., crushing it instantly. The ancient human weapon was reduced to a pile of smashed pieces of metal and wood. Vesta was furious.

Meanwhile, a large group of the direwolves had managed to scale the wall and breach the castle. The massive wolves were now able to deal severe casualties inside of the castle. Small iron weapons could not pierce the hides of the wolves and on the rare occasion they did, not much damage was done. Goblins were torn to pieces without mercy and with every kill Daemos collected more and more souls, no matter what side the creature was fighting on. Mages, goblins skilled in fire-magic, continued to throw fireballs at the direwolves to try and burn their fur.

Daemos watched with interest as more of his beasts were dying and their souls were sucked into his gauntlet. He looked at Nyana.

"Input?"

"This battle is impossible to lose. The king was craftier than we anticipated, but even with higher losses than expected, this battle is still ours. Then again…if you would like to lower our casualties then maybe we should intervene?"

"Very well. Leave this to me, then."

Daemos took a step backwards and without warning, started running as fast as he could towards the castle wall. As Daemos charged, the hydra was finally able to crawl out of the pit of massive spikes and continue its advance. Daemos slammed into the castle walls, smashing a large hole right through the castle wall and let out a triumphant roar like a berserker. The moment the opening was formed, the goblin infantry and the beasts charged towards the large hole their master had created.

Daemos drew his massive blade and held it to his side. Nyana levitated to the top of the castle walls, more interested in watching the fight than participating in it. Daemos started slaughtering the goblins with his massive blade which was larger than two goblins put together. The delicate bodies of the goblins ripped apart and eviscerated as soon as they came in contact with Oblivion. As more and more of Daemos's troops and monsters spilled into the Whitia Castle, the overlord himself once again charged like a bull towards the large wooden gates of the fort. With one powerful charge the gates were crushed against the unnatural strength of the revenant.

The hydra crushed the castle walls completely and reared back in triumph. The trolls smashed goblins until they were reduced to red and green blobs spattered on the ground. The direwolves too continued their carnage and were ripping the small goblins to shreds, leaving intestines and limbs scattered about.

Vesta was now truly overwhelmed and terrified. Gogba nervously bowed as he looked to his king.

"My lord... t... this is not going as planned. Perhaps we should start peace talks a—"

"NEVER! I REFUSE! I REFUSE TO PUT ALL THE YEARS OF UNDERCOVER WORK AND PLANNING TO NOTHING! I spent too long serving that old decrepit fool. Biding my time to take over this kingdom. I didn't wait that long just to be overthrown by a horde of mutts!"

Gogba was taken aback. He was still distraught over the assassination of his brother. Hearing Vesta speak of his recently murdered brother so poorly enraged him. He squinted his eyes and shook his fist. Vesta stared Gogba down.

"Now. We must prepare to defend the castle. Grab a weapon and —"

Before Vesta could finish, Gogba used his large body to push Vesta right off the top of the castle and watched as the goblin king tumbled to his death. With a loud thump he hit the ground, dying instantly.

Gogba took a moment to catch his breath. He looked at the flabbergasted Nomai, who was unable to believe what he had just witnessed.

"This is a fight we cannot win. I want to live," Gogba said to Nomai.

Daemos skid to a halt as he stood in the throne room. He expected to find the king there, but it was completely empty inside. Daemos gripped the hilt of his blade tightly. The entire sword was smeared in blood and organs. Suddenly, an obnoxious, high-pitched laugh could be heard coming from behind the empty throne.

"HAHAHAHA! COME NO FURTHER, SWINE! It is I! The unstoppable! The unbeatable! The magnificent Cling Clang! I shall make sure your death is slow and painful for the damage you have caused my great land!"

Cling Clang's face suddenly drooped, his usual manic smile reduced to a grimace. It was as if something in his brain had clicked and changed him in an instant. Maybe an old life resurfacing above his madness in a time of need.

"You're hurting too many people. Die now," he said in a quieter voice with an eerie calmness to it.

Daemos was unamused. He still couldn't fathom how a buffoon like him was even alive till now. He drew his blade, ready to kill the goblin. Cling Clang did the same with his dagger. It had a strange, ethereal glow to it. It was most likely a magical dagger. Daemos calmly walked forward. He held his massive sword with a single hand as easily as one would wield a dagger.

Cling Clang started moving towards Daemos with surprising speed and before he could even react, Cling Clang leaped into the air and slashed Daemos where his neck would have been. Daemos attempted to counter, but Cling Clang easily evaded the attack and slashed Daemos's wrist. The attacks barely hurt, but the places where Cling Clang slashed Daemos were glowing red, a glow that wasn't fading. Daemos was taken aback. He was not fighting the same way he was before. It was almost as if he had been completely changed. Daemos was not prepared for this. He held his guard up.

RAMPAGE: THE RISE OF AN EMPIRE

Both stood in a standstill, waiting for the other to make a move. Daemos was still confused and distracted by the bizarre change that Cling Clang had undergone. He couldn't stand still anymore. With a monstrous roar, he charged forward. Cling Clang did not move an inch. Daemos was beginning to become more and more distracted by the strange change he felt inside him until suddenly…

"BOOM!"

The two glowing slash marks on Daemos's body started to glow brightly until…

"BOOOM!!"

The slash marks on his body exploded. Chunks of Daemos's armor flew across the room, parts of his bony exterior now visible. The slash on his neck had broken a major section of his helmet and revealed his skeletal face. Cling Clang seemed completely unfazed by Daemos's appearance, almost as if he were in some kind of trance. Daemos threw his damaged helmet to the side and stared at Cling Clang.

"You are more worthy than I thought. Why did you not fight like this in our first battle?"

Cling Clang did not answer his question and instead continued to attack with lightning speed. Daemos tried to block the attack but once again was slashed by Cling Clang on the leg and a fiery explosion followed. More chunks of Daemos's armor blew off his body. He growled in frustration.

"You know it would be really embarrassing if I had to come to the rescue, right?"

Daemos looked behind him to see Nyana leaning against a wall. In a split second, while Daemos was distracted, he got slashed again.

"AAAARRGGHHH! The fool in the forest was more powerful than I expected! How can a pathetic goblin stand against me?" Daemos said as he tried his best to block Cling Clang's nonstop flurry of slashes and strikes.

Cling Clang threw a knife at Nyana but it uselessly bounced off an invisible shield she put around herself before she entered the castle. Cling Clang ignored her and continued to attack Daemos.

"That's your problem right there. You underestimated him just because of his race. It's true that different species are born with different amounts of magika in their bodies. Some races are better at magic and are physically capable of casting larger spells that take more magika. That doesn't mean they are lesser or inherently weaker. Any race can be a powerful warrior."

"ARE YOU DONE LECTURING ALREADY?! HELP ME CRUSH THIS MAGGOT!" Daemos roared as he was finally able to land a punch to Cling Clang's gut. His fist shot the goblin's small body several feet back and it slammed into a wall. Cling Clang shakily pushed himself back up and went into a combat stance. Daemos did the same.

"My job is not to help in battle. It is to mentor you. You're not going to be an all-powerful overlord if you can't overcome this. You have the Gauntlet of the Overlord. Use it."

"He is too fast. I can't react to his m—"

Cling Clang attacked once again, not giving Daemos the time to finish his sentence and slashed him across the chest. The fiery blast that followed broke off more chunks of Daemos's armor. The explosions themselves were not doing much damage to his bones, though. Daemos grunted in frustration and the goblin regained his stance.

"Stop standing there and help me kill him."

"No."

"What?!"

"You have to do it yourself. Your size and strength are impressive, but they won't help you in this fight."

Daemos groaned in frustration and held out his gauntlet. Cling Clang held out his hand as well. The two stared each other down, waiting for the first move to be made. Daemos was getting more impatient by the second and blurted out a spell.

"FIREBALL!"

"Fog!"

A massive fireball shot from Daemos's gauntlet and headed right for Cling Clang. With precise timing and movement, the goblin used his fog spell and disappeared from plain sight. The massive ball of flame threw up smoke and violently slammed into the stone wall behind the fog with a loud and powerful explosion. A hole was left in the wall surrounded by rubble and debris. Daemos stepped back, confused, and before he could move another inch, he was slashed on the back and once again hit by an explosive attack. He stumbled forward.

"This has gone on long enough. You will perish."

"Not until I splash your blood along these walls and crush your bones to dust. "

" LIGHTNING!"

A bolt of lightning shot from Cling Clang's palm, breaking off into several electric bolts which started to deflect from various surfaces around the room, hitting everything but Cling Clang himself. Daemos held his sword to his side and was ready to charge at him before he was stopped by a force field.

Nyana slowly drifted down in front of Daemos. "Pathetic. This was such a disappointment. You're not ready yet. You need more training."

"AAAAARRRGGGGHHHH! LET ME OUT OF HERE!" roared Daemos.

"You will die if you challenge me like your strange undead friend. I don't know what kind of magic allows one to control the minds of monsters and make the dead live again, but I will find out and destroy it," Cling Clang addressed Nyana, his next target. He moved with lightning speed and just as he was about to slash her...

"Paralysis!"

Cling Clang was frozen mid jump and he fell to the ground. She gently walked towards him, took out her dagger and plunged it into his throat with a smooth elegance. The goblin gurgled blood and died almost instantly. She reached down to grab his knife and put it into her satchel. She turned to Daemos and removed the force field entrapping him.

"You're not ready. You need more training. Come on… let's get this over with," she said, thoroughly annoyed.

Daemos angrily punched a wall, leaving a hole in it, and walked in front of Nyana to get to the top of the castle. She was getting on his nerves again and he didn't want to admit that she was right. He pushed his feelings to the side, ready to confront the king of the goblins.

Daemos kicked down the doors with ease and was surprised to see no king. He found a goblin dressed in lots of gold and jewels and another that was incredibly obese. Both looked with horror and confusion at the strange skeleton that stood before them.

"You… you're the black knight who leads this army?" Gogba asked, stuttering.

"Yes. Now you shall—"

Before he could finish, both Gogba and Nomai were bowing in front of Daemos. Daemos was taken aback, but not displeased. He could see the shocked and confused faces of the two goblins after seeing his skeletal head. They were probably thinking that he was some kind of god or all-powerful being.

"We see… that you are the superior ruler. Please spare our lives so that we can serve you with the utmost loyalty."

"And how will the two of you be of any use to me?"

Both of them scrambled to try and get their word out first. Nomai pushed Gogba to the side as he presented his case.

"My lord, I am what would be called a pirate. I have been stealing from the orcs for most of my life and will gladly lend my skills to you. I am also one of the greatest frontline generals in Whitia."

RAMPAGE: THE RISE OF AN EMPIRE

"And I am one of the most influential merchants on this corner of the continent. I have great relations with the dwarves of Gluth and have the knowledge of the many forgotten trade routes that lead out of the Duma Forest."

Daemos looked at Nyana, who gave him a nod.

"Very well. If you prove yourselves useful to me, your lives shall be spared. Now, we have much work to do. Whitia is now mine. I shall shape this small country into one to be reckoned with… soon, all with fall before me."

CHAPTER 8

The cold wind was like a sharp knife to Ashehera's cheek as she followed king Renas and his small herd of salamanders up the frigid mountain. The travel up the mountain has been incredibly hard, even with the salamanders being used for warmth and for melting away the snow and ice impeding their progress to meet the dragon queen Voxis.

Ashehera calmly walked near the front of the traveling band with Renas. A small group of royal guards trudged behind the king and queen, barely able to keep up with their pace. The only reason they have not completely fallen behind and succumbed to the frigid temperatures and cold was because of the melted path the salamanders had left for them.

Ashehera looked at Renas and cleared her throat. "When will we be arriving?"

"We still have a long way to go, cruel one."

"Do you have an estimation, at least? My meeting with Queen Voxis is of the utmost importance."

Renas sighed. "No, cruel one, I do not have an estimation. We will arrive when we arrive. I cannot make our arrival any quicker with this weather. Let us camp here for the night."

Ashehera already regretted this decision. Getting the assistance of the Nagas was the safest bet, but it for sure was not the quickest or easiest. The salamanders were put to rest and given a meal to recuperate while Ashahera made her guards set up the tents. The royal carriage was brought along, but Ashehera herself couldn't stay inside since it was being used for storing the tents and supplies.

When the tents had been set up, Ashehera crawled inside and stared at the roof of her tent. She was already hating this. She was used to sleeping in the most luxurious beds and rooms to ever grace Harmonia. Now she was sleeping in a tent during a blizzard.

The salamanders were sleeping around the camp, forming a protective barrier of heat around the camp, keeping the Naga and elves warm. Ashehera kept her trident at her side as she lay on the ground and started thinking to herself, *I hope Arun and Adamar are safe. Was this a bad idea? What if I'm too far away to protect them? What if…* She cut herself off. She pinched her cheek and reminded herself that she has been having these thoughts since the first day she left Shatterstar. There was nothing she could do about it. All she could do is continue with her journey to get the information she needed and then return to her children as soon as possible. She refused to lose them like she had lost her eldest son.

Suddenly, the camp residents heard a loud scream. Ashehera shot up and grabbed her trident. She burst out of her tent with great speed to find strange creatures apparently made of ice attacking the salamanders. Their bodies looked like they were made out of icicles with sharp jagged edges. Their heads were shaped like that of a demon with faintly glowing green eyes. Their arms were long and ended in long talons.

King Renas hissed and backed away. "You have to stop those things! They are ice wraiths. If they kill our salamanders, then we are dead for sure! Don't let them bite you!"

Queen Ashehera held her trident in the air and barked orders to her soldiers. "Kill those creatures! Protect the reptiles with your lives!"

The small band of golden armored elves charged and clashed with the six ice wraiths. The ice wraiths let out an ear-piercing scream and attacked the soldiers. Ashehera grabbed her trident and was ready to join her soldiers when suddenly an ice wraith jumped onto her back and dug its claws into her shoulder. She screamed as the ice-cold talons sunk deep into her warm body. The wraith was so cold that when her shoulder started to bleed, the blood instantly froze around the wound, making it all the more painful.

She held out her hand and yelled, "FIREBALL!"

A destructive blast of flame shot from her hand and melted a hole right through the body of the ice wraith. She stood up and looked at her knights. One of them was already dead, his throat ripped out. The blood bubbling from his neck froze, forming strange abstract shapes. Another wraith bit into a knight, who screamed in pain as her body started to twitch and her bones made loud cracking noises. Her armor started to crack as suddenly a fountain of blood erupted, her spine snapped and from her back started growing a new ice wraith.

Ashehera was dumbfounded. She had a general knowledge of monsters, but she had never witnessed much in her long life since she had been sheltered in the capital of the Harmonian Empire most of her life.

When she watched the wraith grow out of her knight's spine, she shuddered and called her forces back. "RETREAT! RETREAT! DON'T LET THEM BITE YOU! PROTECT KING RENAS WITH YOUR LIVES!"

The soldiers fell back and made a circle around Renas. Ashehera stepped forward with a determined look in her eyes. Her trident twirled in her hand and suddenly came to a stop.

"You will not impede my progress. FLAMING CYCLONE!"

Ashehera's spell created a massive flaming tornado that wreaked havoc in the ice, destroying most of the wraiths. When one of them died, it let out a scream that could shatter glass. After Ashehera's tornado died down, only two wraiths were left standing. One wraith lunged towards Ashehera, only to be instantly impaled by the queen's strange crystal trident. While impaled, the wraith squirmed and shrieked.

The second wraith ran on all fours towards the queen and attempted to bite her, but she moved with expert reflexes and slammed the impaled wraith into the other one.

"FIREBALL!"

Both of the wraiths died in the flames of her spell and were reduced to water. Ashehera let go of all the tension in her body. With a shaky breath, she assessed the damage. Two casualties and the salamanders were also injured. The power of the salamanders had weakened and they had started to give off a lesser amount of heat. The group could already feel the difference, especially Renas, who slowly started to lose colour, his body curling on itself.

"KNIGHTS! I WANT KING RENAS IN PERFECT HEALTH! WARM HIM! NOW!"

As the knights rushed to make another fire and grab as many blankets as possible, Ashehera went to check on the injured salamanders. Luckily, neither of them was killed in the battle.

King Renas struggled to speak. "Fire… bathe them in fire."

Ashehera held out her hand and started bathing the salamanders in flames one after the other. The fire started slowly closing their wounds.

She gave a weak smile as both the salamanders were healed from the fire and gave her a contended, grateful look. She was somehow reminded of her children, realizing how much she missed them. She wanted to get this over with as soon as possible so she could return to them. She wondered what they were doing right now.

In the absence of the queen, the Harmonian Empire has been in a state of panic. Ever since the unprecedented attack on the capital with completely unknown magic and the revelation that Harmonian citizens were the majority of the attackers, mistrust and paranoia has set in the lives of the citizens, many of whom have been trying to use the panic to their advantage. Some citizens have called the imperial guard to make arrests on 'suspected terrorists' almost every day. With the queen gone, most of the decision-making has been left to the nobles and high-ranking officials, but even they cannot keep complete control over the massive territory. Even when new laws and rules are set into place, it takes too long for them to be fully implemented due to the sheer size of the empire.

Order was mostly maintained in the capital since only the richest and most privileged lived there. They were the first to gain aid and protection from the government, since they live in the same city as them. The further out in the empire's territory one goes, however, the more social and political unrest is found. Despite this, paranoia and panic has had a foothold in the capital as well.

It was late in the night and Arun had just put Adamar to sleep in his bed. He smiled weakly as he brushed his brother's hair and tucked him beneath the covers. He has been trying to spend as much time with his brother as possible to distract him from all of the negativity swirling around. Not that it has been of much help, though. Ever since their mother left on her quest, Adamar has been down in the dumps. Arun is glad that Adamar still had such a strong parental bond with their mother – something Arun had lost a long time ago because of their many disagreements and differing viewpoints. He found it insulting that his mother gave charge to a group of bumbling nobles instead of him, who was next in line to the throne of the Harmonian Empire. Arun looked at his brother again and left the room. He gently closed the door and let out a big sigh. Arun now had Adamar out of the way. He didn't want his little brother to worry too much about what he was doing.

Arun was told to not join the royal meetings, since it was not in his jurisdiction. Arun found this insulting. It made no sense. He was next in line to the throne. What power did they have over him? He had a suspicion, but there must be a reason as to why they did not want him to be there. He needed to find out.

"Invisibility!"

Arun's body blinked out of view in an instant. He took the opportunity to run to the meeting room as soon as possible. He needed to learn as much as he could before the spell wore off.

Arun arrived at the meeting room and stayed as quiet as possible. The door was slightly ajar, giving Arun the opportunity to listen. The door was guarded by two knights in golden armor. Arun looked around for a way to distract them. He retreated and ran to the next room. It was the trophy room where his mother kept all of the empire's most prized treasures.

Placed in a display case is Reynard's armor and sword. Sleek silver metal with overlaying gold designs. A massive greatsword. A vibrant blue cape. Arun still remembers Reynard from the little time they knew each other for. He was the strangest elf he ever met. Arun sighed as he put his hand on the glass of the display case and looked at the armor closer. He still couldn't fathom the fact that his brother came back from the dead and was trying to kill his mother, his fellow knights. It boggled his mind in a way he couldn't understand.

"I miss you, brother."

He turned away and grabbed a random display case containing jeweled goblets and tipped it over. The glass smashed on the ground and alerted the two guards. Arun darted to the other side of the room and pressed his back against the wall. The nobles stood up in a startled manner.

"WHAT'S HAPPENING?!"

"ARE WE BEING ATTACKED AGAIN?!"

One of the knights stepped into the room and bowed. "Please do not be alarmed. We will take care of the problem. Stay exactly where you are. You're in the safest place in all of Harmonia. There is nothing to fear."

"'Safest place,' he says. As if the capital was not just was hit with an unprecedented attack," one of the nobles scoffed.

Once the knights left their post to check the crash, Arun dove past the door and carefully entered the meeting room. He hid himself in the corner of the room while still being invisible and continued to listen in.

"I swear these knights get worse at their jobs with every passing day."

"Don't speak ill of our empire's protectors! You would be dead if they were not here."

"Nor did I dispute that, but my statement stands."

"Such insolence!"

"Enough squabbling. We have a meeting to continue. Now, we are having increased problems with overexpansion. We do not have enough troops to fully protect our lands."

"Ah, yes, I know about this. Many of my subjects whine to me about werewolves. They act as if they have never held a blade in their lives. How terrible can a werewolf be? It's just a dog that stands."

"Nevertheless, the problem still stands. Civilians are constantly being raided and slaughtered on the outskirts of our borders. It is hard to call them borders at times. We need to solve this as soon as possible. Her majesty depends on us."

"What we need to do is increase conscription. We need more soldiers!"

"Oh, not this again."

"I mean it! The more soldiers we have, the better we can protect our—"

"If we left you in charge, the entire population would be the military! We need peasants. No peasants mean no food and we are already dangerously short on food."

Arun was taken aback and surprised by this. Was there really not enough food to feed the entire empire? Arun never thought about it. Every morning he woke up in a lavish palace with all the food he could ever want to eat at his disposal. Was there really that many people suffering inside the empire? He knew it was bad. He knew that the borders were constantly attacked, but they didn't have basic necessities either? That was news to him.

"We should try and conquer the Duma—"

"NO! Don't you remember the last time we attempted to go in there?"

"But there are plenty of monsters and plants too—"

"The answer is no! That entire forest is a death trap. Some of the most deadly and powerful monsters in the world live in that forest. We have tried annexing that forest too many times to count, only to end in defeat every single time."

"So what else could we possibly do?"

"…Give up some of our land?" said a younger noble who had been quiet for most of the meeting. The moment he spoke, the entire table erupted in chaos.

"HOW DARE YOU!?"

"TREASON! TREASON!"

"YOU'RE A PART OF THE HOODED ATTACKERS, AREN'T YOU?!"

"SILENCE! Let's hear what he has to say first."

"Um… our borders are too long to uphold. We can't control our own size while also fighting a war, defending against three kingdoms and occupying the Dragon Council's mountains. We have to give up some of this land if we are to survive. The civilian death count is only rising higher and higher. Starvation, disease, murder, robbery, riots – we have even had recent disturbing cases of cannibalism brought to us."

"Peasant brutes. Don't they know we are working as hard as we can?"

"Disgusting animals."

"We can't keep living like this. It would be an improvement even if we cut off the land and made them vassal countries that serve us. ANYTHING! We cannot keep going at this pace. Our farmers are being torn to shreds and even if they were okay and not being raided, we STILL would not have enough food to feed everyone!"

Arun had heard enough. He felt like crying. How could all of this be happening under his nose the entire time? He lived his entire life in this city and just assumed everything was just as clean and perfect there as it was here. He quickly ran out of the room and threw himself onto his bed. He felt tears running down his face. How could this happen? How could his mother have let this happen? He looked at his brother and wiped the tears from his face.

He wanted to leave. He needed to leave. See all of this for himself. But he couldn't abandon his brother like their mother did… like their father did. Or should he? It would be safer for him to stay here, all alone. He said he wouldn't abandon him, but if he took his brother with him, he would be in so much danger. What was he even thinking?

Arun shakily sat up in his bed and stared at the mirror in the corner of the room. Thoughts ran through his head faster than he could process. He wanted to do the right thing… but what was the right thing? He could leave through the window right now and explore his kingdom, learn what was happening outside of the bubble he has lived inside of for 200 years. Was that selfish? Was it selfish for him to do this?

Adamar stirred in his sleep and yawned. He looked at his brother with drowsy eyes.

"Big brother? Are you okay?"

Arun looked at him, surprised that he woke up, and hid his pain with a smile. He sat on the end of Adamar's bed and rubbed his hair.

"Heh... yeah, I am okay, little brother. You should go back to sleep, though. It's really late."

"Okay. I love you."

Aun let out a shaky breath and forced his smile harder. "Yeah... I... I love you, too."

Arun lay down next to his brother, talking to him until Adamar fell back asleep. Arun sat in silence and deep contemplation.

Once the capital of Whitia fell under the control of Daemos and his dark forces, the rest of the goblin country quickly fell as well with almost no resistance. The death toll has been traumatizing to the nation of Whitia and most are terrified of their new king.

Daemos returned to Zithoss when all of Whitia was under his

control and some cleaning up had been done inside of the ancient dungeo full of dust and bugs. He bowed his head to Zithoss and Nyana followed suit.

"Whitia is now ours."

"Good. Now. Give me the souls you have collected."

Daemos stepped forward and placed the gauntlet in the stone groove on the well of souls. Hundreds of souls poured into the well and the green liquid at the bottom started to rise exponentially. As the liquid continued to rise, the entire room started to glow more and more.

Zithoss lifted his arm and the screaming souls of monsters and goblins were absorbed into his body. Zithoss kept greedily absorbing souls until the stream of green fog ceased abruptly. Zithoss let out a weak laugh as he slowly started to stand up from his throne.

Nyana, overcome with emotion, ran to Zithoss's side to help him move, but he held his hand out to stop her. He took one step forward and nearly stumbled. Nyana instinctively went to grab him, but he stopped her again. He took another step forward and then another.

He then slowly walked towards Nyana and put his skeletal hand on her shoulder. "I'm proud of you."

Nyana felt like she was going to pass out. She felt a smile stretch across her face under her mask and watched with excitement as her master walked step by step towards Daemos.

Zithoss put his hand on Daemos's shoulder and looked up at his eyes. "I'm proud of you as well. I cannot begin to express my joy. I have not been able to move my body… for too long. Now is the beginning of a new era. Daemos… what do you think is the best course of action to build our empire?"

Daemos looked at Nyana and then back to Zithoss. He wanted to say that they should continue to steamroll to the next country in the Duma Forest, but he had a feeling it was a bad idea.

"Whitia is ours, but it is in ruins. The capital is destroyed and many have died at my blade. We need time to recuperate. Rebuild stronger."

"You're learning. Good. Continue to do my bidding. Build Whitia as a powerful nation and continue on your rampage."

"Yes, my lord."

Daemos and Nyana left the mountain and Daemos called over a new drake he had taken control of to fly them to the capital. Both of them climbed on the reptile's back and took flight.

"You seemed happier than usual."

"And why shouldn't I be? I was praised by my master and after so many centuries of being stuck in that chair, he can walk once again! It brought tears to my eyes."

"Right. If you're done, we have things to discuss."

"As impatient and joyless as ever, I see. What is it?"

"How do I do this?"

"What?"

"Get them on my side. I can tell they are opposed to my rule. I also know you are more adept with words."

"Well, for one, I try not to be a prick every possible moment."

"Hmph. Whatever."

"I think I know the answer you want, though. You're going to get better results if you rule with compassion and not fear."

"What are you talking about? Do you know how ridiculous this sounds? The mysterious assassin that works for Zithoss the Elder Lich, telling an undead overlord to rule with compassion?"

"I know how it sounds. But compassion can be used as a tool."

"How so?"

"If your people worship you, they are more willing to do as you say. They will work harder and fight harder. I'm not telling you to coddle them. Just don't be a brainless barbarian."

"And how do you know so much about being a leader? You preach about this all the time and yet I have no clue why you know so much."

"It's complicated."

"Complicated?"

"Yes, complicated. I don't want or need to talk about it."

"Fine. I shall try to heed your advice. Especially of the two goblins we spared. They seem useful. Close to the former king."

The two landed their drake on top of the damaged fort and hopped off. Daemos walked with a powerful and confident stride into the fort with his large black cloak billowing behind him. He entered the throne room to see Nomai and Gogba bowing to him and a new throne that was built for him while he had been gone. It was made of stone, furs, and bones. Daemos walked past them and sat down on his new throne. He removed his helmet and placed it next to him. The red lights in his eye sockets had a sadistic glow to them.

"W... w... welcome back, my lord," said Nomai.

"W… we are honored to see you return," Gogba quickly followed suit.

Daemos looked at Nyana and then back at the two. "She deserves a throne as well."

"O… oh of course, my lord! O… our apologies! We will start building right away!"

Nyana turned to him, surprised. She tilted her head to the side and then looked back at the two goblins.

The two were about to run away and start getting the throne built, but Daemos held his hand up to stop them. "We have things to discuss."

"O… oh of course! My apologies, sire!"

"What are the damages? I want to know everything."

"Oh…well…"

Nomai and Gogba looked at each other, deciding who should break the news to Daemos.

Gogba sighed and stepped forward. "There is much panic and confusion. The casualties are… very high. We would be unable to go to battle any time soon."

"Understood. Nomai, what would you suggest we do?"

"M… my suggestion? Well, um… what I always did was conduct raids on the orcs of Nigt and protect our borders from them… but with the damages we have sustained, that may be a problem. More than half of our food comes from the raids."

"Would it be sufficient to use my beasts to protect and raid while your forces recover?"

"Y… yes… yes, it would suffice."

"In the meantime, we shall continue to develop more farmland to make our own food and I shall use my beasts to hunt. Now, Gogba, what about you?"

When Gogba heard his name, he looked forward intently. "Well, I conduct trade and sell goods to the other tribes."

"That will cease as of now. Your trade will continue, but you will not sell these supplies to my own people. We are using these to build and grow. New weapons, better homes and defenses, and anything else useful for increasing wellbeing."

"I… I see."

"Is there a problem?"

"None at all, sire! Forgive me."

"This is going to be the beginning of a new era. All of our resources and energy will be put into construction and development. Go now. There is much work to be done."

Nomai and Gogba bowed before leaving the throne room.

Nyana looked at Daemos, her mask hiding a smile. "I'm impressed. It was like you were a different person out there."

"I don't know how to explain it."

"Maybe you didn't lose as much as we thought you had from your past life, after all. Come on. We are doing more training. If you are going to use the gauntlet, you are going to have to learn to use more than one spell."

"Of course. I shall be just a moment."

Daemos stepped out of the fort and lifted his gauntlet up.

"MY BEASTS! RAID THE NEIGHBORING LAND OF NIGT AND MAKE THEM TASTE THE TRUE FEELING OF TERROR! BRING BACK FOOD AND TREASURE FOR MY PEOPLE! SHOW THEM THE POWER OF DAEMOS!"

A bellowing roar was heard across the forest as the monsters of Whitia started marching towards Nigt to initiate their masters desire.

Smoke rose to the sky as the sound of drums and cheering was heard echoing across the forest. Along the border of Nigt was a new raiding party ready to attack Whitia. The party was being led by the newly crowned queen of Nigt, Lazgar. Lazgar was a muscular woman, her dark green skin covered in scars and calluses from decades of combat. Resting in the sheath on her back was a massive sword made of thick, rusted steel. Red stains that look decades old were still present on the blade, along with dozens of small nicks and cracks. Her hair was raven black and pulled back into a ponytail. She was dressed in heavy leather and steel armor and wearing a cape made of werewolf pelts.

Lazgar had been anticipating the next time she would be able to fight. Lazgar has been filled with curiosity for days now. There have been no counter raids from Whitia and there have been no goblin sightings in days by the scouts.

Lazgar, one by one, started putting war paint on the faces of her raiders and began to give her speech.

"Our people are depending on us. We need food to survive the upcoming winter. I know you will make me proud, my warriors. Shall our mighty swords crush their small bodies and may their food feed our families for months to come."

The orcs let out a thunderous roar of applause. Lazgar was about to send out the raiding party but she was stopped by a gentle and nervous voice.

"Um… w… w… wait please."

Lazgar turned around and saw her younger sister, Shagar. Shagar was slightly shorter than her sister, but was still of a larger stature. She was dressed in a robe made of brown cloth and animal furs. Around her wrists were bracelets made of flowers and small stones. In her hand she held a wooden staff and her hair was blonde, a rare color for orcs.

Lazgar sighed when she saw her sister and looked her up and down in disappointment. "What… what are you wearing?"

"A robe."

"Why?"

"Because it will be easier for me to use my magic this way without wearing clunky armor. Besides the woman in my dreams says—"

"You were destined to save the world with your magic light blah blah blah… IT'S NONSENSE! It's just a dream, Shagar, we went over this! Orcs are not supposed to be mages! Look at your muscles!" she said as she grabbed her sister's arm and pulled her sleeve down to reveal her large biceps. "You were MEANT to be a warrior! Like all orcs! How am I supposed to protect you while you are playing dress up and won't even defend yourself with a sword?"

Shagar looked away with a small tear running down her green face.

Lazgar sighed and put a hand on her broad shoulder. "Why did you really come here?"

"To talk you out of this! We can have peace talks with Whitia and Shimia. THIS DOESN'T HAVE TO BE—"

Lazgar was about to smack her sister across the face with rage in her eyes. Shagar stumbled back with surprise and fear in her eyes as Lazgar stared her down.

Lazgar resisted the urge as her hand shook and quickly lowered her arm. "How dare you? How dare you say that after they killed Mom and Dad? Get out of my sight… NOW!"

Shagar sniffled as she ran away. She felt it was impossible to talk with her sister. Why can't she see that peace is the only option? She continued to run through the forest, away from any villages and leaned against a tree. She let out a shaky breath

"What are you crying about this time, greenie?"

"AGH!"

Shagar looked up and saw a woman watching her from the trees. She had pale skin and long brown hair. She was wearing casual clothing and had two fluffy wolf ears popping out of the top of her head. Her vibrant magenta eyes stared at Shagar and by then,

RAMPAGE: THE RISE OF AN EMPIRE

Shagar already knew who it was. Lucia, the werewolf princess of Shimia.

"Lucia? W... what are you doing here? Your too deep into Nigt territory! What if you're caught?!"

"Oh, calm down, greenie. I got here quickly as possible without anyone seeing me. Besides... I was bored. I wanted to see you."

Lucia jumped down from the tree and placed a kiss on Shagar's cheek. She couldn't help but smile after that. Lucia laid down next to Shagar and stared at the top of the trees with her.

"So... why were you crying?"

"Oh um... it was... my sister again... she... she was going to slap me. I... it's not normal for her she... she's just under a lot of stress, is all."

Lucia let out a low, menacing growl.

"LUCIA! NO! Please... please don't do something dumb."

"Why?"

"I... I suggested we make peace again. I just... I have a feeling in my stomach. Something horrible is about to happen. Weeks ago... or... or maybe it was a month ago... I had this horrible... horrible dream."

"Yeah, I know, sweetie. You already told me about it."

"But... but I don't think it was a dream. I... I think it was a warning."

"A warning?"

"I... I know how it sounds but... I'm really serious. I... I probably sound dumb right now."

Lucia grabbed Shagar's hands gently and looked her in the eyes. "Hey... don't say stuff like that about yourself. I believe you. Now, go on."

"Well... you know... that magic I have been using?"

"Yeah. Strangest magic I have ever seen. I have never seen the magic you do anywhere else. It's pretty."

Shagar blushed as she held out her hand and closed her eyes. "Lantern!"

A small warm and glowing orb of light formed out of thin air in the palm of her hand and started to float. Shagar was already feeling lightheaded. Orcs have incredibly low magika, so they can't cast as many spells until it regenerates, and they are unable to cast more powerful spells that cost more magika.

"In my dream... there was a... being. I couldn't fully make her out. It was... beautiful. So many wings and eyes. It... I think it's a she... she talks to me in my dreams."

"Wait really? Why didn't you tell me?"

"O... oh I am sorry, I... I didn't mean t—"

"Shagar, calm down. You know you never have to tell me anything you are not comfortable with, right?"

"I... I... I know, I am just—"

"Calm.... Down. What does she say to you in your dreams?"

"I have been dreaming of her since I was a little girl. She has been the one teaching me these strange spells in my sleep. I... I can't use so many of them since I am an orc... I don't have the magika to cast them... but there are so many... even a long-forgotten spell that can heal wounds!"

"Woah... really? That's... that's amazing. A spell that can heal others. But... nobody remembers it anymore?"

"Something like that... but... a little while ago, in my last dream, she said something awful is coming... and then I felt it. Something so sinister and dark it was... scaring her. She told me that if we are all to survive... we must work together and stop what is to come."

"This... this is crazy."

"She said that I am the catalyst to start the hope of Harmonia."

"Honey, this is... I... I don't know what to say."

"You think I am crazy?"

RAMPAGE: THE RISE OF AN EMPIRE

Lucia let out a snort of laughter and kissed Shagar on the lips, making her green skin flush pink. "I wouldn't care if you're crazy. I would love you anyways."

"Lucia… thank y—"

"SHAGAR! SHAGAR? WHERE ARE YOU?"

"I… it's my sister! You have to hide!"

"Got it! Love you!" said Lucia as she moved with superhuman speeds to the safety of the trees.

Shagar turned to see her sister looking down at her.

Lazgar pulled Shagar in for a hug and let out a shaky breath. "I… I'm sorry I did that to you. I… I don't know what came over me. I… I'm sorry."

"I… it's fine."

"I… I understand that you want peace, but you know it's not possible."

"But… but my dreams!"

"I know, okay? You talk about them all the time but, at the end of the day, they are only dreams and nothing else. Now come on. Let's get you on a horse to ride back home."

"Okay."

Lazgar returned to meet with her raiding party again. She walked back and forth to inspect them. Two dozen mighty orc men and women stood to attention as she put the war paint on their faces.

"No more distractions. This time we—"

Suddenly, the ground started to shake. The orcs held firmly onto anything to keep their balance. They all started to look around in a confused and panicked state. What could possibly make the ground shake like that?

"Are we about to be raided?"

"Are you kidding me? No goblin can make the ground shake like th—"

Suddenly, from the trees, a massive direwolf lunged forward and tackled the orc who had just been speaking. The wolf shoved its fangs into the throat of the orc, killing him instantly, but was soon killed itself as an orc slammed down a warhammer on the wolf's spine, smashing it. Soon, a whole pack of direwolves appeared. The orcs slowly stepped back and circled around their queen to protect her. Lazgar drew her massive rusty sword and held it close to her side.

From the sky, drakes could be seen circling them like vultures. Trees started falling to the ground and break as trolls started to lumber forward and finally, a massive hydra behind them all.

"WHAT IS THIS!?"

Lazgar was speechless. These brainless monsters were in a war formation. How is that possible? Why are direwolves, trolls, drakes and a hydra all working together instead of eating each other? How are they able to have such a formation and not break form? Why are their eyes glowing red?

All of these questions sped through Lazgar's mind at rapid speeds as she watched her raiding party get ripped apart and eaten.

"Chieftain Queen! You have to leave! We Will hold them off!"

"You think I'm a coward?! I'll rip them apart!"

"NO CHIEFTAIN! YOU MUST LEAVE!" A direwolf lunged at the orc who was speaking to her and before the wolf could bite him, he smashed its head open with an axe. "You need to survive! NEED TO! LEAVE!"

"I REFUSE TO—"

In a sudden moment, the orc was swooped off the ground by a drake and ripped apart in seconds.

The blood dripped on her face and she slowly stepped back. "I... I'll come back... I... I promise."

Lazgar shuddered for a moment and nodded her head. She quickly ran in the other direction. Two direwolves chased after the queen as the raiding party did the best they could in order to hold back the others. Lazgar looked behind her to see the two wolves gaining speed on her. She knew she would never be able to outrun the two, so she skidded to a halt, spun around, and held her ground. One of the wolves lunged at her, trying to bite her head off, but Lazgar used her massive sword to slice the wolf down the middle with blood spraying all over the place. The second wolf successfully pounced on Lazgar and shoved its massive fangs into her shoulder, right through the armor. She let out a scream and angrily shoved her fingers into the eye socket of the wolf. The wolf refused to let go and continued to try and rip out her throat. The wolf was acting insane and despite any pain refused to stop fighting, but Lazgar would not let go. She looked at her other hand and dug her fingers in the wolf's other eye. As she squeezed more, she could feel the wolf's eyes pop and see the blood being squeezed out of its head. With an intimidating war cry, she jolted her arms back hard and ripped off the direwolf's head with her bare hands.

She shakily stepped back and panted. She has never fought a direwolf like this before. Or any monster, for that manner. It didn't feel pain, or maybe it just didn't care about the pain at all. All it wanted to do was kill her. Any other animal would have panicked and retreated. But this was something different. Something sinister.

She quickly tossed the head away and ran back to the safety of the nearest village where she could get a horse. "If anyone survives, follow my trail to the palace!"

Hours later, she arrived back at her castle. It was much larger than the castle that the goblins had. The castle in Whitia was old with age and had not been repaired in ages, whereas the castle of Nigt was a powerful stronghold made for a battle. Strong stone walls and tall stone towers loomed over any would-be invaders. The massive gates of the castle were opened with long ropes. Although tedious-seeming, this poses little problems for the orcs who were born with incredible strength and muscle mass.

Along the walls of the castle were werewolf pelts and skulls that had been crudely nailed to the walls. All around the front and sides of the castle were sharp wooden barricades and guard posts. Orc warriors were constantly patrolling the area and stood at attention once their chieftain queen arrived.

When Lazgar arrived at the upper floors of the castle, Shagar was waiting for her and instantly ran towards her.

Lazgar had a look of confusion and disbelief on her face as she still had been unable to process what had happened hours before. "Sister! Are you okay? What happened?"

"I... I don't know."

"Sister... what's wrong? Your face is... it's..."

"I'm fine... th... there is nothing to worry about. This is for me to deal with."

"Just tell me! I can help! I can—"

"NO! No... no you can't. Just... do what you always do. Just stay in your room talking about your dreams while using your strange magic. That's all you need to and should worry about!"

"What? Sister, what are you talking about? All my life you told me it was nonsense and—"

"Well, I changed my mind! Just... just..." Lazgar let out a cry of frustration and stormed off in an irritated manner, leaving Shagar speechless.

Lazgar went to her own bed chambers and gently loosened the armor off her muscular frame. She changed into comfortable silk and fur clothing and collapsed onto her bed of cleaned werewolf pelts. She stared up at the ceiling, uncertain of what she could do for her people.

CHAPTER 9

Two weeks have gone by since Daemos and Nyana conquered Whitia. There was much destruction still left to be repaired, but there have been substantial improvements since his takeover. The resources of Whitia are no longer privately owned and could now be used to improve all of Whitia. As Whitia's new army of monsters continued to bring back hauls of food and loot from Nigt, the citizens of Whitia have been able to expand and grow more than ever, now that the monsters are no longer against them. That meant farmland expansion and more access to resources. This has proved even more useful because another iron mine in Whitia has been discovered and has been occupied ever since.

Daemos sat on his throne and next to him was Nyana, who now had her own throne as well. Bowing in front of them was Nomai, Fena, and Gogba. Gogba was holding a scroll with all the recent reports on the progress of Whitia.

"So... you three made it. Give me a rundown on what's happening."

"Of course, my lord. Progress on the rebuilding and expansion has been far beyond our expectations. With the beasts using their large frames to aid in the construction, we have been able to speed up building exponentially."

"And my personal request?"

"Of course, my lord. I have personally spoken with my contacts in Gluth and they have sent several crates of metal armor and weapons. Eventually, they are going to send three of their blacksmiths to build for us. In the meantime, the supplies and armaments they have sent over should suffice."

"Good. I want to do away with these wooden weapons and defenses. We have iron and we are going to use it."

"As we should, my lord. Speaking of which, a second iron mine has been discovered in deep woodland."

"This is turning out better than expected. Nomai, what do you have to share?"

"Many in Whitia are still cautious of you, but public opinion is vastly increasing. We have not been able to freely expand and prosper in a very long time."

"And what of our raids of Nigt?"

"Highly successful. We have been returning with large amounts of food and salvaged orc weapons. I'm surprised such beasts would be able to complete such complex tasks despite being… well, beasts."

Daemos lifted his gauntlet up and the moment he did, the eyeball on the gauntlet opened and started to look around the room. It stared at the two goblins, who immediately stepped back, wary of the gauntlet.

"I control them. Their animalistic minds have no factor. They are just bodies attached to my strings."

"O… of course."

"So Nomai, suggestions on when would be the right time to attack Nigt?"

Fena cut in with a report of her own. "I believe I would be best placed to answer you, sir."

"By all means, proceed."

"From what my scouts report, the orcs are incredibly taken aback by the recent attacks and are still very unsure on how to proceed. Orcs have never been openly attacked by an organized force of monsters, nor has anyone else to my knowledge. Morale is at a low for them. I think the best action would be to try and scare them into submission while they are vulnerable."

"I agree. I want all available workers mining out iron and I want these blacksmiths to work overtime. I want swords, shields, armor, and anything that can kill. Our forces will be fully armed. I want armor for the beasts as well. This will be a day to be remembered for ages to come. Nyana, come with me. We have royalty to meet."

Daemos stood up and walked towards the doors to leave his throne room with Nyana in tow. His massive black cape flowed behind him as he moved with haste.

When they left and walked their way to the top of the fort, Nyana tilted her head in slight confusion. "It happened again."

"What?"

"Everything about you. Your personality and demeanor just changed in an instant. I still don't understand why that is happening."

"...Neither do I, truth be told."

"It's possible that fragments of your past life are coming to you but... maybe not? I... I just don't know."

"I could care less. We have a meeting to go to."

Daemos called over a drake and the two of them climbed on its back to fly towards Nigt.

Shagar sat by herself in the forest close to the castle. She has been in a depressive mood ever since her sister's recent return. She has only been able to learn a little bit about what has been happening once her sister returned. More raids were attempted by the orcs, only for them to be crushed. Now, to make matters worse, it was the orcs of Nigt who are being raided, not just by the werewolves of Shimia but also these monsters. Nigt is beginning to starve.

Shagar felt a wave of depression wash over her as the days get more and more and filled with the growing paranoia of her people.

"You looked s—"

"EEEEEEEEEEEEK!" Shagar jumped up in a panic and threw a punch behind her at the voice that had startled her.

It was Lucia.

She whimpered in pain a little as she held her jaw. "Ouch ouch ouch... heh... I guess that's orc instinct for you."

Shagar gasped. "LUCIA! Oh no I am so sorry! I... I... I didn't mean it I s—"

"Oh, stop with the apologizing already, its fine," Lucia said as she rubbed her jaw.

Shagar grabbed her girlfriend and firmly kissed her on the lips, catching Lucia off guard. "Better?"

"Hehehe... more than better. Now... mind telling me what's on your mind?"

"Things are getting bad... the Whitia raids have failed."

"...What?"

"Recently, we have been getting attacked by large monsters... hydras, direwolves, drakes, and trolls. What makes no sense, though, is that they are all working together and fight in formation, almost as if they are intelligent. All of their eyes glow the same unsettling red."

"But... how is that possible? That doesn't even make sense."

"I don't know... I... I just don't know. I... I'm scared. I'm scared for my people and my sister. I just want all of this to stop. I can't talk sense into any of them! War is so built into the culture of my people that... that..." Shagar felt tears form in her eyes but Lucia hugged her tightly and refused to let go.

"Hey hey hey... it's alright. I got you."

Lucia struggled to find the words to comfort Shagar as she watched her girlfriend cry into her shoulder. She let out a shaky breath before pushing Shargar back a little so she could look her in the eyes. Lucia forced a smile to hide the fear she was feeling for the safety of her girlfriend.

"We can leave together."

"W… what?"

"We can leave Duma. Nigt doesn't value you like I do. If you stay here, you are going to get hurt. Come with me. We can finally be together! Just the two of us."

"What? I… I can't! I can't abandon my people!"

"Shagar… you're going to get hurt. You… you mean everything to me. I… I can't stand to see you so upset. Just come with me and everything will be okay, I promise!"

"Lucia… you know I ca—"

An ear-piercing screech filled the sky and a large winged silhouette flew over the orc country. Orcs ran to their battle stations and started blowing war horns.

"DRAKE ATTACK! DRAKE ATTACK!"

Lazgar heard the call and grabbed her massive iron sword. Shagar stood up and ran towards the castle.

Lucia grabbed onto her hand. "Sha, what the hell are you doing?!"

"I'm going to help my people!"

"How?! Stop acting ridiculous! Come with me!"

"The answer is NO, Lucia! My citizens are depending on me!"

As Shagar ran off, Lucia let out an annoyed sigh and vanished into the trees to stay hidden. With her amazing speed and agility, she moved from tree to tree to follow Shagar and to make sure she was okay.

The drake started to circle around the castle, calling attention to itself. As the orcs watched in astonishment and confusion, the drake started to slowly descend to the ground. Lazgar approached it with her massive iron blade resting against her shoulder. She was taken aback along with the rest of the orcs as Daemos and Nyana hopped off the snarling drake which had the same unnaturally glowing red eyes as the rest of the monsters which had been raiding Nigt, eyes they shared with the black-clad knight who had just disembarked from the drake. Lazgar was shaken but held her ground as she stared at the duo.

Lazgar was only a few inches shorter than Daemos. She walked right up to him and they stared each other down. She refused to look weak in front of her people.

"Who are you? What are you doing here?"

"I am Daemos. You and your people will either die or refer to me as 'master'."

"HA! I doubt it, you milk drinker! I can see by your pet lizard that you have been the one trying to destroy us with your little animals. You fail to destroy us! All you have done is provide us with more pelts!" she yelled, raising the morale of her soldiers who were surrounding the two dark beings. They started laughing and clanged their weapons together in anticipation of killing the two strangers. Shagar finally arrived and watched the scene unfolding from a distance. Her head instantly started to hurt once she was near the two strange dark beings.

"Honey? Shagar, what's wrong?" whispered Lucia from the trees.

"Something... something is very wrong with those two. Evil. I... I cannot explain... but... it's wrong."

Daemos looked at Nyana who simply whispered to him, "Don't look at me, *Overlord*. Just remember the plan. We don't want the bloodbath to be too big. Remember what I told you about the orc culture."

Daemos stared at Lazgar and unsheathed his massive blade. Holding it with one hand he pointed it towards Lazgar and refused to break eye contact with her. A strong gust of wind blew behind Daemos, making his cape flow behind him menacingly.

"I challenge you to one-on-one combat, your highness. No magic, no outside intervention, no forfeiting. If you win, I promise to surrender and never bother your people again. If I win, then I shall attack again with my entire army. You shall all fall under my rule."

Murmurs spread across the crowd of orcs but Lazgar did not hesitate. A fire was in her eyes now and it was hungry for combat.

"I accept! I am going to make you my bitch!"

All the orcs around her started to cheer and bang their weapons together in excitement. Shagar was less than thrilled. She was worried. Something did not feel right about this knight.

"Such abrasiveness! Where shall our duel commence?"

"At the combat pit. Come. I grow more and more excited to spill your guts onto the floor after I peel off your armor like a crab's shell!"

"By all means, be as excited as you want, it will only make your defeat more enjoyable for me."

The combat pit was a large crater in the ground that must have taken days to dig with an entire crew. The ground was covered in mud and bones. The walls were a thick layer of rock with skulls and pelts nailed to them. The rim of the pit was covered in spikes to make it impossible for someone to climb out. The only way in and out were the metal gates that led to the bottom of the pit.

Lazgar prepared herself for the upcoming fight. Before all of this happened, she had been scared. Something she did not understand was destroying her nation in a way she could not control. But now… now she has a target and a solution. She doesn't understand magic. She understands swords. Now she has a chance to swing her sword at the problem and bring everything back to normal. Just the way she likes it.

Right before Lazgar was about to enter her side of the arena, she was stopped by her sister.

Lazgar gave her a harsh look but her face quickly softened. "What is it?"

"Sister... I... I don't think this is a good idea. There is something... very wrong about that knight. I felt it. I feel... cold when I'm near him."

"I don't have time for this, Shagar, I have a duel to fight."

"SISTER PLEASE! Just for once trust me! I know you don't like magic but just for once please! Just listen to me! There is something wrong about him! You should not fight him!"

"AFTER HE CHALLENGED ME? I won't look weak in front of my people! I won't throw away our ancient traditions!"

"WHAT HAVE THEY DONE FOR US?! PLEASE SISTER, PLEASE!"

Lazgar stared daggers at her sister and it looked like she was about to smack her, but she refrained and turned away. "I am the queen. My word is law. That is final. Now get out of my sight."

Shagar ran out of the preparation room of the arena and waited to see what would happen in the crowd, dreading every moment. Lazgar's side of the arena opened up and the arena was filled with cheers as she ran out with a devilish smile on her face. She was dressed in iron armor and wielded her old, cracked sword. Despite the condition of the sword, it was still thick and massive, able to smash most swords on a single hit.

The other side of the arena slowly opened to reveal the massive silhouette of Daemos, his gigantic frame further exaggerated by the longhorns on top of his helmet and his large black steel boots. Whenever Daemos took a step forward, the ground shook a little. Nyana watched on in the crowd with many of the orcs throwing her nasty looks. If they wanted to kill her right now, they could have already, but duels in the arena were an important part of orc culture.

Daemos was ready to put on a show. He unsheathed his large crimson blade and wielded it with one hand. This caught Lazgar off guard. If he was able to hold that blade with one hand, he must have incredible physical strength. Both of their swords were massive in their own rights. Lazgar's sword was shorter, but it was incredibly thick and heavy. Probably over a hundred pounds heavier than Daemos's sword.

As Daemos methodically walked towards her, Lazgar charged at him, running at full speed. She held onto her huge blade with both of her muscular hands and slammed it towards Daemos with an overhead strike. Daemos was unfazed, however, and lifted his blade upwards to block the blow. The blades clashed together with an ear-piercing sound. Lazgar was taken aback. She was being held back completely.

Daemos pushed his arm forward to break the clash of blades, making Lazgar stumble back. The crowd was in disbelief as Daemos continued his slow walk towards his opponent. He held his blade to his side pointing outwards and without hesitation slashed at Lazgar several times. His speed resembled that of someone who was using a fencing saber or a dagger and not a massive greatsword. The crowd was flabbergasted at this show of dexterity and strength.

Lazgar barely had the chance to block all of his attacks. She was getting nervous. She quickly glanced at the crowd that was abuzz with concerned and confused murmuring. Lazgar raised her sword in the air and got a delayed cheer from the crowd. She turned back to her opponent and moved with impressive speed. She jumped into the air and slammed her two-hundred-pound-blade downward onto Daemos. A shot of adrenaline filled her as she witnessed her attack stagger Daemos for a moment. She refused to let go. Once her feet touched the ground, she used the momentum of swinging her heavy sword to slam her blade into Daemos's side. He let out a grunt and stumbled back. The side of his now armor sported a dent.

"What kind of armor is that? Not many metals can survive a blow from my sword."

Daemos refused to answer her and started walking towards

her again.

Lazgar let out a laugh. "You know, if you don't start taking this seriously, you're going to end up dead."

Daemos lunged forward and knocked her at the waist with the tip of his blade. The graceful twirls of Oblivion were almost hypnotic to look at as he clashed with Lazgar's blade. His sword was picking up speed and could sometimes be only seen as a blur of red. Daemos performed a circle parry on Lazgar and cut her right wrist. She let out a growl as she dropped her heavy sword.

Lazgar retaliated by kicking mud in Daemos's face and tackling him. As Daemos was blinded and dazed, she was able to wrangle his sword from his hand and throw it to the side. Daemos kicked her in the chest, making her fly back and slam into the pit wall. Daemos got up and wiped the mud from his helmet.

"Are you as formidable without your sword, milk drinker?"

Daemos cracked his neck and knuckles before walking towards her. A strong gust of wind blew as Lazgar charged at him. Daemos was ready to punch her in the head but she swiftly dodged and performed an uppercut. He stumbled back and snarled. Daemos tackled Lazgar and punched her in the stomach. She coughed up some blood and a crack was heard echoing across the arena. The audience was as quiet as a mouse.

Daemos used his metal claws to shred the skin on Lazgar's arm with a powerful swipe. She retaliated by kicking Daemos in the leg and doing a tactical roll-away. Mud got into her wounds, making her wince in pain, but she used this opportunity to grab her sword. Daemos went to grab his own sword but was quickly attacked by Lazgar. She aimed right for his head. The impact was loud.

Daemos's helmet came flying off and his skeletal head was revealed for all to see.

Lazgar stumbled back in fear and confusion along with the audience. "W... what kind of creature are you?"

Daemos did not respond and grabbed his sword. Lazgar stepped back towards the exit, but Nyana intervened. She snapped her fingers and cast a spell.

"Flaming walls!"

Both of the arena's exits were blocked off with a wall of flames. The orcs were about to attack her for interfering, but she lifted her hand and cast another spell.

"Wall of reflection!"

An orc tried to decapitate Nyana, but once his blade touched her invisible shield spell, he was decapitated instead.

All the orcs stepped back in confusion as Nyana spoke, her voice carrying across the arena. "And here I thought orcs were not supposed to retreat from a challenge?"

Lazgar gritted her teeth and looked back at Daemos who stared at the fire with empty eyes. Lazgar was confused. Daemos simply stared at the fire blankly. Nyana was confused as well.

Daemos's mind was going blank as he stared at the fire. He swore he could hear and see things that he couldn't remember. He heard screams and silhouettes of strangers screaming and writhing in pain and agony. Whispers he could not make out filled his mind until one voice that was clear as day spoke in a pained voice.

"Reynard… it hurts."

An uncontrollable rage that Daemos could not control or understand filled him within seconds. He held his sword with both hands and ruthlessly started attacking Lazgar with his full strength. His blade swings were wild and full of hate. Lazgar could barely stand up to his uncontrollable might. With every swing she tried to block, she felt her entire body get more and more tired. Shagar was panicking. She felt like crying. She didn't get along with her sister, but she still meant the world to her. She knew there was something wrong about this knight. So much hate and bloodlust. She could practically feel it radiating off of him like heat from the sun. It made her feel nauseous being around so much rage.

"You can save her."

Shagar looked around, confused.

"Don't be afraid, young one. It's me."

Shagar looked on in astonishment as the strange six-winged woman from her dreams materialized before her.

"Y... you're here! Why can't anyone else see you?"

"Because I only wish for you to see me. Please listen, child. Your magic. Cast it at the knight. You are a special woman. You are the key to setting things into motion. You are the key to saving this world from darkness."

"I... I... what if I..."

"Shh... calm yourself, child. I will never leave your side. That is a promise. Now please move quickly. Use one of the spells I have graced you with."

"Of course... th... thank you. I knew you weren't just a dream... I... I knew you were real."

The six-winged stranger vanished in an instant. The crowd was too loud and panicked to pay attention to Shagar talking to herself. All except Lucia, who was watching her with concern from the trees. Shagar pushed her way to the front of the crowd. Orcs were terrified for their queen as they watched Daemos wildly swing at her without any restraint or finesse he had shown at the start of the duel. Nyana was unnerved as well; this was going against their plan completely. Shagar watched as her sister was on her last legs, trying to defend herself from the rampaging skeleton.

Thoroughly rattled by the duel and afraid for her sister, she cast a spell without even thinking. "Brilliant radiance!"

A blast of light left her body and shined onto Daemos. Daemos reeled back and let out a horrific scream of pain. He dropped his blade and stumbled back. His skull was smoking, his face covered in glowing burns.

Nyana instantly teleported inside the arena and stood next to Daemos as he grabbed his sword. "In the coming days, expect an invasion like none other. You will fall under the rule of King Daemos."

Nyana cast a spell and teleported herself and Daemos away from the arena. The entire crowd was speechless, unable to understand what they had just witnessed. Shagar shot through the gates of the arena and ran to her sister.

"LAZGAR!" Shagar hugged her as tightly as possible and Lazgar shakily returned the hug. "ARE YOU OKAY?! D... DO YOU NEED HE—"

"Hey, I am okay. Your magic... it saved me... you... you were right all along. We need to stop this now. Sha... Sha I am so sorry... I... I"

"Don't worry about me right now. We need to tell everyone about this!"

"...What... what should we do?"

"I have a plan but... but you're not going to like it."

"What?"

"We need to make an alliance with the werewolves."

The crowd instantly protested, but Lazgar did not seem offended this time. "...I...I think I agree with you this time... but... it will never happen. They won't believe us that something like this is even possible."

The orcs went up in yells and the clanks of metal could be heard as another voice called out.

"I will vouch for this alliance."

Lucia, the princess of the werewolf kingdom of Shimia emerged from the trees.

Lucia put her hands up as weapons surrounded her, but Lazgar

CADE SKOBLAR

called out immediately, "Put your weapons down, now!"

The orcs were taken aback, but they did not argue with their queen. "You may speak, werewolf. Why were you here to begin with?"

"I was spying... but... I saw everything. That brute will destroy you all and then come after us if we don't do this together. I will use everything in my power to bring our countries together to fight this."

Lazgar would have never agreed to this, but she didn't see any other option here. She was willing to make an alliance with their sworn enemies.

The two dark warriors teleported some distance away from the orcs and Nyana paced back and forth in a worried and confused manner.

Daemos groaned in pain as the sizzling and burns started to slowly fade away. "What... what was that?"

"A major hindrance in our plans."

"NYANA! WHAT... WAS.... THAT?!"

"Light magic."

"Light magic?"

"A long-forgotten magic that is the opposite of our own. I thought there were no light magic users left in Harmonia."

When Nyana heard the words that came out of her mouth and the reality of the situation at hand, she started pacing back and forth while mumbling to herself. Her glove shakily stroked her cold golden mask and her breathing seemed to quicken. As soon as she seemed to lose composure, though, she gained her wits about her again.

"...Her magic... hurt."

"That would make sense. You're undead. This is a major hindrance. We may have made a grave error. We put on a show all right, but now they know you have a weakness. This won't spread fear as we had hoped. We need to kill that orc as soon as possible. We need to ride the momentum before we can learn. We need to invade as soon as possible."

"How shall we take care of the magic orc?"

"Send some monsters after her. She is the primary target. We need to send creatures that can travel great distances in the shortest amount of time. We need to gather as many new monsters as possible while our forces make a quick strike to kill her. A sense of smell would be viable as well. The drake that brought us here still has her scent. Use that drake as the head of the squad so we can kill her."

CHAPTER 9.5

Ashehera felt her body get colder and colder as their journey up the mountain continued. The temperatures only got more severe the higher they went up. Even the warmth and protection of the salamanders have been dwindling thanks to their food supply being sabotaged by a starving Harmonian knight. He had been swiftly executed for his actions by the queen herself. The journey was now much more difficult. The salamanders' food had to be rationed out in smaller portions, making them hungry, weak, and grumpy. With the salamanders in poor health, they were only able to produce enough heat to keep the group somewhat alive. The same could not be said for the reptilian king Renas. The cold has been greatly affecting him and he has been relying on the magic of the queen herself to keep him alive. Ashehera is no fool. She knows that if Renas were to die before they reach the end of their destination, they would all die. Her top priority is keeping him alive.

"We shall camp here for the night. I want you all to collect as much firewood and meat as possible!" ordered Ashehera. Her few remaining knights rushed off to obey her orders.

Renas shivered as Ashehera tried her best to warm the dying king. She was draining much of her magika to keep a constant flame burning. While she had plenty of magika to spend, it will eventually run out.

Ashehera stared at the king with frustrated eyes. "You better not die, you old fool. Everything hangs in the balance. I forbid you to die."

She looked at the salamanders, who were only able to keep a meek warm environment at best, compared to the raging heat that melted snow during the beginning of the journey. Suddenly, a low growl could be heard from behind them. Ashehera turned around and was tackled before she even had time to react. A large beast with white fur dug its claws into her shoulder and jumped back into the snow. It was camouflaged near perfectly with the snow and was very hard to see.

Ashehera took her trident out and went into a defensive stance. Renas started falling in and out of consciousness when she stopped using her spell. She kicked the king over to the sick salamanders and went back to focus. Before she could even start looking again, she was ambushed and slashed once again. The strange beast melted into the snow again.

Ashehera took a deep breath as she lifted her hand up and slammed it into the ground., "PILLAR OF FIRE!"

From the ground erupted a tornado of volcanic flame that melted the snow around them and reached high into the sky. She hoped that would suffice for a beacon to her knights. She felt most of her magika drain from using such a mighty spell. The size of the pillar was impressive and was quickly destroying cover for the beast.

Slowly, the beast decided to reveal itself from the snow. It walked on all fours and resembled a large panther with a whip-like tail. The tail was incredibly long and made cracking sounds in the wind as it wildly whipped around. Ashehera twirled her trident and waited for the perfect moment to strike. The snow feline lunged with amazing speed and slashed her shoulder before she could hit. The cat lunged again, but this time Ashehera dodged and was able to slash the feline's back. The cat's blood dripped onto the melted rocky ground and slush that had melted from the flaming pillar that was still burning just as hot and bright.

Just as the feline was about to lunge again, arrows and fireballs started shooting towards the cat. The beast turned to see elven knights charging to protect their queen.

"PROTECT THE QUEEN! PROTECT THE QUEEN!"

Knights in golden armor surrounded the beast that was now beginning to snarl and hiss as any threatened animal would. Ashehera took her opportunity with the beast being distracted. She jumped over her soldiers with amazing agility and pierced through the neck of the monster with a downward thrust of her trident.

She crudely removed her trident, spattering its blood all over the ground and looked at her knights. "Cook the beast and whatever animals you hunted in my flame pillar. Keeping the king and the salamanders healthy is top priority."

King Renas was gently stroking the fiery scales of the salamanders who, in turn, rubbed their heads against him. Ashehera watched with interest.

Renas took notice and called her over. "You are taking much care in ensuring my survival."

"My kingdom would suffer from the dragons if I didn't."

"That is most likely true. I am a treasured friend amongst them."

"I can feel your disgust towards me."

"I will not lie, cruel one. Most of this world hates you."

"In due time, you will learn for yourself what I have learned. I don't care if the world doesn't believe me. When the time comes, you will all flock to my empire for safety. It is only a matter of time."

CHAPTER 10

Lucia scouted ahead to show the traveling band of orcs following her the right direction through the forest to reach her to the dwelling of her father Fenrer, king of the werewolves. The group was about to enter Shimia. It had taken them three days to travel to the border. The countries inside the Duma Forest were smaller than most of the others in Harmonia and Lucia was able to lead the orcs forward with the many shortcuts she knew through the forest. The traveling band were on the outskirts of Nigt and only feet away from the border. All around them were spiked walls of rock and wood and tall guard towers made by the orcs to defend their borders from the werewolves.

All along the walls and trees were werewolf skulls and pelts that were nailed against them. Lucia gave a nervous gulp, looking at her kin that were used as decorations. She felt a hand grab hers. She turned to see her girlfriend, Shagar. She smiled, but looked back to see if any of the other orcs were looking.

"Sha? What if they see us?"

"Honestly, I don't care anymore. I'm done hiding what we are. We have more important things to worry about. If our relationship is the biggest thing on their mind right now, then that's honestly kind of sad."

Lucia gave a small smile and a blush came across her face. Usually, she was the more abrasive one in the relationship. She wasn't expecting this kind of talk to come from Shagar.

"Thanks Sha. That… really means a lot." Lucia gave her a toothy smile and held Shagar's hand tightly. She looked deep in her eyes. She was about to give Shagar a kiss until suddenly…

"AWOOOOOO!"

From all directions, massive hulking werewolves jumped down from the trees and surrounded the traveling band of orcs. Some of the wolves were not in their beast forms, with only wolf ears popping out of the top of their heads. They had weapons drawn and magic spells charged up, ready to release. Others were in their massive bestial forms, their bodies towering over the large orcs. Their claws were like daggers and their fangs sharp as swords. The large beasts snarled, their eyes shot with bloodlust.

All of the orcs bunched together, ready to defend the queen and princess with their lives. One of the surrounding attackers slowly stepped forward with a look of confusion and interest on his face. He was an older man with gray hair. One of his wolf ears was bitten off and the teeth patterns could still be seen. One of his eyes was missing as well. He gave off an aura of authority and experience. He wore rusted armor and a red cape. The old man stepped forward and looked at Lucia.

"Princess Lucia? What are you doing in the presence of these brutes?" he asked in an old gravelly voice.

"They have come in peace, Uncle. I am representing them. There is a threat far larger than any I have witnessed before and peace between our countries is the only option in order to ensure our survival. I have witnessed all this myself. I need to speak with my mother and father as soon as possible."

"You may speak with them whenever you may please, but these animals are going into the dungeon, where they belong."

"I cannot allow that. They all must come with."

"Oh? Why must that be your highness? "

"Because.... Because Nigt royalty is in this group... along.... Along with the woman I love! I beg you, General Ferald... no... *Uncle* Ferald! Please... you have to trust me."

Both orcs and werewolves were shocked as they muttered amongst themselves in confusion. General Ferald was taken aback by what he had just heard. She was… in love with an orc? Shagar was in the crowd of orcs. Her face went from green to pink at a rapid rate. Lazgar looked at her completely shocked. She had no clue that her sister was having a relationship with the Princess of Werewolves this entire time. She wanted to speak to her about this, but seeing as they were currently surrounded by armed werewolves, now might not be the best time.

General Ferald watched as Lucia refused to break eye contact. He saw the seriousness and determination burning in her eyes. He gave a grumbling sigh and nodded his head.

"Come, then… but you have much to explain. I want weapons trained on the orcs at all times. One wrong move and I want them dead in an instant. Let's move forward to the castle!"

As the group approached the palace of the werewolves, most of the orcs were intimidated. The palace was built on top of a large cave with massive gothic towers rising from it. Shagar stood closer to Lucia as she stared up at the tall towers.

"I didn't know werewolves built such a place."

"We didn't."

"What?"

"Thousands of years ago, Shimia used to be under the control of vampires, who had enslaved werewolves for their own purposes. Our ancestors broke away from their bondage and defeated the vampires. We have owned their castle ever since."

"Oh."

As the two talked, the orcs and werewolves watched them like hawks. As the group walked inside the cave, they were met with two large iron doors that opened for them. Inside the castle was ancient vampire furniture and architecture. Most of the orcs were left under guard outside of the castle. The only orcs that were allowed inside were Lazgar and Shagar.

They were escorted to the main throne room. It was decorated with statues and red carpets. At the end of the room were two thrones. One of them was empty and the other was being used by Fenrer, the king of the werewolves. His hair was brown and long, his skin covered in many scars and his eyes looked like those of an emotionless predator ready to rip the flesh off of anyone that stands in his way. The king seemed more bestial in his normal form compared to the others. Despite not being in his beast form he was hairier than the others and still had his claws and razor-sharp teeth.

He lifted an eyebrow as he watched his daughter enter the throne room with two orcs. "My daughter. Why have you brought this prey into my throne room?"

"They are not prey, Father. This is the queen of the orcs, Lazgar, and the princess Shagar."

"We have not come here to fight! Merely to talk. We need to make peace." Lazgar interrupted.

Fenrer lifted an eyebrow and sat forward slightly in his throne. "Orcs? Orcs wishing for peace? Now this is something new. I am intrigued, so I shall play along with this childish game. Why would orcs want to make peace with us? Why should I not simply stand up from my throne and drink your blood?"

"Because a threat beyond any I have seen before is going to crush Nigt. After we fall, Shimia will surely be next."

"Is that so, your highness? My daughter… is this true?"

"I saw it with my own eyes. A large horned knight who… wasn't alive."

"Wasn't alive? What nonsense is this? You come to my throne room and make up this ridiculous—"

"IT'S NOT FAKE!" yelled Shagar. She seemed to instantly regret her outburst as Fenrer stood up.

"You step into MY castle dare to yell over ME?! I WILL—"

Before he could finish his sentence, Lucia jumped in front of Shagar to protect her.

Fenrer was taken aback and confused. "What foolishness is this?"

"I won't let you hurt the one that I love! You need to listen to me!"

"The one that you what?" he said with a confused snarl

"I SAID, THE ONE I LOVE!" Lucia said as she pulled Shagar to her side and kissed her on the lips. Shagar smiled and giggled. Both Lazgar and Fenrer were completely taken aback by this.

"How… dare you? You have thrown away our ancient customs FOR A FEMALE ORC?! YOU ARE GOING TO INHERIT THIS KINGDOM! YOU MUST BEAR THE CHILD THAT WILL INHERIT YOU! THIS WILL NOT STAND!"

"W… what? This is not why we are here, Father! A power is rising that will destroy this world! This is serious! We need to—"

Suddenly, the entire castle started to shake. An ear-piercing screech and the horrified screams of orcs and werewolves echoed from the halls of the castle. Shagar held her head in pain and stumbled back. Lucia caught her in a worried manner and looked her in the eye.

"Sha? What's wrong, Sha? What is it?!"

"The… the dark presence… I… I feel it again. I… its them! They followed us!"

"Were they spying on us?"

"I… I don't know… I… I…"

The castle began to shake again and the smell of smoke started to spread across the castle. Fenrer walked down the halls towards the entrance. General Ferak was waiting for him with a bow.

"Brother. The castle is being attacked by drakes, goblins and… dire wolves. Sire."

"Direwolves? That's impossible. We are wolf kin! No wolf would ever harm us! And... did you say drakes and goblins? Working together with direwolves?"

"I did, brother. But that is not all... look for yourself."

Fenrer and Ferald walked forward and witnessed pure chaos. The sky was infested with six large and powerful drakes that breathed fire and death upon the enemies below. On the backs of the drakes were goblins shooting down arrows and spears from their backs. Direwolves ruthlessly rushed at full speed towards orc and werewolf alike and viciously shredded their flesh with fang and claw. The only similarity was that all of their eyes emanated an unnatural red glow. Fenrer was utterly confused. He looked at the sky and watched as drakes landed on the top of the castle, hordes of goblins jumped off their backs and charged into the castle, ready to butcher Shagar.

Fenrer was completely stunned but was snapped back to reality by his daughter, who shook him. She looked scared and had desperation in her eyes.

"FATHER! THIS IS THE THREAT! OUR NATIONS MUST JOIN FORCES IN ORDER TO SURVIVE!"

"MY FELLOW HUNTERS! JOIN FORCES WITH THE ORCS AND PROTECT THE PALACE! THIS IS MY COMMAND!"

The werewolves emitted a beckoning howl that echoed across the battlefield. Some werewolves morphed into their hulking bestial forms while others stayed in the back lines to fire arrows and spells. Werewolves clashed with direwolves in ferocious close-quarters combat. The werewolves' hulking forms gave them more survivability against the direwolves, but the direwolves were under a strange trance that made them fight on no matter how injured or outnumbered they were. The werewolves were shocked to see that they were being outmuscled in some cases by the direwolves, who were pushing their bodies to the most extreme potential. The wolves would run so fast that some of their legs got injured and yet they continued on as if nothing had happened. The bites of the massive wolves would be so powerful that they could crunch steel with ease but in the process would break their own jaws. This did not stop them. It was a disturbing sight to see these animals destroy their own bodies just to deal as much damage as possible. No fear. No animal instincts. Just the desire to injure and kill the enemy as much as possible.

Fenrer morphed into his larger beast form. Since he was the alpha of the pack, he was even larger than the other werewolves. His claws and fangs were longer and sharper and his hide was thicker. He let out a roar and charged into the battlefield. One of the drakes swooped down from the sky and rained fiery death down to all who were under him. The flames easily burnt the werewolves' fur and spread widespread panic across the battlefield.

Fenrer jumped high into the air with his powerful legs and landed on a high tree. He then took another powerful leap and lunged right onto one of the drakes. His butcher knife claws sliced their way through the drake's scaly armor like a knife through butter. The drake let out a screech of agony and was about to bite Fenrer. Fenrer intervened and instead shoved his massive fangs into the throat of the drake. Blood seeped from its neck. The panicked drake tried to shoot fire from its mouth but instead the flame shot from the hole in its neck. As the drake spiraled towards the ground, Fenrer leapt off of its body and landed towards the ground battle. Direwolves lunged on Fenrer, but he was easily able to crush their bones with his grip and fling them off. He watched the panic amongst his soldiers who were slowly getting roasted alive from their thick fur being caught on fire. Werewolves in their normal forms desperately tried to cast water spells to put out the fires, but were being picked off by the direwolves and drakes.

Inside the castle, Shagar and Lazgar took refuge inside of the throne room. Only two werewolf guards were left behind to protect the orcs. Shagar shivered. This was the first time she had ever been inside of an active warzone. Lazgar put a hand on her shoulder and gave her a reassuring smile.

"Hey… calm down. We're going to be fine. I'm not going to let anything happen to you."

The large doors of the throne room were being banged upon. The two guards pressed their bodies against the door to barricade it. Lazgar drew her massive iron blade and Shagar made a small fire in her hand. The ruthless ramming of the door continued until suddenly, it all came to a sudden stop. Just as Lazgar was about to drop her guard, the door started to bubble and sizzle with a sickly sound. The doors started to rot from spells of acid being performed upon it. As the doors melted into a puddle, the room swarmed with enraged goblins with glowing red eyes. Lazgar jumped in front of her sister, ready to defend her. She was surprised to see the goblins were just like the monsters that attacked them. The same eyes and ruthless behavior.

The two guards started to morph into their beast forms, all the while goblins start to pile on top of them and endlessly stab them over and over again with their smaller weapons. The goblins in the back were using their magic to shoot fireballs.

"KILL THEM ALL! RIP THEM APART FOR THE MASTER!"

Lazgar refused to charge forward. If she did, she would leave her sister exposed. Shagar was breathing heavily while maintaining the small flame in her hand. Since she was an orc, she was unable to cast many large spells because of the amount of magika her body could hold. She looked at her sister who continued to hold her guard as they began to be surrounded.

"W…what are we going to do?"

"You have that special magic. How many spells do you know?"

"…I …I've had the dreams since I was a little girl. I… I know a lot of them, but since I am an orc, I can only cast two. So many of the spells I know take too much magika to cast."

Goblins started to charge at her as fast as they could. Three goblins came from the left but with a powerful swipe of her massive sword she cut three goblins in half down the middle Their bodies flung across the room, scraping across the ground. Even as it was cut in half, one of the goblins was still trying to kill the orcs. It was barely alive but trying to crawl towards them and stab them. Lazgar was disturbed and crushed its head with her foot. Another goblin lunged and tried to stab Lazgar's leg. She blocked the attack with her sword, but a piece of the blade got chipped off from the attack.

Lazgar kicked the goblin away with her mighty strength and sent it flying backwards into a wall. She looked back to her sister to see if she was okay and went back to the fight.

"Well? What spells do you have that could be useful? You have two of those strange ones, right?"

"U… u… um, yes. Only one of them may be useful, though."

Four more goblins jumped from the sides and started piling up on top of Lazgar and ruthlessly stabbed her with their knives and short-swords. Shagar tried to cast a spell, but an arrow came flying by and shot her in the arm. She let out a yelp and pulled the arrow out of her arm. Her white cloak was now stained with her blood.

"SHAGAR, NO!" yelled Lazgar as she attempted to reach her sister, but was unable to because of the goblins crawling across her body and stabbing her relentlessly. More arrows came flying towards Shagar. She didn't have the capability of using a shield spell. Before she could let out a scream, Lucia dove into the room in her bestial form and shred the archers and spellcasters in the back to pieces. She turned her head to see two fellow werewolves surrounded by goblin corpses and still trying to shake some of them off. The goblins were enhanced, somehow, and it was harder to pull off their bodies. When they are eventually pulled off, the fur and flesh the goblins were tightly gripping also came away.

Shagar looked at her girlfriend's beast form. She had never witnessed it before. It resembled her father's form quite a lot, but with a slimmer body. The massive wolf-like creature stared down at Shagar and was breathing heavily. Shagar had heard about the tales of werewolves before. It can take them many years of training to control themselves in their bestial forms, but even one that is well trained can lose control with too many emotions or stimuli.

Lucia got closer and closer to Shagar. Lazgar was about to intervene but before she could do anything, Lucia was rubbing her large head against her and licking Shagar's face.

Shagar let out a small chuckle and hugged her large head. "Thanks, Lucia."

Lazgar looked to her sister and then back to Shagar. "Yeah... thanks."

Shagar snarled but gave her a small nod.

The castle started shaking again as drakes slammed the outside walls with massive fireballs. The fight continued to rage on with massive casualties in the werewolf-orc alliance. Many of the werewolves died slow and painful deaths from their fur being caught on fire. Fenrer was able to use his mighty strength and agility to kill at least half of the drakes. His claws easily shred through the tough scales of the reptiles. Even if Fenrer's and Lazgar's forces were victorious, the damage has already been done. Many have died and only from a small force of goblins, drakes and direwolves. Most of them have been wiped out by the sheer numbers of the werewolves, but the battle is not over yet.

Avalanches of ancient brick and stone tumble to the ground falling on all underneath as the drakes started violently bashing their bodies against the castles. Only three drakes and a few direwolves remain of the monster army and out of desperation, all are going after their primary target, Shagar. With a final desperate slam, one of the drakes smashes its body into the side of the castle, crumbling the wall and making a large hole into its side. The exhausted drake fell to the ground, giving the enraged werewolves a chance to pile on top and rip it to shreds.

The direwolves rushed inside the castle to hunt down Shagar. All the wolves moved with incredible speeds. Some were moving so fast they started to slightly trip, only to regain their ground and momentum in seconds. They smelled her and knew exactly where she was.

Fenrer jumped into the air and ripped open the neck of a drake, leaving only one left. The final drake let out an ear-piercing screech and unexpectedly rushed into the castle. The drake blasted crackling flames from its mouth and blocked the entrance it went through, halting the progress of the werewolves and orcs that were chasing it.

"WE HAVE TO FIND ANOTHER WAY AROUND! MOVE! MOVE!"

The drake roared as it smashed its way through the destroyed hallway of the castle. Its large body was too big and the destruction it caused inside of the castle wherever it moved showed. The drake's wings scraped and ripped against the walls of the castle, shredding the thin flesh on the wings. The maddened drake pushed onward with no pain, following the scent of Shagar.

Lucia was about to change back to her normal form when suddenly direwolves lunged on top of Lucia, digging their claws and fangs into her flesh. She let out a roar of pain as she flailed to get them off. Shagar covered her mouth and looked to her sister in a panicked state.

"HELP HER!"

Lazgar was about to rush over, but she immediately changed her targets when she saw that several direwolves were running right at Shagar.

Lazgar lunged forward and impaled a wolf on her thick blade. Another wolf jumped from behind and was able to cut through the skin on her back with ease, but with one slash of her sword, she decapitated the wolf. Panic and disorder filled the five survivors in the throne room as more and more direwolves started pouring in, accompanied by a very loud noise coming from further down the hall. The two werewolf guards did everything they could to protect their princess, but eventually were too overwhelmed by the amount of direwolves ripping apart their bodies and feasting on their flesh. As the two succumbed to their injuries Lazgar and Lucia stepped in front of Shagar.

"Let me help you! Let me fight!"

"JUST… just stay quiet… I need to concentrate."

Three direwolves moved with incredible speed to the left of the trio and four moved to the right. Lazgar took the left and charged forward. She slammed her shoulder into one of the wolves, making it fly backwards into the wall and cracking it. The wolf got back up and charged once again while the other two pounced on her back. Lazgar let out a war cry and slammed her back against the wall with the wolves barking in rage as she did.

Lucia used her bestial strength to throw the direwolves to the side and used her claws to rend their flesh. No matter how hard they fought, the wolves would not back down. No matter how injured the monsters were, they fought to their last breath with strength above what was normal for their species. Shagar gasped as direwolves piled on top of her girlfriend and ripped off patches of her thick hide with their teeth and claws. Shagar lifted her hands in desperation to cast a spell with no real plan in mind.

RAMPAGE: THE RISE OF AN EMPIRE

"BRILLIANT RADIANCE!"

The entire room filled with a blinding light. Everyone covered their eyes but Shagar, who seemed unaffected by her own spell. The moment she cast the spell she could feel a large chunk of her magika drain in almost an instance. She may only have enough magika for one or two more spells until she would have to wait for it to regenerate. She nervously grabbed her sister's sword and sliced apart as many wolves as possible while they were stunned and blinded. She was able to lift the massive blade because of her natural orc strength. Blood splattered all over her fine white robes as she butchered the monsters that injured the one she loved.

Lazgar rubbed her eyes and watched with astonishment as her little sister shredded the wolves apart. She smiled as Shagar handed her sword back to her.

"You did good. I knew you had orc warrior spirit in you somewhere."

Shagar gave a shy smile but ran to her girlfriend, who had several lacerations and injuries all over her body. She hugged the large werewolf, who nuzzled Shagar back.

The loud noises and rumbling were getting louder and louder during the entire fight and the source of the, would arrive soon. Lazgar pushed Shagar behind her.

"Stay behind me."

"NO! Let me help!"

"I'M NOT RISKING ANYTHING HAPPENING TO YOU!"

The hallway was getting brighter and brighter and an orange glow got closer to the throne room. Before Lazgar had the time to realize what was rushing towards them, Shagar jumped toward and put her hands up. She didn't have time to think. She had spent her entire life trying to understand these strange magical powers that nobody else had. In all her life, she has only managed to do one or two spells from that magic. She didn't care if her magic was overall weaker because she was an orc. She didn't care how low her magika was. All she cared about was protecting the ones she loved in the only way she knew how.

The maddened drake smashed into the doorway and blasted a tongue of flame directly at the three royals.

"SHAGAR, NO!"

As Lazgar screamed, the injured Lucia attempted to push Shagar out of the way, but Shagar's hands started to glow white and a barrier formed in front of them. She didn't even understand how it happened. It was instinct. The barrier blocked the flames that violently slammed against the clear, shining magic. The flames sizzled like magma and started melting things inside the room but bounced off the barrier. Furniture and metal started to become ash and liquid from the heat. It was getting harder to breath as fire spread across the throne room.

Lazgar and Lucia watched in disbelief at the amazing feat of the one they loved. She was not going to be able to last much longer, though. The barrier was slowly starting to crack from the nonstop onslaught of the enraged drake. Shagar was barely able to hold up the spell and it looked as if she was going to pass out any minute.

From the hallway, Fenrer in his massive beast form lunged onto the back of the drake and used his large claws to dig into the eyeballs of the drake. The massive reptile wildly swung its head around in confusion and rage. The drake felt the pure agony of its injury but was pushing through it, only wanting to murder its attacker in the most brutal way imaginable.

Following the king was General Ferald with a jewel-encrusted sword. He slid underneath the drake and shoved his blade upwards and sliced open the drake, making all of its intestines fall out of its body and onto the floor. Ferald lifted his hand and yelled "AQUILLUS!"

From his hand sprayed a funnel of water that extinguished the flames inside of the room and filled it with steam. The moment the fire was put out, the barrier shattered into several pieces and Shagar fell to the ground, unconscious. Lucia lunged forward to catch her girlfriend and held her close to her body. Fenrer jumped off the drake, but it was somehow still alive! Whatever was influencing this drake was making it push forward no matter what until it was dead. The drake bite down on Fenrer's arm. Fenrer roared and decapitated the drake with his claws. He reverted to his normal form and fell to his hands and knees. Now that he was not in his beast form, it was much easier to see the number of injuries that were sustained during the battle. Fenrer shakily held onto the wall for support, with Ferald immediately supporting his brother.

"Everyone must attend to themselves… give medical assistance to all survivors, orcs included. Queen Lazgar? I feel there is much that we need to discuss. Tend to your wounds. I am going to call on forces from all across Shimia as soon as possible. Rest. When the time is right, we will have a proper discussion over the future." Fenrer said to Lazgar, who nodded in relief.

Over the past two days, Fenrer has been supplying as much medical aid as possible to all of the survivors, orc or werewolf, and gathering combat-ready werewolves from all over the kingdom to get ready to fight in case of another attack.

All the royals were gathered in the destroyed throne room, locked in a heated discussion. Fenrer paced back and forth as his daughter argued with him.

"Father! Don't you understand? If we don't attack now and defend Nigt, then Shimia is next! If we are attacked one at a time, then both our kingdoms will surely fall! We need to attack NOW with aid from the orcs to win!"

"We are in no condition to attack! Some of our greatest warriors are either dead or injured. This attack crippled our forces and now we are relying on our own civilians to fight as well. We will be walking into a slaughter."

"Father… the choice is simple. We either wait like cowards and accept our fates as a full army of those freaks crushes our kingdom OR we fight and have a chance of surviving with allies on our side."

Fenrer sat in silence as he let the words of his daughter fester within him. He let out a sigh and looked up to her.

"Fine… once preparations are made… we fight in aid of Nigt."

Lucia smiled and hugged her father.

"Thank you, Father."

"It should at least take us a day to make it to Nigt, less if we are lucky. I suggest you start preparing yourselves now."

CHAPTER 11

Daemos and Nyana had rushed back to Whitia as soon as possible to prepare the army. Their entire plan had flipped on its head. Nyana had not been expecting any form of light magic to still be known to this world, or at least none that would be in the Duma Forest. Furthermore, Daemos had nearly ruined the plan when he lost control and almost killed the queen. The two talked things over as they neared the main palace.

"How is this going to be resolved, Nyana? Shall we inform the master?"

"There is no time! Time is of the essence! You must begin the invasion of Nigt NOW and send out a second battalion to hunt down that orc. I will speak to our lord personally. What we need now is speed and momentum."

"I know all that already. You told me. We will use this drake to hunt her down as the pack head." He said as he gently rubbed the neck of the drake they were riding on the back of with his gauntlet.

"THEN GO!"

The drake landed on the top of the fort and Daemos jumped off. He turned back to look at her and nodded. Nyana jumped off as well and was ready to move as fast as she could towards her lord's hidden mountain lair.

"I shall carry out my tasks here. You inform him of what has happened. When the time comes, we shall meet again."

Nyana nodded and leaped off the side of the roof and Daemos lifted his gauntlet. The gauntlet glowed a sickly red which resonated with the already crimson eyes of the drake.

"Obey me. Gather more of your brethren and be on the ready. You will be the pack leader to hunt down the orc with the strange magic."

The drake let out a roar into the air and flew off to do as it was commanded. Daemos entered the castle and called for a meeting. In due time all of his goblin advisors and leaders gathered in the throne room at his command.

"Y...yes, sire? What is your command?"

"There has been a change of plans. The siege of Nigt must start now."

His advisors were immediately shocked and were unsure of how to approach his reasoning. Gogba stepped forward with a worried look on his face.

"I... if I may ask, my lord... what has driven you to make such a drastic change in your plan? Although there have been improvements but... we are still recovering from the damages of the first war."

"Complications in the plan. Don't worry. The orcs are demoralized and weak. The raids have left a toll on them. The attack is a distraction while an assassination party will be dealing with an important mission."

"A... assassination party?"

"Yes. I have drakes waiting on the top of the castle. They have the scent of the target. Nomai, tell me, are any of Vesta's assassins still alive?"

"Um...y... y... y... yes, my lord," he said fearfully, concerned by how little their lives seemed to matter to him.

"Good. They will be useful. Send them to the top with the drakes so that I may instruct them myself. In the meanwhile, I want the main army to be prepared as soon as possible. We shall soon march to Nigt!"

Nyana walked down the dimly lit halls of the mountain fortress. She pushed the doors open to the throne room and bowed her head to

RAMPAGE: THE RISE OF AN EMPIRE

Zithoss. Zithoss was staring into the bottom of the well of souls and was muttering to himself. He slowly turned his head to look at Nyana.

"M... my lord, I must–"

"You scouted the world for me. You promised me there was no light magic on the face of this world."

Nyana lowered her head. Shame and panic filled her body. She felt like garbage. She had failed her master. She was about to apologize profusely, but he cut her off.

"For decades, you roamed the continent to help me plan my return. Now everything is at risk. You have failed me."

Those words rung through her ears like an echoing boom. She collapsed to her knees and felt all hope leave her body. Her only purpose in life has been a failure.

"I... I am not worthy to live... take my soul..."

"No. Your failure is a great hindrance to my plans but there is still a possibility to salvage what you have destroyed."

"Please tell me how, master! I will do anything to redeem myself in your eyes! I... I'm nothing without you!"

"I am not strong enough to leave this place yet. If I was, I would have simply attacked the elves myself to take their souls. My revenant must continue to play his part. I predict... if nothing is done, then we shall surely fail... all because of you. Despicable... you scout almost 100 years... hundreds of years of planning! All down the drain because you couldn't do the one thing I asked of you. Find if any light magic users exist. You failed me."

"Master please! T... t... tell me what I can do! I'll do anything! Anything!"

"You are going to have to bring the souls to me. You can't harvest souls for me and my revenant is too busy. I have to entrust everything to you. I'll have to create glyphs for you using up the power I was already given. Two teleportation spells. One for the trip there and one back to me. Your spells may work for small distances, but traveling across the continent is a task only I can perform."

Nyana was determined to redeem herself, but her stomach dropped when she heard him say those words. She knows what he was implying. To carry over as many souls as possible she needed small bodies to maximize the number she can bring with her.

"You seem unsettled. Are you going to fail me again?"

"N… NO! Never… NEVER AGAIN! I… I'll… I'll do it!"

Zithoss glared at her and turned towards the well. He lifted his skeletal arms into the air and started muttering ancient words from a forgotten language. Smoke started rising out of the well of souls and spiraling around his entire body like a cyclone. Ashes started to rise from the dimly lit well and all formed together to make small pieces of paper. Zithoss started chanting in his strange language, inscribing the strange pieces of paper with his magic to be stored.

Crooked and jagged lines get etched into the paper from thin air and start glowing a sickly green. The moment the glyphs were created, the well went dark and empty. Zithoss collapsed to the ground but was caught by Nyana, who held him in her golden gauntlets. She forgot how light and frail his body had become. She gently placed Zithoss on his throne once again. The only semblance of life in his body was the dimly lit eye that had a constant red glow to it.

"This was your fault, Nyana. You shall make it right. Bring them to me so that their souls are mine. You failed, so now I must salvage this plan. I will need all the power I can muster in order to win the coming battle and… call in an old servant of mine. She went into a deep slumber, hidden from the world after my first defeat. I was hoping to postpone awakening her for as long as possible. She is a wild card. Then again… that is what we are forced to do now, thanks to your foolishness."

The more he berated her, the more worthless she felt. How could she not find any light magic? She was the one that gave him the okay to start his plan. She told him there was no light magic. This was her fault.

"I... I shall not fail you, master. Not again. I can promise you that."

"Then listen well. I need the most powerful souls possible, with the least amount of risk, as soon as possible. Time is not on our side. You better come back with results. You are indebted to me."

"Of course," she said with a bow. She picked up the glyphs off the floor and activated the first glyph. She teleported away to the place of her choosing in order to get what she needed for her master.

The assassin squad had already been sent out and the armies of Daemos marched forward towards Nigt. Daemos knew what he needed to do. Nigt must be crushed as soon as possible and then afterward, he would wait for further instructions.

As his armies marched toward Nigt, the sound of war horns could be heard echoing among the trees. Daemos was ready. He lifted his gauntlet and allowed its power to take the minds of his army. The eyeball on the gauntlet opened wide and stared at his troops. One by one, all of their eyes started to glow red. They felt no pain and will stop at nothing to win now, even at the risk of their own bodies and lives.

Daemos wasted no time. His armies marched into Nigt and were on the lookout for any orcs. From the trees, arrows rained down towards Daemos's forces, but Daemos lifted his arm into the air and casted a spell.

"Precision gust!"

All the arrows shot towards the troops stopped in midflight and instead were shot in the opposite direction towards the ambushers. All the enemy arrows killed their own shooters with perfect aim and their bodies fell from the trees, lifeless. One orc fell to the ground out of fear and looked up with horror at the hulking black knight.

Daemos stared down at the orc and picked him off the ground with one hand. The orc's legs were dangling off the ground as Daemos lifted him up.

"How many more are coming this way?"

"W... w... we won't surrender! Our orc pride refuses to! You will be—"

Daemos simply snapped the orc's neck and violently threw his body to the side. The orc's soul was ripped from his body and absorbed into his gauntlet. Daemos stepped over the body, crunching the dead orc's bones with his heavy metal boots to continue the march forward. The goblins marching behind Daemos were already getting scared of the cold-blooded behavior of their lord.

Daemos turned his head to the side to speak to his generals. "Fena."

"Yes, my lord?"

"Take a scouting party towards the right to find any possible traps the orcs may have left. They are obviously expecting an attack if they had these sad excuses for warriors waiting for us."

"Yes, my lord," Fena said as she lifted her blade in the air to signal her fellow wolf riders to move to the right in the forest to scout and flank the enemy.

Daemos then turned to the left to look at Nomai who stood at attention.

"Nomai."

"Yes, my lord?"

"Your battalion has some mages, but they are weak. Nevertheless, this is an advantage. The orcs only have one mage. Take a battalion of direwolves and some orcs and a drake with you to secure a high ground position. If there is no high ground position, I want you to be ready as a flanking ambush. The main force is going to draw all the attention. Fena is on stealth, so you're going to be the flank. Wait for the right moment. When the main force strikes, you will attack from the side. Got it?"

"Yes, my lord. Nothing gives me greater satisfaction then bringing glory to your name," he said, with only a small wince of fear in his voice.

As Nomai and his battalion left for the left, Daemos pointed his sword forward and yelled. "CHARGE! KILL THEM ALL! BEAT THEM DOWN UNTIL THEY SUBMIT TO MY WILL!"

The army charged, letting out a mighty war cry. The ground rumbled from the heavy feet of trolls, direwolf hordes and the mighty hydra. The sky flurried with drakes flying all over the sky and raining down fire. Trees started to catch on fire and more and more orcs were being forced out of their ambush spots and attacked head on. None of the orcs expected what was coming. More drakes, orcs, and direwolves all in one place than most see in a lifetime. Not to mention the massive hydra.

"D… don't just stand there! We will defend our home! Our orc pride demands that we do!"

The two large armies clashed together in close combat. Direwolves lunged on top of orcs and bit into their flesh like it was paper. Massive trolls crushed the orcs into mangled, crunched-up bodies with the large trees they used for clubs. Drakes rain down death and spray fire into the defensive ditches that the orcs had dug up. Their screams filled the air as they were melted alive, unable to escape from their fiery tomb. The unstoppable hydra was soaking up arrows and slashes from swords and axes. Most of the attacks could not even penetrate the monster's armored scales, but whatever attacks did somehow manage to draw blood on the massive beast healed in moments.

The hydra released concentrated blasts of magika from each of its mouths, spreading destruction and death wherever the beams touched. The beams melted through the bodies of the orcs with complete ease and destroyed any defenses they had set up. The orcs were prepared for a forest siege to protect their villages but they were never expecting the force that was coming for them.

An orc with an eyepatch raised his axe over his head and let out a war cry. Orcs jumped down from the trees on top of the hydra and started cutting into its scales. The hydra let out a pain filled snarl and wildly flailed its long serpentine necks to throw off its attackers. Daemos drew his blade and charged in front of his soldiers to cut down as many enemies as he could.

Daemos climbed up the hydra's tail and used his massive blade to decimate the attackers. An orc tackled Daemos and made him stagger backwards as another orc shot arrows right at the gap in Daemos's helmet. Daemos grunted as the pulled the arrow out of his head, scaring the orcs around him. He grabbed the orc that had tackled him by the throat and snapped his neck with ease. The distraction Daemos had caused was enough. The hydra was using its long necks to bite and eat the orcs that were on its back.

"MARCH FORWARD! HEAD FOR THE FIRST VILLAGE!"

The orc with the eyepatch was shocked by the sheer size and power of the enemy. He took a horn from his belt and blew into it. Moments passed but whatever reinforcements or plans the orc had in mind were ruined.

Daemos chuckled to himself. "Looks like Fena did her job."

The eyepatch-wearing orc was taken aback and immediately started to fall back with as many orcs as possible to get into the defensive positions at the first village.

Daemos could see the first village with his own eyes now. He was ready to start a massacre.

RAMPAGE: THE RISE OF AN EMPIRE

Nyana teleported to where she thought she could follow her orders to the fullest. She knew what her master had been implying. Elven children. Small enough to bring several with her to the trip back and although young, rich with magika. It would also be the safest and the fastest. In that moment when she teleported, however, she just couldn't go through with it.

Nyana found herself in a frozen tundra wasteland. Nyana knew where she was and was already regretting her decision. She was in the territory of the Dragon Council. One of the most dangerous places in all of Harmonia. The most powerful race of all is the dragon. They have more magika than elves and their massive bodies make them powerful enemies. Nyana realized what she had to do now and it made her feel sick. She has no choice now. Her master had gambled everything on this. All of his power went into those two glyphs and she had used the first one to get here. She has no choice now. she has to steal dragon eggs. They are undeveloped, but they still have a soul rich with magika. Nyana clenched her fist and cast a small fire spell around her. She needed to keep the light dim so that she wouldn't be spotted.

As she pushed onward to try and find a dragon nest, the pit in her gut grew deeper and deeper. She really didn't want to do this, but she had no choice now. She knows she is disobeying the orders her master implied but she couldn't have gone through with it. Not small children who were already thinking and breathing. She has used children as hostages before, but it was all bravado. At least with eggs, they are not conscious.

Nyana slowly approached a cave and peeked inside. She dimmed the light from her spell further as she saw a massive dragon sleeping around its nest full of eggs. The dragon had a green and brown scaled pattern and was roughly thirty feet long. The loud snoring of the dragon shook the icicles on the roof of the cave as it slept. As the dragon peacefully slept around its nest of eggs, it blew black smoke from its nostrils.

Nyana knew this was dangerous. Her magic capabilities are nothing compared to that of a dragon. Even with the unique spells she learned from her master, the sheer power of a dragon's magic could overpower her own. She looked at her two daggers. She tightly gripped the handle of the one that she took from the corpse of the goblin Cling Clang near the beginning of their journey. She did not have much use for it up until now and she hoped that would continue to be the case.

Nyana took one careful step after another inside the cave. She was going to use all of her magika to keep this invisibility spell up no matter what. She refused to fail her mission. With every step she could feel her nerves start to fire up. Every small crunch of the snow beneath her boots, or every time she nearly stumbled on the slippery ice beneath her, almost made her heart stop.

The large dragon's head started to move and Nyana instantly froze like a statue. The dragon opened its massive mouth full of several rows of razor-sharp teeth and let out a yawn. Nyana let out a shaky breath, but in a moment, all the calm in her body left as she accidentally snapped a twig that was buried under the snow. The dragon's eyes opened wide and its head shot up. A snarling hiss left the dragon's mouth as Nyana slowly retreated.

"I see your footprints, intruder. I smell you… a smell I am not familiar with. Strange. Show yourself. I would normally not be against visitors, but you seem to be the undesirable type," growled the dragon in a feminine voice. Nyana kept completely silent. Her heart was racing.

"I can hear your heartbeat. You're scared. Normally, I would reassure a traveler not to fear me. Us dragons have learned to lead a peaceful existence. I won't ask again. Reveal yourself."

Nyana was already scanning the entire cave, trying to think of solutions. Whatever the dragon was saying could be nothing but drivel for all she cared. Her mind was completely focused on solutions. Should she retreat? Attack? Grab and run? She still has plenty of magika. Should she wait it out? She does not have forever to do this.

"Still not talking? This is rather frustrating. I don't know what your intentions are, mortal, but I have nothing to offer. All of the rumors about my kind hoarding treasure are simply stereotypes about our species. We have no need for mortal currency."

The dragon's tail started to swish back and forth behind her massive scaly body. Nyana panicked. She would be caught if any of her body touched the dragon. She jumped over her tail and landed in the snow, making a small crunching noise. She was lucky this time since she landed behind a boulder.

The dragon whipped its head around and let out another hiss. "Why are you hiding from me?! What are you planning?" The dragon looked around the cave with an angry expression on its face. "You better explain right—"

Suddenly, the dragon's eyes narrowed and smoke blasted from her nose. The dragon let out a rage-filled roar that made some of the icicles fall from the ceiling and get impaled in the snow.

"You're here to take my eggs, aren't you? Trying to steal my little babies?! HOW DARE YOU?!

The dragon wrapped her long tail around her nest and stood up to investigate the cave. Sparks were flickering inside the angry mother's mouth. Her orange eyes darted around the cave looking for any noise or footprints she could key in on.

Nyana knew that she was running out of time and magika. If she was going to make her move, it had to be soon. She knew that her ticket was already secured. She didn't need to worry about that. She just needed to get her hands on those eggs and soon.

Nyana held onto the dagger that she had retrieved while conquering Whitia and stayed as quite as she could. The dragon was getting more and more agitated by the moment. A small noise came from the opposite side of where Nyana was and the dragon instantly whipped its head around and emitted a stream of crackling flames. The smoke subsided to reveal a small fox, now reduced to damaged bone and cinder.

Nyana took this opportunity to capitalize. She lunged and stabbed the knife into the dragon's tail to release its grip on the eggs. The knife created an explosion that cracked and destroyed several of the armored scales on her tail. The dragon let out a roar full of agony and pain while Nyana quickly dropped her invisibility spell so she could cast another.

"DOME OF TIDES!"

A massive dome of water appeared from thin air and enveloped her body and the nest. Nyana started to quickly loot the nest and horde as many of the eggs as possible in her bag. The dragon slashed at the shield of water, but it did as much good as a sword slashing into the waters of the sea. The dragon started blasting as much fire as she could muster from her maw and aimed all of her power directly at the dome. The flames were so hot that the water was starting to evaporate into steam and rise to the top of the cave. Nyana worked faster, stealing more and more eggs as her dome got thinner and thinner by the moment.

As the barrier was just about to break, Nyana pulled out her glyph and activated it, teleporting away in an instant. The dragon roared in rage, tears filling her eyes at the loss of her would-be children.

In a split second, Nyana returned to where she started not too long ago, in the throne room of her master.

Zithoss sat slumped over in his throne waiting for her. "You returned? I thought it would have been sooner."

Nyana opened her bag and gently let the dragon eggs roll out. Zithoss was silent for a moment. His glowing red eye stared at Nyana.

"...You didn't listen to me..."

"My lord... I... I panicked for a split second. I... I know it was a mistake, but I... I made it worth your while! These souls are more than sufficient! Better than the ones you wanted!"

"I asked you to take no risks... the path of least resistance. Everything is hanging in the balance now. You have jeopardized everything."

"I... I... I am sorry, my lord, I... I... I don't understand... I... I brought back better than what you had asked for! I..."

"ENOUGH! You would be nothing without me! You came crawling to me as nothing and I made you powerful! I granted your truest desire, did I not?! You forget your place! I own you!"

Nyana stood there, speechless.

"Come to me."

Nyana slowly walked towards him and Zithoss looked deep into her eyes.

"You were but a small child when you stumbled upon my lair so many years ago. You are like a daughter to me... I depend on you. I can't risk having you fall back on me now."

"Please... please, my lord... never say that... I would never turn my back on you."

"Then why? Why won't you follow the orders I gave you? If you can't handle this, then how will you fight on to what is going to come? I have groomed you for this role for most of your life. I trained you and nurtured you even when I couldn't move a single inch of my body. Stuck in the very throne that I am stuck in once again. I granted your wish that none other could. Do you still remember?"

Nyana was crying, tears dripped out from the eyeholes of the mask. She was shaking and slowly nodded her head at him. "How... how could I forget?"

"Then why? Why have you been failing me recently?"

"My lord... I... I SWEAR to you... It was a split-second hesitation to kill those... innocent children. I promise you... I.... I..."

"I understand now, child. Come to me... like you used to."

Nyana's heart fluttered. Nostalgia filled her as she slowly stepped towards Zithoss and leaned her head gently on his knee. She was careful not to lean against his fragile bones too heavily.

"For a mortal, you live for a long time, but you are still mortal. Mortal emotion is something you have to deal with. I am devoid of them. For the time you have served me it has been for scouting and assassinations. I did not take into account your... feelings on the matter. If I am to understand how the living work... you need to express your feelings, do you not? Tell them to me. You are permitted to speak freely."

Nyana was stunned by how kind and warm he was being. He has not been so open with her in so very long. Ever since she was a small child. It took her off guard, for sure, but she was nevertheless quick to oblige his request.

"Master I... I don't know. I... I couldn't kill... ch... children. I... just can't. I have done so many assassinations for you but none of them have been children. I have taken child hostages but... never this. I... I panicked in a split second and thought snuffing out the unborn would make this easier."

"I see... but I don't understand."

"W... what, my lord?"

"The living cast you aside, did they not? You are a being that can never adjust to a living society. Why are you unprepared to do what is necessary against what we have planned?"

"You… you don't understand why I was hesitant to kill… children?"

"Correct. They are eventually going to grow up to become our enemies. They will not give the same kindness to you that you gave to them. It is only at a disadvantage to us to show them mercy."

Nyana was taken aback, but before she had time to really think about what he had just said, he interjected.

"All this world has done is push you to the side. No one came to you when you needed it most. They don't deserve your mercy… but I can tell you are conflicted by your mortal emotions. If you find it… necessary to spare others, I won't object as long as it is not of a disadvantage to us… understand?"

Nyana bowed her head and retrieved the eggs for Zithoss.

Zithoss stared at the dragon eggs with anticipation. "Destroy them. Allow me to take their souls."

Nyana took a deep breath. This was far easier for her to do. There was no consciousness inside of those shells. She grabbed one of her daggers and plunged it right through the shell of one egg after the other. As each was egg impaled, a powerful dragon soul was absorbed by Zithoss and floated into the well of souls. With just one baby dragon soul, the well glowed brighter than it ever did when it was only full of goblin and monster souls.

The souls started to swirl around Zithoss and were absorbed into his body. More power than Zithoss has felt in ages filled his body at an alarming rate. He felt his body reinvigorate. Old cracks in his brittle bones started to repair themselves and a powerful aura of magic was now starting to swirl around his body. Zithoss stood from his throne with much more ease compared to last time and it could have brought tears to Nyana's eyes.

"M… my lord… how… how do you feel?"

"Like a fragment of my former self… and better than I have ever been in a long time. Now we must wait. Return to Daemos and prepare for the coming fight. I shall keep a watchful eye. When the time comes, I shall use my power to crush the enemy. I wished to reveal my power until later… but my hand has been forced. Promise not to fail me again."

"Of course, my lord."

CHAPTER 12

The werewolf and orc alliance moved with haste back to Nigt where they would work together to snuff out the current threat. On their travels through the far end of Nigt, they were able to recruit some orc village guards and civilians as well. Most of the orc villages were to the south of the castle but there were some to the north as well, facing Shimia. Both the orc force and the now mostly civilian army of werewolves have been marching nonstop towards Nigt. Thanks to the speed of the werewolves and the stamina of the orcs, the journey was over in less than a day or so. Their numbers were high, thanks to all the civilians that have been brought along for the fight. Even though most of the werewolf army was now composed of civilians, they were still a formidable force and had all the natural advantages a werewolf would have.

Shagar was getting more and more nervous as they got closer to their home. She saw what such a small force of those monsters could do when they were coordinated. She is terrified to imagine what an army of them all together could do. She jumped a little with surprise as she felt a hand on her shoulder. She relaxed when she realized it was her sister.

"O… oh. Hey, Laz. What is it?"

"You seem nervous. Don't be. Me and Fenrer have been making battle plans together. Soon everything is going to be back to normal, okay? I already told you your part in this, remember?"

"I… I know, I'm… I am just—"

"I WON'T let anything happen to you, okay? And I am sure your… girlfriend won't either."

Shagar smiled, happy that her sister finally took the time to acknowledge them being together.

"You got that right!"

Shagar let out a small yell as she was picked up from behind by Lucia. She was still wrapped in bandages from her fight three days ago. She tried to hold Shagar bridal-style, but it was much harder for her to pick up an orc in her non-beast form. Shagar appreciated the attempt, though.

In turn, she picked up Lucia, who scrunched her face up in a pouty manner. "This is not how I had things planned out."

"Pffffft.... hehehe... thanks, Lucia."

Suddenly, screams could be heard in the distance. Everyone stopped what they were doing in an instant. Shagar put down Lucia gently with a look of worry on her face. Smoke was seen rising over the trees. Instant realization and panic struck Lazgar and Shagar. The enemy had already steamrolled their way across Nigt and they were attacking the capital right now!

THAT'S FROM THE CASTLE! WE HAVE TO MOVE NOW!" yelled Lazgar.

Fenrer gave a nod and lifted his sword into the air.

"Nigt's castle must not fall to the enemy! We fight to save Duma Forest from darkness! We fight for a better future for our kingdoms and create a new bright future where we will no longer fight amongst ourselves! CHARGE!"

Hundreds of orcs and werewolves let out war cries and howls as they charged at full speeds towards the castle.

<hr>

After several days of burning and pillaging orc villages, the armies of Duma's new overlord had finally made it to the Nigt's Caste. Their numbers had only increased as Daemos had used his gauntlet to control more monsters and make war prisoners out of the orcs, forcing them to fight for him. Halfway through the conquest, Nyana returned to Daemos and fought with him. The final charge was about to start soon.

Daemos paced back and forth in thought, his large black cape flowing behind him as he did. His unnatural glowing red eyes were filled with frustration and restlessness. Nyana was leaning against a tree, sharpening her knife.

"You are telling me that there was a chance that this campaign could have ended in failure this early and it was because of the panicked orders you gave me?"

"Oh shut up. I don't want to hear your complaining and moaning. I fixed it. Our master will take care of everything."

"Leave everything to the decrepit corpse? Great."

"That's rich, coming from a decrepit corpse."

Daemos glared at her and walked off to speak to his troops. He climbed up the back of his hydra so all his monsters, goblins and orcs could hear him. His gauntlet started to faintly glow as he spoke to his people.

"We are about to crush the fortress capital of Nigt! We have burned their villages, slaughtered all who did not bow and made our names feared through all of Duma!"

A cheer could be heard from the crowd as their king spoke. When Daemos first conquered Whitia, the goblins were less enthusiastic about their king's war. Now that the benefits have been revealing themselves over time and their masters' influence has been slowly spreading to them, they seem much more fervent. Some even seem excited for the coming fight.

"Soon all of Duma will be united under one flag! My flag! A land too treacherous for the outside empires to colonize will be brought together as an unstoppable force!"

The crowd cheered louder. As Daemos got more and more energetic, the gauntlet started to glow even more and affect his troops.

"Nigt will fall to our might! Orc and goblin will be united as one people! One kingdom! All who resist will be brought to the sword! All who bow will be rewarded! We shall rain death upon them until they submit to our power!"

The goblins erupted in manic cheering. Their eyes glowed red from Daemos's malice and bloodlust being poured into them by the power of the gauntlet.

"CHARGE!"

The sound of thunderous marching filled the air as the large force of goblins and monsters charging towards the orcs. Even orcs who had been beaten down and forced to be war slaves fought against their own kind on the side of the goblins. Orcs made a desperate defensive formation in order to protect their capital fort. Many orcs stayed inside of the castle to shoot arrows from towers and windows. Almost all the men and women that could fight took up arms for the coming fight. The only ones that stayed inside the castle for safety were the elderly, the sick, and the children.

Daemos's forces charged forward with Daemos himself and Nyana fighting side by side on the front lines. The orcs had dug trench systems, erected barricades, and spread thick mud to slow the charge.

Daemos charged forward like a maddened rhinoceros, smashing through three barricades with ease. The wood of the barricades splintered into dozens of pieces on coming in contact with the massive black knight. With a psychotic fury, he cut down and obliterated any orc who stood in his path. Oblivion cut open their armor and flesh like a knife going through butter. An orc attempted to jump Daemos, but he grabbed the orc by the throat and slammed him so hard against the ground that it cracked.

Nyana ran by Daemos's side and used her deadly explosive dagger to destroy the orcs' armor with quick and elegant strikes. None could get close to her, for any that tried were instantly killed with crackling thunderbolts and molten volcanic flames of doom. Any that managed to get close to her had no chance. She dodged every attack they managed to throw at her and were killed by her dagger.

Daemos jumped right into the trench full of orcs armed with spears and throwing axes. Daemos ripped apart every orc in front of him with his massive sword. Orcs tried to impale Daemos with their spears and swords, but most uselessly sparked off of his armor.

Arrows rained down from the towers of the castle. Goblins were being shot down quickly and efficiently by the archers.

Daemos turned to Nyana who was slitting the throat of an orc. "Deal with the archers."

"On it."

Daemos lifted his gauntlet to the sky and used its power to call down a drake to land next to Nyana.

Nyana jumped on the drake's back and Daemos pointed to the top of the castle. "You and your brethren will massacre those archers. Go."

The drake let out an ear-piercing scream that alerted two fellow drakes to assist it in its orders. The winged reptiles flew higher into the air while getting shot with arrows and spears. The gauntlet's power made them feel no pain from their wounds.

Orcs fell backward in fear as drakes flew to the top of the castle and began spreading searing flames everywhere they could. Nyana leaped off her drake's back and gracefully landed on her feet. She unsheathed her explosive dagger and without hesitation used her incredible speed and agility to her advantage while attacking the orcs. An orc shot an arrow right at Nyana's face but with stunning reflexes she was able to dodge out of the way and immediately retaliate.

"Acid bolt!"

A thin and lightning-fast bolt of bubbling acid formed in her hands and shot faster than any arrow could. It melted right through the neck of the orc and into the wall behind him that in turn melted as well.

Doors swung open as more and more orcs were forced to leave their arching posts to deal with the intruder. They could not risk her getting to the defenseless interior of the castle. Nyana whistled to call over the drakes. Archers in a vain attempt tried to shoot down the enemy, but

Nyana raised her hand and cast her magic. "CHAIN LIGHTNING!"

A crackling lightning bolt shot from her fingers and bounced from target to target, killing several orcs with a single spell. Their bodies fell to the ground limp and charred in a pile. Nyana kicked down a door and began to search the castle towers for any other archers.

Inside the castle, an orc general was pacing back and forth in a nervous manner. Another orc ran into the room, panting.

"Speak, soldier. How does it go?"

"Bad, sir. One of their warriors has already breached the palace and the attacking force is overwhelming us. Their hydra simply will not die and a large black knight is devastating our defenses. He gets closer and closer to the front gates and is cutting open a path for the enemy force to break through."

"This cannot happen. WE NEED TO HOLD THE LINE! I refuse to fail Queen Lazgar. No matter the cost, we must hold the keep!"

Suddenly, screams could be heard from outside of the room. Blood started to pool from the crack under the door. The general grabbed a massive warhammer and the other orc unsheathed his blade. The door slowly opened to reveal several dead orc guards and no enemy.

The orcs started to look around in a confused manner. Suddenly, one orc fell to the ground, dead from a slit throat. Before the general could even react, a dagger was pressed against his throat, a weapon he couldn't even see. Nyana materialized in the blink of an eye once her invisibility spell wore off.

The orc dropped his weapon and snarled, "I shall not rest until all of you invaders are killed."

"I wouldn't count on it. You're coming with me alive."

The orcs were receiving massive casualties. Daemos's forces were powerfully working together. Goblins ride on top of their monster allies and use spears and arrows while the beasts of nature spread carnage on the battlefield.

Daemos snarled as he jabbed his metal talons into the eye sockets of an orc. He then pulled as hard as he could and ripped off the orc's head. Orcs were known to be violent warriors when they became desperate, but the ferocity of their enemies was surprising even them. The enemy's empty red eye sockets were staring at them with nothing but pure malice and bloodlust. The pure hate and determination of their enemies was disturbing. No matter how injured the enemy was, they would not stop fighting until they were killed. Even small goblins were ruthlessly attacking orcs with limbs missing and intestines hanging out of their body – they fight as if they cannot feel it at all. Their only priority was to spread pain and carnage.

A couple of orcs stepped back in disgust as they watched one of their fellow orcs get dogpiled by several goblins and be ripped to pieces like a pack of piranhas eating their prey. One goblin ruthlessly shoved its fingers deep into the orc's neck and ripped out its vocal cords with a cheer, holding it above his head like a trophy with blood squirting everywhere.

"What… what can compel these goblins to become such animals?!"

"Me."

Both orcs turned around to see Daemos looming above them. They quickly grabbed their swords, but Daemos was too powerful. He backhanded one orc, sending him crashing against a stone wall. The other orc was slowly getting choked by Daemos's gauntlet. As the air slowly left his lungs, the doors of the castle opened to reveal Nyana holding a dagger to an orc general's neck. As she approached Daemos, she cast a shield around them so they may speak uninterrupted. Several orcs were attacking the shield to try and break it as they talked.

"Call off your warriors and surrender to me. You have lost this fight."

"I will not betray my queen to some horned reaper!"

"…Horned Reaper? I rather like that name. I think I will take it along with your capital. This one does not seem to want to bend his knee. Slit his throat."

As Nyana brought the dagger to his throat, the entire battlefield was distracted by a war cry in the distance. Hundreds of roars and howls, all at the same time.

>-!-<)>-·-O-·-<(>-!-<

Charging down the hill was a massive combined force of orcs and werewolves, taking Daemos and his army completely off guard. The new attacking force came from the side and clashed against the unsuspecting goblins and monsters. Werewolves lunged high into the air and slashed at the throats of large trolls and direwolves. The physical strength of the werewolves was impressive. Their talons were sharp as knives and their reflexes second to none.

Werewolves jumped on top of the hydra and sent the massive reptile into a frenzy as the wolves tore through its scales and flesh. No matter how much damage was done to the hydra, it continued to heal. However, the werewolves had now halted the hydra's assault.

Lazgar and Fenrer spotted Daemos and looked to each other.

"That's him. That is the black knight I spoke of to you. The one that is… not alive."

"A couple days ago I would have been convinced you were mad… but I must assume the worst. If this knight is undead, how will we stop him?"

"My sister's strange magic somehow hurt him… we can do this, but we have to work together. His strength is incredible and he has the capabilities of magic as well."

Lazgar looked behind her and watched as Shagar and Lucia were speaking to each other. She gave a nervous sigh and called Shagar over, who quickly rushed to her sister's side.

"Do you remember the plan, Shagar?"

"Y… yes. Stay behind you and weaken the knight while you and Lord Fenrer defeat him."

"Just… stay safe, okay?"

Lucia stepped forward with a determined look in her eyes. "I won't let anything happen to her."

"Good… see to it that it doesn't."

Fenrer turned to General Ferald, who was overlooking the battle. "Ferald. Stay here and lead the troops."

"Of course, your highness."

"Alright… let's do this," said Fenrer as the four royals charged into battle, ready to kill Daemos.

Daemos whipped his head around and snarled, "Deal with him. I shall attend to this issue. Our lord better have this solved soon."

Daemos charged out of the magic shield to attack the new army head-on. Nyana slit the throat of the general and continued to kill those she could at the castle. As Daemos charged forward, he was collecting more and more souls inside of the gauntlet, both from his allies and foes.

As he charged forward, he was watching as the tide of the battle was no longer in their favor. Their forces were now taking heavy casualties from the surprise werewolf and orc attack. Daemos was getting angrier just watching it and in turn, the gauntlet made his forces fight even more ferociously.

As Daemos ran forward, he was killing werewolves in a brutal fashion: decapitation, maiming, and dissection. A werewolf lunged toward Daemos but he split the werewolf down the middle in midair, covering himself in the wolf's blood and innards. Daemos skid to a halt when he came into contact with the royals who were charging at him. Daemos lifted his gauntlet up and pointed his massive blade towards them. His crimson blade was dripping with blood as red as his glowing eyes.

"I must commend you all for pulling off such a valiant attempt at victory. Because of your tenacity, I shall give you an option others don't receive. Surrender to me now and I promise all of you will be spared. Raise your blade to me and I will personally assure your deaths."

Fenrer stepped forward and drew his blade. "We reject your mad grab for power! You have lost this fight! The number of lives you have taken is inexcusable! Prepare to die!"

"Then you have chosen your fate. COME THEN! BE PREPARED FOR THE HORNED REAPER!"

Fenrer and Lazgar both attacked at the same time, one from Daemos's left and the other from the right. Daemos in turn used the length and size of his blade as a defensive play and blocked both of the attacks. Lazgar headbutted Daemos and he slashed at her with his blade in response, cutting her cheek. Fenrer snarled as he clashed blades with Daemos.

"You're going to pay for everything you have done."

"Soon you will either be dead or bowing before me. All of Duma will be united as one. Then Harmonia is next."

"Prepare to die, 'horned reaper'," mocked Fenrer. "Lazgar, take charge for a moment."

Lazgar clashed blades with Daemos as Fenrer began to transform into his bestial form. Lazgar looked towards her sister, motioning for her to enact her part of the plan, until suddenly…

"FIREBALL!"

A massive ball of flame came hurtling towards Shagar. Lucia quickly tackled her out of the way of the spell and looked up. Nyana was levitating high off the ground with her cloak billowing in the wind. Her golden mask glittered in the sunlight.

"I'm afraid I can't allow you to do that. We just need to wait for a couple more bodies to hit the floor. Doesn't matter which ones. I won't allow you to interfere any longer, orc. You have caused enough trouble as it is."

Lucia stood in front of her girlfriend protectively and drew her blade. "If you want to do anything to her, you're going to have to go through me. You won't lay a finger on her."

"Then I suppose both of you will die. THUNDER!"

Crackling lightning shot from the tips of her fingers and Lucia once again pushed Shagar out of the way of danger. Shagar was terrified, but she knew she needed to help her sister and Fenrer.

"Brillia—"

Before she could finish the spell, a dagger went flying right for her neck. Lucia took the attack, grunting in pain.

"LUCIA!"

"This isn't going to work! She's too fast!"

Nyana gave them no chance to recover. She flew right above Shagar and cast another spell.

"SPEARS OF HAIL!"

In a small area around her, razor-sharp shards of ice started to rain down over Shagar. Shagar was slightly hurt, her blood spilling on the grass, but Lucia got her away from the rest.

Lucia snarled, "You hurt her! I'm going to kill you!"

"I highly doubt it. I have not been impressed so far."

Lucia roared as her body began to morph into her bestial form. She bared her fangs and let out a terrifying growl. Her eyes squinted at Nyana, who patiently waited for her opponent to strike.

Daemos ferociously attacked Lazgar to the point where she was barely able to keep up with his constant battering. She was being forced onto the defensive as Fenrer was finishing his transformation. Daemos was trying to push Lazgar out of the way to kill Fenrer while he was vulnerable, but Lazgar continued to play the defensive despite the great strain being put on her muscles. Not many can overwhelm an orc. She was still in awe and fear that such a strange being was capable of doing so.

Daemos snarled as he was pushed back by Lazgar. He watched as more and more of his soldiers were being killed. His goblins were indeed made more powerful by the Overlord's Gauntlet, but they don't stand a chance in open combat against angry werewolves. Their fur was thick like leather armor and their claws were as good as blades in their own right. Daemos growled in frustration and turned around. It was too late, though. Fenrer, now in his massive beast form, tackled Daemos. His claws slashed and rend Daemos's armor. Daemos kicked Fenrer off of him, making the werewolf alpha grunt slightly.

Daemos held his gauntlet out. "FIREBALL!"

The ball of flame that was formed in his hand was much larger than any fire spell that Nyana had seen before. Then again, she had never seen her master's fireball spell either. Daemos chucked the fireball at Fenrer and Lazgar. Fenrer dodged out of the way but the flames made a direct hit on Lazgar. She screamed in agony as the flames started to roast her alive. The ball of flame made a massive explosion on impact that pushed everyone near it back from the sheer force.

"SISTER, NO!" screamed Shagar in complete horror as she ran away from the safety of her partner and towards her sister.

Lazgar was burning alive and life was rapidly shrinking away from her. Lazgar could barely comprehend the world around her as all of her flesh was rapidly being seared off by the flames. Tears ran down Shagar's face, but they almost immediately evaporated from the sheer heat of the flames engulfing Lazgar. Shagar's hands shook. She was about to cast a spell, but before she could even open her mouth, a dagger came flying towards her face.

Lucia slashed the dagger out of the way in midair and roared. Shagar turned towards Daemos, who was locked in a deadly stalemate with Fenrer. Every time Fenrer landed a blow on Daemos, Daemos would retaliate with an equally powerful strike from his massive sword. Shagar lifted her hands up, ready to try and cast again. Lucia was doing everything in her power to keep Nyana away from her.

"BRILLIANT RADIANCE!"

A warm and angelic white light streamed from her palm and gently caressed Daemos's armor. Daemos let out a scream of agony as the light penetrated him. He wildly swung his blade around, trying to hit anything he could but the pure agony of the light was driving him mad. It was a pain that was so excruciating it made his mind go completely blank.

Daemos fell to the ground and snarled. Even when he was fighting Fenrer he had felt no pain at all. His armor was thick and even when it was damaged, his bones were greatly strengthened by his master's magic. Fenrer's claws could scrape against his bones and create sparks on contact, but the bones refused to shatter.

Nyana floated around Lucia, who had been pinned down. She could not go on the offensive against Nyana, or else Shagar would surely perish. Nyana turned her head quickly as she watched Daemos get struck by Shagar's spell and grunted in annoyance. She flew towards Shagar at a lightning speed. Lucia was ready to once again go on the defensive, but Nyana moved her body to instead attack Lucia.

Nyana slashed Lucia's arm with the explosive dagger. Her arm was shredded apart in an instant. Bone cracked and blood splattered across the ground.

"LUCIA, NO!" Shagar screamed in a traumatized voice as she ran towards her.

Nyana was ready to slit Shagar's throat, but Lucia fought through the agonizing pain and slashed at Nyana with her claws. Nyana dodged back but was almost too late as the claws shredded the end of her cloak.

Daemos let out a hate-filled roar as he fought through the agonizing pain. He forced himself to stand. He looked at his sword and held it in a defensive stance. He has had little use for this sword's main ability so far. Now was the time to show its power.

Shagar, with tears in her eyes, yelled once again, "BRILLIANT RADIANCE!"

The ray of light shot from her hands, but Daemos was prepared this time. He put his sword in the way and destroyed the spell with a slash of his sword. All those around were taken aback and confused, except for Nyana, who already knew about its power. Daemos clenched his fist and turned to see his army. Complete disarray. Mass death. The army he had worked so hard to build was in tatters.

Rage filled Daemos. "I won't... let you steal this from me... right when I started."

Fenrer let out a roar and Lucia protectively huddled around Shagar. Nyana gently levitated down to Daemos's side and twirled her dagger in between her fingers. Daemos held his gauntlet up in an intimidating pose. Nyana said there was a plan and he was sure he had figured out what it was. It was a gamble, whether his gloat was going to work or not.

"You have tried my patience, mortals. For eons I have waited for this moment to once again face the living in combat. To rebuild this empire that was once mine so long ago."

Nyana looked at Daemos completely confused. What the hell was he talking about?

"I must be honest... I was surprised to see someone who can use magic such as yours, orc. It doesn't matter anymore. I wanted to restrain myself this time, but you have proved worthy enough for me to display the full extent of my power. Every single death on this battlefield has only made me stronger. Even her majesty's soul is now swirling around in a vortex of death and agony," he said, pointing to Lazgar's charred remains.

Shagar's tears fell down her face quicker and she screamed, "YOU'RE BLUFFING! YOU HAVE NOTHING LEFT, YOU EVIL WRETCH!"

"Oh but I do... now... WITNESS THE POWER OF AN ELDER LICH! THE POWER OF DAEMOS, THE HORNED REAPER!" Daemos yelled to the sky as he held his gauntlet into the air.

Zithoss watched with great interest as Daemos made his proclamation. He sat on his throne, using magic to watch the fight from a bird's eye view, quite literally. With ease he was able to control the minds of hundreds of crows flying in the sky and see through their eyes. As Daemos yelled, Zithoss started to chuckle. Soon that chuckle turned into a manic laughter that filled the halls of his dusty and empty mountain dungeon.

"I knew I chose you for a reason, prince of elves. I know now that I chose right. Alright... you figured out the plan... I mind this as much as I commend you for it. Bring victory to your name, *elder lich*! HAHAHA! THE DEAD SHALL RISE! SERVE YOUR NEW MASTER TO THE FULLEST!" Zithoss exclaimed and then proceeded to chant in an ancient language.

A thunderous boom filled the room as a massive pillar of green light rose out of the well of souls and into the sky.

The sky started to turn green and overcast with dark, ominous clouds. Crackling lightning shot in random directions as an amount of magic so large started to fill the area that almost everyone still alive got goosebumps. Shooting down from the sky was a massive pillar of green magic that slammed right into Daemos's gauntlet. The sheer amount of power blasting down from the sky pushed away Shagar, Lucia, and Fenrer. Ferald quickly joined the others to protect the royals and see the spectacle for himself. The fighting ceased as they were witnessing a power unlike any they had witnessed in their entire lives.

"NOW WITNESS THE POWER OF THE HORNED REAPER!"

A mighty shockwave of energy blasted from Daemos's gauntlet. At first there was nothing... and then... movement. The bodies of the dead started to writhe. Goblins, orcs, werewolves, and other beasts that lay dead on the floor began to slowly rise from the ground. The spell did not stop there. The bones of the long-forgotten dead, buried deep under the ground, dug their way to the surface. Warriors of long-forgotten countries and kingdoms crawled to the surface. The living on both sides of the war crawled back in horror and confusion at the display of power.

After the zombies of the freshly killed came to life, the forgotten remains of knights and beasts under the ground rose in their skeletal bodies. Dozens of holes were opening up in the ground and skeletons of different shapes and sizes crawled from the dirt and mud. All of them had different weapons and sets of armor. Some were even riding horses that had been resurrected as well. Next were the ghosts. Appearing in their light bluish green tint, they stood in a trance, rocking back and forth. Their eyes were empty and void-like. The corpses of three armies and the long-forgotten dead had risen once again in service of one master.

Shagar was speechless. Magic of this caliber should be impossible. On the level of gods! Not just that, magic to bring back the dead does not exist. It makes no sense!

Lucia was still in great pain because of what had happened to her arm, but all of her attention was focused on the madness that was happening in front of her.

Fenrer snarled as he stepped back in caution and confusion. He watched as the massive amount of morale his army possessed vanished in an instant. They trembled in fear and confusion from the unnatural movements of the undead.

Daemos pointed his gauntlet finger at Fenrer and in unison, all of the undead turned towards Fenrer. "Listen and listen well! I present to you a proposal. Bow your heads in service of me, or die and become one of the walking corpses you see now. Either way… you will serve me. Now choose!"

Silence filled the battlefield. Panicked murmurs filled the field as the survivors picked their sides. Most of them decided to join Daemos. Orcs and werewolves hurriedly stepped off the battlefield in a panic as the ones that stayed loyal went back to protect the royals. Fenrer was ready to order a retreat when suddenly a thunderous roar echoed across the battlefield. Fenrer and Daemos turned to see the source of the noise.

From the forest, the sounds of trees being cracked in half invaded the eardrums of everyone nearby. A ghastly heavy breathing started coming from the woods. Disgusting weeds and vines started to grow out of the ground and wrap around Fenrer's legs. The vines had thorns that punctured his thick hide with ease. Daemos was confused, but he assumed this was one of his master's undead. Nyana, however, knew that this was much more.

From the forest emerged a beast that was beyond all reasonable explanation. Its head was that of an elk's skull with massive serrated antlers. The inside of its mouth was full of uneven razor-sharp teeth. Its eye sockets contained beady green eyes. Its body was made of a strange material. Its flesh resembled bark or scales colored jet black. Running along the beast's back was thick, matted fur, ending with the tail of a serpent. Its arms and legs were unnaturally long, making it tower even above Daemos. Its fingers were long and tipped with long talons that were the exact same color as its strange skin.

The monster's reptilian tail rattled behind her as it first looked at Daemos and then at Fenrer. A brave werewolf charged into the fray and attempted to slice the monster with his claws. The werewolf's claws sliced open the monster's skin and revolting black sludge started seeping out of its wound, squirting all over the werewolf. The wolf started whimpering, roaring in agony as the monster's blood started to melt through the werewolf's face and went directly into its brain, killing it instantly.

RAMPAGE: THE RISE OF AN EMPIRE

Fenrer snarled as the large monster approached Fenrer. The beast tackled Fenrer with incredible speed, taking the werewolf off guard. He could barely hold back the strength of the horrific abomination, already locked to the ground with the black vines that had arrived just before the monster did. Fenrer ruthlessly flailed about, snapping the vines and slashing the monster's face. His claws sparked against the skull of the monster uselessly.

The beast punched Fenrer in the chest, making the werewolf fly backward and slam against a tree. He slowly started to morph back into his normal form as the monster approached. Fenrer coughed up blood.

Lucia started to run to her father, but he held his hand up to stop her. "You must run! Warn the world! Take your woman with you! GO! Ferald... protect them... please."

Lucia was about to attack the monster and Nyana geared up for attack as well, but Ferald grabbed the two girls quicker than lightning and cast a spell before she could do anything.

"GREATER TELEPORTATION!"

The three vanished in an instant and Fenrer let out a small laugh. The monster's arm started to crack and crunch into different shapes. Its bones were breaking and reforming at its will. Its hard black flesh peeled open as its bones were being reshaped. In mere moments, the monster's arm had transformed into a massive curved blade that was almost as large as its already colossal body.

Daemos stepped forward and looked the werewolf king in the eyes. He removed his helmet and chuckled. "Your kingdom... is mine."

"All of Harmonia will band together once they know what happened here."

"I'm sure they will. Let them try. I want all of Harmonia to know that the Horned Reaper is coming."

CADE SKOBLAR

The monster roared and without any mercy sliced Fenrer in half. Daemos kicked the mutilated body to the side. He then chopped off Fenrer's head and held it up for all to see.

"YOUR KING AND QUEEN LIE DEAD AT MY FEET! ORCS! WEREWOLVES! YOU ARE NOW IN MY TERRITORY!" He threw Fenrer's head to the side and continued to give his speech. "All who surrender will be shown mercy All who resist will be put to the sword. Duma will now be united as one nation. No more will goblin, orc, and werewolf fight for scraps. No more will we hide in the shadows of this forest. Together we will build a new future as a united people. Our allies and citizens shall reap rewards beyond your imagination and prosper. Our enemies will be shown no mercy, no compassion. A new power is rising in Harmonia. The forest that has been feared by even the elves has now been united into one almighty force. A force that will soon breach the borders of the outsiders. Today and for many more days, we rest! We heal. We build our strength. Then we shall show Harmonia the meaning of power. We show Harmonia the meaning of terror. We show Harmonia the meaning of dread. We shall bring glory to our new empire. The Duma Empire!"

The battlefield was filled with cheering from Daemos's troops. The orcs and werewolves that had surrendered stay silent. Daemos now had a mighty army of the undead along with a new army of the living. War has been costly, but in one fell swoop both Nigt and Shimia have been annexed into Daemos's dark empire. The Duma Empire. Nyana looked at Daemos and then at the hulking beast who was staring at Daemos. It seemed more conscious than the other undead, who only seemed to move slightly on their own unless given orders.

"Daemos... that orc escaped."

"Yes... I saw. It was surprising to say the least to know a werewolf had learned teleportation magic. Not many werewolves are mages from what you told me."

Nyana fidgeted at a loss of words because of what she thought was her fault.

"Now is not the time to fret. We must see to our people... and learn of whatever this beast is."

"My master spoke of her returning. She is one of his servants that was in a deep slumber. His magic reawakened her."

"Is that so?"

The beast growled, sending the goblins standing nearby scurrying in all directions.

"Let's return to Zithoss. We have a lot of work to do. Duma shall be rebuilt into a paradise."

Daemos lifted his gauntlet into the air and sent a command to his undead. "My legion of death! Secure my empire and spread out across the land! Bring stability to my lands and protect my people! Violence against my citizens is forbidden! This is my command!"

The undead marched the moment the command was made. They would spread across the Duma Empire and secure each village, city, and town.

Daemos turned to Nyana and nodded, "Now, let's reunite with our master."

In a sudden flash of light, Ferald, Lucia, and Shagar were all teleported a fair distance away from the battle and were now in Shimia.

Ferald helped the two royals to their feet and was already rushing them off. "We don't have much time. Shimia has fallen and we must escape as soon as possible. I used all my magika in that spell to teleport us as far away as possible."

"WE CAN'T! OUR PEOPLE! WE CAN'T ABA—"

Lucia put a hand on Shagar's shoulder with a sad smile. "We have to go."

"NO, WE CAN'T! YOUR ARM! Y... YOU'RE GOING TO BLEED OUT!"

Lucia's arm had been completely mangled by the explosion. Blood dripped on to the ground in puddles and bones were sticking out of her arm. She had already lost a staggering amount of blood and it was amazing that she had not already perished.

"I can't lose you... I can't lose you like I lost Lazgar... please..." Shagar shakily held onto Lucia, who gave a weak laugh.

Ferald lowered his head in shame. "I am sorry, your highness... I failed to protect you by ordering the troops. I have failed you and Her Highness Shagar. If it would please you, I will happily take my own life as punishment for this inexcusable event."

Lucia sighed, "Oh, Uncle Ferald... don't be an idiot. None of this was your fault. I need you to protect Shagar... she is everything to me... okay?"

"Of course."

Shagar was about to interject but suddenly the world around her froze. She stepped back in confusion, only to see the familiar six-winged woman whose body seemed to be made of pure light. Her blinding light made it hard to make direct eye contact with her.

"Your life is beyond valuable, young mortal... and your love for this woman is strong. Your power... it will allow you to save the one you love."

"W... what? You... you really mean it!? PLEASE! PLEASE TELL ME HOW! But..."

"Is there something on your mind, young one?"

RAMPAGE: THE RISE OF AN EMPIRE

"...Yes... you have been with me... for almost my entire life, but I have been taught so little... with what little of my power I could use I have finally been able to help the ones I love... for... for what I could... oh Lazgar..." Tears dripped from her face as she continued to talk to the mysterious figure. "Why have you taught me so little? This new enemy is going to bring death and pain to so many... how will I be able to stop him if I don't know how to?"

A warm light radiated off the body of the strange figure. A peculiar feeling washed over Shagar. She could feel the patience and love the extraordinary being had for her. Although Shagar couldn't see any facial expressions on her, she could practically feel a kind and warm smile radiating off the being, like a mother would give to her child.

"You were born special. This world has grown dark. Too many in this world have forgotten my existence and my influence on this world has shrunk day by day. You are purehearted. Full of kindness and passion. My light was not sealed off to you. You are the chosen one. However... you are an orc. Your body cannot handle the strain your powers will put on your body. You simply don't have enough magika. Most of the spells you have access to are simply locked off because you don't have enough magika in your body. I have been... scared to teach you some. They can put much strain on your body and possibly hurt you with only little results."

Shagar fell to her knees as despair started to fill her. She had already lost her sister. Even though they fought and disagreed a lot, they were still sisters. Right when her sister had started to accept her, she was taken away in such a cruel and unforgiving way.

Before she fell deeper into her pit of pain, the entity continued, "Your love for her is inspiring... I can teach you what you want... but it will put great strain on your body. Your magic is unique. No one has what you are able to do... same as the enemy. The magic you have is capable of wonders beyond your imagination, including the magic to heal."

"…H… heal? But… that's impossible. No magic is able to heal."

"You will have to trust me, young one. Now… walk towards me… reach out and touch my light. Let its warmth and knowledge spread through you. You need to stay alive… you need to never give up hope. You are a purpose. A destiny you must complete. There are people to the east. The Holy State of Aidiel will guide you and protect you. The last followers I have. You must seek them out. They can help you fulfill your purpose."

Shagar shakily walked forward and touched the light. Her skin felt warm and soothed. The light started to wash over her entire body and in an instant, time unfroze and the world returned to its normal state.

Shagar shook her head quickly to snap out of her state of confusion and ran to Lucia. "Lucia… please hold still… okay?"

Sure… I can't really move anyways… I… feel cold."

Shagar closed her eyes, aware that she had only moments to save Lucia, and breathed slowly. Her hands started to shimmer a golden color and her hair started to float up, forming a cloud around her face.

Her eyes opened, only their whites visible, as she spoke aloud the spell, "HEAL!"

Golden light started to spread across Lucia's arm and the pain vanished. The wounds instantly cauterized and stopped bleeding. Slowly, bones were being pushed into their joints and the skin started to close. Lucia and Ferald watched with complete astonishment at the display of unknown magic happening before them.

Halfway through the healing process, Shagar started to sweat heavily and blood started to drip from her nose. She fell backwards and Ferald caught her. Shagar felt terrible. Her body felt cold and full of pain, but none of that mattered to her as she saw her beloved's arm. It had not completely healed, but the wound was not bleeding and the bones were in the correct place.

"SHAGAR!" Lucia said in a panic as she held her close to her body. "H… how did you do that? A… are you ok?"

"…Yeah …I had help from a friend." Shagar tried to push herself up but she coughed up some blood in the process.

Ferak used his cape to wipe her face. "Your majesty… are you alright? How were you able to cast such wondrous magic?"

"My friend… told me… we have to go to the east. We have to find the Holy State of Aidiel."

Daemos, Nyana, and the large beast teleported to the mountain dungeon. The beast seemed to know everything and was in fact leading them back to the throne room. When the two massive doors to the room were pushed open, the large monster ran on all fours towards Zithoss and sat beside his throne like a dog. Zithoss placed a bony hand on the monster's head while sitting in his throne and looked at his other two servants. Daemos lowered his head and gave his report.

"Master, in a few days all of Duma Forest shall be annexed to our empire. It is one of the few places in this world that has been impenetrable to annexation for almost all of time. Duma is a name that radiates power. Because of this, I petition that our empire shall be named 'the Duma Empire'."

"I care not for names… your request is granted. Before we speak of anything else, I would like to congratulate you on your recent victory. Not only did you show an impressive display of force, but you have successfully taken all suspicion off my existence by proclaiming yourself as an Elder Lich. I am most pleased by this."

"Thank you, my lord... now if I may ask... who is this beast? When your spell was cast, she came on her own to fight alongside us. She is unlike any creature I have ever witnessed."

"That is because there is no creature like her.. Hundreds of thousands of years ago I created her, trying to create a second elder lich... but failed. Nevertheless, what I created instead has been loyal to me. Her name is Chindi. Once I was defeated, I am sure Chindi went into a hibernating slumber until I returned."

"Why was she not with you during your defeat?"

"In my arrogance I had allowed Chindi and my top generals to do as they pleased as a reward. I was so certain of my victory I did not see when defeat came. Besides Chindi, there are three other great warriors who are still bound to me, just as you and Nyana are now. Victory will be certain if you are to find them and work together."

"We will see to it. My forces have taken major casualties from the last battle. We will need time to recuperate in order to spread outside of the Duma Forest. How long should we wait?"

"I feel multiple forces may be against us, now that we have drawn such attention. Rumors of this battle will spread. You will need to be precise and calculated. Take Chindi with you. She is a powerful ally."

Zithoss pointed forward and Chindi walked to the side of Daemos and Nyana.

"You have a legion of the dead now... use them to your advantage, my revenant."

"...Master?"

"Yes, my revenant?"

"Can you teach me the power to bring back the dead?"

"I am the only being to have ever been able to accomplish such a feat. One of my generals was able to summon and control the dead, but not awaken them. As far as I know, this is impossible. Then again, you are the first revenant to use the Overlord's Gauntlet, my revenant, no less. Only time will tell."

"Thank you, master. I shall start rebuilding our forces at once."

"I will be looking forward to your next report. Find my generals, Overlord. They are your key to victory and the path to power. Go now, Overlord of the Duma Empire. Show all of our enemies the meaning of pain and despair!"

CHAPTER 13

After several months of traveling through the treacherous mountain paths of ice and snow, Ashehera and King Renas finally arrived at the Dragon Council. The two members of royalty, along with the escort soldiers and salamanders, were all exhausted. King Renas had gotten quite sick from the cold during the long trip. During the journey, four of Ashehera's elven knights had died from the cold and King Renas had received frostbite on the tip of his tail. All of them would have suffered if it were not for the salamanders that kept them warm and melted a path forward for them.

King Renas has seen this place many times in his life, but this was the first time in Ashehera's life that she has ever witnessed the home of the dragons. Even in her millennium-old life she had never seen this place. It was a valley of dragons farther than the eye could see. In the middle of the valley was a massive chasm full of caves and crevices. At the far end of the valley was an enormous castle made out of ice and crystal. All around the sky, dragons of different shapes and sizes could be seen flying around. Suddenly, a dragon spotted the group and swooped down from the sky. It had black scales and vibrant green eyes. Its four strong legs firmly landed on the snowy ground. The dragon was massive, easily thirty feet long. What was more surprising was that there were dragons that seemed even bigger, reaching about 50 feet. The dragon bowed its head when it saw King Renas. "Lord Renas. It is quite the unexpected pleasure to have you visit us, my friend. Your body must be freezing. I will have you tended to in a moment, but before I do…"

The black dragon let out a bellowing roar and four more dragons swooped down to surround them. The black dragon's tail swished back and forth. The elven knights formed a circle around their queen with fear in their eyes. One of them was shaking in his boots as he was stared down by several massive dragons.

"I need to know why you are with these greedy backstabbing elves."

"Do not harm them… I am under a deal to bring these elves to Queen Voxis.

Queen Ashehera of the Harmonian Empire wishes to speak with her."

"Is that so? What would this meeting be about, my friend?"

"I do not know. My people were under threat if I did not partake in this journey myself."

Ashehera wanted to lash out and kill Renas for leaving her in the lurch in front of the dragons. She took a deep breath. She needed to play this cool.

"Of course I was not going to harm your people. It was an aggressive tactic made necessary by the urgency of the matter."

Ashehera walked in front of Renas and stared at the black dragon. She was terrified, but she didn't let it show. She had enough confidence in her own magical abilities to stay safe.

"I need to speak to Queen Voxis. This is a matter that is more important than territory or politics. Voxis may be the only being who can help all of Harmonia right now."

"And why should I take the word of the woman who has constantly pushed into our territory? You lay claim to our mountains and plant your flags there and expect us to cooperate with you? We dragons have stayed hidden from other societies to lay rest to our bloody pasts. We stay away from war as much as possible only for you elves to push us. The longer you stay here, the temptation to gut you alive grows stronger. Make haste while my composure lasts."

RAMPAGE: THE RISE OF AN EMPIRE

"I am willing to negotiate terms I cannot stress how important this meeting is."

"Your greed shall not infect these lands. I shall rip you apart myself!"

Ashehera's guards started to protectively get closer to her until suddenly, the entire chasm started to rumble, a low growl emanating from it. All the dragons turned their heads towards the noise.

The black dragon sighed and turned back towards the elves. "Queen Voxis shall meet with you. Know that she does not consider you a friend and will kill you if she so pleases. Now come with me, your majesty, we shall warm you and feed you," said the black dragon as he gently picked up King Renas and started to fly towards the large crystal castle in the distance.

Before leaving, the black dragon turned to look at Ashehera. "She is waiting for you at the bottom of the chasm. I do hope you are eaten alive."

The dragon spread its massive wings and gently flew away with King Renas shivering on his back.

Ashehera pushed past her soldiers and lifted up her hand. "Fly!"

Ashehera gently started to float down the chasm. The further she got down, the more nests full of eggs and caves with sleeping dragons inside she encountered. She could hear her soldiers crying out in terror once their queen left them.

"NO WAIT! DON'T LEAVE US!"

Ashehera could care less about them. She had a goal in mind. She needed answers. There is only one creature in Harmonia that has a longer lifespan then an elf to her knowledge and that is a dragon. Her best option was to speak to the oldest dragon to have ever lived. Voxis, queen of the dragons.

The further she floated down; the more eyes were focused on her. Ashehera was a mighty opponent, but she was surrounded by dragons who were fully willing to rip her apart. She was terrified but kept her face stoic. The nests she passed were full of eggs of different shapes and sizes. Half of them were already hatched with tiny dragons squirming around in their nests and on the bodies of their mothers and fathers.

Ashehera could see the bottom now and her stomach dropped. What she saw was the body of a dragon almost double the size of the others around it. Lady Voxis was truly massive. Ashehera gently landed on the icy ground and cleared her throat. Queen Voxis's body is covered in light blue scales and icy shards of armor. She was curled up like a snake.

Ashehera let out a breath to calm her nerves. "Queen Voxis of the Dragons! I, Queen Ashehera of the Harmonian Empire, wishes to speak with you and negotiate with you on incredibly important matters. Your endless wisdom will prove useful not only to me but to all of Harmonia."

The entire ground started to shake and icicles started to fall from the ceiling. The massive body of the old dragon started to unwind itself only for Ashehera to discover that what she had seen was not Voxis in her entirety. She had only seen her neck. Voxis was so colossal in size that it was too much for someone of Ashehera's size to comprehend.

Voxis stretched her neck and shook the snow off her head. Her eyes were a vibrant and sharp green. Her mouth was so large that she could eat several dragons with a single bite if she so desired. Dragons never stop growing in their lifetime. Their size changes depending on the amount they have eaten and how much magical power they have accumulated. Voxis is the oldest dragon to ever live. She lowered her head and stared at Queen Ashehera. She started to telepathically speak to Ashehera.

Her voice sounded old, but intimidating and commanding. "So. The queen of elves dares to set foot on my land after she wrongfully intrudes on our mountains. You are a foolish queen. What had you hoped to gain from my presence, surrounded by my dragonkin? I suggest you explain yourself before I crush your tiny bones under my claw." She said as she slowly moved one of her fingers. Just one of her claws were massive enough to kill a large beast.

Ashehera let out a breath and stared up at Voxis. She was scared and outmatched, but she was determined to get her answers. She had not been anticipating this. She was so much larger than she had ever thought.

"I come seeking your wisdom. Something beyond my understanding has occurred and seeing how you are the most ancient in our world, you would be able to help me."

"Why would I ever help you?" she asked as a gust of icy wind shot from her nostrils.

The wind pressure of the icy air almost knocked her off her feet and the cold air felt like sharp knives against her skin. Ashehera grit her teeth and regained her posture.

"Because if you don't, I fear it will tear apart this entire world."

"Then speak. Speak before I change my mind. But know this. If this turns out to be a waste of my time, I shall take it as an insult. I shall break the long peace I have made my kin endure and burn your pathetic empire to the ground. There will be no mercy and you will watch as everything your greedy race has built will crumble."

"Very well. I was mourning the death of my son… but… a magic I have never seen before was used and… and brought my son back from the dead."

Voxis was instantly intrigued and seemed to change her stance to listen better. She seemed almost agitated. To see one so powerful and wise have a fleck of panic in their eyes was an astounding sight.

"Almost none of our weapons worked. Only… this."

Ashehera took out her crystal trident and Voxis's emerald eyes grew wide. The massive ice-colored dragon got closer until her eye was right up to the trident.

"These crystals look to be the same that grow in your lands. I wish to acquire as much of it as possible."

"I had never thought I would see this trident again. It's been so long I can barely recognize it... except for that aura of power radiating from it... that amazing power. There is no doubt that this is the trident from the War for Harmonia. I can assure you that the crystals are not what give that trident its power nor are they naturally grown in any fashion."

"War for Harmonia? What do you mean?"

"I indeed have all the information that you require, but I refuse to give you any of this information until you promise to withdraw from our mountains."

"Deal. Now... what do you know?"

"That is a trident that was crafted by the Goddess Aidiel almost seventy-five thousand years ago."

"Aidiel is... real? What... what about the seven gods?"

"I'm surprised you even know her name. Yes. She was once very well-known and openly worshipped in this land. As the years went by, her name fell into obscurity and was lost to the sands of time, as many things of this world have been. As for the seven, they are part of just another religion that was formed over time, like many others yet to come and the many that have already been forgotten." Voxis brought her massive head slightly closer to Ashehera. "Is what you say true? You saw your son... rise from the dead? And only this trident was able to hurt him?"

"It's true."

Voxis dug her claws into the ice and her body began to tense up. Panic filled her as dark memories started filling the corners of her mind. Memories that she had tried to lock away and forget for thousands of years came rushing back to her.

"A darkness unlike any alive today was witnessed... I thought... I thought we killed him."

RAMPAGE: THE RISE OF AN EMPIRE

"Who?"

"Zithoss... the Lich King. Son of the Goddess of Death, Nioxis. He is a monster among monsters. A violent storm that spreads nothing but pain, misery, and death to all that are near him. There was a time where all of Harmonia was his..."

"That's...impossible."

"It's more real than you would like to admit. I was there to see his downfall... or... what I thought was his downfall."

(75,000 YEARS AGO)

The sky was engulfed in a sickly green fog, thick enough to blot out the sun. All of Harmonia has been engulfed in chaos and death after being conquered by the Lich King Zithoss. Five kings and queens came together in a brave and last-ditch effort to defeat him. Millions were dead and only a few were left alive. At the farthest corner of Harmonia was a final stronghold for hope. Whatever remaining survivors were left were gathered at Queen Voxis's crystal castle. Entire races and species have been driven to extinction and millions of the undead are roaming Harmonia under the rule of Zithoss.

Thousands of civilians from different kingdoms and races huddled together in fear inside the safety of the crystal castle while the remaining leaders of Harmonia's greatest kingdoms conspired together.

On top of the tallest tower was a room overlooking the lands of the dragons and farther beyond. Inside the room was a large clear table made out of ice and crystals. There were almost thirty chairs at the table, but only four of them were used. At the far end of the table was Lady Voxis. She used shapeshifting/illusion magic to make herself look like a humanoid version of herself. Her skin was fair and smooth with a pale complexion to it. She was wearing a dress made of ice and snow that gracefully wrapped around her body. She was surprisingly tall in her human form being at least six and a half feet tall. Her hair was as white as the snow that adorned her dress.

On the right side of the table was King Firebeard of the dwarves and King Eric Sargon of the humans. On the left side of the table was King Tarron of the elves and Queen Lyra of the werewolves. All of them had a serious look on their faces. Serious looks that signaled that they were ready to die.

King Firebeard was about three feet tall, but he was heavily toned with bulging muscles. His hair and beard were red and his skin had a darker tone to it. His armor was made out of a grey steel with a smooth and shiny texture to it. His eyes were a deep and vigilant blue. Some of his teeth were missing and in their place were golden ones. His crown was gold and encrusted with dozens of gemstones. He was covered in a variety of expensive rings and necklaces. Resting by the side of his seat was a massive, Warhammer made of gold and embedded with jewels, just like his crown.

King Tarron was a tall elf with incredibly pale skin. He had a long white beard and his face was covered in wrinkles. His body was very skinny and frail. He had chocolate brown eyes and a long pointy nose. His ears were taller than most elves and almost reached the top of his head. He wore a majestic outfit made of the finest silks and furs. A grey cloak was wrapped around his body as he stared intently at the others at the table. His attire resembled those of the old wizards of song and tale.

Queen Lyra of the werewolves was a short but muscular woman. She was much younger compared to all the others, because her parents had died in the war and she was forced to become the new leader of her people despite her young age. Her black hair was so long that it practically touched the floor and she had two wolf ears sticking up at the top of her head. Her eyes were blood red and sticking out from her mouth are fangs. She was wearing armor made out of the thick scales and furs of monsters from the Duma Forest. Her skin was a warm ivory color. The tips of her fingers ended in razor-sharp claws that could most likely shred through steel like it was paper.

Last is King Eric Sargon of the humans. He had dark almond skin and lush brown hair. He was wearing golden armor with a long red cape that could wrap around his body. Upon his head was a golden crown encrusted with sapphires. He sported a thick brown beard and his eyes were a deep black color. He had a very serious and intimidating look on his face. Leaning beside him is a large sword with a golden hilt.

Voxis started to talk. "The evacuation was a success. We have as many living civilians as possible safely inside of the castle. As for royalty, however… it would seem we are the only leaders left in this land. Zithoss will find out we survived soon. Until then, we need as much time as possible to prepare for the worst. Harmonia has been a land full of conflict for as long as I can remember, but now is not the time to fight amongst ourselves. If we are divided, then we shall surely all perish."

"Aye, I agree with ye. We have no room to fight amongst ourselves if we wish to vanquish the dark lord who has wrought such death to our homes. My mines are at your disposal as well as my hammer," said Firebeard.

"Elf and dwarf have never gotten along… until today. I consider you all family. What we face today may be the end of all times. It is a shame that it took such carnage to bind our alliances together. Know that for as long as I breathe, the elves shall consider you all as one of our own. It is my hope we all get out of this fight alive, but if dying for my home is what is destined for me then I accept it. I consider it an honor to die with you all," said Tarron.

Lyra rolled her eyes and stuck her feet on the table. "Yeesh, melodramatic much? Don't worry, we got this in the bag. I'll show Zithoss to never mess with my citizens ever again. I'll teach him to never destroy my home again! I'm going to rip off his stupid horns and then shove them down his neck!" she barked in a loud and abrasive manner.

On the outside, she looked confident and proud…but her eyes showed it all. She was terrified.

"QUIET!"

The room fell silent as King Eric Sargon the Third stood from his seat to speak. He looked at Lyra with intimidating eyes. His pupils shrunk slightly as he stared at her.

"You're nothing but a child."

"Huh? WHAT?! YOU CA—"

"In an unseen amount of time, the deadliest being to ever walk this land is going to find us and do everything in his power to squash us like ants. All of you sit here and talk as if we are all going to die. I know I won't. I have a reason to live. I have watched as women and children were brutally ripped apart from limb to limb. I watched as those mangled corpses rose from the dead soon after and did the exact same to others what had been done to them. I refuse to allow myself to die in this fight because I swore, I will avenge my people. I will stop at nothing until I have his head ripped off and placed upon a pike."

"Calm yerself, human. Of course, we're all fightin' till de end!"

"Whether you all fight or not is none of my concern. All I care about right now is vengeance and victory. It is the only reason I have agreed to work with all of you and share the latest of our human technology with you."

"Yes indeed. These 'ballistae' 'and 'catapults' are most intriguing, for sure," said Tarron.

"BUT this does not change the fact that we have a foolish queen who acts like a child when everything is being put on the line."

"HEY! He... he hurt my people... and... and he burned down my kingdom! My forest! My home! I have every right to be here, Eric! You're not the most important one here, human!"

"AM I NOT?!" roared Eric as he slammed his armored fist against the crystal table.

"I sit at a table with elves, dwarves, werewolves, and dragons and yet I come here as an equal! A better, even! You were all born with powers beyond imagination and lifespans that are more than triple of my own. And yet we are just 'equals'? You want to know why? Humanity prevails! As you soar high and mighty, humans crawl through the muck, fighting for survival. Fighting to be on equal footing among the beings that walk this land. And we will do it by any means possible. Without our technology you would have fallen ages ago. I will not allow childish nature and your egos get in the way of my victory."

Voxis growled and a burst of cold icy wind filled the room. "You shall hold your tongue, Eric Sargon the Third. We are an alliance."

Eric stared with cold eyes. His stare was filled with hate and was colder than the wind blowing into the room. Voxis was shocked. As the others shivered with the cold air cutting into their skin like a freezing knife, Eric stood firm and stared her directly in the eyes.

"Alliance? That's... that's funny. You all see yourselves as so important and mighty. Meanwhile, us fragile humans with our short lifespans and lack of magic are getting all of the work done to actually get a victory."

Everyone at the table was appalled. Firebeard slammed his fist on the table and snarled at Eric. "HOW DARE YE!? The brave men and women of me kingdom have been dyin' to supply all the ore they can give ye! They fight till the very end!"

"I find it insulting and preposterous that you think my fellow elves have not contributed to this war. Our spellcasters have been working around the clock to give medical aid and bombard the enemy."

"YOU'RE A JERK! The werewolf brothers and sisters rip apart those undead pansies! We can fight off a bunch! You human losers die so easily."

"My dragonkin have also died... we dragons are mighty but... their numbers are immense. I find it insulting that you insist you have been the most valuable member of this alliance while we have been working hard to ensure victory. You humans have received the least number of casualties in all of this. Perhaps it has been you who has not been contributing."

Eric glared at Voxis as she made her last comment. "We humans are survivors. Yes, we have had the least number of deaths. While you attack the enemy, we planned. We have pulled off something that can win the fight for good."

"OH REALLY? Why don't you show it to us then, huh?"

"I agree with the wolf! If ye have something so important, show it."

Eric reached into his cloak and pulled out something that made everyone at the table nearly have a heart attack. It was the Gauntlet of the Overlord. The personal gauntlet of the Elder Lich Zithoss. Eric held up the gauntlet and then placed it in his own hand. The eyeball on the gauntlet looked around the room as everyone got up from the table and stepped back. Even Queen Voxis took a single step backwards.

"How... how in de blazes did you get your hands on that... evil thing?"

"Are... are you working with the enemy?" asked King Tarron.

"We humans have our ways... and no, you paranoid old man. As you know, this gauntlet was made by Nioxis herself. The goddess of death and chaos. It allowed Zithoss to trap the souls of those he had killed to use for his spells and influence the morale and emotions of his soldiers. By using human craft, we have made this gauntlet so much more. Before this gauntlet was nothing but a tool. Now… it is a weapon. Observe." King Sargon held up the gauntlet and pointed it towards a wall. He smirked as he pointed his finger. "Fire!"

A massive blast of flames erupted from his hand in a fiery explosion that collided with the wall, destroying it instantly. Everyone in the room were shocked and left speechless.

"Now… we can use his power. It's all in the gauntlet. The gauntlet is alive. It learns. It thinks. It knows the lich's magic by heart. It casts the magic for you. All you need is a basic understanding and a power source."

"P… power source?"

"Yes. Souls. This gauntlet was filled with them when we stole it."

Voxis slowly sat back down at the table and stared directly at Eric. "We can't do this."

"And why is that queen of the dragons?"

"This is too dangerous. You are using the craft of a goddess and you tinkered with it using your human ways. I doubt not the intelligence and determination of humanity, but I also know how easy it is for the human mind to get corrupted. This power cannot be allowed to stay here. It must be destroyed. That gauntlet is pure evil."

King Sargon looked at Voxis with disbelief and anger. He walked up to her and was holding back the urge to do something irrational.

"If anyone here is insane, it's you, your majesty. Too… too many of my comrades died to get this gauntlet. We executed the most dangerous mission to ever happen on this land. We stole Zithoss's gauntlet. Without this, he cannot control his forces efficiently and take souls the moment someone perishes. It's ours now… not… not only that, but I IMPROVED it! We have his power now! AND YOU WANT TO DESTROY IT?! Me and my people gave you

THE ANSWER… how to bring this world back to the way it's supposed to be. HUMANS DID THIS! NOT ELVES! NOT DWARVES, AND CERTAINLY NOT DRAGONS! You wish to take away this monumental achievement of humanity? To steal the glory?"

"Lord Sargon, please listen. None of us understand the ramifications of using such an artifact in combat. Your achievements are nothing less than spectacular, but how about we—"

"Greedy elves…trying to steal the glory to gain which we have sacrificed THOUSANDS. DO YOU NOT UNDERSTAND!? THIS RIGHT HERE?! THIS IS OUR TICKET TO WINNING! TO SURVIVING! AND YOU'RE ALL READY TO THROW IT AWAY!? HOW… HOW DARE YOU!?"

Voxis slammed her fist down on the table and cracked some of the thick crystal. "Sargon… compose yourself!"

"You're all mad. You hide in here like rats… even when we have exactly what we need you—"

"ARE YE DEAF IN THE EARS!? Who knows what that thing be doin' to yer noggin'…"

"Do you think I care about what happens to me at this point?

"What? I… erm… I don't think I understand."

"I made a promise to my people as they were butchered alive and resurrected as those… things. I promised I would avenge my people. This gauntlet… it's how I am going to do it."

"But at what cost? Did yer even think about it before you started casting the magic of a lich?"

"I don't need to justify my a—"

Suddenly a warm glow filled the entire room. A light so blinding and bright that everyone had to shield their eyes. As the light dimmed enough for vision to return, everyone in the room was greeted by a strange being. Its body resembled that of a woman and yet it had the proportions of a creature that did not exist in Harmonia. Instead of its arms were six massive wings that were larger than its own body. On the wings were large unblinking eyes that constantly looked around. Its face was completely blank with no features whatsoever. All of its skin and feathers were the color of pure white. The strange being's hair was constantly floating and moving around, defying the laws of gravity. Its feet never touched the ground, keeping it constantly levitating.

King Tarron watched with astonishment and disbelief. The old elf slowly stood from his seat and fell to his knees in front of the strange being.

"Do… do my eyes deceive me? Are… are you… Aidiel?"

When the name Aidiel was uttered, the room began to fill with surprised gasps and whispers. The strange being spread its wings wider across the room. Although it had no mouth, it was able to speak. Its voice started to echo across the room.

"Yes, my child. I am the one you call Aidiel."

The moment the being confirmed who it was, everyone in the room bowed, except for King Sargon. Even the mighty dragon queen Voxis bowed. Aidiel was a greatly respected and worshipped goddess. She was the creator of Harmonia and life itself. Sargon was given dirty looks for not bowing to Aidiel. Tarron was the first to break the silence. He shakily looked up at the glowing goddess with tears in his eyes.

"Oh, benevolent one. What honor do we hold to be graced by your presence?"

"The dark armies of my nephew are fast approaching. He has come himself to personally watch you all die. I have made an oath to never interfere with the world of the living… but I cannot bear to watch my children suffer any longer. I have come to aid you all on your monumental fight for the fate of the world I have made."

"Thank you, we will take whatever aid you are so willing to give us."

"Aye... 'tis truly a blessing to lay eyes on ye."

"We are not worthy of such kindness, goddess. I will do whatever I can to please you."

"In all my years of ruling over the dragons I have never been given such a privilege. I will fight in your name, my lady."

Aidiel spread her wings apart and let five of her feathers fall to the ground. "My feathers are made of my pure essence. These weapons will prove to be one of the only useful tools to defeat my nephew and his undead legion. Please. Take one of my feathers each and allow it to seep into your soul.

Firebeard was up first. He excitedly picked up one of the feathers. The feather started to turn into a white liquid and change shape into something completely new. Soon, the feather transformed into a mighty warhammer made out of blue crystals.

Firebeard looked at it with astonishment and bowed his head. "Thank ye kindly, with all me heart. I shall treasure it and fight in your name until me last drop of blood is spilled."

The next was Tarron. The old elf bent down and picked up the feather. Just like with Firebeard, it changed into a white liquid and morphed into a mighty trident made out of blue crystals.

Tarron bowed his head. "I shall pass this gift down generation after generation, so your glory will never perish."

Lyra jumped forward and picked up the feather with excitement, accidentally snapping it in half. Her heart sank and tears filled her eyes. The feather turned to liquid which soon turned into two crystal daggers.

"There was no need to feel ashamed, my child. I have many other feathers and no wrong came of it."

"O... o... of course! I... I will slash a bunch of people with these! I promise!"

Voxis slowly stepped forward and held the feather in her hand. She didn't like being stuck in this small body during the meeting and she hoped that her gift would not be a small weapon for a small hand. The feather's liquid started to overflow, covering her body from top to bottom. She was taken aback at first, but was surprised to see her body now covered in crystal armor.

"Do not worry, my child. Your gift will work in your true body."

"I... I... thank you from the bottom of my heart, goddess."

Aidiel turned to King Sargon, who stared at her.

"The last feather is for you, my child."

"I don't want it."

The room instantly erupted in an uproar. Tarron was the first to explode at Sargon. "HOW DARE YOU!? THE GODDESS GOES OUT OF HER WAY TO BLESS YOU AND YOU TURN IT DOWN?! THE INSOLENCE!"

"Lad, this is a once-in-a-lifetime opportunity and you turn it down? I'll say one thing to ye. Ye have fuckin balls."

"I already knew you were a jerk and a moron, but this is pushing it."

Voxis stayed silent but watched with annoyance and disapproval.

Sargon said nothing until they were all done with their berating and yelling. He held his gauntlet up and pointed it at the goddess. A sign of aggression to most in the room, who seemed ready to kill Sargon.

"Why should I trust the word of the goddess of life? You watch us suffer and die like a coward. You watched as my people were brutally ripped apart and brought back as undead abominations and did nothing. Why should I even acknowledge your existence?"

The room was about to explode with outrage, but Sargon continued to speak in a louder voice to drown them out.

"The fact that I am wearing this gauntlet is proof enough that I don't need the help of a sniveling coward who is content with watching her world and especially children be resigned to a fate worse than death. Unlike everyone in this room, I am not a blind, scared sheep looking for directions in time of crisis. I am a human. One of the 'weakest' of your children, just as you made us be so. Yet here I am, leading the charge to fix your failure. Hiding away wherever you go to, you don't have any responsibilities, do you? Just watching us suffer and die. Well, I do have a responsibility, saving humanity from the fate you doomed us to. I'll take responsibility because our 'mother' will not."

The room was completely silent. Taken aback by the pure brazenness of King Sargon, whose eyes were filled with determination and anger. He took a step towards her and stared directly at her blank and empty face.

"You're afraid, are you not? Of facing someone who can actually reach you? Actually, harm you? That's why you leave it to us to fight him for you?"

Aidiel still said nothing.

"Well, your holiness... I need you to do something for me. Stay afraid. I want you to go back to your hiding spot and watch as we kill your nephew. When he is defeated by my own hand, humanity will see you as an enemy because of your inaction. Then... one day... humanity will rise to the point where we can touch you. Where we can harm you. Until that day... be afraid. Humanity will catch up with you. That's the promise of a king."

Everyone in the room was completely speechless and mortified of the audacity of Sargon. How can someone have the courage to say such heinous words to the goddess that created them? It was abhorrent!

Aidiel stared down at Sargon with her empty and blank face. Her six wings curled inwards, the eyeballs on her feathered wings stared at him. Without a face to look at, it was nearly impossible to tell what Aidiel was thinking or feeling. She stared at Sargon before finally spreading her wings and leaving in a flash of light without uttering a single word. Everyone in the room stared at Sargon, who simply stared back at them. They could not even fathom what they had witnessed just now.

Sargon broke the silence. "Pray to your goddess. I care not how you waste your time. I must speak to my troops. The armies of Zithoss are fast approaching and I have a war to win."

Sargon left the meeting hall through the large icy doors and closed them behind him, leaving the room with nothing but the lingering cold air.

"What... what just happened?"

"Well, young lass... we just witnessed the rage and arrogance of humanity firsthand."

"It was rash and insane for that buffoon to act in such an unruly manner. The goddess was gracious enough to give us these weapons made of pure light... and he chose to spit in her face instead of falling at her feet."

"I... I know that humans were supposed to be kind of mean and untrusting but... that was the Mother. That was everyone's mom right there. He just threatened to kill her. It just seems... wrong," said Lyra as she carefully observed the two daggers she got from Aidiel.

"I have lived for a long time, my friends. In that time, I have seen many generations of humans live and die. Out of all of the creatures in Harmonia, humans have some of the shortest lifespans among us. They have a hunger for knowledge that outweighs all of our own combined and the progress they have made is staggering. Some of the weapons they have created are pure genius and I would not be surprised if they outdid themselves in the years to come. Some would even say humans are the smartest of the races... yet I disagree. Their unwillingness to cooperate and their hostilities and biases get in the way of them making true progress," said Lady Voxis as she gently caressed her new crystal armor.

"I have heard this before... humans end up making the same mistakes over and over again... because they don't live long enough to see the patterns," Lyra interjected.

"Exactly, young one. I urge everyone to please heed my words. Even though it continues to be... unendingly difficult to work with the humans, it would be wise to try to cooperate with them to the best of our ability. Despite their rude demeanor, hostile personalities, and isolationist mindset, they have accomplished what none of us have been able to do. Steal the Gauntlet of the Overlord from Zithoss himself. Not only that, but they have managed to somehow improve on it as well."

"This is what I don't understand. How can humans improve on an all-powerful artifact crafted by the gods themselves? It makes no sense!"

"Humans are indeed strange, but also resourceful. It doesn't help that they don't share their secrets and methods with us. I still yearn for the day that human knowledge can be added to the great elven libraries."

Suddenly, the ground started to shake. A loud rumbling could be felt across the entire castle and the lands outside. An echoing voice could be heard in the air, chanting.

This instantly made Voxis and the rest of the table jump up in a panic as they recognized the chanting instantly.

"HE IS CASTING THE SPELL AGAIN! GET EVERYONE INSIDE! NOW!"

Voxis ran to the window as fast as she could and let out a thundering voice echoing across the icy valley of dragons.

"EVERYONE GET INSIDE, QUICK! THIS IS A DIRECT ORDER FROM YOUR QUEEN!"

Once the civilians of all races that were hiding in the valley heard the chant, panic started to spread quickly. It was Zithoss with his chant of death. A powerful spell only available to him. Able to instantly kill anything within a large radius and bring them back from the dead as his undead warrior slaves. He chanted the spell every time before he would attack. The world was lucky that he had to wait for several days before using the spell again.

All manner of creatures, even dragons, ran in a panic towards the safety of the castle, where the spell would not reach them. From the windows, a large tidal wave of black fog started rolling towards the castle and the valley. The ones that were too slow to reach the castle instantly died and fell to the ground, lifeless. Voxis watched with pain as two of her dragons were not able to make it back. She watched as the dragon's bodies slowly started to twitch to life and move.

Suddenly, Voxis's eyes filled wide with horror as she remembered something. "THE NESTS!"

She started pushing everyone aside as she ran through the castle to find a window where she could see the nests. She knew that she couldn't leave the castle until the powerful chant ended. She would die if she did. She reached a window, hoping a dragon would be able to salvage the eggs before the fog rolled in, but it was too late. All the eggs had started to crack and falling out of them were undeveloped dragon fetuses drooling blood and covered in egg white. Voxis's eyes filled with tears and horror as the tiny fetuses were made into the undead. They uselessly squirmed and crawled around, trying to bite and kill anything near them.

Voxis returned to the meeting room to see all of the other guests watching through the windows as they saw the fog dissipate and the armies of Zithoss approached. She heard footsteps behind her and turned around to see it was Sargon.

"The time has come. Let us go."

Sargon turned to leave and speak to his forces before the battle would commence.

Sargon stood in front of his forces. A small number of knights and able-bodied peasants. The rest of the humans were not able to fight due to sickness, age or because their bodies were unfit for combat. A small force of elves, dwarves, werewolves, and dragons was all that was left. All the other kingdoms have been damaged so badly that the survivors were unable to fight and had to take refuge in Queen Voxis's castle.

All of the kings and queens that were gathered began their speeches to prepare their soldiers before the battle started.

King Firebeard held up his crystal Warhammer for all of his dwarven soldiers to see. "With de power of the Goddess Aidiel on our side, we shan't fail! We will crush the skulls of the undead to a fine powder an' light the future for our kin! May our forges never grow cold and our mines stay ever rich!"

"HUZAAAH!"

King Tarron stepped forward and addressed his elves. He held his crystal trident in the air above his head. "The enemy is large and mighty, but we must have faith now! With Goddess Aidiel on our side, we have nothing to fear! My brave elves, we must support our friends in battle. Rain down powerful magic to burn our enemies and heal our friends! Let the sky rain down with our arrows to skewer the enemy."

"HEAR, HEAR!"

Queen Lyra of the werewolves stepped forward with her two crystal daggers. "Alright guys! I just got knives from a goddess and I am going to use them to stab Zithoss in his stupid face! The enemy is the prey and we are the predators! Rip them apart and scatter their bones so nobody can ever find them!"

Her werewolves howled and cheered.

Lady Voxis calmly stepped forward. All of the dragon soldiers were currently in their human forms so they could fit amongst their allies in battle. Voxis was wearing the crystal armor she had been given by Aidiel. She took a deep breath and spoke to her people.

"This will not be an easy battle. Many of us will perish. But now we have hope. Use me as your shield. This armor will not only protect me but also the ones who use me for cover. I shall protect as many of you as possible. We must rain down fire and ice from the skies and use our powerful magic to end this fight as quickly as possible. Let us avenge our sons, daughters, wives, and husbands as soon as possible… we will make this monster pay for everything he has done."

"TO VICTORY!"

King Sargon walked back and forth as he addressed his soldiers. A fire burned in his eyes unlike any other. A raging flame that refused to stand down or surrender under any circumstances. As he watched his soldiers stand at attention, he made a fist with the Overlord's Gauntlet.

"Defeat is not an option. Today, we are about to make history. We are going to kill a god amongst men. We are going to use his own weapon against him and bring humanity back to where it rightfully belongs. We fight for our children. We fight for our homes. We fight for justice. We fight for glory. We will fight so that one day our future generations can look back on this day with pride. Failure is unacceptable."

"YES SIR!"

"Then… let us proceed towards our destiny."

As the doors to the castle opened, the five armies came together in unison, ready for the final battle with Zithoss. As the armies stood ready at the gates, the faint sound of marching and demonic chanting could be heard from the distance. The undead that were created by Zithoss's spell stand there like statues, waiting for their master to approach. Voxis felt sick just looking at them. Motionless corpses standing straight and staring at them with unblinking eyes. The moment the spell hit them, parts of their body had started to rot away.

One could see some of their bones and muscles. Maggots and bugs were already crawling over their body.

Firebeard pointed towards the distance. "Look 'ere! I think I see somefin'!"

On the other side of the battlefield was a large icy hill where two undead trolls were carrying the throne of Zithoss himself. Zithoss was dressed in his red robe and his hood was up. Most of his face was hidden because of the hood, but even from the other side of the battlefield, his glowing red eyes and antler-like horns could be seen. His hands were skinny and had paper-thin skin with a greenish-brown tinge to it. His claws were long and razor-sharp. Morale started to quickly plummet as more and more undead started to gather. All together there may only be thirty thousand soldiers left in the alliance of the five kingdoms. Zithoss's army must run into millions. Dragons, werewolves, humans, elves, dwarves, and the undead of so many other kinds of races and monsters are all gathered.

"This… this is madness. There… there are so many of them. How… how is this possible?"

"So much for faith in your goddess, elf. I have prepared for this moment. I know what I must do. READY, MEN?! DEFENSIVE FORMATIONS! PREPARE THE CATAPULTS AND BALLISTAS!"

The humans on the top of the castle armed the siege weapons that had been recently invented.

Zithoss slowly pointed his finger towards the enemy. He has grown arrogant and full of himself. Constant victory after constant victory. He does not know failure. Even though the humans had managed to steal his gauntlet, it serves them no purpose. He only used it to speed up the process of him collecting souls and to easily give orders to his undead legion. It does not matter to him. Surely, he can win with numbers alone.

"CHARGE!"

"FIRE!"

Without warning, massive arrows and giant boulders were shot at incredible speeds towards the now advancing undead army. Undead dragons were knocked out of the sky and smaller units were being crushed under the weight. Zithoss was taken aback. What kind of weaponry was this? Before he had a moment to ponder further, a massive boulder was being hurled towards him by the catapult. Zithoss simply held up his finger and the boulder froze mid-flight. All were stunned by his power.

"How powerful of a magic-caster is that monster? He doesn't even need to utter the name of the spell?"

"And despite using such a weak levitation spell, he was able to stop a boulder moving at such a high speed. How can one use such a weak levitation spell in such a manner?" Tarron added.

Zithoss opened his mouth and whispered, "Rot."

The entire boulder turned to dust. The army of Harmonia was quickly losing morale, seeing the complete magical dominance of Zithoss firsthand.

"DON'T LOSE YOURSELVES IN THE MOMENT! FIGHT!" Sargon screamed as he held up the Gauntlet of the Overlord. The gauntlet's eye opened and started looking around. Sargon's eyes started to glow red and soon all the soldiers' eyes started to glow as well.

Zithoss sat forward in his throne with surprise. "They figured out how to use my gauntlet? How can a mortal use such an artifact for themselves? This is actually starting to become interesting now."

All the soldiers on the battlefield, regardless of their race or species, started to fall under the influence of the gauntlet. They started snarling and foaming from the mouths, soon having all fear and doubt leave them in an instant. All that remained was the desire to win and destroy.

Firebeard looked on with horror as he watched his soldiers start to act like wild animals, viciously starting to rip apart and smash the enemy. "What have ye done to them!?"

"I shared it."

"What are ye talkin' bout?! Speak, dammit!"

"I shared my desire for revenge and victory with all of our soldiers. They were losing morale… I won't have it."

"Are ya bloody mad, mate?! They need to surrender if it comes to that! You're dooming them all to die!"

"I already told you, dwarf. I won't lose."

"WHY YOU?! I'LL RIP YOUR BLOODY HEAD OFF!"

Firebeard tried to run and tackle Sargon but he was pushed back. Some kind of barrier was protecting him now.

"What the… how in the—"

"Are you going to try and stop our victory? Or are you going to use those weapons you cared so much about? I need more enemy casualties for my plan to work. So, get to killing already."

"I can't believe I am saying this, but I agree with Sargon. The glorious Aidiel has granted us these weapons to harm Zithoss. We know normal weapons will work but they are not as effective. This is our chance."

"Fine… let's go."

As the kings run to get to the battle, Lady Voxis jumped out of the window of the castle and changed into her true form. A massive blue ice dragon. Her body was so massive that she was about the size of five normal dragons. She was in her crystal armor given to her by Aidiel. She swooped down and blasted a current of icy breath down on the enemy, freezing hundreds in a moment. Although she destroyed so many with a single attack, it all seemed fruitless with the sheer number of enemies she was facing right now. Hundreds of arrows all shot at Voxis, but they were uselessly destroyed against Aidiel's crystal armor.

RAMPAGE: THE RISE OF AN EMPIRE

Two undead dragons flew right into Voxis and one of them bit down on her with their razor-sharp teeth, but the armor was so strong that the only thing that broke was the jaw of the undead dragon, snapping and uselessly hanging downward. This did not kill the zombified dragon, however, only enraging it and making it continue its attack against her. Voxis used her massive size to her advantage and swatted away one of the dragons with her tail. Three more undead dragons swooped down to attack Voxis, but the massive bolts of the ballistae shot down the dragons mid-flight and saved Voxis.

From behind the castle, a flock of ally dragons took to the sky and flew over the battlefield to bombard the ocean of undead warriors with fire and ice.

Zithoss slowly raised his hand and with a flick of his wrist cast a spell. "Burn"

The power of Zithoss's spells was too powerful to fathom. He was the supreme magic caster. Not only that, but he was able to use some of the most powerful spells ever conceived with complete ease and only by saying a single word. Nearly no one was able to use the powerful spells that the lich used, but the few that could have would have to prepare with several supporting casters and it would take several minutes to cast correctly.

A massive flaming tornado erupted from the ground in response to Zithoss's spell. It killed and roasted several ally dragons, leaving their charred corpses on the ground. Some would think the fire dragons would be able to survive this, but this fire was unlike dragon fire. It was a strange grey flame that existed outside the laws of nature. As the dragons started to die, Zithoss attempted to take the souls from the dragons. Dragons have the most powerful souls of any living creature in Harmonia. The amount of magika inside a dragon soul is immense.

Suddenly, Zithoss watched as the souls were being absorbed by someone else. It was Sargon! Zithoss had killed over two dozen dragons and now Sargon was taking the souls for himself. Zithoss angrily slammed his fist against the side of his throne. Even if Sargon was unable to use those souls, he was depriving Zithoss himself of them.

"Burn!"

"FRIGID HURRICANE!"

For the first time in a long, long time, Zithoss was truly struck dumb. He could not believe what was happening. A human used the gauntlet to replicate his magic?

The two spells collided with each other and canceled each other out in a massive explosion that shook the battlefield. Zithoss slowly stood up from his throne and stared down at Sargon who stared back.

"Fog!"

A massive tidal wave of black fog rolled in from the mountains and started covering the entire battlefield and castle. All the living started choking and dying from the poisonous fog, but the power of the gauntlet allowed them to continue pushing forward with their battle rage and lust.

"BREATH OF THE GODS!"

A titanic gust of wind started to blow away all the fog. Zithoss growled. He started speaking in a strange, ancient language that echoed across the battlefield.

All the undead started to go into some kind of frenzy as they charged towards the castle. Sargon held up the gauntlet to give orders to his troops.

"They are aiming for the castle. Protect it at all costs."

All the alliance troops slowly retreated to better protect the castle. Voxis was racking up a body count in the thousands now. She was an amazing warrior and the size of her body was an excellent aid in crushing the enemy. Of course, body count was not always a good thing while fighting a lich. The more undead soldiers and living soldiers were destroyed, the more souls were up for grabs between Zithoss and Sargon.

The doors of the castle slowly started to open. Firebeard, Tarron, and Lyra have finally arrived. Sargon sent orders with the gauntlet.

"We must destroy Zithoss NOW! Everyone else must protect the castle and the civilians inside at ALL COSTS!"

The moment the castle gates opened, the horde of undead charged as fast as they could towards the gate. The alliance soldiers under the influence of the gauntlet charged as well with a bloodlust unlike any other seen before. Pure rage and anger weaponized into fighting spirit and morale. The soldiers became more combat-focused, more deadly and more willing to sacrifice everything if it meant victory.

The two armies clashed right outside the castle. The gauntlet-controlled soldiers were incredibly efficient and kept on fighting no matter what. Even with arrows sticking out of their bodies or large chunks of their flesh missing they continued to fight. Did they feel pain? No. The rage of Sargon was being spread to all the troops through the gauntlet. They were too enraged to care about the pain right now. Too enraged to allow themselves to feel famished and tired. All their minds were put to a single goal. Destroy the enemy. They will push their bodies to the absolute limit in order to have this victory, even if it puts themselves at risk of death.

The empowered troops were successfully cutting down the undead and with the help of the gauntlet, their numbers were not falling as quickly. Still though, normal weapons were not very effective against the undead. It took several mighty and empowered swings of their iron weapons to destroy the skeletons and zombies.

The royals took their opportunity. Firebeard took a desperate charge right through the enemy lines. Lyra moved with lightning speed, flipping over one of her soldiers and diving right into the front lines of the undead. She swung her crystal daggers and watched in astonishment as the knives slashed through the necromantic bones like water. The skeleton was instantly destroyed.

"These weapons are amazing! Keep up, you old geezers!"

Firebeard roared as he charged right through the skeletons and smashed their bones with ease using his new hammer. "Don't be callin' me an old geezer, ya pup! I've been itchin' for a fight all night and now's me opportunity!"

Flying above the both of them was Voxis who blasted her powerful icy breath across the battlefield. The sky flashed with incredible colors as Zithoss and Sargon exchanged mighty spell after mighty spell. Explosions and blasts filled the sky nonstop as the battle continued to rage on from the ground.

Tarron moved with astonishing speed despite his old age and cut through the enemy with ease. His eyes locked on to Zithoss, who was distracted with the magical tug-of-war he was having with Sargon.

"IGNORE THE TROOPS! THE MORE YOU KILL THE STRONGER HE CAN GET! WE NEED TO DESTROY THIS FOE NOW!"

Lyra nodded and started running over the heads of the skeletons, hopping upon one after the other until she got closer to Zithoss.

Firebeard called out to Voxis. "Lady Voxis! Give us a lift, will ye?"

Voxis dived downwards and grabbed Tarron and Firebeard, but several other undead warriors climbed up as well, sticking their swords into her massive body to haul themselves up. She roared as the undead climbed up her body and she wildly shook around. She shook off several of them, but a dozen or so were still able to reach her back and began to attack the two kings. Six skeletons moved to the left and the other six moved to the right.

"Ye take the left and I'll take the right."

RAMPAGE: THE RISE OF AN EMPIRE

Firebeard charged towards the right and slammed into three skeletons. He swung his mighty warhammer and crushed one of the skeletons' skulls to dust. While making the swing, he accidentally left himself open enough for a skeleton to stab him in his side. He let out a grunt of pain and retaliated by headbutting the skeleton with his thick skull. He then wound up his body and swung his hammer, smashing into two undead skeletons and sending their broken bodies airborne. Before he could control the momentum of the warhammer, he got stabbed again. He let out a mighty war cry as he body-slammed a skeleton and then smashed its head in. He finished by winding up his swing one more time and decimating the last two skeletons.

Tarron moved with a lightning speed and expertly dodged several attacks. He lunged towards a skeleton and cut right through his body. He then landed on the side of one of Voxis's spikes and jumped off it to lunge once again. His undead adversaries started to adapt and dodged this time. Tarron didn't quit and bounced off another spike only for it to backfire this time. One of the skeletons grabbed onto his long white beard and used his claws to dig into the flesh of his chest. Tarron let out a yelp of pain and rolled on Voxis's back. He squinted, took aim, and threw his trident. Catching three of the skeletons off guard, it went through all three of them and cracked their bones as easily as a chicken's egg. Tarron jumped high into the air using his elven agility and grabbed the hilt of the trident mid-jump. He then grabbed the trident and started to swing it as he was falling. When he landed, his slash went through both the skeletons, cutting them straight in half.

"Ye did well for an elf," panted Firebeard.

"I can say the same for you, my dwarven friend."

"There is no time for idle chat! Zithoss has caught whiff of our plan!" said Voxis as she saw Zithoss turn his head towards them and lift up his hand. Voxis tried to steer out of the way but it was too late.

"Fall."

It felt as if every single muscle in Voxis's body was on fire. She couldn't move a single inch and started falling out of the sky, plummeting with an increasing speed. With a mighty boom, Voxis landed on the ground on top of hundreds of the undead. She roared in pain as hundreds of claws, bones, and swords stabbed into her side in areas not covered by her new armor. Tarron and Firebeard were flung off Voxis and slammed into the ground. Lyra was quick to arrive at their location after she saw Voxis. She dragged Firebeard and Tarron behind her and took a defensive stance as she was being surrounded by the enemy.

"Come on, you old losers! You have to get up! Please! We can't lose now! Not… not after everything!"

Dozens of undead skeletons started to surround her. Lyra trembled a little before composing herself. She looked behind her to see how Voxis, Tarron, and Firebeard were doing.

"Please! Please get up! We are almost there!"

Suddenly, the sound of Zithoss's chanting could be heard over the noises of the battle.

The skeletons charged towards her and Lyra did everything she could to protect her allies. With precision she slid through enemy attacks and parried with deadly stabs and slashes. For every ten enemies she could destroy, at least one would be able to slip past her defenses and stab her. Lyra continued slashing and stabbing, again and again and again until she was barely able to stand up. She held one of her daggers close to her as the horde closed in on them. Lyra felt tears run down her face.

"A… Aidiel… p… p… please, help us… I… I… d… don't want to die."

There was no response.

"AIDIEL, PLEASE!"

An arrow flew right into Lyra's shoulder and she fell to the ground. Voxis coughed up blood and used her wing to try and pull out the hundreds of sharp objects stuck in her side. She protectively covered her allies with her wing, ready to feel a great amount of pain until suddenly...

"VOLCANIC BLAST!"

A massive blast of lava erupted from the ground, melting the enemies closing in around them. King Sargon was levitating over them and slowly landed on the ground. He turned to look at them and then towards Zithoss, who was now closer than ever before. He was staring right at them.

"I will not be stricken down by failure because of the incompetence of my allies. You will follow me in a direct charge towards Zithoss."

Lyra was shaking and spit up some blood. "W... we can't... we're hurt."

"The gauntlet is locked off from the magic of Aidiel. I can't heal you. Voxis... can you?"

Voxis could barely move. She looked at Sargon and motioned towards the castle, where the elves were still casting healing spells from the top of the castle along with the ballistae and catapults.

"I shall return soon. Lyra... everything is in your hands now. Keep them alive. I am going to bring some elves here and they can heal you."

"I... I'm scared. I... I don't want to die."

Sargon was annoyed, but he understood the situation. Lyra was forced to be queen because her mother and father had died. All she had ever done was lead small raiding operations against the smaller forts that Zithoss made around Harmonia. It was only a matter of time before the adrenaline and fake bravado wore off and fear and the realization of the situation settled in. He understood she was young. A young adult, but still a child on the inside. He wanted to comfort her, but he couldn't waste time. She was either an ally or an obstacle and he couldn't waste time on the field of battle. He refused to fail because of the weakness of others.

Sargon stared down at her. His eyes were cold and unforgiving. It was as if he were staring directly into her soul and judging her worth.

"Then die."

"W... what?"

"Die like a dog in the street. You will be forgotten and just be a cobblestone in the path of my victory. If you don't want to die, then pick up your blade and hold out for a few more minutes. Just know that if you give up, you give up on Harmonia and doom us all."

Lyra shakily picked up the dagger with tears in her eyes. When Sargon looked at her, all he could see was a scared girl. He reached his hand out, wanting to comfort her, but realization kicked in. His desire to destroy Zithoss was stronger than anything else.

"Fly!"

He clenched his hand into a fist and flew away towards the castle. Lyra was left alone with her three unconscious allies bleeding slowly to death on the floor. Lyra watched the lava bubbling around her. She saw the skeletons on the other side blankly staring at her like sharks, waiting for their prey to come out of hiding. The ring was small. Enough for Tarron, Firebeard, and her to be safe, but Voxis was obviously too large. Only a part of her head was safely in the ring. Her neck was not burned by the lava because of Aidiel's armor.

Lyra's eyes went wide as she watched the skeletons start to climb up Voxis's body and use her neck as a bridge in order to get inside the ring of lava. She shakily lifted her dagger and held it out at them.

"I... want to live... I want to live... I WANT TO LIVE!"

As Lyra charged towards the advancing undead, Zithoss watched with great interest. Soon his soldiers would have killed the remaining royals and all he had to do was stop Sargon.

Zithoss lifted his hand and pointed his finger towards Sargon. "Kill him!"

Undead dragons flew directly towards Sargon. Sargon stopped in his tracks and turned around as the dragons started to fly around him. He looked at his gauntlet. He did not have much power left. If he could kill these dragons, he would be able to use their souls. He needed to act wisely. Zithoss was still on a victory high. He thought it was impossible for him to lose this battle right now. He had already conquered all of Harmonia and now there is but a small army left for him to crush. His numbers were near unlimited and he had access to some of the most powerful undead troops and magic that this world has ever known. He needed to use that to his advantage.

Sargon charged up his gauntlet as he was flying backwards towards the castle. A dragon spread its wings and charged towards Sargon.

"FIST OF THUNDER!"

His entire gauntlet was smothered with large electric bolts and with it he punched the undead dragon's head so hard it exploded. The lifeless body of the dragon fell to the ground and he quickly absorbed its soul before Zithoss had the chance to do so.

"Struggle as much as you want, little ants. My victory is inevitable."

As two more dragons swooped in, the catapults launched just in time and were able to knock both the dragons out of the sky. One of the dragons whipped Sargon with his mighty tail before he was knocked out of the sky. Sargon was shot back with incredible speed and slammed against the icy exterior of Voxis's castle. He spit up blood and felt as if several of his ribs had smashed.

Elves rushed to him and helped him stand up.

As they rushed him off, Sargon struggled. "No, you fools! Heal me quickly and then come with me! We need to heal the others so we can finish this!"

Lyra was in bad shape. She was holding off the enemy barrage of arrows being fired over the lava as she was also fighting off the skeletons using Voxis's body as a bridge. Lyra fell backwards and scooted away as the skeletons were almost about to get inside the lava circle.

Lyra looked at her daggers. These weapons were incredibly effective against the undead, able to kill them with complete ease, but she was about to die soon. In complete desperation, she dropped the daggers and allowed herself to change her form. Her body started to crack and pop into different positions. Hair started to grow all over her body into a thick and powerful hide. Her nails grew into claws that were several inches long. Lyra's eyes became a thick and dark yellow color with focused and intense pupils. Her back arched and her legs bent into the shape of an animal's. Emerging from her back was a bushy tail. Lyra slowly stood up on her hind legs and let out a roar so mighty it pushed back the enemy slightly. In her werewolf form, she felt more confident.

A volley of arrows shot at Lyra, but her hide was so thick that the arrows simply stuck out of her thick fur and didn't penetrate her flesh. She let out a ferocious roar and charged at the skeletons on all four limbs. Her attacks were full of mighty strength and ferocity. She effortlessly threw around enemies like they were nothing. Her powerful claws dug into the bones of the skeletons, but they seemed unfazed. Her claws were not destroying them as quickly like the dagger was able to. She kept slashing at the head of one of the skeletons until finally she was able to destroy it. She had made a tactical sacrifice. She couldn't fight off the enemy and destroy them as easily now, but in return her defenses and survivability had gone up significantly.

Lyra pounced on another enemy and then kicked them into the lava that was surrounding them. Her massive arms were able to swat away enemies like flies, but she was starting to become overwhelmed by their numbers. Lyra was trying her best to dodge attacks and keep them away from Firebeard and Tarron. One skeleton was able to jump on Lyra's back and started hacking at her with its axe. He was able to dig the rusty blade deep into Lyra's shoulder. She let out an enraged howl and threw the skeleton off of her and into the lava.

Lyra was being pushed back as more and more skeletons started to pile on top of her. She felt cold and rusty metal stab into her flesh again and again and again. Voxis started to stir and came back to consciousness. She moaned in pain as she opened her mouth and unleashed a blast of icy breath. The skeletons were frozen instantly and Lyra started pushing them into the lava.

From the sky, Sargon levitated down with several elven healers who instantly ran to the aid of the royalty and started healing them. Voxis started pulling out the dozens of weapons and bones impaled in her side as Tarron and Firebeard came back to consciousness.

Sargon started to speak to them as they recovered. "Listen closely. Zithoss is underestimating us. He thinks this fight is impossible for him to lose. We need to prove him wrong. He will most likely start this fight going easy on us for his own amusement. We need to use that against him to earn an advantage right at the start of the fight. This fight means everything. We can't fail now. Let's go."

Sargon helped his companions back on their feet and stared up at Zithoss, who was still sitting on his throne on top of the hill to watch over the battle. Sargon used the gauntlet to start levitating off the ground and flew towards Zithoss. Voxis slowly stood up once she was healed to the best of the elves' ability and shakily spread her wings. Lyra, Tarron, and Firebeard all ran in the direction of Zithoss. Lyra turned into her human form again and grabbed her daggers.

As the group ran towards Zithoss, who was staring down at them with great interest, several more powerful undead ran in front of them. Lyra slid under the legs of an undead troll and stabbed her daggers into the troll's back. She then used the daggers to climb up its back and stabbed the large zombie in the neck several times until it collapsed.

Voxis sent icy breath down towards Zithoss but the lich simply flicked his hand and sent the attack directly back at Voxis. Luckily for Voxis, she was an ice dragon and so her own attack did nothing to her.

Firebeard tackled an undead werewolf and smashed its legs with his hammer. The undead werewolf squirmed around, trying to slash Firebeard, but he took his mighty hammer and smashed the monster's head in.

Tarron clashed with an undead knight in heavy armor. He flipped over the knight and started casting spells.

"FLASH THUNDER!"

A powerful blast of blue lightning shot from his fingers and slammed into the knight. Then while the large knight was stunned, he decapitated him with a clean and precise cut.

The group of five arrived on top of the hill where Zithoss was waiting. Beside the throne were two more undead skeleton knights in black armor. Resting on the side of his throne was an intimidating blade, Oblivion. Zithoss was dressed in a red robe made for royalty. It had several rips in it and it seemed to be incredibly old.

Zithoss slowly lifted up his red hood to fully reveal his face. His head was skull-like in appearance with old mummified skin covering it. His mouth was full of razor-sharp fangs and the top of his head had two large antler-like horns. His two glowing red eyes stared at the five royals.

"And so the ants have gathered up enough courage to face me. A last desperate push to save Harmonia. All you have done is doom your people. Look for yourselves," Zithoss said as he lifted his hand and pointed towards the castle.

They turned around to see that the castle was almost fully overrun. The defenses and infantry were almost fully gone. The only reason the castle had not been taken over yet was the elven spell casters, catapults, and ballistae on top of the castle. Sargon clenched his fist and turned around.

"This is over. Today, you are going to die. I will personally cut your head off and stick it on a pike."

"Ye are gonna pay fer everythin' you did!"

"So many innocent lives taken by your greed and madness. It will end tonight."

"YOU SHALL PAY FOR THE DEATHS OF MY CHILDREN AND CITIZENS, YOU WORM!"

"You took my parents… I shall bring honor to my wolfkin and make you suffer!"

"You can try."

Zithoss flicked his finger at them and a massive invisible force knocked them back. Lyra moved with an incredible speed towards Zithoss and went for the neck, but she slammed into an invisible shield. She slid back and gripped her knives tightly.

Firebeard jumped into the air and sent his hammer slamming down on Zithoss, for it to once again do nothing thanks to the strange invisible shield. Tarron jumped high into the air and sent fireballs raining down towards Zithoss, but he swatted them away with ease. Voxis let a powerful current of icy magic breath slam into Zithoss, but he simply held up his hand and deflected the blast.

"How do we stop him?!"

"Nothin' we be doin' is workin' at all!"

"Calm yourselves! We attack all at once! NOW! FIST OF THUNDER!"

Overlord's Gauntlet was enveloped in electricity and he gave the invisible shield a mighty punch that cracked it. Before Zithoss could even react, others coordinated their attacks with Sargon and the shield shattered.

Zithoss stood from his throne. "Those weapons... I can smell my aunt on them. So... she has decided to have pity on you all?" Zithoss lifted his sword from the side of his throne and motioned to two skeletal knights standing guard near him. "She is more of a desperate fool than I could have ever imagined. I'll need you all to hand over those weapons."

"You are more crazy than I thought if you think we are going to hand these over! I will stop you for what you did to my mom and dad!" yelled Lyra

"You can try, but you will surely fail. I have been waiting for this opportunity for a long time. I will not allow this moment to be stolen from me now. This fight is impossible for you all to win. I didn't even need to bring my generals to this fight. I wished to see the end for myself. I won't have it any other way. So come hither, if you dare."

All of the royals attacked at once. Sargon made an overhead swing with his sword, Tarron slid to the side and stabbed with his trident, Firebeard slid to the other side and swung his hammer, Lyra threw her daggers and Voxis blew out a powerful blast of icy flame. Zithoss raised his blade and clashed with Sargon, but he started to get overwhelmed by all the attacks coming towards him at once. Though his body was thin and frail, normal weapons were very ineffective against him, just like the rest of the undead he controlled, but Aidiel's weapons dealt incredible damage to him. He felt Lyra's dagger slice into his mummified rotting skin and he snarled. Despite his skinny body, he had incredible strength. He backhanded Lyra and sent her flying ten feet backward.

Zithoss let out a hiss as he levitated from the ground and sent lightning bolts shooting from his hands. The lightning electrocuted all five of them and pushed them back. He then sent the two knights standing by his throne to attack them. Sargon lifted the gauntlet and made a shield of rock to protect his allies. Tarron and Firebeard jump towards the right and battled one knight. The knight took a large two-handed swing with its great sword towards Tarron. Tarron expertly flipped over the sword strike and countered with a fireball and slammed into the knight, making him fly backward. As the knight flew back, he slammed right into Firebeard's hammer that smashed the side of his head. The knight then grabbed Firebeard and slammed him into the ground. The large armored undead stomped on Firebeard's stomach and was about to run him through with his sword. Just in the knick of time, Firebeard was saved by Tarron, who threw his mighty trident and pinned the knight to Zithoss's throne, giving Firebeard enough time to smash the knight's head.

As Lyra and Voxis fought against the other knight, Sargon shot Zithoss with a powerful shard of ice from his palm.

Zithoss smashed the shard of ice with his own magic and clenched his fists. "This has been entertaining… but now… you shall all die. My victory is inevitable and your castle with the last remaining living is about to fall."

Lyra had just finished off the knight who was frozen in a block of ice by Voxis. She gritted her teeth hearing Zithoss talk and jumped on top of the frozen knight, using it to boost her next jump. She landed on Zithoss's back and continued to stab him in the back over and over again. He let out an enraged growl of pain and grabbed Lyra by the throat. He slashed her in the gut with his claws and threw her to the ground. She started coughing up blood but forced herself to stand up again.

Zithoss was shaking a little. He had been stabbed several times by Lyra and each stab wound hurt more than he imagined it would. Pain was not something he was used to anymore. Without even being able to steady himself, he was already under attack once again. Firebeard slammed Zithoss on his head, cracking one of his bones. Tarron lunged at him but he countered with a thunderbolt, making the elf fly back. Tarron's body was burned and he was wheezing with pain. Lyra stabbed Zithoss again, but he grabbed her wrist and twisted it until her arm bent backward, making her scream in pain. Voxis roared and let out a beam of pure concentrated magika from her mouth. The beam grazed Zithoss, making him roar, but he quickly deflected it and burned a hole right through Voxis's chest. She let out a terrifying cry of pain and collapsed. Despite falling back down she refused to stop attacking Zithoss and continued to slow him down with a stream of icy breath. Morale was at an all-time high. After months and years of not being able to leave a scratch on the lich, they were finally able to hurt him. This was their final chance.

Zithoss was being pushed back with every new strain of attacks linked together by the allied royals. Each attack ended with one of them becoming more and more injured, but bringing Zithoss closer to his final defeat. For every attack he landed on one of the royals, he was hit three more times from being outnumbered. Every time he tried to take them all out at once with a mighty spell, Sargon would nullify the spell with one that was equally powerful, wasting his magika in the process.

Sargon stayed in the back lines, making sure that Zithoss could not cast any more powerful spells that could end the fight quickly. Lyra was on the ground, unable to move from the amount of pain she was in. Her arm was bending in the opposite direction and she was bleeding all over. Voxis was restricting Zithoss's movement with her ice breath to allow her allies to land more hits on him. Firebeard and Tarron continued to land attack after attack, no matter how injured they were.

Zithoss snarled and grabbed Firebeard by the throat. "THIS IS NOT POSSIBLE! YOU MORTAL INSECTS DARE DEFY ME!? I HAVE ALREADY WON! I—"

Before Zithoss could finish speaking, Tarron threw his trident right through Zithoss's body. He let out a weak groan of pain. His body erupted into dust and screaming souls that fluttered away into the sky. Zithoss's sword clattered to the ground and fell in the pile of dust. The moment Zithoss was defeated, every single undead warrior fell to the ground, lifeless. As the battlefield was filled with joyous screams of victory and relief, the royals stayed in silent shock.

Lyra was the first to talk. "Did… did we get him?"

"…Aye… aye, we got 'im all right!"

Tarron collapsed to the ground with exhaustion and Sargon collapsed right next to him.

Voxis shrunk down to her smaller human-like form and let out a breath of relief. "W… we did it… we actually did it."

"This day…. shall go down in history as the greatest fight to have ever been waged… we beat the odds. May the friendship and alliance between our kingdoms never break." Tarron said as he held his hand out.

Lyra crawled over to him with a smile and placed her unbroken hand on his. Firebeard coughed up some blood and smiled as he added his hand as well. Voxis joined in, her face bearing the look of a mother who was playing along with her children's game and was happy to do so. All the others looked at Sargon. The dark-skinned human looked at them and then back to the Overlord's Gauntlet. His eyes looked at it longingly, as if he was about to part with a dear friend. His eyes then moved towards Zithoss's sword.

"L… laddy? What are you doin'?"

Sargon ignored him as he coughed up blood and walked towards the sword. He slowly reached down and struggled to lift the massive sword. It was large, but he was able to hold it with two hands and looked at it with a smile on his face.

"Laddy… put the sword and gauntlet down."

Sargon turned around with a weak smile on his face. He held his gauntlet up and his smile widened. "May we be allies till the day we die…" he said with a smile. "Teleport!"

"NO!"

Voxis screamed as Sargon teleported away to an unknown location, escaping with the Overlord's Gauntlet and the sword of Zithoss, Oblivion.

Ashehera held her trident close to her side and felt her heart pound after hearing the story. The older and now much larger Voxis stared down at her with a look of remembrance and nostalgia in her eye. Ashehera gripped her hand to make it stop shaking and opened her mouth to speak. She found it hard to find the words she was looking for but eventually, she was able to grasp what she wanted to say.

"I… I thought you destroyed him… you said he turned to ash… how… how is he…"

"I do not know. All this time, I thought he had been dead as well… but the power to bring back the dead to do your bidding is a power only a lich has access to."

"T… this is madness… utter madness… that monster has my son… h… how do we fight something so… so… so powerful?!"

"Only the weapons of Aidiel can harm him and his undead. Currently, the Holy State of Aidiel hordes all that relates to her. You must find them. They are the key to saving Harmonia… despite their brutality."

"Brutality?"

"They are a new religious empire forcing their beliefs on others with death and fire. They are heavily disliked by those in the east. They remind me of another empire."

"Hmm… Lady Voxis, I propose an alliance. We need to work together if we are to ever stop Zithoss or whatever lich is going to destroy this world."

"You have harassed our kingdom for ages…"

"YOU SAID IT YOURSELF! THE FATE OF HARMONIA IS AT STAKE! EVERYTHING! MY SON! I will stop all hostilities! We need to work together!"

"I shall think upon it."

Ashehera took a deep breath. She felt like screaming, but she held it in. "I guess that will have to do. I shall seek out the Holy State of Aidiel… it shall be a longer trip than this one. If we are to survive, we must build an alliance even more powerful than the first one. We need to do this to survive."

CHAPTER 14

Several weeks have passed since the annexation of Shimia and Nigt. For the first time in history, the entire Duma Forest has been united under one flag. Goblin, orc, werewolf, and beast are all forced to live together. All across the Duma Empire, undead soldiers of all varieties have secured the borders and act as the guard in towns and villages. Despite Daemos's new soldiers being spread across his new empire, many are still available for battle in the main army.

Many are still traumatized by the bloodshed and destruction that took place weeks ago. Many farms and homes were destroyed by claw and flame inside Nigt. Shimia was lucky since the siege never reached their kingdom. The only real damage in Shimia was in the royal palace during the assassination attempt on Shagar. Mass reparations have been taking place for weeks to repair homes and farms. These have surprisingly been completed at an exceptional rate, thanks to all of Duma's workers and resources working together for one goal. Many were still scared of their new emperor and were wary of his plan to expand their borders, while others were already seeing an improvement in their lives. Now that they were united, all of their ways of life and skills were being used together. The goblins were teaching orcs their advanced farming techniques so that the harsh and volatile environment did not destroy their crops. Orcs no longer have to send their young men and women to die by raiding Whitia and Shimia for food. The werewolves were slightly under-average magic casters when they were not in their bestial forms and now they could teach the goblins and orcs what they were physically capable of. None of the three former kingdoms have to worry about monster attacks anymore, thanks to all of them serving their emperor.

Daemos has been using most of his time finding and controlling more monsters to fill up the loss of numbers from the last war. Casualties were high and he didn't plan on being caught off guard like that ever again. He has been training every day on top of recruiting the beasts, refining his sword play and increasing his collection of powerful spells. If he could eventually learn the necromantic magic of his master, he would become unstoppable.

As the days passed on, Daemos became more and more restless. He could swear that every so often, faint voices were speaking to him in the back of his head, but they were too quiet and muffled to fully make out. Voices crying out in pain, voices loving and calm, voices screaming and filled with rage. Too many to count. None he could understand. They aggravated him. Something about hearing these voices made something boil inside of him and wanted to drive him towards violence.

It was the middle of the night. The full moon shone brightly in the sky. Daemos was overlooking the repairs of the Shimia castle, soon to be his own royal palace. Large trolls carried loads of boulders while others painstakingly chipped away at the stone to shape it into bricks. This process was difficult, but thanks to Gogba's contacts in the dwarven kingdom of Gluth, they have been able to trade the rare resources of the Duma Forest for an abundance of construction tools and gold. As of now, nobody knew that Duma was a united empire except for the royals of Gluth. Gluth was already a valuable trading partner of Whitia before it became the Duma Empire. It changed nothing for Gluth, except that they now had more trade opportunities.

Grindstones and tools chip away at stone with loud clinks and clanks. Daemos paced back and forth, overlooking the construction of the castle when suddenly, he felt a tap on his shoulder.

He turned his head to see Nyana levitating off the ground so she could meet his height. "Yes?"

"I wanted to speak to you about some things."

"As you wish. We might as well speak in private."

The two of them walked into Daemos's new castle. He had developed somewhat of a liking towards the old castle already. According to his subjects, it used to be a castle owned by the vampire kingdom, known as Vojhan, several thousands of years ago. The vampires used to live inside of the Duma Forest but were forced to flee their home after the uprising of the werewolves. The werewolves were subjugated by them and treated as slaves. When the werewolves were victorious, they took the castle for themselves and made it their own capital.

Daemos liked the ancient gothic aesthetic of his new palace, but after being under the control of werewolves for so long, they had made the inside more… primal for his tastes. He would see to it that the inside of his castle would be proper for an overlord in time. In the corner of the throne room was Chindi, eating a large elk by violently ripping into its flesh.

Daemos sat down on his throne, another thing he intended to fix in the future and placed Oblivion next to his throne, leaning against the wall. Chindi sat down next to Daemos's throne with blood all over her face and intestines hanging out of her mouth.

"Now we may speak in peace. What is it that you would like to discuss with me?"

"First, we talk business. I must admit I am impressed. I would have expected you would jump in and try to attack the elves the moment you won."

"I still want to... but now is not the time."

"I know. Listen to me. Your empire..."

"Our empire... you're crucial in this as well."

"...Our?" Nyana was thoroughly taken aback.

"Is that not what I said? I don't intend to keep the spoils for myself. You have been a valuable ally."

"Thanks... I already knew you were helpless without me, but if you're trying to butter me up this much, then you must be truly hopeless... but thank you nonetheless. Ahem, now, yo— our empire is going to expand more and more. In that time, there is going to be friction with the leadership. It's impossible to govern over all of Duma by ourselves. We need kings. Ones that are powerful and loyal to us. Ones capable of taking charge while we are expanding our territory."

"You're right. I think Whitia is already taken care of. Fena is an exceptional choice fo—"

"No, Daemos, you're thinking too small. If we divide the leaders into the previously existing borders, that will only cause more friction and even the possibility of civil war. No, we need ONE king for the forest. Right now, the dwarves are having a civil war and are split into three kingdoms. When we defeat them, we would need ONE dwarf king so that the same problem doesn't happen again."

"...Of course. Then I know what we must do. We will call out to find suitable candidates for the role. Then we will find ourselves a king for the forest. Once the forest is properly secured and restored, we will continue our conquest."

Daemos sent word out across Duma that he was in search of a king. Many were surprised by this. In Whitia, Nigt, and Shimia it was all decided by royal blood. Now any of them could have the chance to become royalty. Many rushed to avail the opportunity. Many were turned down. In the end, only three made it to the final pick to be king. After the tireless trials and tribulations of picking amongst the three candidates, it was finally time. All three candidates for the new King of Duma arrived one by one into Daemos's throne room. To the left of his throne was Nyana, who was leaning against the wall and to the right of his throne was Chindi, who gnashed her fangs. Black infected sludge dripped from her mouth.

The first candidate was Fena. She was the only candidate that had been personally requested by Daemos himself. He saw potential in her leadership abilities. She had proven to be a valuable asset in the past. What she lacked in size and muscle she made up for with brains and quick thinking. She wore new iron armor, thanks to the few iron mines inside of Whitia now being distributed to all instead of a few. Ever since Whitia became a part of the Duma Empire, all of the iron mines have been put to maximum production. Her hair has been tied back into a braid and she was now properly equipped with stronger weapons. A large direwolf stood by her side, panting.

Fena lowered her head and knelt. "I have come to your summons, my lord."

"Fena. You are the only one I personally called to participate. I expect you will perform most ardently."

"I shall not disappoint, my lord."

"See to it that you do not. I am looking forward to what you will do in the coming trials. Bring in the next one."

Walking through the large doors to Daemos's throne room was a massive orc. His eyes were cold and calculating. He was a head taller than most of his fellow orcs and was dressed in thick hide and metal armor. Sheathed upon his back was a massive chunk of jagged sharp metal that was too thick and heavy to be called a sword. It had several spikes protruding from the blade, which was very uneven and discolored.

The massive orc knelt down and bowed his head. "It is an honor to meet you, my lord. I am Gortem. We have met before, but I doubt you would remember. You cut me down on the battlefield and soundly defeated me. I was lucky to survive."

He took off a piece of his chest armor and showed Daemos a large slash mark on his chest. He put the armor back on and continued to speak.

"You have gained my respect, my lord. I would be honored to govern the forest in your name while you are bringing glory to the empire."

Daemos was impressed. "I am pleased by your dedication. I am sorry I—"

"Please don't, my lord. We fought fairly and you bested me. Something that many in the past have tried to do and failed. For every enemy I have defeated, whether by killing them or sparing them in the end, I took their blade as a trophy and then smelted their weapon into my own."

Gortem reached behind him and grabbed his massive weapon. It was so much bigger than both Daemos's blade and the late Lazgar's blade. Hundreds of swords, daggers, axes, and other weapons have been crudely melted to form this amalgam of iron weapons.

Fena observed this with concern. He was powerful. When the orcs and goblins used to be at war, he was a main target. He had killed many of her soldiers in the past. She gritted her teeth and glared at the orc. Gortem ignored her completely.

"Quite an impressive and unique weapon. I look forward to seeing it in action soon."

"As you wish, my lord."

"The last contestant may now enter."

The final contestant was a large man that was almost the same size as Gortem. His skin was dark brown and his hair was white as snow. His yellow eyes were rigid and full of focus. The man was dressed in simple clothes and was unarmed. He had white wolf ears on the top of his head that were folded back. The man lowered his head and took to his knee.

"I am Tiamet, the winter wolf," said the large werewolf in a deep voice.

Fena was getting even more nervous now. She excelled when she had troops at her command and time to plan. She does not know what these trials were going to be, but her anxiety over them was growing more and more. Gortem broke into a smile when he saw Tiamet.

Daemos stood from his throne and walked towards him. "Now this is interesting. I don't remember seeing you on the battlefield. Where were you?"

"I did not participate. I was an outcast in the kingdom because of the color of my fur. I have lived in isolation ever since I was a child. I saw the battle from the sidelines. Yours is a new power rising in Harmonia. I have learned how to become a survivor. I intend to be high on the food chain."

"An outcast because of your fur? I won't let stupidity like that get in the way of my goals. You have powerful ambition, but keep it in check. I am your master."

"Understood, my lord," said Tiamet, refusing to show any weakness.

Nyana scoffed to herself at what Daemos said. He didn't have much authority to speak about discrimination when he himself possessed an all-consuming hatred for elves.

"Good. The three of you have gone through many trials to arrive at this position. One of you will become the king of this forest and rule as my vassal while I continue my rightful conquest. The dead now roam these lands. They are eternally loyal to me. If you try to betray me once you have tasted power… there will be no mercy."

"I would never dream of betraying you, my lord."

"You have gained my respect and loyalty on the battlefield. I have found a blade stronger than my own. My allegiance is with you and you alone."

"I know the natural order… the food chain of power. I will obey."

Daemos nodded, but something about Tiamet made him suspicious. He seemed willing to climb this 'food chain' no matter what. He was going to keep a close eye on him.

"Very well… we shall commence with—"

Before Daemos could finish his sentence, the doors to his throne room were thrown open. A goblin ran as fast as he could and bowed before Daemos.

Daemos was unamused at the interruption. "What is it? This interruption better be worth my time, maggot."

"Umm… m… my lord, e… e… elven settlers with armed guards a… are trespassing y… y… y… your borders."

Daemos's glowing red eyes widened as he came closer to the goblin. "WHAT?!"

Nyana was starting to get nervous. If he loses control like when he was first resurrected in Shatterstar, then this could become very problematic.

Nyana looked at Chindi, who was crunching down on the last of her meal. She hoped Chindi would go along with whatever Daemos probably was about to do. "Y… y… y… yes, my lord! They have brought several axes with them. I think they intend to expand the borders of their nearby outer villages. What are your commands, my lord?"

Daemos was pacing back and forth while muttering to himself. Daemos's head was starting to fill with the same voices he could not make out. They invaded his mind by the dozens to the point he wanted to explode.

"They... encroach on... my land? Filthy elves... pathetic filthy elves... THEY WILL BE ANNIHILATED!"

"W... what?! But s... s... s... sir, they are of the Harmonian Empire! We... we can't—"

Daemos snarled and lifted the goblin messenger off the ground. His eyes were glowing brighter and brighter to the point they hurt to look at. "WE CAN'T WHAT?! FILTHY DEGENERATE ELVES THINK THEY CAN TAKE WHAT BELONGS TO ME?! ELVES?! I'LL RIP THEM APART! COLLECT ALL THEIR SOULS TO ROT AWAY IN MY GAUNTLET FOR ETERNITY!"

Nyana stepped forward. She grabbed Daemos by the arm and Daemos whipped his head around to stare at her. He threw the goblin against the wall and allowed him to scurry away. Daemos was trying hard to restrain himself, failing miserably at it.

He snapped at Nyana, "WHAT?!"

"This is insane, Daemos! We are not ready t—"

"I WILL NOT TOLERATE THIS! YOU THINK I SHALL STAND IDLY BY WHILE FILTHY ELVES TAKE WHAT'S MINE?! THEY WILL ALL DIE!"

Daemos's gauntlet violently started to shake on his hand and was glowing red. The eyes of all of his soldiers in the throne room started to glow as they became affected by the gauntlet. Chindi arose from the side of the throne and snarled with rage as the power of the gauntlet invaded her mind. Nyana fell back in pain as the power of the gauntlet had even started to affect her. Daemos was out of control.

"WE MARCH TO SLAUGHTER THE ELVES! EVERY SINGLE ONE OF THOSE DEGENERATE PIECES OF GARBAGE WILL DIE AT MY SWORD! EVERY ABLE-BODIED MAN AND WOMAN WILL COME WITH ME! WOLF, ORC, GOBLIN, BEAST, AND UNDEAD!"

Gortem, Fena, and Tiamet all let out a war cry in approval. Their personalities and thoughts had been completely washed over by the desire to rip apart and mutilate their enemies, no matter the cost.

Daemos kicked down the doors and turned back to look at Nyana. "Stay here if you so desire, weakling. Tonight, my blade shall taste the blood of elves!"

Daemos charged down the halls with his three candidates and skidded to a halt when he made it outside. His gauntlet sent shockwaves of power across the land around his castle. Civilians who were repairing the castle and soldiers standing guard dropped what they were doing and went into a frenzy. Daemos's bloodlust, hate, and rage was being poured into each and every one of them. His desire for violence and his disdain for elves were all being forced into their minds. In the previous battles, the soldiers had felt like they were in a daze or a dream while under the influence of the Overlord's Gauntlet. But this… this was far different compared to those times.

Daemos lifted his sword into the sky and called out to the crowd of blood-starved soldiers and workers. He was shaking with rage and anticipation. As angry as he was right now, he found himself excited and happy as well. A chance to kill elves. He still did not even understand why elves made him so mad. He didn't care.

"AT THIS VERY MOMENT, THE ELVES ARE TRYING TO TAKE OUR LANDS! YOUR HOMES!"

The crowd roared and banged their blades together.

"FOR HUNDREDS OF YEARS, THE OUTSIDE HAS FAILED TO TAKE THESE LANDS FOR THEMSELVES! NOW IT WILL BE IMPOSSIBLE, FOR WE ARE NOW UNITED AS AN ALMIGHTY EMPIRE!"

The crowd wildly cheered. They were incredibly hungry for violence now.

"THE BEASTS BOW TO MY CALLS! THE DEAD MARCH IN MY NAME! NOW THE LIVING WILL BECOME UNITED AND UNSTOPPABLE! WE WILL MURDER THESE INTRUDERS! TAKE EVERYTHING THEY OWN... AND THEN... WE WILL PAY BACK EACH INSULT A THOUSAND TIMES OVER!"

The crowd was becoming wilder.

"WE WILL BURN THEIR HOMES! WE WILL HORDE THEIR FOOD AND GOLD! WE WILL KEEP THEIR WEAPONS AND TOOLS! AND WE WILL SLAUGHTER EVERY ELF THAT DARES TO LOOK US IN THE EYES!"

Werewolves were morphing into their bestial forms and orcs banged their swords and shields together. Goblins started to mount beasts and ready them for combat. Drakes let out horrifying screams that echoed in the night.

"WE WILL SHOW NO MERCY! NO COMPASSION! WE WILL HOARD EVERYTHING OF USE AND THE REST WILL BE KINDLE FOR THE FLAMES! WE WILL START TONIGHT! THE FIRES WILL BE SO LARGE THAT THE SMOKE WILL BE SEEN ACROSS ALL OF HARMONIA! IT WILL BE A MESSAGE TO THE ENTIRE WORLD! WE ARE HERE! WE ARE COMING! AND WE WILL NOT BE STOPPED! THIS WILL BE A NIGHT ALL WILL REMEMBER AND ALL WILL FEAR! WE SHALL BE THE HARBINGERS OF DOOM TO ALL THAT DARE OPPOSE US!"

The crowd was going ballistic like a starving dog being held in place by a chain with a piece of meat inches out of its reach.

"IN THE NAME OF THE DUMA EMPIRE! IN THE NAME OF DAEMOS THE ELDER LICH! IN THE NAME OF DAEMOS THE HORNED REAPER! CHARGE!"

Daemos gestured and a drake swooped down and let Daemos climb onto his back. The moment he gave the order, all those in his presence charged towards the entrance to the Duma Forest. Nyana ran outside, only to see Daemos flying away with his horde of maddened warriors. She felt the pit in her stomach grow. How far will he go? Nyana quickly ran after them, but made sure to shadow them and not be seen.

This was the day he had been waiting for. An excuse to attack. The strange voices in his head have been driving him mad and urging him to do violence. The elves are right at his doorstep now. Now is his chance to let loose the impulses that have been driving him mad for so long. He doesn't understand why he feels the way he does and he doesn't care. Now is the time to go on a rampage.

CHAPTER 15

Commotion and rumors were spreading around the Duma Forest from the villages that were stationed right by the entrance of the infamous woods. A small platoon of village guards was set out to investigate, along with a group of workers who intended to make use of the situation. Many times in the past, the Harmonian Empire has tried to expand its borders into Duma, only to fail. Government-wise, the empire has temporarily given up on expanding in that direction, but desperate farmers and militia have still constantly attempted to expand their borders to have access to better farming soil and resources. Since these villages are on the very border of the empire, they are the farthest away from receiving any aid or protection from the government. For the most part they are on their own. Despite failure after failure, the villages continue to try and push their borders into Duma. Every year their population grows and with it their supplies dwindle more and more. This is their only option.

A small convoy of elves walked through the thick abundance of trees and exotic plants. Some were village guards with low grade weapons and armor, but most were just common villagers. They brought wooden handle axes with them in an attempt to cut down some trees and push back the forest by a little. Any little bit of land they could get would be valuable for them.

"Let's stop here. We don't want to venture too far. Do what you can but be quick. We should not stay in these accursed woods for long," said one of the guards, readying their sword in case a monster attacks them.

The villagers hurriedly started chopping down trees and foraging for anything valuable or edible on the ground. Suddenly, a faint sound was heard. The guards whipped their heads around and drew their weapons at once. The sound was soft, but it soon got louder and louder. One of the guards turned to the villagers with a panicked look on his face.

"Get behind me. Don't run until we give the signal to do so."

The villagers rushed to hide behind the guards, unsure of where the noise was coming from, or what it even was. A large shadow blocked the moonlight and shrouded the elves in darkness. The shadow was gone in an instant, but something was falling from the sky.

BOOM!

With a powerful and thunderous sound, Daemos jumped down from the back of his drake and landed on the ground. His iron boots cracked the ground and created a small crater beneath his heavy feet. A dust cloud formed that temporarily hid his features, allowing for only his threatening silhouette to be visible to the elves. The titanic figure stood up straight and allowed his large black cloak to wrap around his body. From the other side of the dust cloud the only thing that could be made out was his silhouette and his two glowing red eyes.

The guards stepped back in a panic. Most of them were already frightened by the massive figure before them. Others were bolder, stepping in front of the group and pointing their weapon right at Daemos.

"Identify yourself!"

As he spoke, the sounds stopped and from the darkness of the forest more glowing red eyes popped out from the shadows. No bodies could be made out. Just eyes that intently stared at them. More and more eyes started appearing until it seemed that the group of elves was completely surrounded.

RAMPAGE: THE RISE OF AN EMPIRE

The dust finally dissipated and Daemos became visible in his full glory. "The Horned Reaper has come for you."

Without warning, Daemos moved with lightning speed and decapitated the first guard. All of the monsters and soldiers waiting in the shadows charged forward and began ruthlessly ripping apart the elves, whether they were armed or unarmed. The souls of the elves were drained into the Overlord's Gauntlet. A sudden surge of exhilarating power filled Daemos as the souls were absorbed into him. This sensation of power felt so different compared to the others. Their souls were nothing compared to the ones he just consumed. He was getting drunk off the power from every elven soul he absorbed. There was an entire village close by for him to further increase his power.

Daemos stared down at the now mutilated and torn open bodies of the elves lying at his feet, his boots drenched in their blood. He felt nothing but joy and anticipation for their deaths. He was already overwhelmed by the amount of power in his gauntlet that trumped anything in comparison to what was there before. The thought of increasing it twentyfold made him more and more excited.

His violent impulses were forced into the minds of his soldiers. Daemos did not even need to utter a single word for his orders to be heard loud and clear. Daemos pointed his blade in front of him and all of his forces charged towards the village.

On the farthest outskirts of the Harmonian Empire were its poorest villages. With the empires borders spread out so far, it was near impossible for any of the villages to get the support and protection they needed. That is why most of the bordering kingdoms sent raiding parties against the defenseless, villages while the empire fumbled over itself, trying to go in more than one direction, acquiring more territory than it could handle.

The small village of Dry Leaf was one of the most desperate of these villages. The empire has failed to help them time and time again, so they have had to take measures into their own hands. Dry Leaf has been heavily militarizing their town guard and consistently trying to expand the borders of the town without the knowledge of or orders from the queen. They have, in a sense, become a semi-independent entity. They have even gone far enough to push into the outer territories of the Dwarven kingdom of Gort next to them.

Dry Leaf faced a desperate struggle for resources and land. Every year, the population rose with no increase in production or resources. The town has been barricaded and small watch towers have been constructed around the town. They have gotten so used to being raided that they were now well prepared. The citizens have also been learning how to fight as best as they can with zero professional training. Magic-wise, the elves were incredibly gifted and had a mass abundance of natural talent, but without proper training they only had access to the most basic of spells.

Starving elves gathered around a fire, waiting for the search party they sent to Duma Forest to come back. Many of the wooden shacks have even begun to collapse from recent raids. Some elves had begun to wonder if the village elder was only sending more foraging parties into Duma Forest just so that the population would go down and beasts wouldn't leave the forest if they were fed. Food has been rationed out to as many as possible.

Guards patrol the walls and towers when suddenly, one squinted his eyes at a strange orange light in the sky. The guard was approached by an older elf with a slightly different helmet compared to the other guards.

"You see something?"

"Yes, captain. Look at the sky! What is that?"

"I don't know… but I am not taking any chances. EVERYONE TO THEIR BATTLE STATIONS! GET THE CIVILIANS INSIDE!"

A panic spread across the populace as they were ushered away, but the dull and broken looks on their faces were proof that this was a routine occurrence for them.

"READY, ARCHERS AND SPELL CASTERS! Have you figured out what it is yet?"

"D… d…"

"HUH? Speak up, boy, I can't hear you!"

"D… D… DRAKE! INCOMING DRAKE ATTACK!"

"DAMMIT! WE HAVE A CODE SCALE! CODE SCALE! EVERYONE GET—"

"N… no… t… there's more of them! I… I see more drakes! A… and trolls! A… a… … a… and werewolves, a… a…"

Before the guard could finish his sentence, an arrow whizzed past his head and into the wood tower he was standing in. Another was shot and went right into the guard's eyeball. The captain stepped back in a confused panic. He had never seen so many different monsters together in one place.

Drakes began to swoop down from the sky and blast fire across the village. The flames began to quickly spread and engulf the walls. Panicked guards ran to the front gate to try and barricade it. It was useless. Even with ten guards holding down the gate, it was instantly smashed open by Daemos. The gate splintered to pieces and sent guards flying backward.

"KILL EVERY BREATHING ELF!"

Werewolves barreled through the splintered remains of the gate and violently shoved their fangs into the flesh of elves. Goblins swarmed inside, riding the backs of wolves, and pounced on top of the innocent bystanders. Orcs used their brutish strength to smash down any defenses in their path. Monsters caused absolute chaos amongst the guards. Chindi let out a gurgling roar that made the ground shake. Serrated vines ripped from the ground and started coiling around and impaling guards. The sharp thorns ripped through the dull metal armor like paper. One vine impaled a guard's leg and lifted the screaming elf towards Chindi's mouth. The massive abomination chomped down on the guard's body, making blood ooze and seep from her teeth.

The captain was in complete shock and confusion. Goblins, orcs, and werewolves… and beings that he had never witnessed in his entire existence… working together? Monsters serving them? What in the world was happening?

A guard shakily ran to the captain and began shaking his shoulders. "CAPTAIN! CAPTAIN, SNAP OUT OF IT! WE NEED YOU RIGHT NOW!"

The captain snapped out of his frozen state and was ripped back to the reality of what was happening.

"WE CAN'T WIN THIS FIGHT, CAPTAIN! WHAT ARE WE GOING TO DO?"

"W… we need to draw our forces together. If we are divided, we will be massacred. We need all the guards in one unit. And make sure the villagers are safely escorted out of here!"

"YES SIR! Let's move!"

The captain ran with the guard down the guard tower and into the bloodbath beneath them. The captain was stunned by what he was seeing. Werewolves have raided them several times, but they never harmed a hair on the townspeople's head. They only killed guards and raided food. But now, they were ignoring the supplies and food and going out of their way to kill them.

The captain watched as the fire started to spread faster and faster across the entire village. Black thorn vines were rapidly growing and blocking exits. Even with the fire blazing, the vines refused to burn away. Every citizen was in complete panic, going their own separate ways and fleeing for their lives. The captain was starting to lose control of the situation rapidly and had to quickly gain footing.

"GATHER HERE! WE MUST PROTECT THE—"

Suddenly, a massive bolt of lightning shot like a speeding arrow right through the captain's head. His body was engulfed in crackling fire. Within moments, the captain's body was charred black and it fell to the ground in front of Daemos. Daemos lifted his foot and stomped on the head of his prey, splattering his cranial remains across the floor.

"DON'T LET A SINGLE ELVEN MAGGOT ESCAPE! SLAUGHTER EVERY LAST ONE OF THEM!"

As the fire spread, Daemos's head started becoming foggy. More voices cluttered his thoughts and mind in the middle of the battle.

"None of them deserve to live!"

"They took you away from me! I thought I lost you."

"You're one of us… don't forget that."

"THEY TOOK EVERYTHING!"

"STOP BEING A COWARD! PICK UP YOUR SWORD OR LEAVE!"

"There isn't anything I wouldn't do to protect you…"

"YOU'RE NOTHING TO ME ANYMORE! YOU TOOK EVERYTHING! I HATE YOU!"

"Reynard… it's not your fault."

Daemos felt a rage growing inside of him that was larger than any he had ever known. These voices… he didn't know who they were. He didn't recognize their voices and yet he felt such an uncontrollable rage from them. He roared in frustration.

"BRING ME ELVES! BRING ME THEM!"

The ground started to shake as the hydra walked right through the village walls and started lowering its long necks to eat the villagers close by. In the complete carnage and confusion of the situation, many went their own paths. Some started barricading themselves away in their homes, some tried to fight back, some even lay on the ground to play dead.

Daemos was becoming more and more overwhelmed with the amount of power he was gaining from every elf that was killed. It was beyond his wildest dreams and it was only increasing by the moment. This, along with the rage that was overcoming him like a fog, made him almost unrecognizable. His mind was practically on autopilot. All he cared about was raising the body count.

A group of elves have frantically started to climb up trees in a vain attempt to escape. The children were the first to climb up and they climbed as high as possible. Goblins rode in on their wolves and started throwing torches at the trees. Parents, in an adrenaline-filled panic, tried to put out the fires and fight back. Many elves tried using ice spells and water spells to quell the flames, but they were spreading too quickly. Children cried and screamed as they watched their parents being butchered alive and the flames rise higher and higher. By the end, the climbers either fell from the trees into the fire or forced to wait in dread as the flames came to them.

The villagers were being massacred. Even with this many elves shouting out spells, they are outnumbered and after all, mere villagers. Their bodies were beginning to pile up across the battlefield and blood was soaking the soil and grass.

"FIREBALL!"
"ICEWALL!"
"SHOCK!"
"WIND!"
"WATER BARRIER!"

"FLAME WALL!"

Daemos pointed towards a barn that was barricaded from the inside. Elves barred the large doors with anything they could find, frantically hiding their children inside the hay and grabbing anything they could use as a weapon. Many elves tried to find some high ground to blast spells at the attackers.

"BREAK OPEN THE BARN! BRING THEM TO ME ALIVE!"

Orcs gathered together to use themselves as a living battering ram. Ten orcs all came together and ruthlessly charged towards the barn doors. The first charge cracked the doors, yet they still held. Chindi used her vines to start ripping at the walls of the barn. At this point, she was not doing it for food, but rather to enjoy watching her prey squirm about in a panic.

"AGAIN!" ordered Daemos as the orcs stepped back and charged once again. The barn doors broke apart and terrified civilians screamed and cried as they were beaten to a pulp and dragged out of the barn to be thrown at Daemos's feet.

Nyana flew at incredible speeds to try and find Daemos. She couldn't help but be scared. What if he did something that jeopardized everything they have fought for? She couldn't help but remember what her master had told her, that these were the same mortals that had cast her aside. They won't show her the same mercy. And yet, she couldn't help it. She was fine murdering an adult, a soldier. She could not understand the mindless slaughter of civilians, of innocent men, women, and children.

As Nyana flew across the skies, she was halted to a stop. Her body froze as she witnessed an entire village engulfed in flame. Bodies strewn across the ground, ripped apart, and mutilated beyond recognition. There was no discrimination from the killers. The bodies of children were amongst the dead. Nyana landed on the top of a tall tree and felt herself getting sick to her stomach. Her eyes were stuck on the body of a little girl with her legs crushed under rubble and her eyes pulled from her head. A direwolf was ripping into her stomach and chewing on her intestines. Nyana shakily moved the bottom of her mask slightly to the side and vomited. She moved the mask back into position and continued to watch in horror. She started to look for Daemos in a panicked state until she finally saw him.

Daemos paced back and forth as elves were forced to their knees before him in a line, their hands bound behind them, no matter the age. Elves begged and cried as Daemos continued to pace.

"Today is the final day of your measly and worthless existences. Your village will be the first foothold of my new empire. Your bodies will be used as food and your bones as catalyst for the undead."

More of the strange voices filled Daemos's head as he was speaking. They drowned out all of the noise around him.

"Why should we spare them? After everything they took from us?"

"They are hypocrites, afraid to share power."

"I think I am pregnant."

"I won't give up… not on you and not on them."

"Did you ever realize you were lied to?"

"You are pathetic."

"I never should have trusted you!"

"I love you more than anything!"

"They didn't spare a single one… yet you hesitate… do you even care?"

"I WONT STOP UNTIL YOUR ENTIRE RACE HAS BEEN MASSACRED!"

"Reynard… you're scaring me."

The voices quieted down and Daemos could feel the strange rage overcome him once again. It won't let him think straight. He took out his blade and pressed it against the throat of an elven woman crying, trying to be close to her son.

"You love your son… don't you?"

The woman shakily looked up at Daemos and shook her head in a terrified fashion. Her eyes reflected pure terror. "Please… d… d… do whatever you want to me… just… let my boy g… g… go."

Daemos tiled his head to the side and turned his head towards the small child tied next to his mother. He gripped the hilt of his sword as tight as he could. He hesitated for but a moment, slowly stepping back. But the whispers again started muttering in the back of his head and it drove him mad. He took his blade and ruthlessly impaled the small child. He tossed the dead body off his sword and onto the lap of the mother. Her eyes grew wide, her heartbeat stopped. She was completely silent as her brain could barely calculate what had just happened. Tears streamed down her face and the moment she was about to scream, Daemos grabbed her by the throat and pulled. He slowly ripped her head from her shoulders with her spinal cord still attached to the neck. He held it into the air over his head and his maddened soldiers cheered.

"Slaughter them all."

All of his soldiers darted towards the captives and began ripping them apart. Nyana was crying. Her body was frozen as she helplessly watched. She finally started to understand. Understand why her master chose Daemos instead of her. This was why the Overlord's Gauntlet refused to work for her. This pure hatred and cruelty was what Daemos had and she did not. Nyana couldn't watch anymore. She jumped down from the trees and used a spell.

"TELEPORTATION!"

Nyana teleported right in front of Daemos and got right in his face. Tears dripped from the eye sockets of her golden mask.

"WHAT DO YOU THINK YOU'RE DOING?! WHAT IS WRONG WITH YOU?! WHAT THE HELL IS WRONG WITH YOU?!"

"Get out of my way, wo–"

Nyana jumped up and grabbed Daemos's helmet by the horns. She pulled the helmet off and grabbed Daemos by his skull.

"WHAT HAPPENED TO YOU?! LOOK! LOOK AROUND YOU!"

Daemos stared at the fires. The bodies. He shook his head slightly, confused. As blind anger turned to bewilderment, the gauntlet's power dissipated from Daemos's warriors. Some of them instantly fell unconscious from the utter strain their bodies had been subjected to and being on a constant adrenaline rush for so long. Some that had sustained grave injuries instantly fell to the ground, dead. Most were confused as if the battle and the entire march to the small settlement was a complete haze. Some of the werewolves, orcs, and goblins immediately got sick and vomited the flesh of elves that they had bit into during the fight. Mass confusion and sickness spread amongst his army as the realization of the bodies around them began to sink in. The only one of them that was not fazed or bothered by any of this was Chindi, who continued to dine on elven flesh with glee.

Nyana gripped Daemos's skull firmly and yelled, "WHAT HAPPENED?! WHY WOULD YOU DO THIS?!"

Daemos heard but one final whisper in the back of his mind as she asked this.

"I don't even recognize you anymore…"

A pain filled Daemos as he stared at the mangled bodies of children. The high of battle died out of his system. The power of souls he had gained from the slaughter seemed less exciting. Daemos looked Nyana in the eyeholes of her mask and simply muttered,

"…I…I don't know."

The next morning, rumors of a massive, horned demon called the Horned Reaper started to spread like wildfire across all of Harmonia. Neighboring villages came to investigate the tower of black smoke, only to find the most gruesome sights left behind. Fear and paranoia spread across the land like a plague. Despite this, the Harmonian Empire has failed to take much action as of yet, with the queen still gone.

The coming days were incredibly quiet for Daemos and his army. Some were still in denial of what took place several nights ago. Nyana was still furious and stricken with pain over what she had witnessed. The two of them barely spoke the entire journey back to Zithoss's lair in Whitia.

The two of them walked past skeletal knights that now guarded the massive doors to Zithoss's lair. The undead stepped aside as the two approached and allowed them both to go inside. The ominous halls and floor of the dungeon were blanketed in a thick layer of fog. Zithoss was in his throne, resurrecting more bodies that he had ordered the undead to dig up. A pile of skeletons and rotting corpses are piled at the side of the room.

Daemos and Nyana both bowed as they approached Zithoss. He was already intrigued by the amount of power he sensed inside of the gauntlet.

"I see you have been busy. The power you have accumulated is most impressive."

"Thank you, my lord, but…"

Daemos turned his head to look at Nyana. She wasn't making eye contact with him. She was still mad.

"In the field of battle, I have lost control. Something took over me. I could not control myself. I slaughtered everyone inside of a village just outside our borders and have attracted attention to ourselves. "

"Why concern me with your victory?"

Daemos and Nyana lifted their heads up. Daemos was confused and Nyana was once again angry.

"I... don't think I understand?"

"What is there to not understand? You won. You have gathered a lot of souls as was your purpose and gained your first foothold out of the forest."

"B... BUT WERE COMPROMISED! THEY ALL KNOW WE—"

"This forest is a peninsula. The only way ahead was forward. None of your conquests could be masked by these woods any longer. You have spread fear and doubt among the people. That is another step to victory."

Daemos was torn. Nyana was heartbroken by what he had done. Daemos felt confused and unsure of himself after what he did at the village and now he is being congratulated?

"I... I don't understand... I thought I had—"

"Do you really think sparing elven civilians would have done us any benefit? There was a choice to make. Spare the defenseless or make use of them. This power you have conceived has done nothing but benefit us."

Nyana quickly stood up and rushed out of the throne room.

Daemos growled and turned around to chase after her, but Zithoss raised his hand to make him stop. "Leave her."

"But she just disrespected you!"

"Worry not, my son. I wished to speak only to you anyways, but first... give me those souls. Keep some for yourself."

Daemos looked at the gauntlet and nodded his head as he approached the well of souls and inserted the Overlord's Gauntlet into the socket. The wall exploded with power as green fog erupted from the pit like a volcano and what seemed to be hundreds of spirits with screaming distorted faces swirled around it like a cyclone. The souls funneled into Zithoss as he let out a decrepit laugh. The cyclone of energy swirled around the elder lich and finished with a mighty pulse that even managed to push back Daemos's mighty frame.

Zithoss stood up from his throne walked towards Daemos. "Now... we may talk." Zithoss looked towards the doors to his throne room, that Nyana had just run out of and gave a small laugh. "Do not worry about her. She is a powerful asset and tool... but you... you are my chosen one. You were worthy of my gauntlet while she was not. You have the power and determination to build the empire that I once had for yourself. You are more than I hoped for. I made a desperate gamble in sending Nyana to make you my revenant and it paid off splendidly. As for your claim of 'losing control', it is of no importance. You are experiencing what all new revenants experience. Flashes of their old lives taking influence over them. You have no mind to control because you are already mine. You were once a mighty warrior in your past life. That man is dead, but his instincts still remain... that is all."

Zithoss put a bony hand on Daemos's shoulder and looked him in the red eyes with his own. Daemos broke eye contact to look towards the agape doors.

Zithoss lifted his finger and with a mighty force both doors were slammed shut. "Do not let her mortal emotions stray you from the path that I have predetermined for you to follow! Sparing the worthless will only prove fruitless! The defenseless would have risen up to become warriors. Thorns in our side. Now they are out of the picture and both of us are more powerful than ever because of it. You are undead. The emotions you once had serve no purpose to you now. What you are feeling are short-lived moments of your old self breaking through, but he has been dead for over a hundred years. Let him rot away, Daemos."

"Yes, my lord. I will not allow these distractions to get in my way again."

"Most excellent. Now, continue to slaughter in the name of your empire. You are the face of the empire. You are elder lich, as your proclaimed. When you are out of these halls, I don't exist and you are the true overlord. Understood?"

"Perfectly well, my lord."

"Then do what must be done. Find my three generals who have now awakened just as Chindi has. Find Urcon, the merchant of doom, Dulahan, the headless rider, and Madam Nestella of the night stalkers. Where they reside, I do not know. All I know is that they have not perished… they are a part of me… I could sense them all of this time. They are like branches of myself, as you are, Daemos. Do what must be done. Find my generals and show no mercy."

"As you wish, my lord."

A woman sits on a throne made of stunning blue crystals. Her skin is white as snow and is covered in stretch marks. She is dressed in ceremonial robes of white and blue and a tall cap. Her robes bear the symbol of a hummingbird with six wings. A large smile was stretched across her face. Her eyes are bloodshot and, in her hand, resides a steel staff with an empty glass container on the top. The throne room was beautiful. Everything shined like jewels and had a mesmerizing effect on those that stared for too long.

The doors to the throne room slowly open. A shy and worried messenger enters the room. As he opened the door, he could hear moans of pain coming from inside. He has skin just as snow-white as the woman on the throne. The woman slowly turned her head towards the messenger and her smile widened, her mouth spread so wide that saliva seeped from the corners of her mouth.

"Hello there, young man. What can this humble chine do for you today?"

The messenger looked around the room with fear. Blood was all over the floor and walls. The walls have several chine and vampire prisoners nailed to the crystal walls. They were nailed to the wall by their wrists, but all the skin has been peeled from their arms. Their legs have been peeled of skin as well. The skin from their arms and legs is nailed into their sides, the other end nailed to the wall. It is as if the skin from their arms is being used to fashion another two pair of arms. Two large dogs with white pelts and icicles protruding from their spines and chins were crushing bones that have been left in a pile next to her throne.

"U... u... u... umm, Priestess Mestifa... I... I..."

"Poor boy, please don't be scared. These are just heathens who refused to let the glorious Aidiel into their hearts. They have taken the lies of the seven false gods into their hearts and are now tainted by lies. To think anyone would be audacious enough to blind themselves from the obvious truth is.... Revolting. You have allowed Aidiel into your heart... have you not?"

"YES! Y... Y... Yes, I have, your greatness!"

"Shhh... be calm, my child."

"I... I... I... I am terribly sorry."

The poor boy found it nearly impossible to look the woman in the eyes. They look glossed over and are probably infected. She refused to close her eyes so she would never be forced to shy away from the wonders of Aidiel.

"Please don't be sorry, young one. Such manners are good for a growing man. Now, what is it you have come to tell me?"

"There… there have been reports… of a massive black demon with horns. The Horned Reaper. He… massacred an entire village in the territory of the Harmonian Empire… even the children. He had an army of different kinds of creatures working together and had a strange monster with him, unlike any we have seen before."

"I see… so it has already begun… Aidiel's prophecy has come true. Things have started to set into motion quicker than expected."

She let out a sigh as one of the large dogs ripped at the flesh of one of the chines nailed on the wall. The chine's screams and cries echoed across the crystal room, making the messenger shake. Mestifa stood up from her throne and one of the large dogs stood by her side to help her down the stairs.

"We should clean the halls. We are going to have visitors very soon."

TO BE CONTINUED